THE SKELMERD

Charles Cutting formerly lectured in English and Communication Studies at a Northern University in Great Britain. In 1998 he was a visiting professor in New Mexico. He now lives quietly in Greece where he runs a small wine business.

Praise for Charles Cutting's *The Surleighwick Effect*

'A campus novel of wild comic caricature which bounces along with unflagging zest' (*Times Literary Supplement*)

'Comic but chilling Jonsonian satire' (*The Library*)

THE SKELMERDALE EFFECT

Charles H. Cutting

ZOILUS PRESS

First published in Great Britain in the year 2000
by Zoilus Press
PO Box 9315, London E17 4UU

ISBN 1 902878 76 0

Typeset by Electrograd

Printed in Great Britain by Antony Rowe Ltd
Chippenham, Wiltshire

British Library Cataloguing-in-Publication Data
A catalogue record for this book is available from
the British Library

ZOILUS PRESS
London

to Sandra

namque tu solebas
meas esse aliquid putare nugas.

CONTENTS

CHAPTER ONE

THE ROAD TO SKELMERDALE

'The call of the Leader is to us a Holy Command.'
(Propaganda Slogan)

'In a melancholly studdy
None but my selfe,
Me thought my muse grew muddy,
After seven yeares reading.'
(Robert Wild, 'Alas poore Scholler')

Autumn Term

Ms Fawn Fern, BA (Oxon) and Ms Florinda Morrison, BA (Surleighwick), were sitting, somewhat tired and disconsolate, in the latter's tiny 8' by 6' office on the bleak, windswept campus of the University of Skelmerdale, at 4 p.m. on the third Tuesday of the Autumn term. Both women, the bloom of youth now well behind them, were sipping a restorative cup of jasmine tea, and gloomily ruminating over the latest irritating memo from Freddie Frowstie, the fidgety, officious Professor of English and head of the department of English and Communication Studies at the University of Skelmerdale.

'Dear Colleague' (he had written), 'It pains me to have to write to you yet again about 'Performance Indicators' but I have no choice in view of the imminence of the next Academic Audit and Higher Education Funding Council for England Selectivity Exercise, on which, as you will know, funding for the department for the next five years will depend. The department's publication record is much improved of late, and details are, as you will know, now being collected by the university on a termly basis. But more and more, I am advised, HEFCE will be influenced in its decisions by 'Other Performance Indicators'. I must therefore, regretfully, and at the risk of seeming intrusive (which it is far from my wish to be), ask each colleague to report activity since the end of last summer term under each of the following headings:

2   The Skelmerdale Effect

a)   Literary and other prizes received (eg, Nobel Prize for Literature, Booker Prize, the Hawthornden, Whitbread Prize for Non-Fiction, Romantic Novelist of the Year etc etc.)

b)   TV programmes made, hosted (e.g. *Bookmark*; colleagues should note that quiz shows are to be excluded), or on which you have appeared (in an academic capacity, not as a member of the general public)

c)   Broadcast talks on radio

d)   Other Media Interviews

e)   Dedications of books received

f)   Honorary Degrees received

g)   Official Honours (e.g., CH, OM, Chivalric Awards), from home and foreign governments

h)   Scholarly Honours

i) Home (eg. Fellowships of the British Academy or the Society of Antiquaries or the Royal Society of Literature)

ii) Overseas (eg. membership of the Hungarian Academy of Sciences)

i) Citations in the *Arts and Humanities Citations Index* (Colleagues should in their own interests check their figures for the last five years and let me have a note of them)

j)   Software developed (eg. computer programs written, videotaped lectures, audio tapes produced)

k)   Universities at which you have acted as External Examiner, whether for undergraduate or higher degrees

l)   Conference Papers delivered

m) Speakers whom you have invited to the University

n) Playreadings organised external to the University

o) Other forms of public activity

p) Conferences organised

with apologies for having to trouble colleagues once again with these tedious, but alas now necessary queries,

Yours,

Freddie Frowstie
Professor of English and Head of Department

"Another impertinent missive from Frowsty Fred," sighed Fawn Fern, sipping her hot jasmine tea cautiously, and looking out of the tiny window of Florinda's office as the rain swept in from the moorlands, and dead leaves were scooped up by the biting winds that surged around the desolate Skelmerdale buildings, and the dank early evening fog rose from the swampy marshes of Skelmerdale's abundant lakes.

"But what are we to do about it?" enquired Florinda, smoothing her brow with her fingers, and straightening out her smock as she spoke. "Come on, let's have a honey cake while we think about what to say. You know how sarcastic Frowsty Fred was about our 'nil' returns on publication for the last productivity exercise. Damn the man! Just because his book on *Hardy and Melancholy* - and a terrible book it was too! - was reprinted two years ago, he thinks he can come down hard upon us, even though he does very little himself. It's just not fair!"

And indeed, Fawn and Florinda were beginning to feel ever so slightly on the defensive in this, the eleventh year of scrutiny of the activities of lecturers in the British university system. They had been appointed together, twenty-five years previously, as bright young chatterboxes of the type so keenly in demand in the early 1970s, in the Department of English and Communication Studies, one of the University of Skelmerdale's trendiest and chicest and most fashionable departments, with a glowing future confidently predicted for both young women, pert, bright and beautiful as they then were, with a witticism for every text, four quotable quips for every tutorial, a simper for every seminar, and a laugh for every lecture.

But things had not turned out as once was hoped. Their beauty had faded, the once-bright future was now behind them, the clever critical books that, at interview, were to have been written up from highly praised undergraduate essays, and made their names for sharp, dazzling perceptive *aperçus* were still in process of gestation - and truth to tell were well out of date. In their heart of hearts, Fawn and Florinda knew that their books would never be written. Each of them had, it was true, once published a note in *Notes and Queries,* and Fawn had once had a letter published in the *Review of English Studies* - but that was ten years ago, and thus too early for any of the recent publication surveys. And so their 'nil' returns had been a black mark for the department - or so Freddie Frowstie had maintained, in his irritating and supercilious and condescending manner.

"I'm not trying to criticise a colleague, of course," he had said pompously. "But I feel I would be failing in my duty as head of the department if I did not draw your attention to what this may mean for us."

"We've got to do something, Fawn," said Florinda firmly at last, pouring out her fourth cup of jasmine tea, and sadly eating a tiny sliver of honey cake. "But what? Let's look at the list again."

With something like despair they went down the list. Literary prizes, certainly not. They had never been on TV or the radio. No one had thought to dedicate a book to them. They were unlikely to be honoured. Unaccountably, no one had ever cited their contributions to *Notes and Queries* in the *Citations Index* (though - and this was a sore point with them both, Florinda had cited Fawn in a review she had once done for the *Skelmerdale Literary Review* - but that journal was not covered by the *Index,* so credit could not be claimed - which, as they both agreed, showed how absurd and unfair the system was!).

At length Fawn said, "I suppose we could organize a conference?"

"What on?"

"How about on a feminist topic? What about 'Women in Victorian Literature and Painting'?" (For Fawn was interested in Dante Gabriel Rossetti, and liked his striking pictures of women. There was, she was sure, an article waiting to be written on the interface between poetry and painting in Rossetti, if only she could be given another sabbatical to write it.)

Florinda looked doubtful.

"I'd say yes to that but for one thing. That would bring out all of the *Lady of Shalott* gang and they'd virtually take it over and we'd be quite eclipsed. And I don't know about you, Fawn, but I've had enough of that dreadful Deirdre and those awful Whitepool people," (naming Skelmerdale's deadliest rival in the struggle for prestige, the University of Whitepool, sixty miles away on the other side of the moors).

Slowly Fawn nodded her head. She could see the force of that argument. The insufferable Deirdre Prout would be sure to come, and just because she had written a book on the *Lady of Shalott* she always lorded it over them terribly whenever they met.

"No," continued Florinda thoughtfully, "if we're to organise a conference and do ourselves a bit of good under 'Conferences Organised', I think we've got to think a bit bigger than that. And we ought to try to get some big names to attend. And perhaps extend the range a bit. Maybe we need to go back as far as the medieval mystics, because, after all, mysticism is very much a women's thing."

"Julian of Norwich," suggested Fawn.

"Yes, women have always been interested in him," answered Florinda. "But even better if it was a woman - say someone like Florence of Worcester. And there haven't been all that many women conferences that have gone from the middle ages to today. And as you know, since Skelmerdale has always had such a good reputation for its undergraduate medieval programme, that might get that ghastly Frowstie off our backs for a bit. We could call it 'Writing Women'."

"Or how about 'Writing Women in Review'," suggested Fawn, warming to Florinda's idea as the conversation developed, and happy for once to be able to make a positive response to Frowstie's interminable questionnaires.

"Or better still - 'Writing Women Re-Viewed' - that sounds better, don't you think?"

They wrote down the title on a piece of paper, and looked at it, pleased with themselves.

Then Florinda had an inspiration.

"'Writing Women Re-Vued'," she said triumphantly. "That's what we'll call our conference. We could include a participatory Revue in the conference entertainments. And we could have it in the Castle Island complex - I saw in the *Newsletter* that that was free in May."

For the University of Skelmerdale, situated as it was in a popular and much visited tourist town in the north of England, had long since turned its locale to good account. Term had been reduced to seven-and-a-half weeks, so that student rooms could be let to conferences for a greater and greater portion of the year, and the profits from these lettings ploughed back into constructing accommodation of a superior standard, with en-suite facilities, and fitted carpets, for use throughout the year, not by students but by visitors and conferences in term time. And Castle Island was the latest of these, a complex set in the middle of one of the vast lakes that dotted the Skelmerdale campus, approached by a long low bridge over the water. The Castle Island complex had only opened that very month.

"Yes," Florinda elaborated, "May would be a good time. We could have it in the gap between the end of teaching and the start of exam. marking. And if we time it right, we could maybe get the Americans to come too - their semesters are usually over by mid-May."

Excitedly the two women reached for their pocket diaries, and drew a piece of paper towards them. They pencilled in the dates Tuesday 13 May - Sunday 18 May, wrote 'Writing Women Re-Vued' at the top of a piece of paper, decisively phoned the conference office to make a definite booking for the Castle Island Complex, and then started to map out a programme. The first part was easy enough: Tuesday 13 May, 4-6 p.m., Registration, 6-7 p.m., Sherry Reception, 7-8.30 Conference Dinner, 8.30-9 p.m., speech of welcome, 9-10, opening lecture, 10-11.30 p.m., Cash Bar.

Soon the main points of the programme were fixed, slotted in around morning coffee, 10.30-11 a.m., afternoon tea, 3.30-4 p.m., Excursion I, the City of Skelmerdale, Thursday p.m., Excursion II, Châtelaines and their Castles in the County of Skelmerdale,

Saturday p.m., Saturday evening, reception, dinner, farewell speech, Sunday a.m., departure.

"Now," said Florinda at last, "all we have to do is get some speakers."

"I could revamp my piece on 'Dante Gabriel Rossetti, Poet and Painter," suggested Fawn.

"And I'll revamp my *Notes and Queries* piece on Emily Brontë as a mystic," put in Florinda. "Now, all we need is the other speakers."

"And how do we get those?" asked Fawn

"It's easy - we just issue a 'Call for Papers'," replied the knowledgeable Florinda, who had attended some conferences, though she rarely spoke at them. Satisfied at last with their labours so far, the two women gathered up their books and marking, pulled on mackintoshes and scarves and overshoes, locked their rooms, and tramped across the cold, deserted campus towards the cottage they shared in the nearby village of Skittleton, on the very edge of the university. And there, after two cups of broth and three more cups of herbal tea, the two women, tired but happy, retreated to the privacy of their bedrooms and the untroubled dreams that follow a day well spent.

Next morning they eagerly button-holed Professor Freddie Frowstie at coffee time in the Senior Common Room of Grace Darling college, which housed the Department of English and Communication Studies at Skelmerdale. And there that tired and harassed figure, with lined and careworn face and greying hair, whose fading eyesight stood in need of powerful spectacles, was so astonished, and at the same time so pleased at the enthusiasm for their project of 'the weaker sisters', as he had mentally dubbed them, that he needed little persuasion to release £1000 of departmental money to 'prime the pump' of the project, and enable the call for papers to be inserted in various journals, and cover postage expenses to get the project off the ground. Already Professor Freddie Frowstie was composing some publicity releases in his mind, and thinking that this scheme might put him in well with the sisterhood at large.

*****

'I have a journey shortly for to go'
(Shakespeare, *King Lear*)

Over the next few weeks, in dribs and drabs at first, and then in a steady stream, the responses trickled in. In Surleighwick, Arkansas, Mrs Ruth Hanwell, sitting one early evening in mid-November at the computer terminal in her study, and logging on to the Bulletin Board of the Society for Shaman Studies, found the conference listed as a 'Forthcoming Event' in the 'News and Notes' section. It had been copied there from the electronic Mystics Ethernet, which had got it from 'Francesca' the Bulletin Board of Feminist Medievalists, to which it had been input by Dr Annabel Archer, who had learnt early of the event whilst visiting Skelmerdale as a visiting speaker from Whitepool, and had seen an advance notice in the *Skelmerdale Newsletter*.

Mrs Ruth Hanwell, cool and elegant in a light-blue tailored cotton frock, with white lace collar, cuffs and jacket-pockets, jotted down the dates, and went out into the yard of her spacious up-scale villa in the countryside, five miles out of town, where her husband, Professor Charles Hanwell, Research Professor in the History of Scientific Poetry at the Baskerville Institute for the History of Science, Surleighwick, Arkansas, was just preparing to char-grill a juicy porterhouse steak on his barbecue set.

Mrs Hanwell looked indulgently at the tanned and youthful figure of her husband, as he stood there in khaki-coloured lightweight slacks and chequered shirt. She gave him a little wave, and then went into the kitchen to put the ice into their favourite pre-dinner drink, a large gin and tonic with ice and lime.

"Thanks, darling," said Professor Hanwell, giving Ruth a loving kiss as he took the drink and enjoyed its familiar icy tang. "No one can make a gin-and-tonic better than you."

For Professor Hanwell, seventeen years older than his twenty-two-year old bride, had been married only for two years, and he and his wife were both still very much in love. Ruth had been his pupil at the University of Surleighwick, England, and he had married her in Bath, just as that university was being closed down. As soon as their honeymoon was over, he had arrived with Ruth in Surleighwick, Arkansas to take up the chair that he had been offered as a result of his monumental book on *Scientific Poetry*.

The marriage and the move had been a great success, and the characters of Professor Hanwell and his wife had mellowed and matured as a result. The first glow of deep sexual fulfilment had put the bloom of vibrant health upon Ruth's cheeks. What there had been of the gamine-like and innocent school-girl in her character had now been transformed. Ruth had put away childish things, and her favourite stuffed animal toy, Timmy the Tiger, had been banished to the third guest room. Gone were the donkey-jacket and the black woollen tights and the spiky hair. Professor Hanwell, a generous man who was not dependent on his salary, had made over to his wife a handsome dress and personal allowance of $80,000 a year. And Ruth, who had excellent taste which as a student she had never been able properly to indulge, had used some of that money to good effect.

Professor Hanwell too had assumed a more relaxed attitude to life, now that his big book was published at last and he had a really solid work of scholarship to his name. He had settled in well at the Baskerville Institute, and had no duties other than to give the occasional lecture and seminar whenever he felt like it, and offer words of encouragement to such occasional graduate students as sought him out. In the autumn Arkansan sunshine, he had started to read widely in the excellent holdings of the Baskerville Institute, and already had on the stocks the basic outline of a book on *Crocodiles and Insects*, a learned and amusing survey of poems in five languages on these topics. The laid back lifestyle of the States suited him, and he was enjoying the novel sensation of no longer being subject to the endless damp, rain and cold of Surleighwick, England.

Contentedly he savoured the delicious aroma of the grilling steaks, and, whilst Ruth freshened his gin and tonic, he pulled the cork of the bottle of excellent Cabernet Sauvignon from the Napa Valley that was to accompany it. Ruth meanwhile sat happily by the heated swimming pool on a comfortably padded sun lounger, watching the skimmer perform its intricate patterns as it gently scoured the surface of the water.

At last it was time to eat, and they sat down to enjoy their juicy and tender steaks, seated at a wooden table in the open air in a sheltered area of the patio. All around the air was silent, save for the distant cawing of exotic birds. The steak was followed by fresh Hawaiian pineapple, washed down with a full-bodied and buttery Australian Chardonnay.

"Charles," said Ruth, at peace with the world, as she sipped her second glass of Chardonnay, "it says on the Shaman Bulletin Board that there's going to be a conference on 'Writing Women Re-Vued' at Skelmerdale next May. How about us both going to it? They're calling for papers, and it would be a chance for me to make my conference debut and put in order some thoughts on Agnes of Anieto." (Ruth, after her excellent First in Theology, had been accepted by the Open University, which had taken over the outstanding student commitments of the defunct University of Surleighwick, to do a research M. Phil. on the Latin and Italian writings of that voluminous and obscure prophetess.) Her husband pulled a face.

"Writing Women Re-Vued?" he said doubtfully. "It sounds a bit trendy to me. That's the kind of conference that would be sure to bring the sisterhood out in force. I'm not sure that's really your scene at all."

The sun was now beginning to fall below the western horizon. Ruth took her husband by the hand and led him back into the house. She sat next to him on the deep cushioned sofa, kissed him passionately on the lips, and then snuggled up against him in a close embrace.

"Don't be such an MCP, Charles," she rebuked him. "I think it would be amusing to go. You could give a paper on Matilda the Hermit - call it 'The Woman in the Cave' or something like that. It would be a change, and I'd like it. Do let's go. It would be an experience to spend a week or two in Skelmerdale next May. I've got friends there, you know. My bridesmaids Tamsin and Fiona are second-years in the Department of English and Communication Studies. And two more of my friends from the Bath School for Girls are also studying there now. And furthermore, great-aunt Florence - you know, the one who couldn't come to the wedding because she was ill - lives only ten miles from Skelmerdale. She's longing to meet you, and this would be the perfect chance."

Ruth sipped the remnants of her glass of Chardonnay, before returning to the attack, running her hands through Charles's hair before slowly starting to unbutton and remove his shirt.

"Anyway, I think you ought to go," she resumed, coming up for air, pretending reluctance to continue their love-making till she had carried her point. "After all, part of your duties here are to go to conferences - they've given you a fifteen-G travel-grant to do that after all! Then, the semester will be over by next May - and even if it weren't, you have so few duties you could still go anyway. Let's face it, Charles," she smiled mischievously, pretending to give him a lecture, "you're doing pretty well at the Professor Game, aren't you? In fact I'd say you're one of the winners. You've got a prestigious job with a good salary and no duties! And even in Surleighwick, England, you had it pretty cushy! Very little teaching, no administration, no worries, with just one clever, pretty, female student who adored you! You couldn't have had it much nicer than that!"

She settled down to give him a serious kiss.

Professor Hanwell did not need much persuasion.

"Very well, my darling smoochy Ruth, we'll go," he smiled, silencing Ruth's little criticisms with a long passionate kiss, as they settled down to make love on the sofa.

*****

Assistant Professor Libby Cyoote, of Florida State, read about the conference as she lazed by the pool of her country club in Tallahassee, sipping iced tea, reading the latest weekly copy of the *University Women's Gazette*, in which Fawn and Florinda had paid for a small advertisement to be inserted. 'Call for Papers on all aspects of Writing Women' it had said. Libby thought for a moment. Her speciality, as a historian of science, was Madame Curie. And she was certainly a writing woman. It would be pleasant to have an excuse to go to England. And anyway, she was coming up for tenure shortly, and giving a paper at a conference abroad would certainly not do her case any harm. Next day, she sent off a fax to Fawn and Florinda, outlined her paper, stressed her interest in the plight of female scientists, and pleaded winsomely for a special personal invitation to deliver the paper that she proposed. Fawn and Florinda were delighted to comply with the request, unused as they were to being able to bestow favours. Libby's departmental chairman was impressed and flattered when she fluttered her eyelashes at him and uncrossed her legs invitingly, as she sat in his office armchair and showed the invitation to him the next day, and he impulsively and recklessly promised her $1200 to cover her expenses.

"Oh Professor Handyman, you are so sweet," she cooed, before returning home to phone her friends and gossip about the disadvantages under which women laboured in the American Higher Education system.

The last person whom she called that night was Assistant Professor Laura Harington, another historian of science and old friend of hers, far away on the west coast at Caltech. Libby and Laura enjoyed going to conferences together, where they could let their hair down a bit in places where they were unknown, and idle away the evenings in woman talk.

It was 10 p.m. in Tallahassee when Libby made her call, sipping the tiniest, tiniest splash of Jack Daniel's poured over a mountain of crushed ice, to relieve the stresses of the day. In California it was 7 p.m.. The lovely Laura took the call sitting on the balcony of her condo overlooking the Pacific Ocean. After her sixth Daiquiri, she was beginning to feel a little light-headed, but was delighted to hear from her old friend Libby Cyoote. Laura had had a long day. Her lecture to the freshwoman class that morning on 'Alchemy and the Beginnings of Modern Science' had not gone down very well - indeed some of the men in it had fooled around a bit and wolf-whistled when she turned her back! Typical sexist behaviour of the male students, she thought angrily to herself, though one had to admit that it was flattering that the boys still found her attractive! "Hi there Libby," she called, stretching out comfortably in her lounger, listening to the rolling surge of the Pacific breakers, and twirling her ice cubes with a swizzle-stick. (Laura had a hands free telephone.) "It's great to hear from you! How's things?"

"Laura, guess what?" exclaimed Libby. "I've had a personal invitation to deliver a paper on 'Writing Women' at a very prestigious international conference in England, no less! At Skelmerdale, that lovely old town way up in the north of England - you must have heard of it! And guess what? My chairman has given me $1200 to cover the cost. Why don't you come and read a paper too? We could have a great time together over there. Go to those lovely old pubs, and do a little drinking maybe! It would make a change, after all!"

"Hey, I'd love to, Libby," exclaimed Laura. "But as you know, alchemy's my thing, and there aren't any women alchemists."

"Well then, there's your paper," answered Libby excitedly. "You can do a feminist paper on how women were prevented from being alchemists because the men wouldn't let them be! Bring in something about transformations and the union of opposites and the quest - it's a gift!"

"Hey, I believe you're on to something there, that really is an idea! I'll call it 'All-Chemical Women' or something like that and see what I can do! It would be fun to have a holiday in England!"

Excitedly, the two historians of science began to discuss their travel plans, and what they would see when they got to Skelmerdale.

*****

Fawn and Florinda's plans were succeeding beyond their wildest dreams. As the responses to their call for papers came in increasing numbers over the next few weeks, they began to feel, cautiously at first, that for once they might be doing something that was a success and would gain them credit in the department. Even Freddie Frowstie was impressed in spite of himself when he learned how many people would be coming from the States.

"Look," chattered Fern excitedly to her head of department over morning coffee one snowy January morning in the second week of the Spring term, "there's Professor Libby Cyoote from Florida State, and Laura Harington from Caltech. And Ruth Henderson from Surleighwick, Arkansas (for Ruth had chosen to respond under her maiden name) - and then there's Professor Charles Hanwell, also from Arkansas - he's a big name - you must have seen the rave review of his big book on *Scientific Poetry* in the *TLS* a year or so ago! We've had thirty-five definite responses from the US now, five from Canada, eighty-two from this country, and ten from the continent! And all areas of 'Writing Women' are covered from the Sybil to Sylvia Plath!"

Freddie Frowstie could not help but be pleased. Since, under the HEFCE 'Public Activity' rules, a university could claim credit for the distinguished visitors who visited it, Skelmerdale would really pick up some brownie points from this event. Who would have thought that anything organised by Fawn and Florinda could have been so successful? Emboldened by their success, Fawn and Florinda went to the former's room to reply to their great enemy Deirdre Prout's proposal for a paper on 'The Problem of Female Identity in *The Lady of Shalott*'.

"It's typical of Deirdre to have waited till she'd heard it was going to be a big and successful conference before deciding to come," grumbled Fawn. Then, greatly daring, tongue in cheek, she wrote a catty letter to her old Whitepool University enemy.

Dear Deirdre,
    Thank you so much for so kindly offering to read your paper on *The Lady of Shalott* again. The response to our call for papers has been simply overwhelming. Everyone seems to want to come, especially from overseas. I'm sorry to have to say that the organising committee felt that your paper would not quite fit in with the main themes of the conference as it is developing, and we must therefore, with the greatest possible regret, decline your very kind offer. So very sorry! We will, though, put you on the reserve list, and if any of the speakers who have accepted falls ill hope very much to call on you then. We're counting on you to come and contribute to the debate, of course, and do very much hope that that will be possible.

with fondest love,

Fawn and Florinda

"There!" said Fawn gleefully, as she mailed the letter to the University of Whitepool, "that's one in the eye for Deirdre and no mistake. If she has any self-respect at all, she won't come now!"

Receiving the letter a day later sixty miles away in Whitepool, Dr Deirdre Prout, sitting in the university refectory in her jeans and white smock, uttered a stream of imprecations, blaspheming and cursing and swearing, as she started to plot her revenge against the hated University of Skelmerdale and the dreadfully uncharitable, nasty, mean, hateful, spiteful sisters of the Department of English and Communication Studies.

*****

Mrs Pauline Quick and Dr Antonia Crumpet, proprietors of the Magic Women bookshop at Hay-on-Wye, returning to their country cottage one January evening, saw the conference announced in *Sistersheet*, a fortnightly journal of feminist news.

"You know, Tony," said Mrs Quick thoughtfully, "we ought to think about going to that. It would be fun to keep up our academic acquaintance, and maybe we could take a van of books there and sell some of them to the delegates."

For Mrs Quick and Dr Crumpet had lectured in English at the University of Surleighwick, England, until two years ago, when they had taken their redundancy money and left that unfortunate institution a little ahead of its demise under the government's privatisation scheme.

"After all," continued Mrs Quick, "if you remember, Tony dear, we were going to go to Skelmerdale to that conference on feminism in nineteenth-century writings, but we never got to it because the department at Surleighwick ran out of funds - and anyway we forgot all about it what with all the excitement of selling up at Surleighwick and settling in here. I think we ought to go - we deserve a holiday, and we could do a bit of business on the side. We wouldn't need to be away for more than five days, and Samantha can cope whilst we're away."

The Magic Women bookshop had been an inspired idea, and Mrs Quick and Dr Crumpet were now able to employ female students, usually from Hereford Polytechnic, to help out at weekends. Dr Antonia Crumpet was as always eager to comply with the suggestions of her mentor and lover Mrs Quick.

"What a good idea, Pauline," she readily agreed. "Why don't you read your paper on 'The Women of *Villette*', the one that you were going to give if we had gone to Skelmerdale?"

"That's a good idea, Tony dear," said Mrs Quick, busily pouring two large tumblers of Manzanilla sherry for them both. She was trim and elegant as ever in a white blouse and dark-grey flannel pencil-skirt that fitted snugly around her still-youthful hips. Mrs Quick, leaning back on the sofa, sipped her Manzanilla pensively, as Dr Crumpet busied herself in setting the table, going to and fro from the kitchen with knives and forks, place-mats, coasters, wine-glasses, and a set of condiments. It was always a pleasure to Mrs Quick to sit and watch the glamorous Dr Crumpet walking around the room, clothed or unclothed. Today, Dr

Crumpet was wearing a full-sleeved black velvet dress, belted at
the waist, and black leather boots. A mass of golden hair cascaded
angelically down her back. Yes, Mrs Quick could afford to feel
quite pleased with herself, after the sudden shock of losing her job
as Senior Lecturer in Charlotte Brontë at the University of
Surleighwick. Hay had not had a bookshop specialising in books
by and about women before - and with the enormous explosion of
critical and other books on feminist topics in the last twenty-five
years, there was no shortage of books to be bought, sold, and
exchanged. And the large stock of items on sympathetic and
natural magic, on were-women and witches, on Haitian voodoo
and prophetesses, had been informative and useful to Mrs Quick as
she pursued her studies of the occult, gaining an ever deeper and
broader knowledge of the subject. Mrs Quick had become an
accomplished witch at Surleighwick, and, together with Dr
Crumpet, had successfully hexed several of her former male
superiors at the university!

Since the first day that the Magic Women bookshop had
opened its doors, freshly painted in black, with its name lettered in
gold, and a delightful sign swinging in the wind showing a witch's
hat and broomstick on either side of an idealised outline of Dr
Crumpet's face, the business at Hay had prospered. Young women
in particular were, to Mrs Quick's satisfaction, frequent visitors to
the store. Hay was within an easy day's drive of several British
universities, and many students visited it to buy cheap copies of the
books they needed for their courses. And then there were the
students from the polytechnic at Hereford, and the colleges of
further and higher education too....And Mrs Quick was so friendly
and welcoming and sympathetic, greeting every attractive young
woman with a sincere smile, offering them a cup of coffee, and
enquiring charmingly about their interests, and casually letting it
slip that she was herself a former university lecturer who had
written a much-admired book on *The Women of 'Shirley'*, that
soon many of her customers adored her, and visited the shop more
often than they would otherwise have done, just in the hope of a
few encouraging moments' conversation with the sage Pauline
Quick!

'Yes,' thought Mrs Quick to herself with satisfaction, 'running
a bookshop is not all that different from being a lecturer in English.
Both jobs involve sitting around all day and talking to pretty young

women about books, and give the opportunity to guide and direct tender and untutored minds into the correct manner of thought....' She lost no opportunity to lead her favourites casually towards the subject of sympathetic magic and the occult, and had great hopes of expanding her coven next Walpurgis Night, when the climate would once again permit a naked moonlight dance in the secret folds of a valley hidden away on the far side of the Brecon Beacons....

Mrs Quick's pleasant reverie came to an end, as Dr Crumpet came out from the kitchen for the final time, bringing with her on a tray a Spanish omelette, a lettuce and tomato salad, a tureen of boiled and buttered potatoes, and an uncorked bottle of Chianti.

Mrs Quick and Dr Crumpet ate their meal in a leisurely fashion.

Two hours later, when the second bottle of Chianti had been consumed, and the first of the evening's glasses of Strega had been consumed, Mrs Quick made tender love to Dr Crumpet before the flickering flames of the open log-fire.

"And if you give your paper on 'The Women of *Villette*'," said Dr Crumpet, standing naked in front of the open fire and enjoying the sensation of its warmth that chill January night, "then maybe I could give a paper on Emily Dickinson too."

"No, Tony dear," said Mrs Quick in tones of mild reproof, gazing at Dr Crumpet's beauty, "if you will take a word of advice from me, I think you need to do a little more work before you're ready to give a paper on that topic. After all, it's an important conference, and it would be a pity for you to give a paper that was not worthy of you. Anyway, you'll have to spend a good deal of time on our little stall, you know."

"Of course, Pauline, I see that you're right," replied Dr Crumpet, glancing admiringly at her mentor, before joining her again on the sofa and snuggling up inside Mrs Quick's loving and enfolding arms.

Two days later Fawn and Florinda had accepted Mrs Quick's paper, and noted that Dr Crumpet would attend as a non-speaking member of the conference. Two more names were thus added to their list.

CHAPTER TWO

ENGLISH TODAY, PART I

'thou shalt find in women virtues lie,
Sweet supple minds which soon to wisdom bow
Where they by wisdom's rules directed are
And are not forc'd fond thraldom to allow.'
(Sir Philip Sidney, *Arcadia*)

Grace Darling College,
University of Skelmerdale
SK2 5DJ

14 November

Darling Mummy,
I'm still very much enjoying the course! Everyone here says that English and Communication Studies is the best course there is at Skelmerdale, and all our tutors say that this is the place to do it. We're now into the first 'Performance' term, when apart from a few lectures that not many people go to all the classes consist of us acting out works of Eng. Lit. We did *Henry V* all of yesterday, and guess what, I played Henry! (Mrs Quick nodded approvingly as she came to this section of her daughter's letter - so good that they were avoiding stereo-typical casting at Skelmerdale!) I loved that bloodthirsty speech before the walls of Harfleur, just before the citizens decided to surrender the town. The wooing scene with Katherine was fun too, because guess what, she was played by Tristram, and he's really very dishy. (Mrs Quick frowned slightly at this.) I must sign off now, because tonight's the St Vitus's dance, when all we Grace Darling girls get dressed up a bit and go rather wild - (again Mrs Quick frowned). And then I have to prepare my readings for next week's classes. Next week we take 'Performance' a stage further, and act out little scenes in

the seminar rooms. We all get dressed up a bit to get us into the mood, and have long sessions, five or six hours at a time. Next week we move on from Old English like Shakespeare to the Victorians. We're acting out readings from *Wuthering Heights* where I'm playing Heathcliff, and I get to make love to Piers who's playing Cathy, and then all the women get together with my tutor, Fawn, for a session on *The Lady of Shalott*, whilst the boys do *Tom Brown's Schooldays* with Dr Stammer. Must dash now, have to meet Tamsin in the bar,

with love,

Blanche

Mrs Quick made herself a cup of coffee, and then sat down again in the lounge of her cottage. That mid-November morning, a pale, watery sun was shining coldly on to the distant Black Mountains. It was always nice to hear from her daughter, and she was glad that Blanche was getting on so well at Skelmerdale. It was in fact quite useful to have such a conduit to the Skelmerdale Department of English and Communication studies, for although she was no longer a full-time lecturer, Mrs Quick was still very interested in the gossip of the profession. Her daughter certainly seemed to be enjoying the course, and doing a lot of acting-out of texts....Mrs Quick thought for a moment. That was not a teaching technique that she had ever employed herself, but maybe she could do so in some of her classes. For soon after arriving at Hay, Mrs Quick had made contact with Hereford Polytechnic, a mere ten miles away, and that still-expanding institution had gladly offered her some part-time teaching in English. So, every Friday since last October, Mrs Quick had driven to Hereford. She was in truth glad of the opportunity to keep her hand in and maintain contact with the young. It was certainly interesting that at Skelmerdale the women seemed to play men and the men women - that was to be sure one way of making the students think about gender-stereotyping, and maybe it offered other possibilities too...Sipping her coffee, Mrs Quick settled down seriously to think.

*****

'Young scholars nowadays enbolned with the fly-blown blast of the much vain-glorious pippling wind...have delectably licked a little of the licorous electuary of lusty learning, in the much-studious school-house of scrupulous Philology.'
(John Skelton, *A Replication*)

Mrs Quick was ever an opportunist, a dynamic, go-getting schemer, sharp in appropriating any new idea or new acquaintance that came along. She was intrigued by what her daughter had told her about studying English at Skelmerdale, so intrigued in fact that she had telephoned her daughter at Grace Darling college, and after several attempts had found her in.

"Oh yes, mummy," her daughter had informed her, "most of our classes are concerned with texts in performance in one way or another. In the summer we act them out of doors, in the winter we have play-readings in tutors' rooms and convert the seminar rooms into a kind of drama workshop...."

Mrs Quick was attracted by this as a teaching method. In the first place, it would be very much easier to prepare for such classes, which were obviously less demanding on the teacher, since so much class-time would be occupied by the students reading and declaiming. And that would allow her more time for her to develop her theories of literature, and to write articles. For Mrs Quick, though made redundant from her job at Surleighwick, had not yet given up all hope of returning to full-time academic life, to the chair that her little book on *The Women of 'Shirley'* so richly merited. And, re-reading some of the great works of English literature in her spare time, she had started to develop certain interesting theories. Surely Heathcliff, whose dynamism and ruthless self-seeking she so admired in *Wuthering Heights*, was a woman? Mrs Quick scanned the text for clues in vain, but the novel really did make more sense if Heathcliff were a woman, and thus a transvestite. Then the novel, through Heathcliff's love for Cathy, became one of the great Lesbian love stories of the world, which was no doubt why she, Mrs Quick, had found it so attractive as a schoolgirl! And the fact that Heathcliff was a woman was the reason why his marriage had not worked out, because the offspring that had been produced were clearly a result of the wife's unfaithfulness! It was obvious, once you had the vital clue of his true identity. And then take Goneril and Regan - surely they were the real heroines of *King Lear*? They were dynamic, go-ahead women of the world, who had been unjustly thwarted by a male-dominated society, whilst literary critics, again predominantly male, had been prejudiced against them, naturally enough, for the last four hundred years! There were so many works of English literature which made much better sense if one posited that the hero was really a heroine in disguise!

Musing thus to herself that early November morning, Mrs Quick made herself another cup of strong black coffee, and sat at the desk of her study, gazing thoughtfully out to the Black Mountains, watching the rain spatter on the windows, as she mulled over her classes for the next three Fridays. What were they due to study in their somewhat quaintly-named 'Great Books' course? - though this blanket designation really did not stop the teacher from regarding any writing whatsoever as great. *A Room of One's Own*, later in the term. Well, that was easy, they could just take it in turns to read it out aloud in class, as apparently happened at Skelmerdale, according to Blanche. Although Mrs Quick had always been somewhat sceptical of the boastful claims which the Skelmerdale English department made for its teaching, maybe they did have a certain panache if they could carry off teaching methods such as that as innovative! And then there was *As You Like It*, an absolute gift for acting out certain scenes. And then there was the novel, starting with *The Return of the Native*, which was the book scheduled for the very next Friday. Well, surely that was easy enough, all she had to do was photocopy it, cross out the linking narrative, highlight the dialogue in coloured ink, and the whole thing was as good as a play! Thinking hard, Mrs Quick drew a pad of paper towards her and bending her head, began to make notes upon it.

*****

Bright and early at half-past-nine, Mrs Quick awaited her Friday class at Hereford Poly with an air of expectation. Teaching in a Poly, she felt that it was appropriate to dress in a slightly more bohemian, casual way than was her custom, so that day she wore a bright red blouse, two enormous turquoise earrings, a voluminous skirt of mottled tweed that billowed out below her knees, and brown leather boots. She had applied a liberal dose of *Quelques*

Fleurs to her neck, wrists, temples and cheeks, and its aromatic essence drifted round the sparsely furnished room. As a temporary part-time lecturer, Mrs Quick did not of course have a room of her own. But at Hereford Poly a room was reserved for the part-time lecturers, who used it whenever they had their classes. It was furnished with little more than a desk, a broad flat table, and chairs. Mrs Quick had however brought in a tin of instant coffee, some biscuits, and a pile of paper plates and cups, so that she could present her usual hospitable face to her students.

She was getting on well with her group, which consisted of seven young women and two boys, which was exactly the proportion between the sexes that was to her liking, for she could then make the boys the targets of her subtle ironies and jokes - which were however so subtle that most of her students, with the exception of the rather brighter ones, did not realise what was going on.

Her students drifted in, casually, as was normal, during the ten to fifteen minutes between 10 o'clock and 10.15 - first Jonathan and Clare, in scuffed blue jeans and sweaters, hand in hand. Then Tamarantha, a bright, alert and highly intelligent Nigerian, protected against the cold by a layer of thick brown sweaters, corduroy trousers tucked into thick fishermen's socks that came up to the knees, and heavy mountaineering boots. Mrs Quick very much approved of the radical and assertive Tamarantha, the boldness of whose views took even Mrs Quick's breath away. ('What's so wrong with necrophilia?' Tamarantha had once remarked, 'So long as the live partner is a woman, of course.') And then there was Lucy, a demure blonde of good family in whom Mrs Quick could see many possibilities. Bill, Wendy, Elizabeth, Dominique and Beatrix, a Dutch student spending a year in England, made up the rest of the group.

Mrs Quick quickly made them all some coffee and served them biscuits on this cold November day, to break the ice and get the conversation flowing along.

"I thought today we'd have a kind of play-reading," she said at last, getting down to business, and handing round photocopies of thirty pages of *The Return of the Native*, with the narrative blocked out, and the dialogue highlighted with felt pens of different colours. "It's an approved educational technique, you know," she lied, flashing them all an intense and sincere smile. "The *British*

Journal of Higher Education has had a series of articles writing of it in terms of high praise, so I'm sure that just for the next two or three weeks you won't mind joining in this little experiment."

And Mrs Quick explained that they would each take a part, and declaim it in class, during and after which she would herself provide a linking commentary and critical enlightenment.

Her class, most of whom had not read the chapters of Hardy's novel they were due to discuss, were happy to fall in with the ideas of the sympathetic Mrs Quick.

"You remember of course that the novel is set in the wild spaces of Egdon Heath," Mrs Quick began. "One of the most utterly remote and numinous places in England - you know what numinous means I am sure, Jonathan, if you don't, look it up, it will be good for you to increase your vocabulary. Have you ever been there? I went there once with my husband, just before he abandoned me and my marriage broke up." Bravely she wiped away an imaginary tear, and all the class warmed to her.

"Yes," she continued, "it's a place where one can feel very close to nature. Stretched out on the grass, one can feel almost that the earth has certain powers, and is conscious of one's presence. One feels that there, if anywhere, the great Mother Goddess Cybele has her home." She paused for a moment, to let the thought sink in. "But I mustn't digress on the Mother Goddess," she laughed, knowing that Tamarantha at any rate would be interested. "Otherwise I should be here all day. I have a little reading list, though, which I can give to anyone who wants to know more at the end of the class." She laughed again. "Though it's probably not the kind of topic that would interest Jonathan and Bill here. Anyway, let's turn to page 126. Tamarantha , you can read Eustacia Vye, that's marked in purple, and Jonathan, you can be the reddle man, that's the dialogue in red. I have some lipstick here if you feel you would like to enter into the spirit of the part. And Bill, you can be Gan'fer Cantle."

Mrs Quick allocated the parts, and then, satisfied for the moment with that auspicious beginning, sipped her coffee and sat back to admire covertly the beauty of the female members of her class. Every fifteen minutes or so, she stopped the reading to make a comment. The class was a great success. The students enjoyed reading out the dialogue in broad Wessex accents, and threw themselves enthusiastically and empathetically into their roles.

At the end of the class, Mrs Quick said:

"Well, I can see that this class has been a great success. Thank you for making it so. Next week we're due to do *As You Like It* in the 'Great Books' course, and if you're all agreeable I have a little idea that you might find amusing. I think that to act out scenes from *As You Like It* we really need a little more room. Now it happens that at my cottage, not far from here, I have a barn which would give us much more space. Why don't we have the class there? I'll pick you up here and drive you there and bring you back at the end - it's only a short drive, and there's room for you all in the back of my Land Rover. And those that have time are welcome to stay on to a finger-and-fork lunch afterwards."

Everyone thought that this was a great idea, and how lucky they were to have Mrs Quick for a teacher.

And then the class broke up, except that Tamarantha and Wendy and Clare and Beatrix and Elizabeth stayed on to ask Mrs Quick some questions about the Great Mother Cybele, and soon she was sitting with them in the student snackbar on the ground floor of Hereford Poly, deep in conversation with her acolytes, and handing out and explaining her reading lists about the White Goddess.

*****

The energetic Mrs Quick devoted the next weekend to clearing out her barn and putting it in good order. A carpenter was called in to assemble an elementary stage made from a variety of planks, and an electrician to rig up a couple of simple spotlights to supplement the natural light that came in from the skylights and the high window at the far end of the barn.

Then, fired with enthusiasm, Mrs Quick took a couple of afternoons off from the Magic Women bookshop, and toured the town of Hay and Hereford itself in search of a variety of costumes to add verisimilitude to her production. Soon a huge pile of dresses, cloaks, hats, scarves, muffs and other items were tossed into the back of her Land Rover, purchased in the main from charity shops like Oxfam, though she had also lashed out a little and purchased one or two special items new.

Promptly at half-past-nine next Friday morning, Mrs Quick was present as arranged in the car-park of Hereford Poly, ready for her class. For once her students were all there on time, stimulated perhaps by the prospect of a change in routine and the little excitement of a trip to their tutor's cottage. Mrs Quick, bright and cheerful as ever, hopped out of her Land Rover. Today she was wearing a black corduroy skirt against the cold, with fur-lined black boots, and a white woollen jacket with a coloured choker wrapped raffishly around her neck.

"Hullo there," she called gaily. "I can take two in the front - Tamarantha and Wendy, you come up here - the rest of you will have to go into the back."

Obediently Tamarantha and Wendy clambered into the high passenger seats in the front, whilst Mrs Quick held open the door for Jonathan, Bill, Clare, Lucy and the other female members of her class.

"You'll be all right there, it's only a short journey," she remarked with satisfaction as she closed the door. Soon Mrs Quick was driving steadily northwards through the suburbs of Hereford, delighted to have the chance of a few minutes conversation with Tamarantha and Wendy, two of her favourite pupils. Half-an-hour later she was turning into the drive of her cottage. There, hospitable as always, she first invited her students into the kitchen, where she enlisted the help of the boys to pour out the coffee she had left gently percolating before she had set out, and distribute biscuits.

"And then at 10.20 Mrs Quick called out:

"Right! Now to work! Bring your coffee with you if you want." She strode out of the house, and lead the way across the scrunchy lightly frosted grass to the barn.

"It's a little cold in here, but we'll soon get warmed up when we start acting," explained Mrs Quick.

She thrust her hands deep into the pockets of her skirt, and as her students perched on boxes or leaned against the wall, she gave them a few minutes introductory talk on *As You Like It*.

"And so the whole play really sets out to subvert conventional notions of gender," Mrs Quick ended by saying. "That is why Rosalind dresses up for most of the play as a boy. And of course on the Elizabethan stage, when women were denied their role on the stage as in most other areas of life, Rosalind would have been played by a boy anyway. So you had a boy pretending to be a girl pretending to be a boy - and later when the boy-Rosalind pretends to be a young woman, we have a boy pretending to be a young woman pretending to be a boy pretending to be a young woman, don't you see? And that's why Rosalind is always making remarks like 'doublet and hose ought to show itself courageous to pettycoat' in Act II. Don't you see? It's Shakespeare's way of exploring gender-stereotypes. Of course, it's a theme he often dwelt on, like in *Twelfth Night* with Viola. And of course in *Antony and Cleopatra* too Antony wears Cleopatra's 'tires and mantles', whilst she dons the sword he wore at Philippi. And then again, Ophelia tells us that Hamlet was wearing stockings that were 'ungartered', so he was a secret transvestite too."

Mrs Quick's students listened, entranced and inspired by her insights and her enthusiastic teaching.

"So Shakepeare is definitely encouraging us to think in non-stereotypical terms, and that of course has to come out in performance. Now, I think it would be fun to try a little experiment to capitalise on these deliberate ambivalences. If I were directing the play, I would try to subvert the audience's expectations in a Brechtian way. So I thought what we would do is this. Rosalind ought to be played by Jonathan there, but to exploit the gender ambivalences, he ought to start out as a man and then become a woman, so as to point up the contrast between what we see on the stage and the words we hear him/her speak.

"Here's what I mean. We'll read first the final scene of Act I, when at the text's literal level Rosalind is a woman - and you can play that more or less as you are, Jonathan, though here's a cloak to add authenticity. Tamarantha, you can play the Duke, and Dominique, you can be Celia - again, here are cloaks for you, and a little crown for you as Duke, Tamarantha."

Mrs Quick distributed her photocopies of the play, and eagerly the students put on the simple props; Tamarantha tried on the crown at various rakish angles, and looked at her black face in the old cracked mirror which Mrs Quick had thoughtfully provided for just that purpose. The rest of the class watched appreciatively, as the three students stood on the stage and read out their parts with what expression they could.

"Very good," said Mrs Quick approvingly.

"Now let's move on to Act II scene 4, where in the play at the literal level Rosalind has disguised herself as a boy - or in Elizabethan terms has reverted to the actor's true gender."

Mrs Quick went to a trunk in the corner of the barn, and made a show of rummaging around in it until she brought out one of the long ankle-length dresses that had been popular with female students in the early 1970s.

"Here you are, Jonathan," she said casually. "Now you have to change gender - I think this should fit you all right."

Mrs Quick paused anxiously, but as she had expected, Jonathan did not demur, but donned the flowery dress, his shirt-sleeved arms poking through its sleeeves, his jeans visible for a foot below the dress's hem.

Mrs Quick frowned.

"No, those jeans don't look quite right," she said. "Can you roll them up to the knee, or even take them off? We've got to get this looking right you know. You can change in the lounge."

Obediently Jonathan went into the house, and returned bare-legged, grinning good-humouredly as his fellow students greeted him with a little cheer.

"Very good," said Mrs Quick, smiling and joining in the laughter. "That's very sporting of you Jonathan - we've got to be authentic, you know. Now, let's take it from the beginning of the scene, ''O Jupiter, how merry are my spirits.' Elizabeth, you can play the clown - I have a jester's outfit here, I think, and Wendy, you can be Corin." Elizabeth and Wendy also ran eagerly into the house to change. Elizabeth donned parti-coloured jester's trousers and tunic, waving a toasting-fork that she had seized upon to act as a wand, whilst Wendy squeezed her boyish figure into black ballet-dancer's tights, a leather-jerkin, and a ruff.

"Good!" said Mrs Quick with great approval as they returned. "Now we can get to work."

Holding their parts in front of them, the students declaimed their lines enthusiastically and theatrically. What a splendid teacher Mrs Quick was! This certainly made the text much more approachable now that she had shown them how modern it all was really.

The time sped by. It turned out that Lucy could sing, so Mrs Quick went into the cottage and brought out Dr Crumpet's guitar. Soon Lucy too was on the stage, strumming at the guitar and singing 'Under the greenwood tree, and 'If it do come to passe, that any man turn Ass'. From time to time Mrs Quick stopped the action to explain a point or ask a question. Before she knew it, it was 1 o'clock.

"Well, I don't know about you, but I need a break," laughed Mrs Quick. "I think I promised you a buffet lunch - let's go and get it."

Mrs Quick strode confidently into the cottage, and the assembled troop of student thespians followed her. Jonathan seemed quite unselfconscious now in his floral dress, and Elizabeth too clearly enjoyed her jester's robes.

True to her promise, Mrs Quick had provided thick, white, crusty loaves. A large pan of excellent home-made soup had been simmering very slowly all morning, and cheese, tomatoes, pickles, cucumber and lettuce were spread along the kitchen table. Eagerly the students clustered round the table and helped themselves to food on cardboard plates. As ever, Mrs Quick had laid on wine in abundant quantities, and soon large tumblers of potent Chianti were loosening her students' tongues.

Mrs Quick leaned against the wall, sipping a half-glass of Chianti diluted with Perrier, for she would have to drive her students home in due course. She was pleased with the way her class had gone, it couldn't have worked out better. She was glad, too, that she had de-natured Jonathan by getting him to wear a dress, it had been easier than she thought! She had gained a little secret victory in thus reducing one of the boys on her class to the status of a woman. It opened up all sorts of possibilities.

"The class isn't over, is it?" asked Jonathan pleadingly. "We will go on and do a bit more, won't we?"

"Oh yes!" chorused the others.

Mrs Quick smiled sweetly, in the manner that so endeared her to her students.

"Well, this morning's class certainly took longer that I had expected - but if you're game, then I am too! I must finish by 4 p.m., though."

"Oh, thank you, Pauline, that is good of you!"

Mrs Quick basked in the admiration of her students.

At 4.15 p.m., the class came to an end. Mrs Quick took them into her lounge for mugs of tea, and then said:

"I think we ought to continue exploring this theme of gender next week."

She handed round some carefully selected extracts from Sidney's *Arcadia*. "This is a work which really explores the theme, more than *As You Like It* in many ways. Would you like another class here?"

"Oh, yes please, Pauline" they all exclaimed.

Mrs Quick smiled indulgently, and luxuriated in her secret thoughts and plans, sipping her tea sparingly, as the students chattered around her, and darkness fell. She watched with cat-like eyes as first Elizabeth, then Jonathan left the room to change back into their normal attire. And then at last it was time to go, and the laughing group clambered back into the Land Rover and returned to Hereford.

*****

Mrs Quick threw herself with great energy into the preparations for her class on the Arcadia the following Friday. Sitting in her office in the Magic Women bookshop next Monday morning, she skimmed through the work and photocopied selected passages, and marked them with the usual coloured felt-pens. From some of the books in her shop, she found illustrations of one of the romance's heroes, Pyrocles, in his disguise as the woman Zelmane, whom he pretended to be for much of the action of the work. From other books of costume she photocopied sketches of Elizabethan ladies' attire - full-skirted dresses, gloves, hats, ruffs, shoes. Then that evening, rummaging through the wicker-baskets full of clothing that she stored in her barn, Mrs Quick selected a bundle of long dresses, and took them back into the house, and there she and Dr Crumpet busied themselves with their sewing machines, adapting the garments to match the illustrations as closely as possible. Both of them were accomplished needlewomen. Samantha, the assistant in the Magic Women bookshop, and other of Mrs Quick's young female acquaintances, were mobilised in this task too, and every evening a regular and cheerful sewing circle met at the cottage. By the Thursday evening, Mrs Quick was satisfied that she had a passable wardrobe for her class the next day.

Promptly at half-past-nine, Mrs Quick drove to collect her students in the car-park of Hereford Poly. Her laughing, chattering group was waiting to meet her, with the exception of Bill, who had a bad cold and had sent word that he could not come. Mrs Quick was no whit perturbed by this news. Tamarantha and Beatrix joined Mrs Quick in the front, the others climbe into the back in high spirits, and soon the Land Rover was on its way to Mrs Quick's cottage outside Hay. After the usual coffee and biscuits, Mrs Quick was soon holding forth about the *Arcadia*. She had not actually read very much of the work, and had the greatest difficulty in keeping the plot in her mind. However, she did not see that as a difficulty, since she knew for a certainty that her students would be in just the same position. Moreover, the main themes of the work were self-evident to her.

"It's an unusual and important work," she enthused to her class, as they squatted down on the floor of the barn. "Most writers of this time are not sympathetic to women, but Sidney is. Maybe it's because he was brought up by his aunts and other female relatives. Sidney is attempting to show a way for women to break out from the conventional bonds of gender. That's why there's so much cross-dressing in the play. And of course the work was written for a predominantly female audience. Now, Jonathan, as the only chap here obviously you've got to play Pyrocles, disguised as Zelmane the Amazon. I've got your costume here, you can change in the lounge. It's quite authentic by the way, look, here is a wood-cut from an early edition."

Mrs Quick passed round photocopies to the rest of the class, as Jonathan eagerly sized the bundle of clothes and dashed into the cottage to change. Whilst he was away, Mrs Quick allotted other parts.

"I'll read Cecropia," she continued ingenuously, "and Wendy, you can read Pamela. Elizabeth, why don't you read Philoclea. Tamarantha , you can be the Queen of Corinth, and Beatrix, you be Gynecia. Here are some costumes for you. You may as well change here, as Jonathan's still in the cottage. Lucy, stand at the door and keep him out till the others have put on their costumes."

Mrs Quick looked on nonchalantly as the girls eagerly stepped out of their dresses and jeans and rushed to done the quite elaborate costumes which Mrs Quick and her helpers had fashioned. Soon they were jostling around the mirror, trying on hats, and trying to fix ruffs in place, squealing at each other in excitement and admiration. As a finishing touch, Mrs Quick fastened a large bundle of keys on an iron hoop around the waist of Wendy/Pamela.

"This is how ladies carried keys in Elizabethan times," she explained. "Look, I have a picture here."

The girls clustered round with interest, as Mrs Quick pointed to a contemporary illustration in a large modern folio-sized book taken from the stock of the Magic Women bookshop, illustrating the history of women's costume.

A few moment's later, Jonathan, dressed as Pyrocles/Zelmane, hurried back to the barn, the ankle-length hooped-skirt swaying around his feet, his chest bare, but with a fur-leather jerkin round his shoulders, holding a breadknife to represent an Amazonian sword.

Mrs Quick looked on in approval, as Tamarantha and Lucy let out a loud wolf-whistle.

Mrs Quick smiled.

"Right," she said, "let's start by reading the passage on page 152."

She handed round photocopies of the text, and for fifteen minutes they read one of the love-scenes between Pyrocles and Philoclea in Book III.

Then they paused for discussion, and soon Mrs Quick was discoursing about the story's magical elements, Demagoras's poison, Gynecia's aphrodisiac potion, and other similar themes.

"So there's no doubt at all that the *Arcadia* is one of the most important, though strangely neglected, Elizabethan works," explained Mrs Quick. "It supplied the plot elements of many later plays and novels, and as an exploration of the sensibilities of women it's quite unparalleled. Now, let's consider some of the many details of costume in the romance."

She handed out more photocopies illustrating Elizabethan costume, and soon the class was zealously pawing them over, gossiping amongst themselves as to which hat and ruff they liked the best. Tamarantha and Wendy pirouetted around the room, and by degrees the discussion veered well away from the text to considering whether satin or linen felt nicer to the skin. The conversation grew to a hubbub as the girls gave vent to their deeply held opinions on these important matters.

Soon it was 1 p.m., and time for a buffet lunch once more. The excited throng of Amazons and Elizabethan gentlewomen thronged in costume still to Mrs Quick's kitchen, admiring each other's outfits and chattering excitedly to one another. Mrs Quick presided over the festivities with great enjoyment, pouring out glasses of Chianti, urging her students to take helpings of home-made pâté, and enjoying the opportunity to talk informally tothem.

"That hat suits you, my dear," she said admiringly to Clare. "Its colour matches your hair so well."

Clare flushed with pride at being singled out for praise by Mrs Quick.

"I was thinking of doing my long essay on Elizabethan hats," said Clare. "Would that be OK for a topic, do you think, Pauline?"

"An excellent idea," responded Mrs Quick approvingly. "I'll put you down for it. I can give you several references to get you started. I have some of the books in my shop, as a matter of fact. Why don't you try to look in tomorrow afternoon? The bus service from Hereford isn't very good, but if you time it right you can get an afternoon in Hay. That would get you started, at any rate."

"Oh, thank you, Pauline!" Mrs Quick squeezed Clare's shoulder approvingly, and passed on to talk to Tamarantha.

"What about you, Tamarantha?" she enquired of the petite Nigerian. "Have you thought about a topic for your long essay?"

"Yes," said Tamarantha firmly. "I'm going to write on the interface between sexism and racism in the *Arcadia* - you know, like why is there a character called Melampus, or Black Foot. It's a terrific work - I am enjoying it Pauline. I don't suppose I'd have read it if you hadn't made us do it."

"I chose it specially with you in mind, Tamarantha," replied Mrs Quick flatteringly. "I knew that you would like it even if no-one else did. But it seems that everyone likes it."

"Yes, but not as much as me," answered Tamarantha happily, basking in the admiration of her teacher. "I say Pauline, I read your book on *Shirley* last week - I did enjoy it!"

Mrs Quick gave Tamarantha a little hug, and passed on.

"Well, Jonathan," she enquired "and how do you like being an Amazon? I hope that the role has made you think again about the gender stereotypes."

"It sure has," said Jonathan easily, reaching out for a Chianti bottle and helping himself to his fifth large tumbler of wine. "These skirts are kind of constricting aren't they. It must have made it difficult to move about in those days."

Mrs Quick patted Jonathan on the chest, and said:

"You're learning quickly, Jonathan. Yes, women's attire was deliberately made constricting in Elizabethan days, so as to keep women in their place, and stop them leading a life as free as men. I'm so glad that our performance has got that point over. Now, with your experience of the role, I think that there's one very obvious topic for you to write about for your long essay - Male cross-dressing in the *Arcadia*. OK?"

She passed on to Beatrix.

"What about you, Beatrix, what are you going to write about?"

"I thought I'd write about villainy in Cecropia," said Beatrix, in her fluent English with just the trace of an attractive Dutch accent in her voice.

"Excellent," approved Mrs Quick. "And I hope too that you will consider the social factors that made her what she was. Don't be too hard on her, my dear. Remember, she was a woman trying to make her way in a man's world, just like Goneril and Regan."

"Oh, but of course, Pauline. That was what I had in mind from the beginning."

Mrs Quick gave Beatrix a little kiss.

"I'm so glad my dear."

By 4 p.m., Mrs Quick had fixed up all her group with a suitable essay topic. Mrs Quick made coffee for the group, and they lingered on in the lounge till 5 p.m.. And then it was time for the class to go home. The girls returned to the barn to put on their normal attire, and Mrs Quick stacked up dishes in the kitchen whilst Jonathan changed out of his Amazon's outfit in the lounge. By 6.30 p.m., Mrs Quick had driven her group back to Hereford, and was happily sipping a large gin-and-tonic. All in all, it had been a successful day. Teaching by performance was certainly great fun, and she was grateful to her daughter Blanche for dropping her the hint. No wonder that Blanche was enjoying life at Skelmerdale; maybe, after all, the reputation for teaching of the Skelmerdale Department of English and Communication studies was not as hyped-up as she had once believed.

CHAPTER THREE

WITCHES THAT WOULD BE

'"We are neither temptresses, nor terrors, nor monsters."
"Some of our kind, it is said, are all three. There are men who ascribe to 'woman' in general such attributes."'
(Charlotte Bronte, *Shirley*)

All through the Spring term, as bookings for their conference mounted, Fawn and Florinda boasted about the event to Freddie Frowstie, and made their plans. And he in turn magnified it to his professorial colleagues, and puffed it to the Vice-Chancellor as a sign of the distinction and activity of his department. Already Freddie Frowstie had drafted several press releases lauding the occasion.

'The 'Writing Women Re-Vue Conference', which has just ended was one of the most successful in the history of the University of Skelmerdale, and in the subject throughout the world. Attended by the most prestigious leading names in women's studies today, it demonstrates the high reputation of the Department of English and Communication Studies at Skelmerdale in this area of study. Participants in the conference agreed that it was the most successful event of its kind that they had ever attended. Several delegates said that they would encourage their own children to apply to Skelmerdale as a result, even though it is well known that competition to get into the department of English and Communication Studies at Skelmerdale has always been extraordinarily high. We confidently anticipate that this successful conference will be the first of many...'

"Yes, it certainly reads very well," thought Freddie Frowstie to himself with satisfaction. This statement would appear in the University of Skelmerdale *Factfile*, and would be issued as a press release to the local and national press before the event took place, regardless of the outcome of the conference, and without regard to its success or failure. Even cancellation of the conference would not delay Frowstie's press release, unless the fact that the conference had been cancelled had itself been reported in the press as a prominent news item.

*****

As increasing numbers of books passed through her hands in the
Magic Women bookshop, Mrs Quick read more and more widely
in the occult, and broadened her interests to include esoteric and
fringe religions, folklore, fairies and Melusines, poltergeists and
otherworld journeys, curses and taboos. Already an accomplished
witch, she devoured all the books about witchcraft that came her
way. She browsed in Shamanism, and in the works of medieval
mystics such as Richard Rolle of Hampole, who, Mrs Quick had
been fascinated to learn, had walked around Yorkshire naked, in a
trance-like state of religious fervour, before donning a woman's
dress, an act of de-and re-gendering of which she thoroughly
approved. The diligent and enthusiastic Mrs Quick learned about
the history of secret societies. The goddesses Isis, Astarte, and
Diana fascinated her, as she embraced the religions of paganism.
She studied magic charms and incantatory spells in world literature
(in translation). And all the while she pondered on the enlargement
of her coven. So far, it was a small one. Last Autumn, before the
nights finally drew in, on two occasions only, had Mrs Quick
donned her Welsh girl hat, put on her grey, woollen, ankle-length
dress embroidered with mysterious signs, and driven to the
secluded valley which she had espied on the other side of the
Brecon Beacons. And there Mrs Quick had raised her arms
outstretched in supplication to the Moon and its virgin goddess
Diana, whilst Dr Crumpet and Dr Veronica Chamberlain knelt
naked on the ground with palms upstretched, and Dr Janet French,
who did not believe in witchcraft, looked on in tolerant
amusement, warmly dressed in black leather boots, tweed skirt,
white polo-necked sweater and windcheater, and stood guard at a
distance further up the hill. Doctors French and Chamberlain were
old friends from Surleighwick, where they had been the medical
officers at the University Health Centre. They now ran the medical
centre at Hereford Polytechnic, ten miles away. So Mrs Quick had
two devotees, and a sympathetic confidante. But she knew that
ideally a coven should consist of thirteen women....This was a
problem which she turned over methodically in her mind, night
after night, as she and Dr Crumpet ate, drank, and made love in
their cottage, when the day's work of the bookshop was done. And

in the end the solution seemed obvious. The recruits for her coven would have to come from her students or her customers.

Mrs Quick's students had always adored her from the start of her university teaching career, perhaps because she had always been genuinely interested in them, and they sensed that this was so. Then too, she had been a pretty young woman herself when first appointed as a lecturer, with slim features and dark black hair and lively eyes. The hair had now turned grey, the face was lined, but the friendliness and openness of expression was still there, and so the students liked her - 'the lovely Pauline', as they had called her behind her back at Surleighwick. Surleighwick was paying her a token sum in the last year of its existence to carry on supervising her three postgraduate students, Margaret, Cynthia and Naomi. There might be promising material there for a start, for those students had always fallen in with her suggestions. It was probably best for her to start with her post-graduates, but there were also her students at Hereford Poly, and there too, when she had got to know them a little better, was food for thought, and material that might be malleable, given time, in the right circumstances.

As Mrs Quick read and dreamed of Celtic Fairy Tales, pantheism, the New Age, the numinous world of tree spirits and standing stones, it was clear to her that nudity was important in rituals, especially ones involving magic. For clearly the removal of shoes and clothing made the link between woman and Mother Earth more potent. And Diana, goddess of the Moon, the goddess whom Mrs Quick admired and venerated above all others, had bathed naked with her maidens. And in fertility rites, women had walked naked through the fields to make the crops grow, or through streams to make the rains come. And the goddess Nerthus was said by Tacitus in the first century A.D. to have paraded through Denmark in her covered waggon, naked inside it, as scholars had shown. And nudity was an important part of the initiation ceremonies of young witches, symbolising as it did the putting aside of the old way of life and the surrender to the new. And the mystery religions of the later Roman empire too had practised cultic nudity. And Mrs Quick had learned from reading the books that came into her shop that nudity was important even in Christian initiation. For Cyril of Jerusualem had written a letter explaining to newly baptised Christians why they had been naked when they had received baptism. And John the Deacon, writing in

500 AD had said that converts were commanded to go naked into the water even down to their feet, so that they could show that they had put off the earthly garments of mortality. And Narsai, founder of the Nestorian school at Nisibis, had commented that the candidate for baptism should stand stripped before the judge so that his nakedness might win pity to cover him. And the Pseudo-Dionysius had described a Christian baptism in which the deacons had undressed the new converts completely, whilst the priest had rubbed oil into their bodies, just as she herself had done with Dr Crumpet's salve the previous summer....And the initiates had been immersed in water three times whilst the priest invoked the names of the Trinity. St Francis, too, making his vows to Lady Poverty, had symbolised this by taking off his clothes. The Abbess of Ramsey, in the twelfth century, had prayed standing naked in a stream. And some Christian writers had interpreted nudity as a symbolic imitation of Christ on the Cross. And since *kosmos* in Greek meant both ornament and world, by putting aside garments, one was putting aside the world. In pagan and secular initiation ceremonies too, nudity was an essential feature. In a fertility rite in ancient Rome, at the Feast of Lupercal, the young men had run naked through the streets, striking with their thyrsus such women as wished to conceive.

Yes! Maybe she ought to try these ideas out first of all on her postgraduates. She would invite them down for a weekend break in the country, at which she would serve one of the meals for which she was so renowned, where mouth-watering and succulent dishes would be accompanied by provisions of alcohol in truly liberal quantities. In these relaxed circumstances, Mrs Quick would see how her favourite female students responded to her ideas on cultic nudity....

*****

'Hell hath no fury like a woman scorned.'

In the University of Whitepool, Deirdre Prout was still seething with fury at Fawn and Florinda's rejection of her paper. The malicious, spiteful, bitches! How dare they! Two complete unknowns rejecting a paper by her, Deirdre Prout, the author of a book on *The Lady of Shalott*! How best to get her own back? That was the problem that was vexing Deirdre's mind day by day, as she brooded malevolently on the possibilities, alas all too limited, that were open to her.

"I could go along with a big pile of copies of my book, I suppose," she remarked to her friend and colleague Dr Margaret Jacquasse of the German Department, as they sat drinking coffee in the Whitepool Staff Club, one February morning during a break between classes. "That would make them feel pretty small."

"Yes, Deirdre, I suppose it might," responded Margaret. "But what if they found out that you only had so many copies because the book had been remaindered? If that happened, the whole thing would misfire."

Deirdre scowled at Margaret's tactlessness, but she had to admit that Margaret had a point.

"I could go along and ask some awkward questions at the sessions."

"Yes - but then you'd be attacking the speakers, not Fawn and Florinda."

"I could let white mice loose during the reception?" continued Deirdre hopefully.

"Possibly," replied Margaret. "But don't you think that that would savour too much of a schoolboy prank? Anyway, it would be sexist, because it would frighten the women far more than the men."

"There's a lot of water at Skelmerdale," hinted Deirdre darkly. "Maybe I could find a chance to push them both into the lake. That would serve the silly cows right."

"Now that's more like it," agreed Margaret "You want to find a way of disrupting the conference that also makes Fawn and Florinda look silly. So you could tip itching powder down their dresses, or maybe throw a custard pie at them. You're not going to do it by scoring intellectual points, you know. People forget what was said at conferences almost instantaneously - I know no one remembers what I say at conferences, anyway. You want to try and make them look ridiculous - like say sawing through the leg of their chair so they fall over when they sit on it, or even better, how about putting super-glue on their chairs so that when they sit down they can't get up again. Something on those lines perhaps?"

Irony was lost on Deirdre, and the possibility that Margaret was joking did not cross her mind.

"Yes, I believe you're on to something. Thanks, Margaret, you've given me one or two ideas. Of course, it will need some careful planning, and I shall need help. But I'm not the only one at Whitepool who hates Fawn and Florinda and would be glad to see them taken down a peg or two. And even at Skelmerdale there are people who don't like them. Damn! I've got to go now for my class on the stereotypes of gender and genre in *The Odd Women*. Let's talk more about this soon."

Deirdre Prout picked up her books and flounced briskly away, delightful visions of a tarred and feathered Fawn and Florinda flitting through her mind.

*****

'We must go onward, ever onward
Beyond that last blue mountain barred with snow.'
(James Elroy Flecker, *Abu Hassan*)

0214146207 Lance-Corporal Dr Crumpet, returning to Hay late that April afternoon thankfully tossed her brown beret with the winged-dagger cap-badge into a corner of the sofa, and sprawled out, tired but happy, in a deep armchair, propping her legs, still clad in combat fatigues and black calf-length laced boots, on a convenient chair, whilst Mrs Quick, neat in a fawn blouse and the beige skirt of a new costume suit, busied herself in preparing two extra-large gin-and-tonics for them both. Since moving to Hay-on-Wye Dr Crumpet had become a weekend soldier. For Mrs Quick, feeling that the Daughters of Glendwyr (the Hay-on-Wye chapter of which liberation movement Mrs Quick had founded shortly after arriving at Hay) would benefit from practical military knowledge on their midnight escapades, had urged Dr Crumpet to join the Territorial Army. As Mrs Quick had pointed out, she herself, at thirty-nine years old, was a few years too old to volunteer. Somewhat reluctantly, Dr Crumpet had fallen in with the suggestion, and, rather to her surprise, had found that she enjoyed the life greatly.

Dr Crumpet, a moderate eater who took plenty of exercise, had always been fit and healthy, and was now in the peak of physical condition. She had passed all her fitness examinations and selection tests with flying colours, and had proved to be of above average intelligence. After a rigorous forty-mile route march carrying a 56lb pack across the Brecon Becons a month previously, she had been accepted into her local territorial unit, none other than no. 22 SAS Regiment (Artists' Rifles) (TAVR), based not ten miles away, at Bradbury Lines, Hereford. Lithe, alert, and inured to hardship and discomfort, L/Cpl Dr Crumpet was making great progress in unarmed combat, in silent killing, and in close-quarter weapons training. She had also learned by heart the whole of Flecker's *Abu Hassan*, from which the Regiment took the motto that graced the memorial to the fallen inside the camp.

Her lovely auburn tresses spilled down her combat fatigues, freed now from the ribbon which normally kept them rucked up neatly under her beret. Mrs Quick looked proudly at her protégée. There was no doubt that uniform suited Tony, whether it was combat fatigues, khaki trousers and battle-dress, olive-green skirt, blouse and shoes, or the wonderful white blouse and full ankle-length evening skirt worn for formal functions in the mess.

"Oh, thanks Pauline," said Dr Crumpet, taking the gin and draining a huge gulp all at once. "That feels good." She lay her head back against the chintz cushions, and closed her eyes.

"You sure you won't be too tired for tonight's festivities?" enquired Mrs Quick anxiously.

"No, I shall be all right, thanks, Pauline," replied Dr Crumpet, holding our her glass for a refill. The wonderful savour of one of Mrs Quick's delicious casseroles filtered through the house. It was cooking in a cauldron, for tonight there were to be seven for dinner - Cynthia, Margaret and Naomi, Mrs Quick's three postgraduates, Doctors French and Chamberlain, and herself and Dr Crumpet.

Mrs Quick replenished Dr Crumpet's glass, and then moved over to the sideboard. She uncorked the nine bottles of Barolo which she had judged would be about right to accompany her cauldron of casserole - for she was a firm believer that alcohol in abundant quantities contributed greatly to the success of any dinner party. In the fridge, six bottles of heady, grapey, Muscadet de Beaune et Venise were quietly chilling, whilst on the sideboard three bottles of vintage '63 Dow's port were lined up in gleaming decanters. An abundant array of cocktails and aperitifs awaited her guests for consumption pre-dinner.

Cynthia, Naomi and Margaret had travelled down from Surleighwick by an early Saturday train, arriving at Hereford a little before lunch. Mrs Quick had met the train and had then driven them to Hay for a light repaste of omelette and salad. The girls had clambered happily into the front and back of Mrs Quick's long-wheel-base Land Rover, for which she had traded in her Peugeot last December. As she had explained to Dr Crumpet, the great advantage of her new vehicle was that it could seat twelve in the back, not indeed in comfort, but an important point all the same.

Chattering, Mrs Quick's postgraduates had arrived at the cottage, looking forward to their weekend away with whole-hearted pleasure, and Mrs Quick had shown them to their tiny rooms under the eaves of the cottage, before giving them a glass of white wine, gossiping away as the girls helped her to shake the salad. Afterwards, over the fruit, they had retired to the lounge, with its peaceful views over the Brecon Beacons, and there Mrs Quick had given her informal seminar on folk-elements and myth in the novels of the Brontë sisters, and had started to prepare the ground for what she hoped would be the culmination of the night's events.

Slowly she sipped at her wine, and handed round the fruit. She did not want to drink too much as yet, for she had a long day ahead of her.

"Of course one has to think of what it would have been like for women living as the Brontës did - so remote, so alone, so intense. I'm inclined to think they had abnormal powers. You remember, I'm sure, the tale of Emily cauterising a wound with a red-hot poker. Now there's a real triumph of mind over matter! And Charlotte too was interested in the paranormal. You remember the mysterious voice which Jane hears at the end of *Jane Eyre*? Of course, living up there in the remote fastnesses of the Yorkshire moors, where the whole landscape is numinous, full of the mysterious powers of Mother Earth, it would be hard not to feel an affinity with it, don't you think? Oh," she laughed, "to lay one's face against the stones, and caress the heather, and feel the breeze tickling one's skin under the cold light of the sun! Yes, it would be hard not to feel in tune with Nature living that way."

Cynthia, Naomi and Margaret had eagerly agreed with Mrs Quick.

"Even here," continued Mrs Quick, "even here in Wild Wales, as Borrow called it - you do know Borrow's book, don't you? Possibly as an American you don't, Cynthia, but I expect the others do. My dears, he was a wonderfully unconventional free soul, who lived quite the gypsy life - even here in Wild Wales, one feels so close to nature." Mrs Quick crossed to the window and opened it, letting a cool slipstream of air whoosh into the room from the west, and breathing in deeply. "Yes," she continued, "life can be so very peaceful here. One can be so in tune with nature. Tony and I often feel, when on our solitary walks into the hills, that we are very much at one with Mother Nature.

'I'll walk when my own nature would be leading:
    It vexes me to choose another guide:
Where the grey flocks in ferny glens are feeding,
    Where the wild wind blows on the mountain side.'
You recognize the lines I'm sure."

Mrs Quick paused for a moment.

"Yes," she continued, "the free, simple, unconventional life. Oh, I don't know, it makes one somehow want to strip off all conventions, and live like a child of nature in the wild hills." Mrs Quick sighed an artful sigh.

"But I suppose we're all very much the prisoners of convention nowadays, aren't we?"

Satisfied that she had started her group thinking on the right lines, Mrs Quick suggested that they take a stroll by themselves into the countryside outside Hay, whilst she herself continued with her preparations for the evening's meal, and awaited the return of Dr Crumpet from her weekend duties.

*****

'There in cold remote recesses
That nor alien eyes assail
Thou, O queen and holiest,
With reluctant lengthening tresses
And with sudden splendid breast
Save of maidens unbeholden
There art wont to enter, there

Thy divine swift limbs and golden
Maiden growth of unbound hair,
Bathed in waters white.'
(A. C. Swinburne, *Atalanta in Calydon*)

Mrs Quick had bathed and changed into a long black ankle-length dress of the type that she found so appealing. She had placed a string of pearls around her neck, and had pinned a golden brooch over her left breast. Now, with the sweet savours of the casserole filtering through the cottage, she could put her feet up and indulge herself with a large gin-and-tonic. Her guests, Margaret, Cynthia and Naomi, had returned from their walk, and were now bathing and changing for dinner. At 6 p.m. Dr Chamberlain and Dr French arrived in the latter's Ford Fiesta, both prepared for the ceremony of worshipping Diana that was to be the culmination of the evening. Dr Chamberlain was ready to participate again in the earthy rites, and Dr French in resigned amusement had agreed to drive Mrs Quick and her party to the hidden valley.

"Hullo, my dears, come in, let me get you a drink," Mrs Quick greeted her guests as they arrived, as she laid aside *Lesbia Brandon*, her favourite Victorian novel. The two doctors sat themselves down on the chintzy sofa, whilst Mrs Quick went into the kitchen to pour her guests the glass of Chablis for which they had asked as an aperitif. She returned with two tall-stemmed round-bowled glasses, each just over half-full. The portions were nonetheless generous, and contained between them just over a half bottle of wine.

"Cheers!" she said, raising her own glass. "Tony should be down soon - she's taken her drink upstairs whilst she gets changed. And my other guests, Margaret, Cynthia and Naomi should soon be here too. I think you'll like them - you may even know them if they were your patients at Surleighwick."

Mrs Quick looked approvingly at the two attractive Doctors. Dr Chamberlain was dressed simply in a dark grey-skirt, slightly pleated, with white silk blouse and cardigan. Dr French, knowing that a midnight expedition was on the cards, had prepared for it by wearing a dark-purple tweed skirt and a polo-necked sweater that showed off her full breasts to advantage. It was a pity, thought Mrs Quick longingly, that poor Janet still had scruples about joining her

coven, but sporting of her nonetheless to act as chauffeuse and
general guard. Her reverie was interrupted by the entrance of Dr
Crumpet. Dr Crumpet had prepared for the evening with some
care. Gone now was all trace of the weekend soldier, gone all
traces of spartan toughness. Her auburn hair framed her etherial
face, and tumbled, well-brushed but riotously down the back of her
flowery Laura Ashley dress, making her look like a pre-Raphaelite
heroine from one of Millais' paintings. The dress curved in at her
waist, and billowed out full-skirted to below her knees. The
fragrant aroma of a sandalwood perfume drifted round the room.
Dr Crumpet gratefully took the large goblet of gin-and-tonic that
Mrs Quick prepared for her, and sat down in a chintz armchair
opposite the two doctors, one elegantly-stockinged leg crossed
decorously over the other beneath her long dress.

And then her three guests came downstairs in a group. Dr
Crumpet they of course already knew, but they had escaped having
to consult the two medical doctors during their time at
Surleighwick, so introductions were made.

Mrs Quick looked around in great satisfaction.

"Well, it's ladies' night tonight," she laughed. "But I don't
think any of us minds that, do we? I did think of inviting one or
two boys for tonight," she lied, "but I thought it would be so much
nicer without them, then we can all get down to some woman-talk
so much more easily! And tonight is anyway, as it happens, sacred
to Diana, the virgin goddess, so boys wouldn't really have been
appropriate, would they?"

Her guests hastened to agree with her.

"No," continued Mrs Quick determinedly. "For far too long
men have made decisions at all-male dinner parties. It's time for us
women to catch up with them. So here's to us all!"

Mrs Quick lifted her gin in a toast, and the whole party raised
their glasses. Then she led the way to the dining room, and
disposed her guests around the table. She herself sat at its head,
and placed Naomi on her left and Margaret on her right. Dr
Crumpet sat at the far end of the table opposite Cynthia, whilst
Doctors French and Chamberlain faced each other across the table
in the middle. Aided by Margaret, Mrs Quick speedily served her
guests the opening course, a fish pâté, and poured them all a glass
of Chablis with it.

Over the first course, Mrs Quick asked her student guests to bring her up to date on developments at Surleighwick in the final year of its existence.

"Well, as you can imagine," said Margaret, "morale is very low. Everyone who can get out either has done so or is doing so, and the first and second years are very fed up about having to finish their course at the Open University. The whole place is going to pot. The library is being disposed of in chunks, so you can never find any books there. It's a mess. They say the VC went mad and got put away. And now no-one knows who's in charge."

Mrs Quick laughed.

"Yes, you have to thank Veronica and Janet there for that. They committed the VC to a madhouse, you know! He's still there I believe."

"So far as I know, he still is," answered Dr Chamberlain. "Well, he deserved it. Janet and I thought that he must be mad to have agreed as he did to the closure of his own university. He was suffering from paranoid delusions, you know. And he was violent, Janet had to take off his trousers and jab him in the bottom with paraldehyde to knock him out! It was a bad case of indecent exposure on top of that, too" - for Dr Chamberlain had gradually and unconsciously made the story more dramatic in her constant re-tellings of it - "an interesting case, nonetheless, in medical history. As the doctors who committed him, Janet and I still get case notes about him from time to time. They use him for demonstration purposes at medical and nursing schools, I'm told, just so the students know what to expect."

"Men!" said Mrs Quick, with great satisfaction.

Aided by Margaret, she cleared away the first course, and ladled out her delicious casserole. Dr Crumpet poured out the first bottle and a half of Barolo, and the talk became general and lively as the evening progressed. Mrs Quick diluted her Barolo with still mineral water from a large bottle, for she did not want to become too drunk, and Janet French too drank sparingly, switching to Perrier after one glass of Chablis and one of Barolo, for she knew she must keep sober if she were to be the party's driver at the end of the evening.

The talk turned to books, and Mrs Quick was urgent in commending *Lesbia Brandon* to her three students.

"My dears, it's one of the greatest and most important novels of the nineteenth-century! Swinburne is not to everyone's taste of course, but oh, what a poet he was! *Atalanta in Calydon* is the greatest Victorian tragedy, and as for *Les Noyades*! You must read it, my dears, and tell me what you think. And then the *Hymn to Proserpine*! If ever a man could convey the attractions and values of paganism, it was Swinburne. And he was right to do so, I'm sure. It was one way of undermining the conventional Christian-based power structures of mid-Victorian England. And my goodness, didn't they need subverting! He was a rebel, a great poet with a flaming heart, and not afraid to defy the conventions. He was in touch with the real life forces of the earth."

Mrs Quick paused, and cleared away the casserole plates, and returned with a syllabub and a couple of bottles of the extremely potent Muscadet. She poured generous servings of the rich dessert wine into the fresh crystal goblets placed before her student guests. "Yes, a great spirit," she continued, as her postgraduates listened to her every word, and the light and smooth syllabub slipped sensuously down their throats. "Like Shelley, Swinburne had the courage to defy convention and wander naked on the sea shore near his home, communing with nature."

Over the fruit and port, Mrs Quick warmed to her theme. The night had closed in, she had drawn the curtains, and switched on the subdued glow of a corner standard-light, and had lit a nest of candles in the centre of the table. The flickering flames cast giant ghost-like shadows over the walls.

"My, this port is excellent," adjudged Mrs Quick benevolently, sipping a small cut-glass crystal of the dark-red liquid. To think it is nearly forty years old!"

Mrs Quick looked round the table at her happy guests, who had been excellently wined and dined, and were now totally relaxed.

"Let's take our drinks into the lounge," she suggested, seeing that no-one could eat any more. In the lounge a log fire was lit to take away the evening chill. Mrs Quick drew the curtains, and turned on the subdued side-lights on the walls. Her guests spread themselves out on sofas and chairs, and on cushions on the floors. Mrs Quick handed round glasses of brandy, cointreau, and strega.

"What do you think about all this, Margaret?" asked Mrs Quick. "Am I making sense to you?"

"Oh yes, I'm with you all the way, Pauline," replied Margaret dreamily, as she gazed at the flickering flames of the log fire. Margaret was a great admirer of Mrs Quick's and looked up to her as a brilliant scholar and woman of high academic distinction, who always had a helpful comment to make on written work submitted to her.

The moment had come for Mrs Quick to make her play.

"Well, my dears," she said, sipping a highly diluted glass of Chablis and Perrier water, holding it before her eyes and twirling the lightly coloured mixture round in front of her, "some of us here are into a new religion, a true new age religion, a women's religion highly appropriate for right-thinking women today. Tony and I have learned a lot from the books which pass through our hands at the shop, and we have discovered that not far from here is an ancient vale, once sacred both to her Celtic equivalents and to Diana, goddess of the Moon, Diana, par excellence the deity sympathetic to the female sex. Oh!" she continued with a smile, holding up her hand as if to ward off their objections, "you may say that Diana is a pagan goddess who cannot exist. But what she symbolises, the numinous power of women, does exist, and there are sacred places still where our inner female strength can be restored and renewed, our souls healed in a place harmonious to nature. And tonight, when the moon is full, and shines upon the earth, we, the votaries of Diana, feel that we should bathe in her rays, and lay ourselves open to her influence, and kneel before her. So I am going to get my little book of hymns, and offer up a rite to Diana with Tony and Veronica here. Janet is not yet a full believer, but she will drive us there. And you, my dears," - Mrs Quick turned to Margaret, Cynthia, and Naomi, who hung entranced upon her every word - "you may come with us, if you wish, as spectators or participants. One thing I ask, and know I can count on - that you speak of this to no one, for the worship of Diana is for the initiate, and knowledge of it not to be spread to unbelievers. But come, come with us and feel the power of Diana's rays. It's time to go. Like the great Nerthus, the votaries of Diana travel unclothed, but hidden from the world's eyes in our waggon. Join us my dears!" Mrs Quick stretched out her hands with a smile of entreaty.

Dr Crumpet and Dr Chamberlain put down their drinks, and unhurriedly stepped out of their clothes, folding them into neat piles and placing them on the floor. They stood there un-selfconsciously for a moment or two, confident in their beauty. And then Cynthia giggled and said:

"Why not, it sounds like an interesting experience to me." And she too quickly stripped off her clothes, and was rewarded by a tender smile from Mrs Quick. Margaret followed instantly, but, feeling the cold a little, moved nearer to the fire to catch the warmth of its dull red embers. Naomi felt a little more nervous and uncertain and shy, but she did not want to be the odd one out, or to seem prudish, so she too took off her clothes, and joined the others. Mrs Quick took out a cloak embroidered with magical signs, and a gnarled staff from an old oak chest in the lounge.

Dr Janet French put on her windcheater, and received the keys of the Land Rover from Mrs Quick. She looked at her naked companions with tolerant amusement. Really! What a lot of mumbo-jumbo, she thought to herself. Goddess of the Moon indeed. One had one's doubts about Pauline Quick sometimes; last year she had seemed so normal and down to earth, very much a practical woman of the world, direct, straightforward, a real go-getter. And now all of a sudden she was into this new age nonsense, and talking of moon goddesses, and worshipping stones in hidden valleys.

"Oh well, it takes all sorts to make a world," she said to herself philosophically. The Land Rover was drawn up outside the front door of Mrs Quick's cottage. It was now 11.35 pm. Mrs Quick turned out the lights of her cottage, and held open the front door. Dr French opened the back door of the Land Rover, and the five nudes scampered giggling across the grass, and climbed inside. Dr French carefully closed the door behind them. Mrs Quick closed the door of her cottage, and raised herself into the front passenger seat of the Land Rover. Dr French switched on the ignition, engaged the clutch, and the waggon of Nerthus was on its way to the vale of Diana.

Soon Dr French was driving on the long and narrow road that led south from Hay to Llanthony, up into the Black Mountains. Three miles to the south, she engaged the four-wheel drive, and cut the lights, and carefully headed the vehicle across the springy bracken and heather towards a distant rock on the skyline.

"You don't think the girls will be too cold back there, do you

Pauline?" she asked. Certainly, with the moon full, it looked as if it might be cold outside.

"Oh no, they'll be all right, I think," answered Mrs Quick casually. "Religious initiates can stand a little heat and cold, anyway. And we shan't be out in the cold for long - not more than ten minutes."

Ten minutes later the Land Rover approached the edge of the bowl-shaped valley that was their destination. Carefully Dr French drove the vehicle ten feet down its gently sloping sides, so that it was hidden from view.

Mrs Quick slid back the little hatch which gave on to the interior of the vehicle, and said:

"Just stay there for a moment as it's a bit cold, whilst I set up the altar. I'll signal Janet when it's time for you to come out."

Mrs Quick made her way down the side of the valley until she came to a tree, in front of which was a flat dolmen, the sole visible remains, so the local history book said, of an ancient pagan temple. Mrs Quick draped her cloak over the stone to serve as an altar cloth, and placed a small leather-bound volume on top of the cloak. She took up position in front of the tree, facing the stone. She waved to Janet, and Janet opened the door of the Land Rover.

"There she is, she's down there," Janet whispered, for although there was no one there, it seemed appropriate to speak in a hushed voice.

In more solemn mood now, the five young ladies descended from the Land Rover, shivering in the moonlight. Dr Crumpet and Dr Chamberlain led the way, and jogged gently down the hillside to where Mrs Quick stood standing, followed closely by Margaret, Cynthia and Naomi. They took up positions in a semi-circle on the other side of the rock, facing Mrs Quick.

Mrs Quick stretched out her arms, the full sleeves of her dress billowing as she did so.

"Diana, goddess of the Moon, of childbirth, of hunting, and of the crossways, look kindly upon us thy servants gathered here tonight. Pour upon us your health-giving rays."

Mrs Quick bowed her head in prayer.

"Let us now all kneel and pray to Diana," she said.

She knelt, and closed her eyes.

Opposite her, the five young ladies did the same, feeling the harsh bracken brush against their shins and thighs.

An intense look of concentration passed over Mrs Quick's face. Her eyes were tightly closed, she seemed oblivious of her surroundings. The pale moon gleamed coldly on the bodies of her associates.

At last Mrs Quick opened her eyes, her face freed from strain.

"It is enough. The goddess has spoken to me. She has received our prayers, and bestowed her blessing. We will all sleep well tonight, you will see. Now let's go home, before we all catch cold."

Mrs Quick picked up her cloak, book and stick, and leaning on the latter for support began to climb back up the valley. Ahead of her the votaries of Diana ran bare and chattering up the hill, giggling a little and whispering excitedly to one another.

Dr French was waiting for them at the top, and good-humouredly opened the back door of the Land Rover for them. It seemed a pretty adolescent prank to her! In a moment or so Mrs Quick too had arrived at the top of the hill, and Dr French was driving the party back to Mrs Quick's cottage. She met not a single vehicle on the way back, for it was now past midnight, and even in the summer the road was always very quiet.

Mrs Quick opened the door of her cottage and led the party back into the lounge. Once they were all inside, she closed the door and turned on the lights.

"And now absolutely the very first thing you must all do is have a glass of mulled wine," she said. "I put it on the hob especially a couple of hours ago. Quick, drink it down, before you even get dressed, it's delicious, and will ward off any chills."

She handed round pewter goblets of a thick and potent concoction, ladelled from a large pan containing mulled wine, oranges stuffed with cloves, cinammon, nutmeg, a very heady brew indeed of red wine laced with brandy. To this Mrs Quick had added a powerful soporific, so that all the party would indeed sleep well that night, and attribute the fact to the influence of Diana.

Cynthia drained a deep draught and held out her goblet for more.

"It seems hardly worth getting dressed, again as we're going to bed so soon," she remarked, warming her bottom in front of the fire. "If it's all the same to you, Pauline, I'll stay as I am."

"Of course, my dear," responded Mrs Quick with an understanding smile. "You're quite right of course, I don't mind in the least."

The others agreed with these sentiments, and even Naomi had now lost her shyness.

"I feel we've had a great adventure tonight, that was fun. You must tell us more about the worship of Diana in the morning," put in Naomi.

"Of course, my dear, I'll lend you some books about it," said the sympathetic Mrs Quick, feeling pleased with herself as she contemplated the very successful end to her dinner party. She stoked up the flames of the fire with a poker, and threw another log onto the fire. Mrs Quick looked happily at her five naked guests, as they strolled up and down the room sipping mulled wine, warming themselves in front of the friendly flames of the fire, and then flopping down on to sofas and armchairs.

After a few goblets of the potent brew, tiredness crept upon them. One by one Mrs Quick's guests said goodnight and slipped upstairs to use the bathroom and retire to bed. At last only Dr French was left, sprawled out on the sofa in a deep stupor, overcome by the effects of three glasses of the powerful mull. Mrs Quick gently took off Dr French's shoes, undid the zip of her skirt, pulled the sweater off her shoulders, undid the top button of her blouse, and drew a coverlet over her unconscious form. Then, well pleased with the night's works, she did some preliminary tidying up, before, at last, succumbing to tiredness herself, and going upstairs to bed.

CHAPTER FOUR

THE WRITING WOMEN RE-VUE. ACT I

'The fourth city is Skelmerdale, the seat of a bishop, and fifty leagues distant from Scotland. In circuit it is great, but not in population or wealth; in respect of these matters it falls much behind London. It has no lord apart from the king.'
(John Major, *History of Greater Britain* (1521))

Professor and Mrs Hanwell flew from Surleighwick, Arkansas to New York on Sunday 4 May. They checked in to the Carlyle Hotel on Madison and 74th for just over a week to see one or two shows and enable Ruth to buy various items for her wardrobe from the fashion houses, and then boarded the QE2 on Wednesday 14 May for the sea voyage to England. They had decided that a few days' ocean breezes would be good for them, after the by now slightly monotonous heat of the Deep South. Moreover, as Professor Hanwell, an experienced Atlantic flyer, had pointed out to his wife, this would enable them both to avoid the tedious exhaustion of West-East jet lag, and the dreadful experience of arriving at 7 a.m., after a sleepless and uncomfortable night, at either of London's main airports. They had taken a first-class cabin on A deck, and the voyage had been a delightful interlude. Each morning, they had lazily taken breakfast in bed, before walking round the promenade deck for forty-five minutes or so. Then they had sat side by side on sun-loungers, reading each other's conference papers, and arguing over last-minute stylistic changes. An aperitif and a leisurely lunch washed down with a bottle of Chablis had been followed by love-making in their cabin, before a drowsy sleep overcame them. Then they had swum in the pool, before returning to their cabins to dress for dinner in the Queen Elizabeth Grill, overlooking the prow of the ship. And over dinner, gazing deep into each other's eyes, utterly absorbed in each other's company, they had gossiped of hermits and religion, of pantheism and Plotinus, and Pan and satyrs and fauns, of Naiads and Sybils, of Nereids and the naughtinesses of nymphs, of nymphomaniacs and neuroses, until, as the evening drew to its close, they lingered lazily over coffee and brandies and crème-de-menthes, and looked at the dazzling life going on all around them. And then, hand in hand, they had taken a final stroll around the promenade deck, looking at the stars bright in the sky, before retiring to their cabin for another honeymoon-like night.

The QE2 had docked at Southampton late on the night of Monday 19 May, and, like many of the passengers, they had stayed on board until the following morning. Then, after breakfast, they had caught the 9. 30 a.m. cross-country train from Southampton to Skelmerdale, avoiding London. England seemed very green that fresh May morning, as they gazed from the deserted compartment at the settled patchwork of fields and farms. Slowly the train progressed north, stopping at Winchester, Reading, Oxford, Leamington Spa, Coventry, Birmingham, Derby, Sheffield, Leeds, York, and then, a little later on, when the train had looped west north of Darlington, after an eight hour journey, they were approaching the famous and historic city of Skelmerdale, in the north-west of England.

"Nearly there," exclaimed Ruth, glimpsing in the distance the tall spire of Skelmerdale Cathedral. "I'm looking forward to this conference - it should be fun!"

Ruth yawned contentedly, and stood up in the compartment to stretch her legs, and carefully smoothed the pleats of the skirt of the stylish and well-fitting light-grey suit that she had bought in New York. Soon they and their luggage were safely installed in a big black London-style taxi-cab, and were driving slowly through the streets of that ancient city, crowded with late-afternoon traffic, on the way to the campus of the famous University of Skelmerdale, on the outskirts of the city. Ruth had been to Skelmerdale several times, visiting her chums at the university, but it was Professor Hanwell's first visit there, and he gazed with interest at the higgledy-piggledy mixture of architectural styles, Norman, Late Perpendicular, Gothic, Victorian, Georgian, Tudor and 'sixties brutalism, all jumbled together in a pleasing mess. Professor Hanwell was startled to see, suddenly, six of Cromwell's Ironsides walking down the street, with iron helmets and visors on their heads, wearing brown leather jerkins surmounted by metallic breast-plates, with massive pistols tucked into the sashes around their waist, and high, black, leather boots. And there coming towards them were an equal number of cavaliers, with feathered hats and lace ruffs and blue silk coats! What was going on?

But Ruth was quite unperturbed.

"Oh, it will be the Sealed Knot," she remarked casually. "They re-enact the battle of Skelmerdale Moor every anniversary, you know. And yes, that's it, today is the anniversary of the famous Civil War battle, when the Cavaliers were routed by the New Model Army, and after a fortnight's siege surrendered the city intact to Cromwell's men. Don't be so surprised, Charles, people are always getting dressed up in Skelmerdale!"

At last the taxi emerged from the central mass of Skelmerdale traffic, and soon it was driving them through the tranquil and spread-out campus of the University of Skelmerdale, past gently undulating hills, and modern buildings hidden away between the trees, with vast expanses of water everywhere.

"'Ere you are squire, that's as far as I can go," said the taxi-driver, depositing their suitcases on the pavement at the entrance to a wide causeway-like bridge that traversed the surface of the water to the island glories of the Castle Island complex.

As Professor Hanwell made to pick up their suitcases, he was astonished at the sight of three dark-haired devil-girls dressed in black tights and bras, with bare midriffs, who surrounded him and Ruth with hissing noises, and joyfully pranced around them, stabbing the air with their tridents. Their faces were masked with Cat-Woman eye-masks, and diminutive black cloaks were draped over their shoulders. As Ruth nonchalantly stepped towards them, they cackled and ran off.

"Student Thespians," laughed Ruth. "Well, I did say people liked getting dressed up at Skelmerdale."

Professor Hanwell looked around in puzzlement. It seemed for a moment that he and Ruth were the only people in modern dress to be seen! Coming towards him over the bridge were a knight and a squire and a nun with a huge badge on her habit reading 'Amor vincit omnia'. Two men-at-arms came to attention and stamped the butt of their halberds on the ground as Ruth set foot on the causeway, the breeze fluttering the skirt of her suit in the wind. Shrugging his shoulders, Professor Hanwell picked up the two suitcases and followed in his wife's train.

Soon they were in the entrance-foyer of the Castle Island complex, signing the registration forms, and being effusively greeted by Miss Fawn Fern.

"So very glad you could come," she said brightly, sitting at the foyer desk in her flowery summer frock, with open sandals on her bare feet.

"Here are your conference packs," she continued. "Your badges and all the information are in those. The drinks reception is at 6 p.m. in the Main Common Room. Meanwhile Tabitha here, one of our student helpers, will show you to your room." Fawn flashed a quick smile and buried her head in her pile of papers again. The Conference was certainly going to be a great success.

Tabitha stepped out of the shadows, and with a little simper lisped:

"Will you follow me thith way pleathe?" She picked up the key to their room, and swayed down the corridor.

It seemed to Professor Hanwell that he must be hallucinating, because as far as he could see Tabitha had not a stitch of clothing on. Surely he hadn't had as much to drink as all that on the QE2?

He looked sharply at Ruth, but she seemed perfectly composed, as if nothing untoward were happening.

"Thanks, Tabitha," she said easily, following in the wake of the naked Tabitha, and leaving her husband immediately behind her with the two suitcases, his eyes distracted by the sight of Tabitha's bare and seductively swaying bottom. Professor Hanwell could not pinch himself, but he made an effort to curl up his toes as he walked along, and he gripped the handle of the suitcases tightly. No, he couldn't be dreaming, he could feel his fingers and toes. But what was happening?

With an effort he caught up with Ruth.

"Why's that girl got no clothes on?" he whispered urgently into his wife's ear.

"Oh Charles! That's not a girl with no clothes on," she reproached him gently.

"But it is! She hasn't. I can feel my fingers and toes. I know it's not a dream!"

Tabitha padded seductively along the polished tiles of the long corridor.

"Thorry it'th thuch a long way," she apologised, pausing for a moment and turning round to face them both, and tossing back her chestnut curls with a self-satisfied air. The dethign of thith building ith quite labyrinthine, ithn't it?"

"Charles! I'm surprised at you," continued Ruth, seeing clearly by his bewilderment that her husband still did not realize what was going on. "You didn't use to be so slow on the uptake. And you a scientist and a historian of science too! Surely you if anyone ought to recognize that what is observed is inevitably and inextricably bound up with the viewpoint of the observer? And after all, we are in Skelmerdale now, and not just in Skelmerdale but in the University of Skelmerdale. Does that make it clearer?"

"Ah," he replied, thinking quickly, constructing a little syllogism in his mind, and trying to avoid being distracted by Tabitha's alluring and unclothed form. "Yes, I think I see. Skelmerdale, chic university, therefore, full of radical and unconventional students from middle-class families: 'Clothes are bourgeois, therefore let's not wear any'. That's it, isn't it?"

"No Charles, that is not it," replied Ruth. "Really! You are slow today! Think! Since we have arrived on the Skelmerdale campus, every student we have met has been in medieval dress. What have we seen? Three female devils, a knight, a nun, a squire, two men-at-arms. Now, does that make it any clearer?"

Professor Hanwell thought for a moment.

"Of course, got it!" he exclaimed. "She's Lady Godiva. How foolish of me not to have seen it before."

Ruth dug her left elbow into her husband's ribs with a friendly grin, as she rolled her eyes at his obtuseness.

"No, Charles! Of course she's not Lady Godiva! Where's her horse?"

At last they arrived at their room, and Tabitha fiddled for a moment with the key, and then held the door open for them before ushering them both into the pleasant, spacious, double room. Tabitha pranced unselfconsciously round the room, opening drawers, showing them the closets, pointing out how the teasmade worked, and finally ushering them into the en-suite facilities in a small room to which a door in the middle of the right-hand wall gave access.

"I hope you will be comfortable here," said Tabitha. "It'th one of the nithetht roomth there ith in the Cathtle Complecth, and you have a wonderful view over the lake." She gestured towards the picture window, from which could be seen a wide stretch of blue water rippled by the breeze, alive with mallards and ducks and water-beetles, and myriad other forms of marine and bird life.

Ruth gestured to her husband to give Tabitha a tip, and, still puzzled, but feeling exceptionally benign towards the lovely and naked Tabitha as she stood before him, cool and lithe and full-breasted, he took a £20 note from his wallet and gave it to Tabitha.

"Oh, thank you tho much, Thir," she said excitedly, putting her arms around his neck and giving him a kiss. "You are thweet!"

"Well, so are you!" replied Professor Hanwell good-naturedly.

"Thank you, O Eve-before-the-Fall," cut in Ruth firmly, holding open the door for Tabitha to depart. "I think we can manage by ourselves now. Don't let's keep you from your duties any longer."

"You recognithed me," exclaimed Tabitha delightedly. "Not everyone doeth, you know. Thome people think I'm Lady Godiva, but that'th thilly, ath I don't have a horthe. I do hope you'll come to thee the thchow. Theven of the Thkelmerdale Mythtery Playth are being put on for the delegateth on the Thaturday evening. I wath lucky to get the part of Eve - there wath great competition for it, but I think the director liked my hair." Tabitha ran her fingers complacently through her long chestnut tresses.

"I bet that's not all he liked," put in Professor Hanwell, fascinated by Tabitha.

"We'll be there," said Ruth decisively. "Thank you Tabitha and good-bye!"

Ruth held the door wide open, and at last the simpering Tabitha left the room.

"Well, Charles," continued Ruth, "I trust you are feeling suitably chastened for not having realised what was going on. Lady Godiva indeed! How daft can you get? There was no horse, after all."

"Sorry, Ruth," her husband replied defensively. "But I've never read the Skelmerdale Mystery plays."

"Well I have," said Ruth. "some of them, at least. I studied several of them in my second-year at Surleighwick. They have a reputation for being by far the most tedious of the extant cycles - much worse than the York or Wakefield or Coventry or Chester cycles. There are 157 of them, and I happen to know that the English department at Skelmerdale makes a big thing of them in its drama option. It was obvious to me at once what was going on! I've had friends who have done the drama option at Skelmerdale. And like in most drama departments, students are really encouraged to become their roles."

"Sorry to have been so stupid, Ruth," apologised Professor Hanwell humbly. "I can see that Skelmerdale will take me a little time to get used to. Is it all going to be like this? And isn't it a little embarrassing for Tabitha?"

"Oh Charles!" Ruth rolled her eyes in mock-exasperation.

"But even so, it must take a hell of a nerve to wander around like that."

"Oh Charles!! Really!! Didn't you notice from her eyes that she was totally stoned on peyote?"

"I wasn't looking at her eyes," replied Professor Hanwell.

"Charles!" said Ruth, affecting to be scandalised. "Anyone would think you had never seen a naked woman before. Now for heaven's sake let's forget about Tabitha." Calmly she drew the curtains. Ruth looked quizzically and mischievously at her husband, took off the skirt and jacket of her suit, unbuttoned her blouse and stepped out of her slip, and stood alluringly in the black seamed-stockings, and peach-coloured bra, panties and frilly garter-belt with soft-pink bows that she had bought at Victoria's Secret in New York.

"Come on, let's make love."

Nothing loath, Professor Hanwell led Ruth to the bed and slipped his hands under her bra.

"How do you know she was on peyote?" he whispered, unable still quite to put Tabitha out of his mind.

Ruth giggled contentedly.

"Remember, Charles, when we got engaged, you asked me what I was now and where I had been. And we both agreed, 'no questions'!"

There were times when his wife was an enigma to Professor Hanwell. Wisely he took the matter no further, but kissing Ruth full on the lips, and removing the rest of her clothes, began to make love to her on top of the bed; and then at last was able to put the Tabitha episode out of his mind.

*****

Afterwards, as five o'clock approached Ruth and Professor Hanwell sat outside on the tiny balcony of their room, overlooking the lake. Professor Hanwell, refreshed and relaxed, lit a Don Diego cigar, and for a moment or two they sat there in companionable silence. Beneath them, on the waters, students in canoes and rowing-boats drifted by, taking evasive action every few moments to avoid the windsurfers in their wet-suits and coloured sailboards.

"It looks just like a holiday resort," Professor Hanwell remarked at length, savouring the tranquil scene, and watching the smoke from his cigar drift lazily over the balcony.

Ruth turned to him, surprised.

"But of course, that's just what it is," she explained. "Didn't you know that Skelmerdale was the first of the English resort universities? All my friends who came here did so because they just wanted a good time. It's a nice, quiet, town, parents think it's safe - though of course it isn't really, they had a bad and still unsolved axe-murder here on campus last year - the courses aren't too demanding, there is no language work, there are opportunities for many sports, they have their own student TV and Radio service, and, of course, there are endless opportunities for dressing up in costumes and acting plays. I expect I could have got a place here too, but I wanted to learn at least something, so I thought I'd go to somewhere more traditional like Surleighwick. Aren't you glad I did?"

Twenty yards away across the lake, and a little to his left, Professor Hanwell's eye was caught by a rather extensive Wendy house, from which emerged a young woman dressed in a flowing white dress, followed by seven tiny figures.

"Ah," he exclaimed, beginning to adjust to the Skelmerdale ambience, "look Ruth, over there, that must be Snow White and the Seven Dwarfs."

Ruth shook her head sadly.

"Sorry, Charles, you're way off beam. Skelmerdale has had an affirmative action programme for little people - or people of restricted growth as they are now more properly called, ever since its foundation. And those buildings over there are their residence block. They live in scaled-down quarters so as not to feel overwhelmed by the furniture you know. And the young woman in white, for a certainty, is just their student carer."

Professor Hanwell began to feel that he would never understand the University of Skelmerdale, and was glad he had Ruth with him to interpret its more curious features.

At length Ruth looked at her watch.

"Well, time for the reception, I think." She rose, smoothed down the folds of the billowing burgundy-coloured frock into which she had changed, and brushed her hair carefully in the mirror. They both pinned on their name-tags, and then walked down the echoing corridors to the stairs, and soon found their way to the sherry and drinks reception, where a buzz of conversation signified that the first event of the conference was getting under way.

Neither Ms Fawn Fern nor Ms Florinda Morrison drank. But they had colleagues who did, and from their own experience of attending conferences, they had learned that part of the secret of conference success lay in ensuring that there was enough to eat and drink, whether of tea, coffee or alcohol, and time enough to drink it in. The increasing subventions that they had extracted from Freddie Frowstie, and the conference fees, had been heavily invested in alcohol, with fruit juices for the teetotallers. The reception had been going on for fifteen minutes when Professor and Mrs Hanwell arrived, and already the lively scene gave promise that this might be a successful and enjoyable conference.

Ms Fawn Fern shook their hands again as they entered the room, and then they passed inside to join the throng.

Once again Professor Hanwell was astonished when an attractive blonde young woman wearing a black corset and suspenders, black bra, black stockings, and polished high-heeled shoes approached with a tray of drinks. Ruth helped herself to a sherry, whilst Professor Hanwell, distracted, tipped the contents of two whisky glasses into a third, and drained a deep sip to steady his nerves as the young woman flashed a smile and passed on to serve another guest.

Once more Professor Hanwell turned to his wife for an interpretation of what he had seen.

"I suppose if I say that I've just seen a girl in black underwear - and - heavens! - there are some more over there - you'll tell me that I'm looking at the matter from an incorrect viewpoint?" He was grateful for the reassuring warmth of the whisky as it trickled down his throat.

"My dear Charles! Of course you are! And you a horror film fan at that! Do you mean to tell me that you never saw *The Rocky Horror Picture Show*?"

"No, I never did."

"Tut, tut, Charles, you surprise me! *The Rocky Horror Picture Show* (1975) became, soon after its release, a cult movie on British campuses. And the real fans of the film are in the *Rocky Horror*

Picture Show Fan Club, and they all like to dress up like the characters in the film. Hence the black underwear. The local campus branch has obviously been roped in to help out tonight with serving the drinks. They'll probably get a course credit for it you know - they're very keen on practical experience of performance at Skelmerdale!"

"How do you know all this, Ruth," asked Professor Hanwell, still disconcerted. "You weren't in the fan club, were you?"

"No," she smiled. "I'd have been too self-conscious, unless I was very drunk. But my schoolfriends who went to Skelmerdale soon joined the club - it's very big here, like all the dressing-up clubs, and that's when I first made my acquaintance with it."

"But isn't it a little strange to be wearing such an outfit at a feminist conference?" asked Professor Hanwell, still not entirely convinced.

"No, Charles," explained Ruth patiently. "It's simply the celebration of the essentially feminine, and a woman's right to choose to wear whatever she wants without men seeing her as a sex-object, so there!"

As they stood there sipping their drinks, two more of the black-corseted Rocky Horror waitresses ran towards them, deposited their trays on a convenient table, rushed towards Ruth, and then shook hands warmly and unselfconsciously with Professor Hanwell.

"You remember my bridesmaids, Fiona and Tamsin, don't you Charles? I told you my friends here were Rocky Horror fans. So nice to see you again." Ruth kissed both her friends. "You must let Charles and me take you out for a really nice meal. If the food here is anything like it was at Surleighwick, I bet you'd leap at the chance of a decent dinner for a change!"

"Ooh, yes please," exclaimed Fiona and Tamsin in unison.

Tamsin in a friendly fashion refilled Professor Hanwell's glass almost to the top with whisky, and as Ruth and Fiona became absorbed in catching up with the news of the last year, Professor Hanwell engaged Tamsin in conversation. And, as the whisky started to take effect, her alluring attire began to seem less startling to him than it had at first.

"So what do you read at Skelmerdale," he enquired at last, as Tamsin poured herself a large tumbler of whisky too, and drained it with a gulp, before proceeding to take a refill.

"Oh, I do English and Communication Studies," she giggled. "That's how I got involved in all this. It's great advert for the department. Smile, Charles, we're on TV!"

And indeed at that moment a young lady in a black cocktail dress approached, with a large video-recorder on her shoulders, accompanied by a young man in tatty jeans holding a microphone and arc lamp.

She filmed Tamsin and Professor Hanwell as they talked, and passed on.

"It's part of her project in communication studies," explained Tamsin. "We're all allowed to do an independent work project in our final year, for which we get extra marks. I believe that Fawn has arranged for Skelmerdale County TV to use one or two shots in its 'Home and Away' local news slot - and then they say that that will help the department get more money from the HEFCE! Well, I'd better circulate again - I'm supposed to get rid of these leaflets advertising our courses." She reached her hand behind her back, pulled out a leaflet from the waistband of her corset, handed it to Professor Hanwell, and moved on.

Professor Hanwell looked at it and read the heading: 'Independent work at Skelmerdale. We at Skelmerdale (it continued) are proud of the many and unique opportunities for independent project work offered in the department of English and Communication studies. Independent work may take several forms. It may be an independently made film or video-project. Strong emphasis is placed on independent collaborative work, working together on small group inter-active collaborative projects'. Professor Hanwell's eyes glazed over, and he crumpled the leaflet into his pocket. He looked around the room, which was now quickly filling with the remainder of the conference delegates. The members of the *Rocky Horror Picture Show* fan club darted eagerly around the room, distributing their wares. And then Professor Hanwell noticed another group of costumed young women, dressed alike in short green buckskin-fringed tunics, belted at the waist, with buskins or open-thonged sandals on their feet, and quivers on their shoulders. One of them approached him, distributing other leaflets from her quiver as she progressed across the room. Professor Hanwell thought carefully for a moment, and correctly divined that this must be a member of the Skelmerdale University Female Toxophily Association, popularly known as the

Merrywomen, as he learned later from Ruth. He took a leaflet, and read: Oppportunities for Graduate Work in English and Communication Studies at Skelmerdale: The department of English and Communication Studies has long been renowned for the vitality of its graduate course in Communication theory, he read, before again hastily crumpling the leaflet into his pocket. He helped himself to another whisky from a passing Rocky Horror girl, and looked around the room to see what had happened to Ruth. She had now finished her conversation with her bridesmaid, and was now engrossed in conversation with a young American lady.

Professor Hanwell went up to them.

"Hullo, it's Laura, isn't it?" he greeted her. "We met early last year in Surleighwick, Arkansas, remember?"

The lovely Assistant Professor Laura Harington of Caltech put her drink on a chair, flung her arms around his neck, and kissed him full on the lips.

"Charles! How wonderful to see you again. What times we had! Oh me oh my!" She turned to Ruth. "Charles and I are old friends," she continued, reaching for a sixth martini from a passing waitress. "He was very sweet to me, and undressed me and put me to bed back in Arkansas when I had too much to drink. Oh me oh my! What must you have thought of me. I'm in room 315, Charles," she said, taking his arm. "Just so you know where to undress me if it happens again!"

Ruth raised her eyebrows quizzically.

"That must have been a treat for you, Laura. Is that a service you offer to all the girls, Charles?" she enquired sweetly.

Professor Hanwell cleared his throat. "It seems some time since we were in touch, Laura," he continued hurriedly. "I expect you know I got a job at Surleighwick, Arkansas, a year last September. "And I can see that you've already met my wife. Ruth and I were married just before I took up residence in the States."

"Oh me oh my, aren't you a sly one," responded Laura, quite unabashed. She gave Ruth a kiss. "I just hope you are happier in your marriage that I am with my brute."

Mrs Quick and her coven - for she had now inducted her Hereford students and made up the full number, and had indulgently treated them to the conference - had arrived not long after Professor and Mrs Hanwell, and were now dispersed throughout the crowded room. Sipping her first whisky, Mrs Quick was glad that she had come, as she surveyed the room, and noted that the conference was predominantly, though not exclusively, female. Mrs Quick was entranced and captivated by the charming Rocky Horror girls, whose costume she definitely approved of. Things had certainly changed since she was a student! It was good that the conventions were breaking down, and that young women nowadays could proclaim their femininity without shame... Opportunistic as ever, she made up her mind to urge her students at Hereford to set up a branch of the Rocky Horror Fan Club as soon as possible.

"Hullo, mummy!" Her daughter Blanche Lucy Guinevere Jane, named at a time when Mrs Quick's enthusiasms were equally divided between the middle ages and the novels of Charlotte Brontë was at her side, in her Merrywoman garb of Lincoln green. Mrs Quick affectionately kissed Blanche, who was now nearing the end of her first year in English and Communication Studies, and looked with pride upon her eighteen-year old daughter, who was glowing with youthful health.

"Mummy, can I introduce my friend Juliette?"

Mrs Quick smiled with approval at the blonde Rocky Horror girl in her fetching outfit whom her daughter presented to her.

"Hullo my dear, so nice to meet you," she smiled. "I do like your corsets, they make you look very smart. What fun this conference is going to be. Everything seems very well arranged so far, and there's lots to drink too!"

"Yes, we're all involved as part of our project work," explained Blanche.

Just then Fawn Fern struck a gong loudly several times, and the conversation slowly faded, and silence fell upon the room.

"Ladies, ladies, and of course gentlemen," she laughed brightly. "May I say a word of welcome to the 'Writing Women Re-Vue'? We're very excited here that so many of you should have troubled to come to Skelmerdale for this conference, which we hope will be a successful one, and will give us all a chance to make new friends, renew old acquaintanceships, and, we hope, learn from one another in this exciting new area of study. My colleague Florinda and I will look forward to meeting most of you individually during the next few days. In the mean time, I should like to invite Professor Freddie Frowstie, head of the department of English and

Communication Studies here at Skelmerdale, to welcome you to Skelmerdale on behalf of the department."

Freddie Frowstie, standing on the stairs that led to the dining room in order to be seen, stroked his straggly beard nervously.

"Ladies and - er - gentlemen," he began uncertainly. "It is a pleasure for me to welcome you all to Skelmerdale on behalf of the department of English and Communication Studies. I think it's pretty generally agreed that we at Skelmerdale have got a superlative record for the way in which the department here has always fostered women's studies - one of the best records in the country in fact - as is proved by the most impressive turn-out here tonight, and the way in which so many famous names have chosen to attend. We have a very dynamic teaching programme in these areas, as I think you will discover during the next few days. It's a pleasure for me to acknowledge the wonderful way in which our students here have rallied round and contributed to the smooth running and organisation of this conference. I think I can say that the quality of our staff-student relationships is deservedly high. I thank too Fawn Fern here and Florinda Morrison, whose initiative it was to hold this conference, and who have put so much work into making the arrangements for it. The programme seems to me a very exciting one, and I'm sure that we will all learn a lot. I know I will. And now, dinner is served in the dining-room next door."

Professor Hanwell collected Ruth, and they proceeded with the throng to the dining room. They found themselves sitting at the end of one of the long tables, opposite a lean, trim, outgoing woman, with greying hair, and her younger, glamorous companion, cool and elegant in a light-blue billowy cotton frock, belted at the waist, a mass of auburn hair tumbling down her shoulders.

"Hullo, I'm Pauline Quick," said that lady to Ruth, smiling warmly as she did so and putting out her hand. "And this is my associate Dr Antonia Crumpet. We're from the Magic Women bookshop in Hay." She leaned forward to read Ruth's name-tag. "Well, well, what a coincidence Ms Henderson. So you're from Surleighwick, Arkansas! Tony and I taught at Surleighwick, England till a year last September, you know, when the university was sold off under the government's privatisation scheme."

"How extraordinary!" answered Ruth. "I thought your faces seemed familiar. I was a student at Surleighwick in its last years myself, reading theology. I used to see you in the Arts building from time to time, though of course we never actually met."

Mrs Quick sighed at a missed opportunity, for she found Ruth rather attractive in her well-tailored burgundy dress.

"May I introduce my husband, Charles?" continued Ruth. "He was at Surleighwick too till a year last September. He was Baskerville Fellow in the History of Science."

Mrs Quick sighed again at learning that the attractive Ruth was married, and flashed a dazzling and insincere smile at Professor Hanwell as she shook hands.

"I'm so glad you kept your maiden name on marriage, my dear," she said to Ruth. "Such a mistake to have done what I did, and changed it. My husband eventually deserted me, of course, but for professional reasons it's too late for me to change my name now."

"Let me get some wine to go with the meal," interposed Professor Hanwell. He strolled to one of the side tables, where the Rocky Horror girls were selling bottles of wine to accompany dinner, and returned with a bottle of Californian Sauvignon and a bottle of Australian Chardonnay.

"It certainly is a coincidence," he remarked as he poured the wine. "I was at Surleighwick for eighteen years, but I don't think our paths crossed at all. "Of course, my office was rather tucked away, and I had little cause ever to visit the Arts Faculty."

Over the Florida cocktail, they reminisced companionably about Surleighwick, agreeing that it was a potentially decent university that had been ruined by poor leadership at the top.

"After all," said Mrs Quick, "you know what they used to say about Gerry Ford not being able to chew gum and walk at the same time. Well, our head of department, Percy Bodgering, couldn't even walk! He's dead now, I believe," she continued ingenuously. "Heart failure, I think it was. He used to be here at Skelmerdale, you know."

"So you went into the bookshop business? Hay is a good place to have a bookshop. Ruth and I often used to visit the town, and bought quite a lot of books there in our last year at Surleighwick. It made such a nice day trip from there, didn't it? Did you use to go there much yourselves?"

"From time to time," answered Mrs Quick casually.

"Wasn't there some trouble involving your department at Hay last year?" put in Ruth. "I used to live in Second Hall, and I remember that some of the boys in Third Hall went on an English trip there, and got arrested. What was it, drunk and disorderly, indecent exposure, or something like that? It got into the *Sun* and the *News of the World*, didn't it?"

"Yes, that's right," answered Dr Crumpet, colouring at the memory. "The boys got horribly drunk, and took off the clothes of Paddy and Simon, two of Pauline and my tutees."

"Yes, it's coming back to be now," said Ruth. "I knew them vaguely, and met them in the Third Hall bar from time to time. I wonder what's happened to them now?"

Mrs Quick extracted a card from the pocket of her skirt.

"Here's our business card," she said. "You'll be most welcome at our shop at any time. Do pay us a visit before you go back to the States."

"Yes, why don't we, Charles?" enquired Ruth. "We're in no hurry to get back are we? Charles is one of those lucky people who have a research chair," she explained to Mrs Quick. "And that means that he does pretty much just what he likes! He's a great book-collector, and I think he'd enjoy looking around your shop."

"Let's see, you're giving a paper, aren't you?" asked Mrs Quick. "I must be sure not to miss that." She rummaged through her pockets again and made a note in her diary.

"Yes, I am - and so is Charles. On Matilda the Hermit of Debrecen, otherwise known as 'The Woman in the Cave'! And if I remember the programme aright, you're down to speak too, aren't you?"

The meal continued on its leisurely and bibulous way, until at length it was time to go to hear the introductory, and mercifully brief, keynote speech on 'Writing Women in the World Today'.

And then the members of the conference dispersed for further drinking in the bar, in preparation for the intensive programme that lay ahead of them in the next few days.

CHAPTER FIVE

THE 'WRITING WOMEN RE-VUE', ACT II

At 9. 30 a.m. next morning, most of the conference delegates had shaken off their hang-overs, showered, and drunk at least a cup of coffee over breakfast. Professor and Mrs Hanwell passed through the servery of the canteen, picked up their breakfasts, and joined Professor Libby Cyoote, whom Charles had also met at a previous conference in Surleighwick, Arkansas, at one of the small four-seater wooden tables in a corner of the room, close to the picture-windows overlooking the lake. Libby was sipping orange-juice and drinking black coffee, feeling a little fragile after her heavy drinking in the bar the night before. A little later they were joined by Assistant Professor Laura Harington, who was wearing a pale-pink light summer frock. Laura too felt that she had as usual over-indulged in liquor the night before in the bar. However, after a couple of cups of coffee, she started to pull herself together.

As it happened, Professor Hanwell and his wife were scheduled to speak in the same morning session before the coffee break, whilst Laura was performing after the break. The conference sessions had been organised on roughly chronological and thematic lines. Hence Professor Hanwell and Ruth were in the section on 'Anchoresses and Female Hermits of the Middle Ages', whilst Laura had been placed in the 'Renaissance Women' section. Libby, dealing as usual with Madame Curie, was to speak in the 'Modern Women' session on the last day. Breakfast was over, and the delegates drifted into the lecture theatre. Freddie Frowstie, Fawn, and Florinda chattered happily, getting a buzz from the presence at Skelmerdale of so many delegates! Yes, Skelmerdale was certainly making a name for itself in women's studies now! After the welcome address and keynote speech, Professor Hanwell delivered his half-hour talk on Matilda the Hermit of Debrecen. Judging that scientific detail was not the main interest of those present at the conference, he had put together an amusing and light-hearted piece about living conditions in thirteenth-century Hungary, based on incidental remarks and obiter dicta in the writings of Matilda. Mrs Quick listened intently, for she had always been interested in the problems of women living alone. From time to time she made notes in a little book. When Professor Hanwell's paper was over, Mrs Quick was the first to enter the discussion, by asking him whether Matilda the Hermit had experienced any difficulties with her periods, something she knew for a fact to have been the case with other anchoresses about whom she had read.

Professor Hanwell disclaimed any knowledge of the subject, stating that so far as he knew Matilda never discussed the matter. Mrs Quick's opinion of Matilda, of whom she had never heard before Professor Hanwell's paper, went down a notch or two.

And then it was time for Ruth, as Ms R. Henderson, to make her conference debut. For her first public appearance, Ruth had chosen to wear a simple white blouse, with an emerald brooch above its left breast-pocket, and a closely fitting navy-blue skirt which reached to just below her knees. She read her paper in a clear and audible voice, without a trace of nervousness. Mrs Quick looked at her with secret admiration, and wished again that Ruth were not married. What an admirable addition to her coven she would be! Ruth contented herself with describing the unusual characteristics of the mystic visions of Agnes of Anieto, pointed out how they differed from other visions of the time, assessed the significance of these differences, and sat down to prolonged applause. Mrs Quick again had a question for Ruth. Had Agnes of Anieto ever experienced any erotic visions, she wanted to know? Ruth explained that Agnes of Anieto had fled the world to escape, among other things, the company of men. Mrs Quick's approval of Agnes, of whom she had never heard until Ruth's talk, rose considerably. "Was she in love with any women?" she enquired hopefully.

"Not in any of the thousand or so letters that I have read so far," Ruth replied. "It is possible that in the thousand or so letters which I have not yet studied in detail, some such references may be found." Mrs Quick's opinion of Agnes rose slightly. She made notes in her black book, so that when the occasion arose she too could lecture to students and student societies on 'Matilda and Agnes, Women against the World'.

"I did enjoy your paper, my dear," said Mrs Quick to Ruth during the coffee interval. "I'm so glad you and Charles are thinking of coming to Hay. Do say you will come. There's so much more I want to ask you both about Matilda and Agnes." Ruth assured Mrs Quick that she felt sure that her husband would agree to come.

After the first coffee interval, Laura Harington delivered her political tirade against the way in which women had been prevented from being alchemists in the sixteenth-century. As all the female delegates in the room thoroughly agreed, this negation had been a crying shame, and Laura's paper was adjudged a great success. Glancing at the programme, Professor Hanwell thought that this was one conference where he need not be too concerned about cutting papers. So he offered to Laura and Libby to take them into Skelmerdale for lunch with himself and Ruth, an offer which the two young professors gladly accepted.

"I think we should go to a wine-bar for lunch," he remarked, as they sat in a foursome in the back of a traditional big black taxi. "It would make a treat for you both, Laura and Libby," he continued, "as I've never seen one in the States. It's where you go when you want first of all to drink wine at lunchtime. All wine-bars have a good selection of thirty or forty wines to choose from, and then you select the food to go with it, rather than choosing the food first and then the wine."

Professors Cyoote and Harington declared that they had never heard of any such thing, and happily agreed that that sounded a really great idea.

The taxi dropped them on the edge of the pedestrianised zone of Skelmerdale, and there Professor Hanwell consulted the driver for his recommendation of a quiet and select wine-bar.

Soon they were in a cool, light and elegant wine-bar, in a tranquil side-lane not far from the centre of Skelmerdale. There, to celebrate the delivery of three successful papers, Professor Hanwell ordered a bottle of Mumm's champagne. Whilst they toasted each other and sipped the cool, foaming liquid in tall slender flutes, Professor Hanwell consulted the wine list, and ordered a couple of bottles of really decent Semillon to start them off. To accompany it he selected a plate of hors d'oeuvres, and the conversation became relaxed and general as the wines started to take their effect upon the group.

Professor Hanwell had ordered a plate of smoked salmon sandwiches for lunch for Ruth and himself, Libby ordered a green salad, whilst Laura tucked happily into a lasagne. The wine-bar was pleasantly uncrowded, and Libby and Laura looked round at the pleasing, and to them unusual, sight of half-a-dozen couples sitting at tables all drinking wine with their lunch, something rarely seen in the United States. The sun shone gently through the mullioned windows of the tranquil room. It was pleasant to sit there in a leisurely fashion, sipping the wine in a relaxed mood. Charles, Ruth and Laura, having given their papers, could afford to celebrate. Only Libby still had that experience before her on the coming Saturday. However, it was clear to them all that the standard of the papers was not very important - all that one had to do was to express the truism that women had been under-emphasised, under-educated, and generally oppressed throughout human history, to be sure of a sympathetic reception for one's paper, particularly if one happened oneself to be a woman.

"It's a real change to get away from the heat of California," remarked Laura, as she drained her glass of Semillon. "My, that was good! Oh me oh my, this lunchtime drinking is fun. I think I shall play hooky this afternoon and do some shopping in Skelmerdale."

She looked through the diamond-shaped panes of glass, and observed two Vikings in loin-cloths and tunics, with sandalled feet, wearing steel helmets, and carrying spears, walking down the street.

"Good heavens," she gasped. "What are those Vikings doing here?"

"Skelmerdale was an old Viking city, I believe," answered Professor Hanwell easily. "So I expect they're celebrating some battle or other. People in Skelmerdale seem to like getting dressed up, as you may have noticed from the helpers on the campus."

"Oh yes," laughed Laura. "When Libby and I arrived we were greeted by a young man who seemed to be wearing nothing but a fig-leaf. I gather he was supposed to be Adam from one of the medieval plays. Oh me oh my, what a performance!"

"We didn't see him," replied Professor Hanwell, "though Ruth tells me we met pre-lapsarian Eve. But Ruth will be able to tell us about the Vikings, I expect. She's been to Skelmerdale before, and knows all about it."

"Oh, yes," answered Ruth. "There was a battle for Skelmerdale - or Skmerdjall as the Vikings called it - in 947. I expect those two are rehearsing for the annual re-enactment of the battle, on May 26th I think it was." The sandwiches and lasagne were followed by fruit, cheese and biscuits, and to accompany them Professor Hanwell ordered a bottle of heady and luscious Trockenbeerenauslese at 18% alcohol by volume. In the distance the bright sounds of a strolling jazz musician were heard. The musical Laura, who loved a catchy tune, started to sway her legs and swing her arms from side to side. Professor Hanwell discreetly removed the bottles of wine nearer to himself, away from Laura's twitching arms, for he knew of old of her propensity to dance on restaurant tables. He didn't mind that so much, but he certainly did not want her to spill the expensive bottle of German wine that he had bought!

Ruth found the behaviour of the two young American academics rather fascinating, for she had met few female academics of any sort in her career thus far. She found their free and easy joking rather attractive, though she felt that their scholarship was possibly rather superficial. Laura and Libby, though, were full of praise for Ruth's paper of the morning.

"Gosh, I wish I knew Italian as well as you do, Ruth," "exclaimed Libby. "I only ever did a bit of Spanish at school, and I don't remember more than a word or two of it. Charles is good at languages too, isn't he?" She sighed. "I guess you were made for each other."

"We're certainly very happily married," replied Ruth with amusement. "But cheer up, Libby, I'm sure you'll find a husband soon enough. There's plenty of time, you know!"

"You don't want to be getting yourself married anyway, Libby" confided Laura, who was now becoming a little drunk. "After all, I'm married, for all the good it does me. I don't care for my husband, and I hardly ever see him."

"So why don't you get divorced?" asked Ruth.

"Because my husband doesn't want to," answered Laura. "He says it would damage his prospects in his firm. So he pays me twenty-five G's a year just to stay married to him, even though we live apart. And it suits me that way rather than go through the trouble of a divorce and getting alimony out of him."

The two young American feminists sipped their wine dolefully, and silently contemplated the difficulties of being a woman in a man's world.

Professor Hanwell ordered coffee for them all, a brandy for himself, a crème-de-menthe for Ruth, a glass of port for Laura, and a cointreau for Libby to round off the meal. And then half-an-hour later the party split up, Laura and Libby to look round Skelmerdale, Professor Hanwell and Ruth to stroll through the crowded streets of the city before catching a cab back to campus, there to enjoy a siesta in their room.

As the taxi entered the Skelmerdale campus, Professor Hanwell observed eight people buried inside enormous papier-mâché heads walking in two in groups along one of the campus paths.

Resignedly he pointed to the strange spectacle, and waited for Ruth to enlighten him.

"The Student Living Puppet Theatre," she explained with that slightly mischievous smile that her husband found so devastatingly distracting. "You've heard of ordinary puppet theatre, of course, Charles? It's like a play, but it deliberately violates the illusion of real people being in a theatre. The most famous example is the fifteen-hour film *Hitler, a Film from Germany* by Syberberg or some such name, I think he was called. All the roles were played by puppets. I saw it once on TV. Now, Living Puppet Theatre takes it one stage further, and is a way of violating that illusion. It's a way of reminding the audience that they are not, after all, watching an ordinary puppet show. Living Puppet theatre is very big at Skelmerdale, you know. I believe you can do a show as an optional extra in English and Communication Studies instead of taking an exam paper."

There were many more questions that Professor Hanwell, who had not understood Ruth's explanation at all, wanted to ask, but, made amorous by the lunchtime wine, he decided that his questions could wait. He drew the curtains, dissolved his wife's teasing expression with a passionate kiss, unbuttoned her blouse, eased her out of her navy-blue skirt and slip, and carried her to the bed in her lacy New York lingerie.

*****

'Nunc est bibendum, nunc pede libero
   pulsanda tellus'
(Horace, *Odes*)

On the Friday evening of the conference, after dinner, a fancy dress party had been scheduled for the conference participants. Fawn and

Florinda had arranged this in conjunction with the university's Medieval Studies programme. Fancy dress was not absolutely obligatory, but free food and wine were offered to all those who turned up in at the event in medieval garb. To Professor Hanwell and his wife, neither of whom liked dressing up, this seemed the perfect opportunity to fulfil their promise to take Ruth's bridesmaids, Tamsin and Fiona, to a meal. So at 7.30 p.m. that evening Ruth changed into her dark cocktail dress, and her husband put on his suit, and they left their room and walked slowly through the corridors of the Castle Island complex, on their way to the bar of Grace Darling College, where they had arranged to meet Tamsin and Fiona. All around them the costumed figures of other conference delegates were making their way to the fancy-dress party.

As the Hanwells left their room, they encountered Assistant Professors Laura Harington and Libby Cyoote, dressed as harem girls, their eyes bright and shining behind their lightly veiled faces, each wearing a blue bra and a pair of diaphanous and filmy harem pants bought that afternoon in the Skelmerdale stores. Painted toe-nails peeped out from open-toed sandals. Laura and Libby had debated long and hard about what they should go as for the party. The previous night, sitting in the conference bar, after her eighth potent fruity cocktail, Laura had expressed her intention of going as Eve in a fig-leaf, but Libby, not quite so drunk as her friend, had dissuaded her from doing that. However, it was a problem for the women. Full-length medieval gowns and pointed hats with veils trailing from behind would have been ideal, but were ruled out on grounds of expense. And then last night in the bar, Laura had impulsively taken off her dress, climbed on to the table, torn her slip from hem to waist in several places, and announced that she would go as Cinderella. Libby had then with some difficulty put Laura to bed, and when Laura woke up, trying on the torn slip in the cold light of sobriety and day, the young Professor had decided that the Cinderella outfit was not really her. At last, she and Libby had settled on the compromise of harem girls, on the grounds that the costume was simple - they would need to buy only the pants - and that furthermore it was important to show that not all the middle ages were western. By dressing as harem girls they would, they believed, be paying a tribute to Arab science.

Ruth and Professor Hanwell caught up with Laura and Libby as they left the Castle Island complex, a slight summer breeze ruffling through their hair and clothes. Laura and Libby were early for the fancy-dress party in Grace Darling college, and happily accepted Professor Hanwell's invitation to join Ruth and himself for a drink in the bar while they waited for Ruth's friends. Soon the four of them were ensconced on the comfortable leather seats of the Grace Darling Heroines bar, overlooking the Lake, drinking Pina Coladas (Laura and Libby) and gin-and-tonics (Professor Hanwell and his wife).

Other members of the conference had had the same idea of fortifying themselves ahead of the official beginning of the party. Several men-at-arms, two milkmaids, a knight in armour, three nuns, an anchoress and four châtelaines were lounging at the bar or grouped at tables near it. And then, theatrically, a witch, with pointed Welsh-girl hat on her head, a long black cloak draped elegantly over her shoulders, wearing a grey robe emblazoned with magic symbols, entered the bar, accompanied by two sinister blonde-haired figures in skin-tight leather trousers, black knee-length boots, wearing leather blousons belted at the waist, with gleaming dirks thrust through the belt.

"I'll have a large gin-and-tonic, please Tony dear," said Mrs Quick decisively, taking the next table to Professor Hanwell, and waving enthusiastically at Ruth.

"Not coming to the party, I see?" she remarked to Ruth, seeing that she and her husband were in civilian clothes. "Well I am. How do you like my outfit? I got it from a theatrical costumiers," she lied, for it was in truth her normal witch's outfit that she habitually took on her travels.

Dr Chamberlain sat down creakingly in her tight leather trousers, and waited for the similarly attired Dr Crumpet to bring a tray of drinks from the bar. For Mrs Quick, feeling in a generous and indulgent mood, had that afternoon bought the outfits that her two favourite acolytes were now wearing. The Magic Women bookshop had sold many books from Dr Crumpet's stall during the first three days of the conference, and Mrs Quick had decided to blow some of the profits. The leather outfits were skin-tight indeed, fur-lined for comfort, and did not allow of the wearing of any garments at all underneath. Mrs Quick had felt like a medieval squire, as she gently eased each of her naked acolytes into their outfit, had carefully drawn up and clipped tight the many fastenings and buttons, had levered their leather-clad legs into tight knee-high boots, and had fastened the straps of these at the top. And assisting them out of their outfits would be even more pleasurable, she had thought to herself, as she had smoothed the leather down around their hips, and swept back their hair page-boy style beneath black caps. Now she looked proudly and with satisfaction around the bar, as Dr Chamberlain sat cross-legged beside her, and as the lithe Dr Crumpet slank seductively towards her with a tray of drinks.

Professor Hanwell and Ruth waved good-naturedly at Mrs Quick and her acolytes - and then Tamsin and Fiona were present, in flowery summery frocks, neatly groomed and dressed up for the enjoyable evening's dining that they were confident they could expect from Ruth's husband. They waved goodbye to Mrs Quick, who called out as they left a promise to tell them all about the party, and then Professor Hanwell's group got into the taxi which he had booked to take them to the Old Station Restaurant, an interesting place a few miles outside Skelmerdale of which he had read in one of the guide books.

*****

After a drive of some twenty-five minutes, first through the suburbs of Skelmerdale, and then through the countryside, sunny and tranquil that peaceful May evening, the taxi deposited the party outside the Old Station Restaurant, a complex of buildings set quite by themselves in the middle of nowhere, behind which six Pullman carriages were parked.

"According to the guide book, it's an old railway station that has been converted into a restaurant," explained Professor Hanwell, as he ushered the party towards the main entrance. "Apparently we eat in one of the Pullman coaches, which are parked by the main Skelmerdale to Scotland railway line."

They entered the building, and found themselves in a waiting room with a pleasant bar, decorated with an immense number of railway memorabilia - signals, station nameplates, railway signs, old advertising hoardings, fireman's shovels and so on. They were shown straightaway into the private compartment of a comfortably padded first-class carriage, and there Professor Hanwell, made indulgent by the company of three attractive young women, ordered a bottle of champagne as an aperitif. Soon they were sipping the coolly foaming liquid, and gazing out of the window at the countryside, in a tranquillity broken every few minutes by the clattering whoosh of a high-speed train rushing past the windows on the main line outside.

"So how has term been going?" asked Ruth of her bridesmaids. "I suppose this is a heavy exam. term for you?"

"Good heavens, no!" replied Tamsin. "They don't believe in a heavy final year at Skelmerdale. We can spread our finals papers over two-and-a-half years. I took my first two finals papers in the summer of my first year. That way, one gets a more representative spread of marks. I took three more papers in February and March earlier this year."

"Me too," interposed Fiona.

"So the summer term of year three is just given over to Performance Studies," explained Tamsin. "We have six weeks to live out a number of our roles, either from theatrical workshop productions, or from social and co-operative projects, or whatever. The course is assessed by the staff on a continuous assessment basis. Our Rocky Horror roles will count towards this, course," she continued nonchalantly. "So it's all quite relaxing for us in the final few weeks."

Professor Hanwell looked from Tamsin, with her jet-black hair and piercing blue eyes, her mouth vividly slashed by red lipstick, to Fiona, with her lighter hair and more ethereal expression. He was glad that Ruth had not gone to Skelmerdale - what was it she had called it, a resort university?

His musings were interrupted by the arrival of the waitress to take their order for dinner. Professor Hanwell listened carefully to what the girls and Ruth had ordered, and then ordered a bottle of excellent Australian Chardonnay, a bottle of Châteauneuf-du-Pape and, for good measure, another bottle of champagne to accompany their various choices.

Their tongues beginning to loosen under the influence of the champagne, Tamsin and Fiona chattered eagerly about life at Skelmerdale.

"The library is not very good, of course," continued Fiona. "But then, the whole emphasis of the department is more on the side of Communication Studies than on English, so that's not too much of a disadvantage. And there's a very good collection of videos of student productions."

"Yes," added Tamsin, "and the social life is good--there's always something going on in one of the colleges, and the bars stay open till 11. 30 p.m., and then there are pubs in the village nearby, and the sports facilities are very good, and there are several collections of theatrical costumes, so anyone interested in theatre can have a good time here. And there's a student TV and radio service too."

The waitress returned to tell them that their table was ready, and they filed out down the corridor of the compartment, through the waiting room where they had first entered the restaurant, and were ushered to their table in a Pullman car on the other side of the building. Dusk was beginning to fall, the table was set with flowers and a lamp. As they sat down, another high speed train whooshed past outside. The first course awaited them on the table, and Professor Hanwell asked for the bottle of champagne he had ordered to be opened to accompany it. Soon the crystal flutes were filled with foaming liquid, and Ruth and her friends were tucking in heartily to smoked salmon hors d'oeuvres, whilst Professor Hanwell contented himself with a pâté. They all had haggis for their second course, and, though a little champagne was still left, the Châteauneuf-du-Pape was opened to accompany it.

The Pullman car was now half-filled with diners. The gentle murmur of conversation was overlaid by the recorded sounds of clanking steam trains, softly echoing station announcements, and the pleasing hissing of steam. Outside darkness descended, and gradually the countryside could no longer be seen; gazing through the windows, Ruth and her friends saw themselves reflected therein in all their convivial and relaxed ease. The waitress cleared away the remnants of the second course, and, in mellow mood by now, they sipped their wine as they awaited the arrival of the main course.

"It's a lovely meal - thanks for taking us out, Charles," said Tamsin. "Fiona and I do a lot of our own cooking, and we don't often eat as well as this."

"What will you do when you get your degree, Tamsin?" Professor Hanwell asked her idly. "Have you made any plans?"

"Oh, I'll probably stay on at Skelmerdale to do graduate work," answered Tamsin. "I don't know what I want to do yet, and it would give me another year to think about it. Besides, there are some good graduate programmes at Skelmerdale - like in Women's Studies, like in Communications (Film and Video), like the M.A. in Embroidery Studies, where you study lovely illustrations of tapestries, and for your mistresspiece dissertation do a six-foot sampler of your own design. I think that's the one for me, I'm good at needlework."

"And I shall stay on too," put in Fiona. "I shall do the taught MA Drama and Communication option that the Department of English and Communication studies offers."

The main course arrived, and they settled down to eat a fillet steak (Professor Hanwell and Ruth) and Roast Duck (Fiona and Tamsin). Outside, by one of those frequent and sudden changes in the weather that are so common in England, it had started to rain, and huge droplets were now spattering the windows of the carriage. This did not however affect either the frequent passage of the high-speed trains outside the window, or the warmth and light and friendly conversation inside the carriage.

Tamsin and Fiona continued to chatter gaily about their life at Skelmerdale.

"It's been fun - great fun," insisted Tamsin. "If you just want a good time, which is what I did, I can't think of a better university to come too. The terms are very short for one thing, only seven-and-a-half weeks, so that means more holidays, and then the number of class contact hours is very small. I've never had more than about five hours a week of formal classes. That's because so much time is given over to the performance options, and they can be combined with other things - like being in the Rocky Horror Fan club, for example. That gains us points for performance - acting out a role, you know - and at the same time we got extra course credits from Fern for helping out at the conference receptions - we'll both be on duty tomorrow as usherettes at the Revue as well, by the way - and then, if I ever wanted to go into modelling, it would look good on my c.v."

"How many clubs like that are there at Skelmerdale?" asked Ruth curiously. "I noticed there were quite a lot of the Merrywomen at the opening reception too."

"Well, there's the High Spirits, for a start," said Tamsin. "Skelmerdale has a lot of ghosts all over the place, and the High Spirits dress up as ghosts - Cavaliers, Roundheads, Roman

Soldiers, Vikings, serving wenches, murder victims, whatever, and
act out the incidents of the haunting. Often they pick up a bit of
pin-money by performing for tourists in the city centre. And then
there are student branches of many of the military societies that
re-enact the battles at Skelmerdale, Sealed Knot, Jacobins" (she
meant Jacobites) "and so on. Then there are the Merry Andrews -
they all dress up as clowns and go around the city and the campus
making people laugh. And then there's the Pirates, where everyone
dresses up as Captain Kidd and his Moll. We're very lucky at
Skelmerdale, the student union has a huge number of clothes and
cast-offs that it has built up over the years, and most of the
departments have a stock of clothing that we can draw on. The
Music department has a great selection of minstrel outfits, the
philosophy department has a collection of beards, Women's
Studies has a vast wardrobe of complete outfits of everything from
a Roman Matron to an ATS girl from World War II - many of
them made by the students as part of their project, of course."

The main course was finished, and, as Tamsin chattered brightly
on, Professor Hanwell ordered a bottle of rich sweet Graves from
France as a pudding wine to accompany the desserts. Himself he
did not have one, but contented himself with sipping his wine
slowly, whilst his wife and her friends, with their more youthful
appetites, tucked into syllabub and meringue and gateaux.

Professor Hanwell and Ruth felt at peace with the world. It was
good for Ruth to see her friends again, and gossip about their lives
over the past year.

"Speaking of dressing up," put in Ruth, "poor Charles here was
quite mystified by Eve-before-the-Fall - he thought she was Lady
Godiva!"

They all burst out laughing.

"Well, it was a mistake anyone could make," Professor Hanwell
put in defensively.

Ruth looked at her friends with a glint in her eye, and in unison
they chorused:

"But where was the horse!"

In a giggly mood, Ruth placed her crumpled napkin on the table,
and led her by now slightly-drunken friends and her husband back
to the main entrance lounge. They took their seats in a secluded
alcove, overlooking the main railway line, to one side of the main
bar. And there they were served coffee and mints to round off the

meal, whilst Professor Hanwell ordered a brandy for himself, a crème-de-menthe for Ruth, and, at his suggestion, a glass of port for Tamsin and Fiona to settle their stomachs.

Everyone was now utterly relaxed, and felt very good-humoured. Even Professor Hanwell, a very moderate drinker who rarely drank to his capacity, felt that he had had enough for the night, Tamsin, leaning her head back against the cushions of her chair, gradually fell asleep, slowly slumping downwards in her seat. Her frock clung to the cushions as she descended, revealing the Rocky Horror outfit that she still wore underneath, with its black stockings and suspenders stretched across her thighs.

Ruth looked at her husband with a smile.

"It's a good job I'm here to keep you respectable, Charles," she remarked with a laugh. "Really, what would people think of you otherwise?"

She decorously pulled Tamsin's frock back over her stocking tops, and gently shook her awake.

Professor Hanwell paid the bill, and asked the manager to call him a taxi. Soon, they were being driven back to Skelmerdale in the warmth of a black London-style cab, Professor Hanwell and his wife sitting on the jump-seats facing backwards. Arriving back at Grace Darling College, Professor Hanwell paid off the taxi, and, at Ruth's insistence, since last year's axe-murderer had never been caught, they escorted the sleepy Tamsin and Fiona back to the very doors of their adjacent rooms on the third floor of the college.

And then hand in hand Professor Hanwell and his wife strolled slowly through the darkened campus back to the Castle Island complex. And, mellowed now, and feeling after the evening's conversation with Ruth's friends that he understood Skelmerdale rather better, he felt that nothing that might happen in this unreal world could surprise him.

In this he was not entirely correct. In companiable silence, he and Ruth strolled slowly through the deep shadows and intermittent pools of light from the standard lamps dotted around the campus. They were overtaken first by the lovely and naked Assistant Professor Laura Harington, shrieking and streaking past them into the shadows ahead, then by Dr Crumpet with dirk at the ready, then by Mrs Quick waving a broomstick, then by four vomiting rugby players. Then, twenty yards ahead of them, they heard a sudden shrieking. Beneath the dim light of the next campus lamp-post, they could just make out the startled figures of Fawn and Florinda, dressed as Cinderella and a milkmaid. And Fawn and Florinda were being forcefully propelled by the shoulders, seized by a stout and burly figure dressed in black, whose face was hidden by balaclava and eye-mask. Before Professor Hanwell could intervene, Fawn and Florinda were pushed into the lake. The masked black figure cackled and ran off into the endless darkness. Fawn and Florinda spluttered in the shallows, and with some difficulty extricated themselves from the thick reedy mud. Shocked and drenched, they refused Professor Hanwell's offer of help, but hurried gasping, sobbing and indignant across the campus to their nearby cottage to dry off and drink herb tea. Peering from behind a tree, Deirdre Prout eyed her handiwork with great satisfaction.

What all these goings-on meant, Professor Hanwell and his wife hoped to find out over coffee in the morning. They reached their room in the Castle Island Complex, and drew the curtains.

"That was a terrific evening, Charles," said Ruth contentedly, snuggling up within his enfolding embrace. She turned around and asked him to unzip the back of her dress. She stepped out of her dress, and took off her slip, and mischievously revealed that she too was now dressed as a Rocky Horror girl.

"A little surprise for you," she murmured. "I could see from the first evening that you liked Tamsin's outfit, so I asked her to get me one this morning."

Professor Hanwell kissed his wife full on the lips and they started to make love.

CHAPTER SIX

THE WRITING WOMEN RE-VUE, ACT III

After their late night, and the rather heavy meal of the previous evening, Professor and Mrs Hanwell slept in late. They neither of them felt like eating breakfast, and neither of them wished to go to the papers in the early 9.30 a.m. session. However, by 10.45 they were up and dressed, and felt fully recovered from all the excitement. Outside, the sun was shining brightly, and gave the promise of another perfect May day. They strolled in leisurely fashion through the corridors of the Castle Island complex, and were soon sipping coffee from paper cups, and munching a biscuit or two in lieu of breakfast. They had decided to go along to support Libby by hearing her paper, and sure enough, they soon found her, sitting by herself at a table, giving her script a last check.

"Be with you in a minute," called Libby as they sat down to join her. "Must just check this last page first."

At last Libby lay aside her script, frowning slightly.

"Don't worry, Libby," said Ruth kindly. "I'm sure your paper will go down well. It will be new to the audience, after all. Not many people know much about Madame Curie nowadays."

"Thanks, Ruth," smiled Libby.

"Say, now tell us about last night," said Ruth, changing the subject in an endeavour to take Libby's mind off her forthcoming paper. "How was the party? Charles and I weren't there, we took some friends out to dinner instead. Did we miss anything? I don't think you noticed us, but when we got back, after midnight, you and Laura ran past us on the path, and I don't think Laura had any clothes on. What was she doing? Not playing Eve-before-the-Fall I trust?"

"So it was you that we passed, was it? It was rather dark, and I'd had quite a lot to drink, so I couldn't be sure. No, she wasn't playing Eve. You know what Laura's like, don't you, Charles?" said Libby, turning to Professor Hanwell. "When she's had a few she gets the urge to dance on tables - but of course you know all about it, it was you that had to put her to bed when she passed out at that conference in Alabama last year. Well, it was a costume party last night, we all had to go dressed up in medieval costume, and Laura and I decided to go as Arab women of the middle ages - a kind of gesture to Arab science, you know. Well, Laura had had quite a few, and sure enough, the time came when she got on to one of the tables and started to dance. And you know, one thing led to another, and then someone suggested that she should do the dance of the seven veils - only she only had four. Strange, really, you'd have thought it would be a man who would make such a suggestion, but the odd thing is I don't think it was. As far as I remember, someone dressed as a witch had that bright idea. Anyway, the end result was that she ended up on the table with nothing on. And then some of the other witches started to close in on her with their broomsticks, and she darted out of the bar to get away from them. It's as simple as that. That's when we must have passed you. Of course, she was absolutely pie-eyed at the time. I'd just die if it had been me, but knowing Laura, she probably won't even remember it - if she does, let's hope she has the sense to pretend she doesn't, anyway."

Attendance at the conference had now started to thin out a little on this last day, as various delegates had begun to move on elsewhere. But Libby still had a respectable audience of thirty-five for her paper, which went down well enough, but elicited little discussion. Assistant Professor Laura Harington tip-toed in quietly when Libby was just ten minutes into her lecture, looking pale and tired.

As the audience dispersed after Libby's paper, Professor Hanwell suggested to Libby that she should lunch with Ruth and himself to celebrate the successful delivery of her paper, an invitation that she was delighted to accept. Laura Harington too gladly accepted his invitation to join the party, and soon the four of them were sitting peacefully in the wine-bar where they had lunched the previous Wednesday.

Professor Hanwell ordered a decent bottle of Frascati to accompany the hors d'oeuvres, and soon they were relaxing and talking free from strain.

Ruth looked anxiously at Laura Harington, who seemed very pale and quiet.

But when Laura had sipped two or three mouthfuls of Frascati, a little colour returned to her cheeks. "Oh me oh my," she exclaimed. "Did I have a head this morning. Wow! Did I drink a basinful last night? Did I! Jeepers-creepers that was a party and a half! And what I need now is a hair of the dog, yes ma'am! Well, anyway, it's nearly all over now, except for the final dinner and Re-Vue. Say, Charles, it's been great to see you again, and to meet you too, Ruth."

An hour or so later, when they had all eaten a light lunch, and sunk a couple of bottles of wine between them, Laura and Libby left to go first to the chemist to buy some pills, then to do some final shopping for souvenirs in Skelmerdale.

Professor and Mrs Hanwell took a cab back to the campus, and there they strolled for a half-hour in the sunshine, watching the windsurfers, sailboarders, skaters, boaters and swimmers, before retiring to their room for a siesta, ready for the final event of the Writing Women Re-Vue.

*****

They both awoke refreshed at 5.30 p.m., and after a lazy cup of tea and biscuits in bed, started to get ready for the final evening's reception, dinner, and theatrical performances. By 6.30 p.m., it was time to descend to the ground floor, and there those delegates who had stayed the course, about three-quarters of the number that had registered initially, were gathering in the common room of the Castle Island complex. For the last time the Merrywomen and the Rocky Horror waitresses were on duty, and as Professor Hanwell and his wife entered the room, Fiona and Tamsin, arrayed once more in high heels and black underwear, greeted them effusively and saw that they were well-supplied with gin-and-tonics. Fiona and Tamsin offered gushing thanks once more for the meal to which they had been entertained the previous night.

"Now what's the programme for the end of term, Fiona?" asked Professor Hanwell, finding it very agreeable to chat to Ruth's pretty friends as they stood there in their alluring black outfits.

"Sun-bathing and recuperating after this conference for a start," she laughed, "Term ends in six weeks time, there's nothing else for us to do after our last performance assessments, so it's just whooping it up and having a good time for Tamsin and me. Then we'll both go to Greece, to lie on a beach in the sun."

Professor Hanwell thought that Ruth's friends were a couple of amiable airheads - pretty and amusing airheads to be sure, but airheads nonetheless. As Professor Hanwell was talking to the black-corseted Fiona, he gradually became aware of an anxious figure hovering uneasily beside him, hopping from foot to foot.

"May I intrude for a few moments?" asked the bearded bespectacled figure nervously, interposing himself between Professor Hanwell and Fiona, who promptly topped up all their glasses with gin, for she was curious to know what Freddie Frowstie could want with her friend Charles.

"We haven't met, I think, I'm Freddie Frowstie, head of the Department of English and Communication studies here."

"Oh yes, of course. I was there at your introductory speech of welcome."

"I was hoping to have a few words before you left," continued Freddie Frowstie, seemingly unaware of the attentive Fiona, whose curiosity was undisguised. "I have a little problem, it's like this you see." He paused nervously and sipped his gin, and ran his left hand uneasily across his beard. "We've been trying for some years now to find a suitable person to give some guest lectures on Poetry and Science. We were left a legacy some time ago to put these on, but, well, you know how it is - none of us here knows much about the subject, and we never could agree on who to invite. Now Fawn Fern here has drawn my attention to the *TLS* review of your book, and it seems to me that you might fit the bill admirably. Will you think it over? It's eight lectures that we want, next Spring and Summer terms. We can pay quite a decent honorarium, about £2500 a lecture I believe, and if you can come we'd give you a room on campus and would provide accommodation. Will you come?"

Professor Hanwell thought for a moment.

"Well, that's a very flattering offer," he replied. "May I think it over? I should like to discuss it with my wife first."

"Oh, do come, Charles," interrupted Fiona. "Tamsin and I will still be here next year - it would be fun having Ruth and you around for a bit."

"I'm not absolutely sure that I could get away from Arkansas." he replied with a slight frown. "But I'll certainly think about it."

"May I write to you about it? We'd be so grateful if you would accept. Not many people want to come to Skelmerdale as visiting lecturers," Professor Freddie Frowstie continued, made doleful and unusually honest for once by the accumulation of gin that had built up in his system in the last few days. "Skelmerdale can be very cold and dismal and depressing in the winter, you know," he soliloquized. speaking into the empty space between Fiona and Professor Hanwell. "The chill penetrates to your bones, and everyone goes down sick, especially the foreign students. It's the river, you know, we're very low-lying here, and there's a kind of miasma that creeps from it and envelops the campus. Skelmerdale can be very gloomy then, that's why no-one wants to come here in February."

Freddie Frowstie was clearly becoming maudlin and self-pitying, and Fiona winked as she refilled his glass and Professor Hanwell's.

"Well, cheers, Charles," she whispered. "Do come, I'll come to your lectures if you do. I'd better get back to my duties now, thanks for a great evening last night." She kissed him lightly on the cheeks, and was gone.

"Well, as I said, I'll certainly think about it," Professor Hanwell responded to the gloomy figure of Freddie Frowstie. "I'll look forward to your letter, my address is in the programme, and I'll be back in Arkansas in three weeks time. Excuse me for a moment, I have to catch someone over there."

He broke off, and joined Libby and Laura, who were drinking glasses of gin with lots of ice and lemon, and were chatting to a tall, pretty, elegant young woman whose lapel badge proclaimed that she was from the University of Whitepool.

*****

Dr Margaret Jacquasse had, on the whole, enjoyed herself at Skelmerdale. At first she had not expected to do so very much, and had come in the first instance purely to offer moral support to her friend the deeply wounded Deirdre Prout, who was still camping in a tent in a remote, thickly wooded part of the campus. But, somewhat unexpectedly, she had found the conference a great success, and had spent the last few days flirting agreeably with such young men as were present. For Dr Jacquasse, a slim, attractive doe-eyed young woman of thirty-one years old, had been a free spirit, since that dreadful day three years previously when, after five years of marriage, she had returned home unexpectedly to find her husband in bed with an air hostess. In a furious rage Dr

Jacquasse had scooped up the air hostess's uniform and lingerie, thrown them on the brightly-blazing fire of their country cottage, and had straightway separated from her husband, and, a couple of months later, initiated proceedings for divorce. Her husband had moved the air hostess in to live with him on a full-time basis, and Dr Jacquasse had started a new life by herself in dull pre-fabricated accommodation on the campus of the University of Whitepool. And there she had started to flirt and lead men on, dressing seductively in lacy diaphanous blouses, in supple leather boots and brightly coloured kimonos, in knickerbockers or slit skirts, in ski pants or in beach attire as the fancy took her. And thus attired she had set herself to make her colleagues and students fall in love with her, to lead them on, all the while herself remaining utterly uninvolved.

So far three young men at the Skelmerdale conference had offered to leave their wives for her in the last three days, which was about par for the course. To all of them she had said that she needed one more year to recover from the tragic circumstances of the failure of her own marriage, but that in the meantime they were free to write to her. And silently she rejoiced in the possibility of breaking three hearts.

As she entered the lounge of the Castle Island complex for the pre-Conference dinner drinks reception, on that final Saturday evening, Dr Jacquasse looked around her to see if there were any young men with whom she might amuse herself for an hour or two. Gratefully Dr Jacquasse took a glass of white wine from a passing Rocky Horror girl, and paused for a moment, sipping at her wine slowly and elegantly. For that final evening of the conference, Dr Jacquasse had chosen to dress simply in a short sleeveless Greek tunic, gathered in at the waist with a gold belt. The white draperies of the tunic ended well above her knees. Her Whitepool colleague Dr Deirdre Prout had declined to attend, but had issued vague threats of disrupting the ceremony. Dr Jacquasse was curious what this might portend. But for a moment she put these thoughts out of her mind, as she spied in the corner Dr Obadiah Ouimpe, a pint-sized, diminutive, balding young man of thirty years of age, who taught Wimmins Studies in the Skelmerdale Sociology department, and whom she had first met at the inaugural reception of the conference. Dr Ouimpe caught sight of his inamorata, and sidled towards her in his sports jacket, cravatte and yellow corduroys.

"Obadiah, daring!" Dr Jacquasse proffered her cheek to be kissed, and Dr Ouimpe, standing on tip-toe, pursed his lips towards his goddess. This brought his eyes on a level with Dr Jacquasse's breasts, scarcely concealed by the filmy material of her tunic. She wrapped her arms around him, and bent her knees, brushing her lips against his, and pressing her breasts against his chest, before releasing him.

"Margaret, darling, when can we meet again, this is our last night you know."

"I know, Obadiah darling," said Dr Jacquasse, secretly laughing at her victim. She rolled her doe-like eyes, and looked at him soulfully. "But Whitepool is only a two-hour drive away, Obadiah, darling. I'm sure that that's not too far away, is it?"

"Oh, of course not, Margaret dearest. I could drive over next Wednesday, and take you out to dinner."

Dr Jacquasse fluttered her eyelashes. "Obadiah, darling, how sweet of you. You are a dear. But Wednesday is not possible for me, I'm afraid, I have a dancing lesson then."

"Or I could come on Thursday, Margaret darling."

"Obadiah! How perfectly sweet of you. But on Thursday I am afraid I have an old school friend coming over for the evening. Just a little get together for some girl-talk. You wouldn't begrudge me that, I know."

"Or Friday?" queried Dr Ouimpe.

"On Friday I have some dreary colleagues coming round for a working buffet supper, Obadiah dear."

"I could come on Saturday."

"Obadiah! How sweet. But on Saturday I'm going away for the weekend."

"I could drive over on Monday of the week after next?"

"Obadiah! I'm not quite sure of my plans for the week after next. Exams are coming up you know, and I may have some meetings and marking to do. Why don't you drop me a line or give me a ring and we can try to fix a date?" She flashed him a smile. "Now, Obadiah darling, I mustn't monopolize you, and I must have a word with Pauline over there." And with that Dr Ouimpe had to be content.

Professor and Mrs Hanwell had now arrived, and were soon at the centre of a group of their friends and acquaintances, including Laura and Libby and Dr Crumpet.

Fawn and Florinda and Freddie Frowstie wandered around, thrilled at the success of the event. Soon the assembled delegates were summoned into dinner by a strangely attired jester.

*****

Professor Hanwell and Ruth found themselves seated with the amiable Assistant Professors Laura and Libby, and as they sat down at the long tables, the Merrywomen and Rocky Horror girls went along the tables pouring out glasses of foaming Spanish cava. As they did so a ragged band of Medieval Minstrels, the men dressed in parti-coloured tights, the women in long white dresses, entered the room, yodelling in high-pitched voices.

"The Skelmerdale Scops," whispered Ruth to her husband and the two American professors. "I heard them last year when I came to see my bridesmaids. They're pretty dire."

And indeed, so they were, at least in the opinion of Professor Hanwell. Fortunately, he had managed to catch the eye of one of the Rocky Horror waitresses, and she had kindly brought a couple of extra bottles of good-quality cava for the party, which she deposited in easy reach of Professor Hanwell's hand, and so they were all able to anaesthetize themselves against the dreary caterwauling of the Scops.

Then the gazpacho was served, and was soon followed by roast pork and crackling, washed down by quantities of fresh young Beaujolais; and again Professor Hanwell's kindly young waitress ensured that his party's glasses were kept well charged. Soon Laura's feet were twitching in time to the music of the minstrels.

Strawberries and ice-cream followed, washed down by the remnants of the cava.

Over the meal the quartet discussed future plans. It turned out that Laura and Libby were both planning to attend the 'Humanism and the Sciences' annual summer colloquium of the History of Science Society in San Francisco towards the end of August.

"Why, Charles and I will be there too, of course," exclaimed Ruth delightedly, for she had grown very fond of the two young American professors. "The HSS summer colloquium is exactly

Charles' thing. How nice that you will be there too! We must all meet up for a meal or two and drinks. Once this conference is over, Charles and I are staying on in the Skelmerdale area for a few days to see one or two relations, and then we'll hire a car and motor around the country for a while before heading back for the States."

As coffee was served, Fawn Fern called for silence, and asked the delegates to note that the performance of the Skelmerdale Mystery play selection would soon begin, and invited delegates to follow the Skelmerdale Scops, who would dance their way to the Great Hall, where the show would be given.

A few moments later, one of the Scops blew three loud blasts on a horn. The male and female Scops then paired off, and danced their way out of the room, playing uncertainly on their pipes and lyres and flutes as they did so. In dribs and drabs, a little self-consciously, the conference delegates shuffled to their feet. The lovely Assistant Professor Laura Harington, seeing the dancing Scops, could restrain herself no longer, but seized Libby by the hand, and skipped happily along in the wake of the Scops, skirt and petticoat flying in the air as she kicked out her agile athletic legs.

Fired by this example, other delegates paired off in a kind of cortège, and drifted out of the room.

Dr Ouimpe eagerly approached Dr Jacquasse and took her by the hand, but she smilingly declined.

"I'm sorry, Obadiah dear, I should love to have danced, but I'm feeling a little faint because of the heat."

"Oh Margaret darling, is there anything I can do."

"Don't worry about me, Obadiah dearest, you go on, I shall be all right."

She shoved the reluctant Dr Ouimpe away from her, recovered her spirits the moment he had left the room, and seized the astonished Freddie Frowstie by the hand, inviting him to join her in a jig.

Professor Hanwell and his wife left the room hand in hand, and soon most of the delegates were waiting expectantly in the Drama Workshop Studio, a large octagonal building behind the Castle Island complex, with four rows of seats surrounding a large empty dais in the middle. Lights and stage paraphernalia were clustered all around, and from the back of the stage a gently inclined ramp led to the back of the theatre. The Skelmerdale Scops danced on the stage for a while, and then there was a silence whilst a lutanist and a flute-girl busked quietly away, leaving the audience to chatter quietly themselves. Then the doors at one side of the workshop opened. A range of spotlights was turned on to a massive pageant waggon, loaded with actors and actresses, which was being trundled slowly down a ramp into the studio by a group of sweating men-at-arms, who carefully inserted and removed chocks in front of the wheels to stop it running away. Mr Twittering, from Skelmerdale's Medieval Studies Centre, whilst this was happening, nervously explained at tedious length that in the Middle Ages the Skelmerdale Mystery Plays had been performed on a waggon which was trundled from place to place throughout the streets of the city, and that that evening's performance was being similarly done on a waggon as a homage to that event.

At last the waggon came to a halt, and the assorted thespians scrambled down from it. The naked Tabitha, as Eve-before-the-Fall, and Adam, excited a sharp intake of breath from the audience, but the actors seemed quite unperturbed. Dr Jacquasse smiled to herself, and left her seat to lounge against the back of the studio, surveying the scene from different angles.

The first part of the Skelmerdale Mystery Plays began - *Noiz Phludde* - as the quaint dialect of medieval Skelmerdale would have it. At Skelmerdale, a particular point was made of doing the plays, not in modern English, but in the medieval dialect in which they were written, incomprehensible to all save specialists. Professor Hanwell was not one of these, and after a moment or two he closed his eyes and nodded off, his head drooping slightly forward. But Ruth, who had studied the plays a little as an undergraduate at Surleighwick, watched with a certain mild interest, as she had never seen them staged before. Laura and Libby, coming from a country where the Puritan tradition still held sway, looked with delight upon the figure of the naked Adam. Professor Freddie Frowstie twisted in his seat and surveyed the scene with quiet satisfaction. What a successful conference it had been! No doubt about it, it would certainly help to keep the name of the Skelmerdale department of English and Communication Studies on the map!

There was a gasp from the audience when two giraffes, led by Noah in a beard, appeared on the stage and cleverly climbed on to the pageant waggon, which by now evidently represented Noah's Ark. Behind them were a couple of cows. The giraffes had been borrowed from a nearby zoo that was shortly to close as a result of animal rights' protests, the cows from a friendly farmer whose land abutted on to the Skelmerdale campus.

Professor Hanwell awoke from his catnap, and would have been astonished by what he saw, were it not that he had now learnt not to be surprised by anything at Skelmerdale.

Suddenly there was a bang and a crash as a wheel slipped off the pageant waggon, and Noah and his animals were tipped on to the floor. The two giraffes bolted down the aisles in terror, and made for the entrance to the studio, causing panic and consternation in the audience. They knocked down Professor Freddie Frowstie, who made a vain attempt to stop them, and trampled him underfoot. Then they charged through the doors of the Great Hall and made their escape, and were soon lost amidst the vast loneliness of the Skelmerdale campus. The two cows, though, were not so intelligent, and charged into the central section of the audience, knocking down and then in their turn trampling upon Dr Ouimpe, two Merrywomen, Elizabeth, a member of Mrs Quick's coven, the university Registrar, and four men-at-arms. Chaos reigned, and Professor Hanwell placed Ruth behind a pillar and shielded her with his body until order was restored. Ambulances were called, and soon the stretchered figures of the injured people were carted off to the Skelmerdale General Hospital.

Eventually Fawn Fern came on to the stage and laughed brightly, holding up her hand for silence to make an announcement.

"Well, ladies and gentlemen, I think that that shows us how lively and interesting *theatre* can be. I'd like to thank the Skelmerdale Scops and the Medieval Players for the splendid performances. And now finally you're all invited back to the reception area of the Castle Island complex for a party with the cast - I'm sure you're all longing to talk to them and tell them how well they've done."

"Hey, Libby, I'd sure like to tell Adam what a great guy he is," giggled Laura.

"Oh, Laura, you are awful!" laughed Libby in reply.

Professor Hanwell and Ruth left the theatre with the other delegates, and were soon drinking a couple of whiskies to steady their nerves.

Dr Jacquasse smiled a broad smile when she reached the safety of the reception area. She suspected that her friend Deirdre Prout had slackened the wheel-nuts of the pageant waggon, and indeed when she returned to Whitepool, Deirdre told her that this was indeed the case. Dr Jacquasse was glad too that the diminutive and boring Dr Obadiah Ouimpe had been carted off to the hospital along with Freddie Frowstie, in all probability with crushed ribs. That meant that she would not have him hanging around her for the rest of the evening making sheep's eyes at her, and that she could amuse herself instead with Adam, a young postgraduate as it turned out.

Fluttering her eyelashes Dr Jacquasse went up to Adam, who, wearing only his post-lapsarian fig-leaf, and drinking a large glass of whisky, was complacently looking around the room..

"Well done, Adam, you were super, you spoke your words with a wonderful accent, and really looked the part," she said slyly, turning her doe-like eyes beseechingly towards him, looking him up and down with secret amusement. "I may come and talk to you, may I not? We haven't met, but I teach medieval German drama at Whitepool, so I was very interested in your performance. You're the best Adam I've ever seen, and your delivery of your lines was superb. I could follow every word - the dialect is very like medieval German you know."

Adam basked in the praise of the lovely Dr Jacquasse, and gulped down a couple of large whiskies. He felt week at the knees at being so close to the lovely young lady. Adam's diminutive fig-leaf did not hide very much, and Dr Jacquasse rejoiced to find a graduate prepared to make such a fool of himself.

Soon Adam was asking if he could see Dr Jacquasse again.

She flashed him an insincere smile.

"I do hope so, Adam dear," she said with secret amusement. "I'll give you my telephone number."

She took a piece of paste-board from her purse, and scribbled a telephone number on it.

"That's my private home number," she lied. (In fact it was her office number, and she spent as little time as possible in her office.) "Or you can fax me at Whitepool. And now I must circulate." Dr Jacquasse wandered around happily, chattering to friends and acquaintances, actors and actresses, happily storing up images of the strangely costumed people that she met, and thinking that her friend Deirdre would be pleased at the disruption that had occurred that evening.

Deirdre Prout was meanwhile spreadeagled on the roof, looking through a skylight, peering down on the scene below, which gradually became more and more drunk. Deirdre had liberally laced the punch with neat wood alcohol, and this was working its effect upon such of the participants as chose to drink it. These did not include Professor and Mrs Hanwell, who did not like punch and preferred their liquor unadulterated. So they stood around quietly sipping whiskies purchased from the cash bar, until the scene became disorderly and they decided to go to bed. Professor Laura Harington and Libby too were now whirling around like dervishes, passing Adam from hand to hand in a kind of wild reel, until Laura mischievously and triumphantly grabbed at Adam's fig-leaf and pulled it off! And Tabitha too was happily circulating among the guests, on a high from the effects of peyote and punch. Fawn and Florinda took but one cup of punch, and then slithered unconscious to the floor, for they were quite unused to alcohol of any kind. There the other party-goers delegates and student helpers tripped over them in a giggling heap of suspendered Rocky Horror legs, dishevelled Merrywomen, drunken lecherous gropers (Mrs Quick and her coven) and departmental secretaries and their partners. Deirdre Prout smiled with grim satisfaction at the drunken scene, and then quietly climbed down from the roof of the Castle Island complex and made her way to Fawn and Florinda's cottage. Spitefully she smashed in the windows with a baseball bat, and then happily dismantled her tiny tent, packed up her camping gear, placed her hob-nailed boots in her rucksack, and climbed into her car for the long return journey to Whitepool, confident that Fawn and Florinda at least had not had everything their own way.

*****

As Professor and Mrs Hanwell strolled back to their room in the chill night air, they could dimly see the two giraffes careering wildly round the campus. Half-a-dozen members of the university security service were trying to catch them in a desultory way, but the giraffes eluded them. Scattered groups of students were however cheering the giraffes on, and trying to impede their capture. In this they were successful. By next morning, when the delegates began to depart from campus, the security men had given up the chase, and the giraffes were standing languidly by the waters adjacent to the Castle Island complex, disdainfully picking over the remains of several student breakfasts.

By noon, the students, thinking the animals cute and saying to themselves 'it's just like Dr Dolittle, isn't it?', had launched an animal rights   petition to 'save our giraffes', and the vice-chancellor had fallen in with their suggestions and purchased them from the zoo to which they belonged for a few thousand pounds out of the university contingencies fund. Dr Winsome, the Skelmerdale vice-chancellor had vague notions that the presence of giraffes on campus could be turned to good account - as a talking point, certainly, and as a source of valuable free publicity for the university. By 10 a.m. the next morning he was smiling into the cameras of Skelmerdale County TV, the giraffes a picturesque backdrop behind him. And then again, he thought, the giraffes might be the nucleus of a safari park - or perhaps they could be incorporated into the university's new logo...And the biology department could do something with the giraffes too, to be sure. Freddie Frowstie, lying with crushed ribs in his hospital bed, was very proud of having been trampled on by the famous Skelmerdale giraffes! He swelled with pride to think that his department's conference had been the first cause of their appearance on campus, and he hoped that they would feature in many student projects and events.

*****

Professor and Mrs Hanwell had said goodbye to Libby and Laura, and agreed to look out for them in San Francisco, and then they too left the campus.

"Well, are you glad you came?" asked Ruth, snuggling up against her husband in the back of the taxi. "It's been fun, hasn't it? I think you should accept that offer of Frowstie's about giving the Scientific Poetry lectures. You could commute if necessary, it's only once a fortnight. I enjoyed seeing Fiona and Tamsin again," she continued, still drowsy from the festivities of the night before.

They arrived at a garage on the edge of Skelmerdale, paid off the taxi, and then went into the office to sign the papers for the Ford Mondeo which Professor Hanwell had arranged to hire.

Soon the lonely spire and tower of Skelmerdale Cathedral disappeared into the distance behind them, as they made their way north to visit Ruth's great-aunt Florence, before returning to the States.

CHAPTER SEVEN

ACROSS THE GOLDEN GATE

'In a few years time, there will be, in the cities of These States, immense Museums, with suites of halls... In these halls the noblest savants will deliver lectures to thousands of young men and women, on history, natural history, the sciences etc' (Walt Whitman, *Democratic Vistas* (Camden, NJ, 1876)).

In the first week of September, Professor and Mrs Hanwell arrived in San Francisco for the Summer Colloquium of the prestigious History of Science Society. Historians of science belong as a matter of course to the History of Science society, famed for the high quality of the articles and the polemical nature of the reviews that appear in its journals *Isis* and *Osiris*. It is one of the most lively and professional academic societies in existence, and Professor Hanwell, who had been a member for several years now, always enjoyed its meetings. He was himself due to read a paper 'On the trail of the Centipede' at one of the plenary sessions.

Some fifteen hundred delegates were expected, and they were housed in a range of hotels in downtown San Francisco. Professor and Mrs Hanwell were booked into the Pan Pacific, centrally located near to Macy's and the other department stores, and just three blocks away from the San Francisco Hilton, which was where the meetings of the Colloquium were to be held. As they collected their electronic pass keys, and made for the high-speed elevator that would whisk them up twenty-two floors to the top of the hotel, they heard a cheery voice call from the open-plan cocktail lounge.

"Hi there Charles! Hi there Ruth! Great to see you again!"

And there was Assistant Professor Laura Harrington, sitting on a comfortable sofa with Libby, drinking Martinis and nibbling potato chips, whilst a pianist at a concert grand played the haunting and catchy tunes of Satie's *Gymnopédies*. Professor Hanwell and Ruth strolled over to say hello.

"We've just got in from Arkansas," smiled Ruth, a little weary from the long westward flight. "Hello, Laura, Libby, good to see you again! I say, you are looking smart."

For Laura, in this most European and sophisticated of American cities, had chosen to abandon the casual attire she had favoured in Skelmerdale, and was now wearing a well-tailored tightly-fitting lightweight tan suit with padded sleeves, which emphasised her elegant legs and trim figure.

"Come and join us," invited the hospitable Laura.

"Thanks," said Ruth. "We will. I could use a drink myself after the flight. Just let Charles and me go to our suite and freshen up, and we'll be there!"

Laura and Libby waved as Professor and Mrs Hanwell were whisked up from the lobby in the glass-walled high-speed elevator. They found themselves in a comfortably furnished and softly-lit suite, with a verandah, a spectacular view over the Golden Gate bridge, a split level drawing-room with a spiral-staircase, and two enormous double rooms, each with two king-sized beds and its own bathroom. Their luggage had already been brought up by the bell-boys from the entrance hall. Ruth unlocked her case, and efficiently placed her dresses and suits on hangers in the wardrobe. Then she stepped out of her clothes, picked up her toilet bag, and disappeared into the bathroom to take a shower. When Professor Hanwell too had showered, he found that his wife had changed into a skirt and blouse, and was sitting at the dressing table brushing her hair. He gave her a kiss, and then himself slipped into a lightweight jacket and slacks, and together they descended in the elevator to the cocktail lounge. Soon he and Ruth were seated with Laura and Libby, drinking gin-and-tonics in extra-large glasses loaded with ice-cubes, stirring the lime with swizzle-sticks.

Laura and Libby had arrived a couple of hours earlier, and had already registered at the Hilton for the conference.

"Now Charles, you didn't tell me that you were to be a plenary speaker," said Laura reprovingly - 'On the trail of the Centipede' - that sounds like a real interesting talk to me. I wanted to give a paper here myself," she continued, "but the organisers turned me down. Oh well, you win some you lose some. Cheers!" She drained her Margarita, and soon the waitress had replaced it with another, the fifth of the afternoon.

"Of course," continued Laura, "this is a real big conference, not like the one in little old Skelmerdale. Oh me oh my, what fun we had there. I wonder if they ever caught those giraffes? Wow! Did I drink some liquor at that conference! But we'll have a good time here, too, I'm sure. Hey, why don't we all have dinner tonight for old times sake?"

Professor Hanwell looked at his watch. It was now half-past six in the evening, and he was not due to speak till the day after next. And, although there would doubtless be talks in the Hilton that first night, there was nothing in the programme to attract him particularly.

"OK, why not?" he said easily. "That would be nice."

Fifteen minutes later, the four of them were crowded into a cab, on the way to a sea-food restaurant that abutted onto the bay from one of the piers in the harbour. And there, seated at a window table overlooking the rippling waters, they sipped another cocktail, lingering over the menu. In front of them was the breath-taking beauty of the bay, serene and calm and untroubled as dusk fell. In the distance were the lights of the Golden Gate bridge, and of the former prison island of Alcatraz. Three freighters slowly crossed the bay, heading towards the Golden Gate.

The seventh cocktail of the day had made Laura loquacious. She put her hand on Charles' knee, and hiccoughed slightly.

"I see your book is getting rave reviews," she said. "That was a terrific one in last June's *Isis* wasn't it?"

"Yes, the reviewers been very kind to me so far," he admitted.

"And I saw a nice one in the *British Journal of the History of Science*," put in Libby.

"Yes, well, like I say, I've been lucky," he replied.

The waitresses came to bring another round of drinks, and to take their order. They all decided to sample the swordfish steaks, and Professor Hanwell ordered a couple of bottles of Californian champagne to wash it down.

"Here's to me," said Libby, raising her glass when the champagne arrived. "My chair told me only yesterday that my tenure has gone through."

"That's great news, Libby," said Professor Hanwell with genuine pleasure, as the party raised their glasses to her. "Especially in times like these when institutions are cutting back."

"Except for the Baskerville Institute," retorted Libby, with a wry smile.

"Well, yes, one has to admit that we've been rather lucky there," answered Professor Hanwell.

Tiredness was starting to catch up on him when the main course was over. Whilst Ruth, Laura and Libby tucked into copious quantities of ice-cream and chocolate sauce, he contented himself with cognac and coffee. An hour later, the party were back at the Pan Pacific. Professor Hanwell and Ruth said goodnight to Laura and Libby, whose rooms were several floors below their own, and returned to their suite, soon after to fall asleep enfolded in each other's arms in one of the king-sized beds.

*****

'Spoken sentences are like sharp nails, which force truth upon us' (Denys Diderot, *Diderotiana*)

The Hanwells awoke at 8.30 am, and after showering, by 9.20 were sitting in the Pan Pacific's elegant dining room, sipping orange juice and eating eggs, Canadian bacon, hash browns, sausage and tomato. Over coffee and toast, they examined the programme - a densely packed, demanding one, with few social functions other than cash bars catering for meetings of special interest groups. Unlike at Skelmerdale, there were no plays, masques, parties, feasts or thespians anywhere to be seen. Professor Hanwell consulted Ruth, and together they ticked out on the programme a not-too-demanding schedule of events for them to follow. Some members of the conference would attempt to attend everything, but that was too exhausting for the Hanwells. By 10.30 a.m. they were ready to leave, and walked leisurely downhill three blocks to the San Francisco Hilton. There they registered on the first floor, and received their name tags. They stood around for a few moments drinking coffee in paper cups, and soon Professor Hanwell was involved in various conversations with academics in the discipline whom he had met at previous conferences. At 11 a.m., he and Ruth broke off their small talk to attend a paper on spiders in literature and science from the seventeenth century to today, a strangely neglected topic, as he explained to Ruth. As always at the HSS meetings, the standard of papers was high, and the discussion was lively and well-informed.

Professor Hanwell's own turn came at 2 p.m. on the following day, when he arose to address an audience of 600 in the Grand

Ballroom with his paper 'On The Trail of the Centipede'. Professor Hanwell had chosen to try out the second draft of chapter 5 from his forthcoming book *Crocodiles and Insects*. Ruth sat with Libby and Laura five rows from the front, to the left of the centre aisle, both proud for her husband but also a little anxious at the size of the audience he had attracted. Many in the field had read one or other of his learned little articles, and those who had not heard of him before had realised from enthusiastic reception given to *Scientific Poetry* that here was a name to reckon with in the field, a man with something to say.

Professor Hanwell started with the well-known names of Conrad Gesner and Ulysses Aldrovandi, and soon he was speaking of an obscure and puzzling footnote in Hieronymus Allopedius' famous work on crocodiles, which had first led him, by indirections, to the Italian manuscripts of the *Insectographia* of that curious polymath, Diego Allati of Seville. And this learned and puzzling poem, in 22,000 lines of Latin verse, contained intriguing sections where passages in hexameters were regularly interspersed not only with cretic tetrameter acatalectics - which was unusual though perhaps understandable - but also with Versus Reiziani, which one had to admit was virtually without precedent. But that was by the way. More importantly, the verses of Allati had thrown light on an obscure passage, which had long troubled scholars in the posthumously printed *Theatrum insectorum* (London, 1634) of Dr Thomas Moffet, the well-known entomologist and father of Little Miss Muffet! And, while checking a virtually unknown contemporary manuscript transcription of this work dating from the 1620s, which had recently been thrown out of Keele University Library, then discovered on a junk stall in the East End of London, and subsequently bought for £8,000 by the London representative of the Baskerville Institute for the History of Science, Professor Hanwell's own employers in Arkansas, he had discovered that this transcription of Moffet's work had marginal annotations which never appeared in the printed version. And these had led Professor Hanwell to the poetry of Hieronymus Zanchius, Pietro di Sanctolio, and to the miscellanies of Alessandro Tassoni (Venice, 1636). And these three works had things to say about centipedes, which, well, quite frankly, were simply astonishing to anyone whose knowledge of the centipede tradition in western literature and thought was confined to the conventional and predictable sources. Professor Hanwell then proceeded to outline the existing tradition, from the earliest references to insects in the Greek and Roman classical writers, through the late-antique encyclopaedists like Isidore of Seville, then on to the Carolingian synthesisers such as the little-read Argobast of Aachen, and so to the bolder innovators of the twelfth and thirteenth centuries such as Honorius of Autun and Henry of Langenstein. Professor Hanwell then discussed Alexander Neckam, in many ways the founder of English natural science, the fourteenth-century speculative scholastics who had had deeper and subtler insights, and then he returned to Gesner, Aldrovandi and Moffet, who stood at the beginning of the tradition of modern naturalism, with whose work the whole subject was put on a firmer basis. But now one had to take account of the work of Zanchius, Sanctolio and Tassoni, where unexpected scientific insights were combined, in the case of Zanchius and Sanctolio, with poetry of a quite unexpected force and vigour, which meant that the whole tradition of scientific poetry in the seventeenth century would have to be re-examined. And this was not without consequences too for a study of the sixteenth-century encyclopaedists such as Béroald de Verville. Professor Hanwell concluded by briefly sketching some ways in which this re-examination should proceed, which would involve not least his changing some of the conclusions of chapter seventeen of his own recently published book on *Scientific Poetry*. Professor Hanwell sat down to enthusiastic applause, as the momentous consequences of his paper for so many different disciplines sank into the minds of the delegates.

"Bravo!" called Libby excitedly, who had not really followed the arguments, but liked Charles and was pleased that his paper had gone down so well.

"Bravo, bravo!" said Laura excitedly, climbing on to her chair in excitement to get a better view of the proceedings as applause surged around the room.

Then the floor was given over to questions, as various specialists in the audience probed Professor Hanwell's thesis from the point of view of metrics, history, philology, etymology, entomology, the Spanish, Italian French, Low German, Hungarian aspects. Professor Hanwell answered or deflected most of the questions, but cheerfully admitting ignorance of the Yoruba oral traditions of insect poetry and the metrical practices of the Polynesian sea dyaks. And then to another round of applause the Chairman of the session set him free.

"Well done Charles," said Ruth proudly, as her husband introduced the session chairman to her. "That was terrific!"

Professor Hamilton Greene, of the Princeton History of Science department, shook her hand, and invited them both up to his suite on the twentieth floor of the Hilton for tea. Soon Professor Hanwell and his wife were drinking Earl Grey served in delicate china cups in Professor Greene's magnificent suite, which had a splendid view of the San Francisco shoreline, and the long bridge over the water to Oakland.

"Wonderful talk, I must say so again, Charles," he re-iterated, as he plopped slices of lemon into their cups. "Perhaps you'd come and give it to my grad. students at Princeton sometime. They'd love to hear it, I know."

"Well, thanks, yes, I'd be perfectly happy to do that," replied Charles obligingly.

"And I can't wait to read *Crocodiles and Insects* when it comes out. Wow! It's going to be a sensation."

Half-an-hour later, descending in the elevator, Ruth dug her husband in the ribs with an impish smile.

"Now don't get too swollen headed, Charles," she said, proffering her lips for a passionate kiss as the elevator came to a halt.

"No chance!" he replied, as they left the hotel and emerged into the pale sunshine of that September day, and strolled slowly up the hill, looking forward to a cocktail in the lounge of the Pan Pacific with Laura and Libby again.

*****

'It was the wide and wave-lashed shore, the black rocks,
crowned with foam,
It was the ocean, vast and deep. The fathomless, the free!'
(Eliza Cook, *Poetical Works* (London, 1869))

Professor and Mrs Hanwell had driven north across the Golden Gate, into Marin county, through the giant redwoods, to Drake's beach. On the way from the hotel to the great bridge, Ruth had paused at a news-stand to buy her copies of the latest issues of *Women and Guns* and *American Rifleman* (for she was a keen markswoman, and had shot with the cadets at Bisley). They drove through the ochred magnificence of the Golden Gate with its spectacular views of the bay, and then headed north on Highway 1, through the scattered, pretty, tourist and fishing villages that clustered along the Pacific shore, and then to the lonely magnificence of Drake's beach. They locked the rented automobile, and Ruth removed her assault rifle and pistol from the trunk of the auto, slinging the rifle in its case over her left shoulder, and thrusting the pistol deep inside the pockets of her anorak. Professor and Mrs Hanwell clambered down a decrepit wooden staircase that led from the parking area to the deserted sea-shore. They walked arm-in-arm northwards along the debris-ridden shore, into the bracing wind that blew off the Pacific, watching the giant waves foam and thunder on to the beach. The powerful wind placed foam capped-tops on the giant waves that came crashing onto the beach. It whistled through their hair, and made Ruth's summery dress cling tightly against her legs beneath her anorak. Sea-birds soared on the breezes, and lazily circled the flotsam and jetsam with which the beach was bestrewn. The air, blowing in from the vast expanses of the Pacific, was fresh and clean. They breathed deeply, relishing the clear tangy breezes and the drops of water whipped up from the waves. For three miles they trudged slowly through the sand and shingle. They were now quite remote from human habitation, in a remote curve of the beach. San Francisco was thirty-five miles behind them. Professor Hanwell, in canvas trousers and leather jacket, sat down on a grassy knoll, and with some difficulty lit a Macanudo cigar. Ruth then unzipped her AK47 from its carrying-bag, put the bag on the beach and weighted it down with stones to stop it from blowing away, took a clip of ammunition from the pocket of her anorak, and loaded it with expert hand, taking care first to eject one of the thirty bullets of the clip as a precaution against jamming, a superstitious ritual perhaps for devotees of the Kalashnikov, but one to which Ruth firmly adhered. Then firing from the hip she loosed off a long and satisfying burst, furrowing the foaming breakers of the Pacific a hundred yards way. The clip was exhausted, and Ruth inserted another, this time firing staccato aimed bursts of four and five rounds at a time, enjoying the freedom to shoot that was not possible in England. She used the third clip in accurate shooting of single shots, the bullets skimming the waves at which she was aiming with precision. When Ruth had satisfied her desire to shoot with the AK47, she took out her 9 mm Browning automatic, and amused herself with target practice at old tin cans that were lying on the beach. The cans jumped and resonated as Ruth's accurate shots bounced them along the beach, until Professor Hanwell, his ears tiring of the sharp crack of the bullets, came up to Ruth from behind, and enfolded her in his arms. With a satisfied sigh Ruth put the safety catch on the automatic and returned it to its holster. She turned into her husband's arms, they embraced and kissed passionately, and still kissing slowly lay down on the dry sand beneath the dunes. Tenderly, Professor Hanwell started to undress Ruth, and they made love above the breakers of the Pacific on that lonely beach. And then, as dusk was falling, satisfied and at peace with the world, hand in hand they returned to the automobile, and slowly and carefully made the tranquil journey to the bright lights of San Francisco. And there, after a shower and a change of clothes in the suite of their hotel, they were ready to face the evening again, with cocktails in the bar followed by dinner for two in a downtown Greek restaurant.

*****

Next morning, whilst Professor Hanwell prepared for a business meeting with his US literary agent, Ruth stood in the lobby of the Pan Pacific hotel and waited for the doorman to whistle up a taxi. The sun was shining again, and the city was bright and gay. The spacious Chevrolet arrived, and Ruth clambered into the back seat, and told the driver to go to the Haight-Ashbury district. At 10.30 a.m. she paid off the cab, put on her white sun-glasses against the dazzling sun, and bought a copy of the *San Francisco Chronicle* from a news-stand. Then she went to a pavement café, and ordered herself a cup of chocolate and a brioche, which she ate with pleasure whilst reading the newspaper and catching up on world affairs. It was a warm and sunny day, in the low 70s, and Ruth felt cool and at ease in her light and flowery summer dress. At last she had finished her chocolate, settled the tab, and gathered up her purse. Ruth strolled up and down Main Street of the Haight-Ashbury district, in the pleasant warmth of the morning, window-shopping leisurely, enjoying the laid-back atmosphere, and entering a variety of shops and boutiques to make some small purchase. She paused from time to time to give a few quarters to the panhandlers. Ruth window-shopped for a few moments outside the alluring windows of La Senza Lingerie, and then entered, emerging half-an-hour later with some lingerie, several pairs of nylon stockings, and a pair of diaphanous harem pants. On impulse, she crossed the road to a gun store, eventually leaving with a couple of hand-guns, which she charged to her credit card, and several boxes of ammunition. The street was a pleasant mixture of cafés, delicatessens, grocery stores, mini-markets, bookshops, furniture stores and other establishments. She spent a happy half-hour browsing in an Occult bookstore, and bought herself an Art-Nouveau enamelled brooch from a costume jewellers. And then, a hundred yards further along the boulevard, she came to Dr Zombie's Voodoo Shop, which announced itself to the world by a skull and two blue shrunken heads in the window, by several packs of Tarot Cards, by pyramids and crystal balls and bright quartz stones to aid meditation. Curious, she pushed aside the beaded curtains and stepped in to the darkened room. The shop was almost empty, apart from a black man in a kaftan who eyed her silently, but with friendly eyes, from behind the counter. Dr Zombie's shop contained an interesting mélange of books, drugs, cards, magic accessories, imitation shrunken heads, pyramids for pyramid power, Tarot cards, hex-dolls, and a wide selection of New Age books on ley lines, flying saucers, alien abductions, Atlantis, the Bermuda Triangle, the Yeti and all the rest. There were works of Theosophy and on astrology and divination, on dreams and tantric prophecies. The cool dark store was pervaded by the smell of incense, and the acrid fumes of cannabis. Ruth browsed away happily, eventually selecting for herself a copy of the two-volume paperback reprint of Madame Blavatsky's *Isis Unveiled*, a work which, although never out of print since the day of its publication more than one hundred years previously, Ruth had never owned. Next she purchased a seventeenth-century edition of Agrippa von Nettersheim's *De incertitudine et vanitate scientiarum*, as well as a handsome set of Tarot cards, for she had been interested in the game since the publication of Michael

Dummett's monumental volume *The Game of Tarot* (London, 1980). Ruth also bought a crystal ball, for she was interested in the theory and practice of scrying, some of the medicaments and magic accessories sold by the store, and several sticks of incense. Soon another plastic bag was bulging with her purchases. The shop-keeper was happy that Ruth had spent over $1500, and offered her a cup of capuccino from the machine that simmered and hissed quietly throughout the day.

Ruth accepted gratefully, and the genial Negro who seemed to be the store's sole attendant busied himself with preparing two foaming cups, as Ruth slid gracefully on to a stool, and rested her shopping bags on the floor. There were still no other customers in the shop.

"So where are you from?" asked the store-keeper, as he leant on the counter and handed Ruth her coffee.

"I'm from Surleighwick, Arkansas," replied Ruth.

"I could tell you had an accent - I knew you was from east of here, that's for sure."

"I guess most people in the States are from east of SF," laughed Ruth. "And where are you from?" she enquired. "Do you come from these parts?"

"Hell no," he laughed, "I was born in BG - British Guiana as was, now Guyana. I emigrated in '66, travelled around the States, and settled here in '79. Say, you have certainly bought a lot of stuff here. Are you into magic and witchcraft and all that stuff?"

"Only historically," answered Ruth carefully. "My husband and I are both academics and into the History of Science discipline - and the history of science and the history of magic are inextricably intertwined. Out of magic came science, so they say. But what about yourself - do you just work here, or do you own the store?"

"I own it. My family practised Voodoo in BG - my father was a witch-doctor, and my mother was a witch. They sent me to study in the West Indies, in Dominica, in Trinidad, and in Haiti. So I learned my trade there, but my heart was not really in it - I decided I would rather follow the Western path, live in the States, earn myself some money and lead the good life." He gave a broad smile with his white teeth, and topped up Ruth's capuccino.

Ruth found him easy to chat too. Christophe from BG - for that was his name, was clearly a character, who knew a lot about his subject, and could converse easily on the contents of his store.

They talked of Thessalian witches who could draw down the moon, of Medea and her herbs, of Albert the Great and his talking head, of ghosts and hauntings, of poltergeists and Zombies, of the I Ching and Swami Muktananda, of Da Avabhasa, of Obeah men and Arthur Conan Doyle, of Novalis and Théophile Gautier, of Eliphas Levi and Dame Frances Yates, of Leadbetter and Besant and Madame Blavatsky, of *Zanoni* and *The Strange One.*

At last, rather regretfully, it was time for Ruth to take her leave. Christophe called her a cab, and as she left proffered her his business card, and also took a small package out from under the counter and gave it to her.

"Have this with my compliments. It's for my special customers - elixirs and such like, you'll find instructions inside. Goodbye, Missie," he said. "And remember, you ever need any advice on magic and all that stuff, you just call or e-mail me at the Dr Zombie Voodoo Shop."

"Thanks Christophe. That's sweet of you. I'll fax, call or e-mail you with any queries."

Ruth waved goodbye as the taxi drew up at the door, gathered together her numerous purchases, and sank gratefully into the back seat as the driver loaded her shopping into the trunk of the car.

*****

Two bell-boys assisted Ruth with her packages when she arrived back at the Pan Pacific. They escorted her into the lift, carrying her boxes, carrier bags, and other packages, gaily-wrapped with ribbon or brightly coloured paper. Soon they were in the entrance hall to Ruth's suite, and they placed the packages in its entrance hall. Ruth tipped them $20 each, and with profuse thanks and smiles the bell-boys left. Ruth felt tired after her intensive morning's shopping. She went to the wet bar, and poured herself a long cool glass of lager, which she sipped on the veranda of her suite with its magnificent view of the bay area. Then she showered and tried on some of the lingerie from La Senza, walking around the cool room, with the net curtains fluttering loosely in the breeze from the open window, enjoying its cool feeling on her skin. Her husband found her thus when he returned, they embraced with a long sensuous and passionate kiss, and soon the recently-purchased lingerie was strewn across the floor as Professor Hanwell carried his wife to one of the king-size beds, and they started to make love.

*****

The conference proceeded on its usual way. Professor and Mrs Hanwell relaxed and enjoyed themselves, taking breakfast in bed delivered to them by room service, lingering over coffee and croissants whilst reading the newspapers and catching up on the morning's news on TV, slowly coming to life, only to shower and emerge ready for the new day at coffee time. Then they would stroll down hill hand-in-hand through the cool softness of the summer breeze, with the temperature nicely into the low-seventies, to reach the Hilton in time to mingle with the delegates over coffee. Ruth was not reading a paper, so this time she could relax, and join in the incessant conversation and chatter without a worry in the world, as she listened to the titles of books and the gossip of the profession being bandied around. Then to lunch, often with the agreeable professors Laura and Libby, or with some of Professor Hanwell's friends and acquaintances. And then back to their hotel for a siesta, or sometimes to an afternoon talk, to be followed by cocktails and piano music in the lounges of one of the hotels; and then dinner in one of the countless exciting restaurants of the bay area. And there it was that conferences were planned, and papers commissioned, and the seeds of forthcoming books disseminated, and lecture series organised. Then, night after night, a nightcap on the balcony of their suite, overlooking the sparkling lights of the vibrant city, before retiring to the delights of the king-size bed and amorous sport and sleep, before the academic caravanserai struck camp, and the delegates briefly went their separate ways, only to reconvene in other cities, under other auspices. And so, after a week in San Francisco, Professor and Mrs Hanwell took a plane east, on the first stage of their journey back to Arkansas, where, apart from conferences and academic visits, he would remain until the end of the year, before leaving for Skelmerdale, where he had decided to take up the short appointment as visiting professor there which Frowstie had offered him.

CHAPTER EIGHT

ENGLISH TODAY PART II

'English Literature gives all who can enjoy it a fund of pleasure.' (Robert Chambers, *What English Literature Gives Us* (London, 1875))

October 19. Blanche Quick was spending her last night at Hay-on-Wye with her mother, before returning to Skelmerdale for the start of the new term. For the University of Skelmerdale, anxious to maximise its income from conference lettings, had gradually lengthened its summer and Easter vacations and compressed the length of its terms. Terms at Skelmerdale were now only seven and a half weeks long, and the summer vacation lasted from the end of May till mid-October. Blanche had packed her suitcases, gathered together her Watchperson portable video and a bunch of cassettes, and was now almost ready. In the morning, Mrs Quick would drive her daughter and her assorted paraphernalia up to Skelmerdale.

Blanche sat quietly in an armchair in front of the log fire, gulping mouthfuls of Frascati from time to time, and putting the finishing touches to one of her glove puppets, a gaily coloured creation of red and purple rags, which ended in a flurry of lacy white petticoats.

"Tell me, Blanche," said Mrs Quick curiously. "Why this sudden interest in glove puppets? You didn't use to be so keen on embroidery and needlework and all that kind of thing."

"It's my project work for the new course in glove puppet theatre," replied Blanche excitedly. "Fawn and Florinda are putting it on. We still don't have a Drama Studio Workshop, so they had the idea for using glove puppets to help put across the literature courses. They've written little scripts based on works of English literature, and we're going to act them out. This doll is Maggie - from *The Mill on the Floss* you know! It's such a good idea of Fawn's - we really get to know the outline of the plot, it's a brill way of learning all about costume, and it saves a lot of unnecessary time spent reading. Do you know how long *The Mill on the Floss* is? I mean to say, how many students are going to read a work like that nowadays? I sure as hell aren't!" Blanche tilted the bottle of Frascati into the air, and swigged the last third of the bottle in a great and satisfying gulp, before lurching into the kitchen to extract another bottle from the fridge.

Mrs Quick leaned back thoughtfully in her armchair, and poured herself another glass of Chardonnay from the bottle in the silver ice-bucket at her side. One had to admit that the Skelmerdale English department was full of bright ideas! Why hadn't she thought of that herself? But, of course, there was less scope for independent project work at a conservative institution like the Hereford Poly. But maybe she could work out something along these lines for her class anyway.

*****

After a leisurely breakfast, washed down with orange juice and coffee in copious quantities, Blanche and Mrs Quick started on the long drive across central and northern England to Skelmerdale.

"Now remember, darling, do look after yourself and always lock your door at night," Mrs Quick advised her daughter. "That campus axe-murderer still hasn't been caught, you know, and we don't want anything to happen to you, do we?"

"Oh, don't worry, mummy," answered Blanche carelessly, with a trace of irritation in her voice. "There's no need for you to fuss so! The university says that its security is very good, so I don't think you need be anxious."

It was late afternoon when Mrs Quick and Blanche arrived at Skelmerdale. The wind was sweeping across the bleak and desolate expanses of the campus, driving sodden dead leaves before it. Drizzle fell in a steady downpour, and a miasma of mist rose from the lake. Mrs Quick and Blanche parked the Land Rover, and between them made several journeys between it and Blanche's room in Grace Darling college, carrying suitcases, a few books, her bag of glove puppets and pet cuddly animals, along with Blanche's tennis rackets, bows and arrows, archery targets, fencing kit and football boots (Blanche played in the mixed and Ladies' elevens, and in the five-a-side Wimmins Scrummage Team). When pots, pans, kettles, plates, crockery and other impedimenta had finally been unloaded, Blanche made a cup of tea for her mother. And then, rather sadly, Mrs Quick bade her daughter a fond farewell and went off to find herself a comfortable bed for the night in a hotel before beginning the long drive back to Hay the following day. Blanche breathed a gentle sigh of relief as her darling mother said her last goodbye, before fixing herself a stiff vodka and lime, which she drank sprawling in an upright chair, her elegant jean-clad legs comfortably resting on the study-desk before her.

*****

Students at Skelmerdale were given a week to settle in before classes started, so during the first few days Blanche lazily unpacked, looked up her old friends, made frequent snacks in the kitchen situated a few doors away along the corridor of Grace Darling College, and drank in the college bar in the evening. By day four, Blanche felt acclimatised to the temperature difference between Hay and Skelmerdale - Skelmerdale was colder and damper in general, but less windy - and so she went in to the department to pick up the meagre collection of mail that awaited her. On the departmental notice-board was a long list of the films, videos, and puppet shows that were being shown and performed that term, together with details of outings to places of literary interest, such as the hostelry where the Brontë sisters had once spent a night, and the burlesque show at the Oldcastle Repertory Theatre. Finally, on day five, she made contact with her tutor Fawn Fern, and discovered the time of her glove-puppet class. Exactly one week after her arrival, Blanche Quick and Maggie the glove puppet were present in Fawn Fern's tiny office. Fawn sat behind her desk, and Florinda perched on one end of it. Blanche squatted on top of a small filing cabinet, and her fellow students sat eagerly on the floor. Tabitha, whom Professor and Mrs Hanwell had first encountered when they arrived at Skelmerdale the previous May for the conference, was one of them, and then there was Isolde, Esmerelda, Jasmin, Juliette, Hugo and Babs, all awaiting expectantly, each with a home-made glove puppet ready to hand.

Fawn Fern laughed brightly. Really, life had taken a turn for the better for Florinda and herself of late. The conference had been a great success, and had put them both well in with Freddie Frowstie. Moreover, it had made a profit, and they had been able to cunningly divert some of the money towards the purchase of materials for glove puppets. But the real joy and triumph was that they had been able to pay to have their glove-puppet scenarios printed! Together they had launched a series, imaginatively entitled at the suggestion of a learned friend at another university *Chronica Skelmerdaliana et analecta borealia*. So now both Fawn and Fern each had five independent publications to their name, each one carrying an ISBN serial number, each of which would moreover rank as an independent item under the HEFCE rules when the next publication survey came along! And that meant that they were now in the top quarter of their department by volume and quantity of publication! Eagerly Fawn and Florinda handed round the first volume in the series, Fawn's ten-page adaptation of *The Mill on the Floss* for glove puppets, with linking plot summary of key scenes. They had given great thought to the design of the work, and it was nicely printed with an old engraving of a windmill at the front.

For the first half-hour, the class admired each other's handiwork. Blanche's glove puppet was passed round from hand to hand, and the swirls of lace petticoat at the end were particularly admired.

"That's really cute, Blanche," said Fawn admiringly, holding it up in front of her face and jiggling the puppet with her fingers, making her class laugh. "And what wonderful material too - I do like that satin lining. Where did you get that from?"

"At a jumble sale in Hay-on-Wye," responded Blanche eagerly. "I bought two square yards for 10p."

"I went to a nithe jumble thale in Augutht," put in Tabitha.

"Jumble sales are so useful for picking up glove-puppet material, aren't they?" agreed Fawn. "I spend a lot of time in jumble sales. Florinda and I bought some lovely chintz for re-lining our armchairs last month. But I suppose we'd better get back to the class." Fawn laughed brightly. "I do so like the eyes on your puppet, Blanche. I think you've captured the spirit of Maggie absolutely. What do you think, Babs?"

Blanche proudly passed her puppet over to Babs. Babs slipped her hand into the puppet, and made it clap its hands together.

"I think it's just great," she said. "I agree Fawn, this is Maggie to a T. But what do you think of my puppet? I did Maggie too, but I interpreted the character in a slightly different way, and tried to make her face more melancholy looking." She held up her puppet with a great feeling of pride and self-importance.

Fawn clapped her hands. "O Babs, isn't that wonderful?"

Gradually the conversation drifted round to that favourite Skelmerdale theme, costume. Most Skelmerdale students liked nothing more than to pore over coffee-table books and exclaim at the brightly coloured pictures. Fawn owned several such illustrating Victorian costume, and these were passed around, so that the students could get further ideas for developing their views of Victorian costume, and could make top-coats and mufflers for their puppets for the next class.

Soon, an hour and a quarter had gone by, and the class paused whilst Florinda went out into the corridor to put the kettle on to make a pot of tea for all of them.

Whilst she was out, gossip became general again, as Fawn started to praise the dress sense of her students.

"I do like that blouse, Blanche," she said admiringly. "Where did you get that?"

"At C and A's," replied Blanche eagerly. "I worked at their Hereford store for three weeks in the holidays, and that entitled me to 20% off their sale items. So I bought three blouses like this!"

"Good for you," said Fawn. "You obviously have excellent dress sense."

"Do you think so?" Blanche flushed with pleasure at Fawn's praise.

"I worked at Marks in the vac. too," put in Isolde. "And I bought several nice skirts and slips there too."

Florinda returned with a large pot of tea, and a few of her home-made honey-cakes which were an attractive feature of the classes for certain students. Talk became general as the class relaxed over tea.

At the end of the tea-break, Fawn took up the main themes of her class once more.

"Now," she laughed, "we come to the second part of the class - the puppet dramatisation of certain selected scenes of the novel."

Proudly she handed out the ten-page scenario which she and Florinda had produced, printed and published. At its core were six pages of about eighty words apiece, containing a little extract of a conversation between Maggie and Tom Tulliver.

"Now, Blanche," Fawn went on enthusiastically, "you do the scene with your Maggie, and then afterwards Babs and Isolde can do it with theirs, and then we'll compare the interpretations. And you, Hugo, can do Tom with your Tom puppet. (The Tom puppet, being of the male gender, had excited rather less interest among this predominantly female class. Moreover, Hugo had found his sewing skills made fun of by his fellow students.) Blanche eagerly threw herself into her role. She sat opposite Hugo in the centre of the room, and holding up her puppet in the one hand, and the scenario in the other, read out her lines with feeling, waggling the arms of her Maggie puppet around. When she came to the end of the scene, she impulsively and mischievously tried to throttle the Tom doll with the hands of her puppet, which made everyone laugh.

"Well done, Blanche," said Fawn delightedly. "I think that's a wonderful interpretation, which certainly helps to put over Maggie's resentment at being a second-class citizen." Then Babs and Hugo did the scene again, and, taking her cue from Blanche, Babs made her doll attack the Tom puppet from the start. Soon Babs and Hugo were involved in a kind of arm-wrestling match, and the class clustered around them in excitement, cheering, with Fawn and Florinda leading them on. Another forty minutes of the class had elapsed.

Then Florinda took over the direction of the seminar. From the corner cupboard she drew out an old epidiascope, and as the students looked on in puzzlement, she erected a small screen, drew the curtains, and switched the epidiascope on.

"Puppet shadow theatre," she began self-importantly. "It's a development of puppet-theatre and living puppet theatre with which you are of course quite familiar, since we've always had a very high reputation for that at Skelmerdale. Some of you I'm sure have acted in living puppet theatre before. Shadow puppet theatre is a development of the same concept, the idea that the essence of a text can be presented in simple yet dramatic form, a form that whilst distancing the reader from the text, allows for a certain measure of creative interpretation of it. Now Blanche and Hugo, will you enact your little scene again for us please? Feel free to alter the interpretation, as naturally we're in a different medium now. And so that you can concentrate, I suggest that Babs and Isolde read out your scripts, whilst you and Hugo operate the puppets in front of the light so as to project their image onto the screen."

Blanche and Hugo gladly took up position, and the class cheered as the shadows clashed on screen, even though physically the puppets did not touch each other.

"Yes, it's a very much more pacific art form, isn't it," laughed Fawn. "The violence on screen has no physical counterpart, it's just an illusion."

As she spoke, and whilst the attention of Fawn and Florinda and the rest of the class was fixed on the screen, Blanche Quick, who took after her mother, impishly thrashed the Tom puppet about the head with her Maggie puppet. Then, in the dark, even more mischievously she crooked her leg around the stool on which Hugo was sitting, and with a sharp tug tipped him off it. Hugo fell to the floor and banged his head, pulling books and papers off Fawn's desk as he fell. Everyone laughed and cheered, as Florinda turned on the lights and drew the curtains, to reveal Hugo sitting on the floor ruefully rubbing his head. It was now 1 p.m., and time for the class to break up. Blanche and Tabitha and Tamsin strolled slowly back to the bar of Grace Darling college for a late lunch.

At 1. 10 p.m. the bar was busy, but not unpleasantly so. Blanche ordered a large Martini and lemonade for herself, and stood Tabitha a vodka-and-lime on the rocks and Tamsin a pint of Roger's Owd Horizontal, the powerful real ale popular with the serious drinkers on the Skelmerdale campus. Contentedly the three young ladies sat at an empty table in the corner of the bar, and gazed out at the wide expanses of the lake, and the birds lazily hovering in the air above it.

Tabitha and Tamsin were quick to tell Blanche that her glove puppet had been super, the best in the class. Blanche basked contentedly in the admiration of her chums.

"I like Fawn and Florinda's classes," she replied. "They're fun...." She swigged her Martini contentedly. "And those honey-cakes were wonderful, weren't they? Anyway, that's our big class over for the week." For the syllabus at Skelmerdale was very flexible, and students could in effect devise their own courses. Blanche, Juliette and Tabitha were taking the 'Glove Puppet' option, and the 'Film and Society' option, which meant that they had to watch a movie and then chat about it the following day with a tutor. This term, the students at Skelmerdale were taking a course on 'Morals and the Movies'. This was a popular option, since week by week there was to be a showing of a soft-porn film, after which the students would speculate about what kind of audience could possibly be shocked by such a thing. But this week's film, *Nurses on the Job!*, was not due for showing till Thursday morning, so that left Blanche and her friends with plenty of time.

Soon their glasses were empty, and flush with money at the start of the new term, Tabitha went to the bar and ordered another round of drinks to accompany the sandwiches, chips and sausage rolls which they had bought for lunch. These they ate leisurely, for now that licensing hours had been abolished in England, the Skelmerdale bars remained open all day long. No longer did students have to drink-up by 2. 30 p.m.. By 2. 15 p.m., the bar was still thronged with a large number of students, some of them playing tiddly-winks on the floor, others playing bar-billiards, others feeding the juke-box which spewed out a constant rhythmical drumming of the latest pops. Soon Blanche and her friends were tapping their feet in time to the music, and banging their glasses on the table to provide a percussion accompaniment. Juliette went to the bar and brought a third round of drinks, which they sipped slowly and languorously. The tiddly-wink players had now started to fight and brawl amongst themselves. Soon a drunken brawl had developed in the bar, as the blue team fought against the green. Blanche, Juliette and Tabitha stood excitedly on the chairs and table, so as to get a better view, as the bar-staff with practised hands quickly pulled down the grilles, waiting for the squabble to end, one way or another, before resuming service. The girl-friends of the tiddly-winks players cheered on their respective teams, and soon, as one of the blue team was punched in the stomach and winded, and another had retired from the fray with a bleeding nose, the green team had the upper hand, three to one. With a roar the green team rushed at their remaining blue opponent, picking him bodily up and hoisting him on to their shoulders. Then with a cry of 'Charge!' and another of 'To the lake!' they surged out of the bar, followed by an excited crowd of camp-followers and other girl-friends. Before the throng had even left the bar, the grilles were raised, service resumed, and Blanche, who was feeling in a good mood, went to the counter to buy a fourth round of drinks.   It was now nearly four o'clock, and Blanche felt sleepy. Blanche waved goodbye to her friends, and wandered sleepily past the long lines of space-invader games, pin-ball machines, and the one-armed bandits that the university had installed in a hopeful bid to increase its revenues by tempting the students to gamble, an entrepreneurial idea that was already paying off handsomely. Blanche arrived safely back in her tiny room on the second floor of Grace Darling College, overlooking the lake, from whence the sounds of raucous horse-play could still be heard. By now rather woozy and boozed-up, Blanche quickly peeled off her clothes and threw them around the room, slipped her baby-doll nightie over her head, and crawled into the unmade bed from which she had risen that morning, succumbing to oblivion shortly afterwards. She awoke at 11 p.m. , splashed a little water over her face, donned a pair of blue jeans and a sweater, and made herself a cup of coffee. Then, at 11.45 p.m., she went downstairs, past the bar again, from which the evening's brawling drunks were just being evicted, smiled to herself, stepped over two comatose and slumped figures, and made her way to the satellite TV room where the late film, *The Zombie Dead* was just starting to show to a large and enthusiastic audience. Blanche snuggled down in her chair with her cup of coffee and was soon lost in the film. It had been a perfect day, and a super start to the new term's teaching.

*****

'There are those who will make you books and turn them loose in the world with as much despatch as they would a dish of fritters.' (Cervantes, *Don Quixote*)

Fawn and Florinda were delighted by the success of their glove puppet class. As they sat in the common room of Tristram de Burke college (named after the well-known catamite of Edward II, who once wrote an excruciatingly bad set of doggerel verses on the city of Skelmerdale from which he hailed) they sipped their glasses of milk and ate a banana and looked out on to the bleak and desolate campus. They began excitedly to plot to gain further publications for themselves. That afternoon, back at their cottage, they started to translate their glove-puppet scenario into French. *La Moulin sur le Floss*, they proudly typed into their word-processors. *'Une joornée Maggie et Tom battayent l'une contre l'autre.'* (Skelmerdale had no language departments, and operated on the principle that no-one would at Skelmerdale would ever be able to detect a grammatical mistake. As for what happened outside the university, if some pedant found a few accents missing or words misspelt, who cared? Certainly not Fawn and Florinda or their colleagues.) By the end of the afternoon, they had set their ten pages of schoolgirl French, and happily turned to the more attractive and important question of whether to alter the illustrations for the French edition.

"I think we ought to go for French illustrations," said Fawn thoughtfully. "After all, our book is for the French market." Eagerly she rummaged through a book on French nineteenth-century costume, and soon she and Florinda were deep into a discussion of chignons and bustles, and were exclaiming happily about the pretty pictures in front of them. Next morning they were proudly boasting about the forthcoming French translation of their book to Freddie Frowstie.

Freddie Frowstie was impressed in spite of himself. Fancy, Fawn and Florinda's work coming out in French translation!

Carefully he jotted down the ISBN number in his diary, and made notes for a puff in the next issue of the *Skelmerdale Newsletter*.

'The international reputation of the department of English and Communication studies at Skelmerdale has been recently confirmed by the translation into French of an important series of experimental texts by two members of the department,' he wrote. 'The use of these texts in class is proving a great success, and is a significant element in the maintenance of the international renown and fame which the department at Skelmerdale has long enjoyed in the eyes of the world, as shown by our high student ratio of applications to places available. It is hoped to build on these developing connections and soon establish a Socrates link with the city of Vichy with which we are twinned...'

Back at their cottage that night, Fawn and Florinda, fired by the success of their schemes, took out a German dictionary and laboriously began to turn their text into colloquial German. *Der Mull auf dem Floss*, they wrote proudly. *'Maggie und Tom worden kampfen über die gummiepuppen'*. By the end of the evening, they had produced a 'German translation' of their work.

Freddie Frowstie was enraptured the next morning, and hastily added to his notes for the Newsletter: 'Links between Skelmerdale and Germany, which have existed from the time of Hengist and Horsa, have been strengthened by the appearance of a new German translation of experimental dramatic texts developed and used as important teaching aids in the Skelmerdale department. Links between Germany and Skelmerdale are of course important in the new Europe, and we at Skelmerdale will be happy to play our part to the full in this. Preliminary negotiations are already underway with the view to the initiation of a Socrates exchange. It is characteristic of the wide-range of qualifications exhibited by the staff of the Department of English and Communication Studies, with its excellent reputation for languages, that the translation was able to be done from our own resources....'

Three days later, when Fawn and Florinda had handed him a presentation copy of *El Molino sopra lo Flosso. Scene di una commedia*, the excited Frowstie wrote again to the *Newsletter*: 'Skelmerdale, as an important city in the Holy Roman Empire [he meant Roman Empire] has always had strong links with Italy. The recent Italian translation of experimental drama texts used in teaching in the department here will, we feel confident, be a significant factor in further developing links between Skelmerdale and Italian universities. We have set up a working-party in the department to consider developing a Socrates scheme....'

That night, pleased with himself, Freddie Frowstie went back home and wrote to Fawn and Florinda, urging them to put in for Senior Lectureships at the next promotion round.

*****

Blanche Quick spent the next few days making clothes for her glove puppets, browsing through books of costumes in the Skelmerdale University library, and just enjoying the abundant leisure that reading for a degree in English and Communication studies at Skelmerdale gave her. She arose each morning about 11 a.m., and when she had showered and brushed her teeth, she went downstairs to join her friends in the Central Snack Bar, which was filled with students from 8.30 a.m. to midnight every day. There she bought herself a cup of acrid-tasting coffee, and then slumped into a battered armchair amidst the filthy ruck of empty yoghurt cartons and crumpled copies of the student newspaper, *The Grotto*. She sipped her coffee slowly, and came back to life to face the rigours of the day, before joining Juliette and Tabitha and Isolde for a long, concentrated game of bar-billiards. Then, after a few pints of beer, a pork-pie and a packet of crisps in one of the college bars, she staggered back to bed at 3 p.m., to sleep soundly till the late evening, emerging just in time for the final riotous hour in the bar of Grace Darling college, with a game of space invaders and a little gambling away of her small change on the one-armed bandits, until it was time for another couple of late-night movies. And so to bed again in the small hours, and the start of another day. Thus Blanche Quick passed her time, until Fawn and Fern's class the following Tuesday.

Fawn and Florinda were in good-humoured mood as their class arrived. Blanche and Juliette and Tabitha slumped on the floor, with Isolde and Hugo. Fawn flashed them a bright smile, and handed each member of the class a brightly coloured cardboard box. Fawn and Florida had easily persuaded Freddie Frowstie to make available departmental funds for another of their experimental drama projects. Two days ago, she and Florinda had been to the Early Learning Centre, and there they had bought twenty sets of the Early Learning Play Theatre, suitable for ages 5-11. And now the class were to use the Play Theatres as vehicles for their own dramatic renderings of the Glove Puppet scenarios in yet another medium. Fawn and Florinda were going from strength to strength. Three nights previously, they had laboriously rendered the text of their *Mill on the Floss* scenario into Serbo-Croatian, translating word for word from a tiny dictionary which they had bought in the Skelmerdale Oxfam shop. And now they had another publication to their names, and would soon have an international reputation for their work! Freddie Frowstie had been overjoyed, and had written to the Newsletter pointing out that a former student of the department had once taught English in Bosnia, and that the Department of English and Communication Studies at Skelmerdale planned to build on these contacts, and when Bosnia had joined the European Union, intended to apply to set up a Socrates link with the University of Scjunk...

Blanche and Tabitha and the rest of the class eagerly unwrapped their packages, and screamed with delight when they saw the prospect that awaited them.

Fawn produced a big pot of glue, some staples and paper-clips, and put on a flowery smock with wide and capacious pockets.

"Right!" she said brightly. "Now I think the first thing to do is for each of us to build our theatres." She laughed gaily. "After all, we can't see how it works on the stage until we have a stage, can we? So...to work!"

Eagerly Blanche riffled through the instructions, squatted on the floor, dipped a brush into a large pot of paste, and started to assemble her cardboard theatre. Tabitha and Juliette and the other students did likewise. Fawn and Florinda looked on contentedly as the class scrabbled around in a disorganised fashion on the floor on hands and knees, bumping into each other, shrieking, quarrelling, fighting over the glue and paste, calling out to each other, pausing to admire each other's handiwork. An hour-and-a-half went by, interspersed by a long interval for tea and honey-cakes. Mischievously, Blanche slipped a brush covered with wet paste onto Hugo's chair just as he was about to sit down. He sat on it, and leaped instantly into the air with an indignant cry, as wet goo spread over the seat of his jeans. Everyone laughed, and Fawn excused him to go back to his room and change his clothes. By the end of the class, all of the students had assembled their theatres, and eagerly waited to act out their scenarios on them.

Thus ended another learning session at the University of Skelmderdale.

CHAPTER NINE

ENGLISH TODAY PART III

'The art of reading is to skip judiciously' (Philip Gilbert Hammerton, *The Intellectual Life*)

The harsh croaking of the Canada geese woke Blanche Quick in her tiny room at Grace Darling College. She buried her tousled head under the blankets for a moment or two, but still the din continued. Then, from next door, through the walls, came the steady throb of rock music from a portable CD player. Glumly Blanche pushed back the sheets, turned on her bedside lamp, and looked at her little alarm clock. It was 10. 30 a.m. Blanche felt like death warmed up, after drinking beer with whisky chasers in the bar the night before till chucking-out time.

"Need a ciggy," she mumbled to herself, as she reached for a packet of High Tar cigarettes from the packet on the bedside table. Then, plumping the pillows, and hunching the blankets around herself, she settled down to enjoy the first cigarette of the day. Blanche had started to smoke in her first term at Skelmerdale, as a small gesture of defiance towards her mother Mrs Quick, who disapproved of the practice. And also through the influence of her first-year tutor, Mr Dedder, who chain-smoked himself, and felt happier if he could introduce his students to the habit too. The thrice-divorced Mr Dedder, (BA Oxon), who had been a founder member of the Department of English and Communication Studies at Skelmerdale a generation ago, had now somewhat run to seed, and passed his days in a hazy blur of alcohol and tobacco fumes. But Blanche, as an impressionable eighteen-year old, had thought him rather suave and worldly-wise, as he greeted his first-year tutorial group, lounging back in his chair with his feet on the table and his hands clasped behind his head, wearing a blue and white striped matelot's jersey, rope sandals with no socks, and blue jeans. And after the fourth glass of Armagnac had been proffered by her bibulous and talkative tutor, Blanche felt quite sophisticated as she sat in Mr Dedder's room on her second day as a student in the department of English and Communication Studies at the famous University of Skelmerdale, nervously puffing away at a

Gaulois. Mr Dedder had a cottage in France in the Dordogne, where he spent his vacations chattering to waiters, and he was the department's resident expert in French communication studies. So Blanche became a thirty-a-day cigarette addict, and did not feel right until she had inhaled two or three puffs of a morning. When she had smoked her first two Gauloises, Blanche summoned up the energy to get out of bed.

She drew back the curtain, and revealed the bleak and desolate windswept campus of Skelmerdale. Below her, the waves of the lake were being whipped up by angry winds. Only a few hardy windsurfers were out and about at this time in the morning. On the other side of the lake, the saplings were nearly bent double by the wind. Blanche ran her hands through her unkempt tresses, and then decided to have a shower. She slipped a towelled bathrobe over her baby-doll nightie, shuffled into her mules, and then flip-flopped down the corridor to the shower. The showers in Grace Darling College abutted directly onto the bedroom corridors, being separated from those who passed up and down only by a thick white shower curtain. At night, when spirits were running high, it required a certain boldness of heart to take a shower, as there was always a risk that a mischievous passer-by would yank back the curtain, exposing the figure within to raucous laughter. But at 11. 15 a.m. things were still quiet in Grace Darling College, and Blanche felt few qualms as she took off her robe and nightie and stepped under the blissful stream of hot water. She soaped herself thoroughly, and even shampooed her hair, which made her feel a great deal better. The heat of the water brought colour back to her cheeks. Soon Blanche was back in her room, rubbing herself down vigorously, and tipping a generous quantity of talcum powder over herself. That done, she donned her Merrywoman outfit of Lincoln green, and descended to the ground floor of the college. Blanche was not going to shoot arrows that day, but she liked the uniform, which she felt showed off her legs to advantage, and it had the merit of being warm and hardwearing, two most important features for life on the Skelmerdale campus. As she went down the concrete and barren stairway, Blanche looked at her watch. It was now ten to twelve, just time for her to get a cup of coffee before the bar opened. At the bottom of the stairs Blanche paused at the pool, pin-table and one-armed bandit room. Feeling in a lucky mood, she inserted a pound coin into the one-armed bandit, and pulled the handle forcefully. She was in luck! Three apples showed up on the screen, and ten one-pound coins clattered into the box. Excitedly, Blanche put another coin into the machine. And this time she got a gold nugget and two cherries, and nine further pounds clattered down. Again she inserted a pound and pulled the handle. And heavens! Three nuggets showed up, and an avalanche of coins, thirty pounds in all, were scooped up by her eager hands. She loaded them into the pouch slung from the belt of her Merrywoman outfit, and tried again. This time, the coin produced no result. Blanche paused, and for once common sense prevailed. She passed on to the coffee machine, and for twenty pence purchased for herself a cup of foul tasting liquid. She sat down in the shabby Junior Common room, which was   littered with discarded polystyrene cups, scattered pages of the student newspaper, banana skins and orange peel. (Skelmerdale had decided to economise by having the common rooms cleaned only once a month.) Blanche swung her shapely legs on to the table, and slumped back in her chair, sipping her coffee, and glancing desultorily at the student newspaper.

AXE-MURDERER STRIKES AGAIN she read with bored indifference.

'Students living on campus were shocked by the sudden death last week of Simon Trebizond, a music student living in Sir Roger de Coverley college. Simon was the fourth victim of the mad axe-person, and the first male. A spokesperson for the Registrar said: "We have always maintained that our security is good, and that there was no evidence of sexual motive in these regrettable attacks, which could have happened anywhere. It is naturally gratifying that the death of poor Simon has proved this theory correct. We are confident that the person responsible will soon be caught, and do not believe that there is any cause for unnecessary alarm."'

"Hi there Blanche!" Blanche's reading was interrupted by Tabitha. Eagerly she tossed aside the boring student newspaper, and accompanied Tabitha to the bar.

"Drinks on me today, Tabby," said Blanche self-importantly. "Had a bit of luck at the one-armed-bandit. Won a packet for myself."

As Tabitha looked on approvingly, Blanche ordered four bags of crisps and two pork-pies, two pints of her favourite Roger's Owd

Horizontal, a whole bottle of Armagnac and two packets of Gauloises.

"Don't feel like work today," laughed Blanche, "such a bloody awful day, feel like celebrating my win instead. "It's a good omen. Anyway, I haven't got any classes today, and I'm up on my reading. How about you."

"Thnap," laughed Tabitha happily. "Much rather thit here with you, Blanche. Anyway, it'th cold outthide."

Blanche carried the tray of drink and food to her favourite corner table, where she could see what was happening in the bar and also observe the not unpleasant prospect over the Skelmerdale lake. She tucked one of her buskined legs beneath her, took a deep swig of beer, and then pulled the cork out of the Armagnac with her teeth. She poured herself and Tabitha two generous slugs into tumblers, and then started to eat the crisps.

"Gosh, that's better," she said. "I need a hair of the dog this morning. I didn't get to bed till 2 a.m. Up gossiping and fooling around in the bar, you know. I slept like a log, but woke up feeling drained."

"Me too," laughed Tabitha. "I didn't get to bed till 4."

Both young ladies drained their Armagnac and washed it down with the potent beer, and then Tabitha offered Blanche some peyote.

Blanche shook her head.

"Thanks, Tabby, but I won't mix it," she said. "Beer and Armagnac's enough for me."

Tabitha smiled seraphically.

"Well I will," she said. "But I exthpect I'm more uthed to it than you are."

Tabitha took a clay pipe from the deep pocket of her smock, filled its bowl with peyote, and was soon puffing happily away. The acrid smell of peyote mingled with Blanche's Gauloises.

By one o'clock the bar was crowded both with student drinkers and with various members of the faculty, among them Mr Dedder, consuming double whiskies at a great rate. A few moments later, Mr Dedder was approaching their table.

"Mind if I join you?" he asked, and sat down without waiting for an answer.

Mr Dedder drained the third double whisky of the lunch hour and looked benignly round the bar, his face flushed and red and mottled. By now the bar was full, and a great throng was struggling to get served. The hum of conversation rose louder and louder.

"I say Johnny," enquired Blanche (Mr Dedder encouraged his students to call him Johnny) "have you ever heard of a novelist called Virginia Wulf? Fawn and Florinda say we're going to be doing her later in the term, but I can't find a Wulf anywhere in the catalogue."

"Virginia Woolf? Oh yes, I've heard of her," replied Mr Dedder. "She's quite well known. I've got a copy of her works in my room somewhere. You can borrow it if you want."

"Thanks, no, I couldn't possibly deprive you of your copy," said Blanche hastily. She did not want to be alone with Mr Dedder in his room, for he had a reputation as sexual harasser, and had indeed several times fondled Blanche's jean-clad bottom in first year one-to-one tutorials, until she had plucked up courage to tell him to stop.

"It's no trouble at all, my dear," relied Mr Dedder, letting his hand slip on to Blanche's green-clad thigh. "If you do find you need it, come and get it at any time. My door is always open."

"Well, thanks - but I'll have another go at the catalogue first. We'll be reading *A Room with a View* or some such title."

"Ah," replied Mr Dedder vaguely. "Yes - I've heard of it, I read it once myself I believe, when I was a student."

Blanche removed Mr Dedder's hand from her thigh in a pointed way, and he sighed, looked at his empty glass and shuffled off painfully to the bar for a refill.

Whilst he was gone from the table, Blanche and Tabitha looked around, and waved gaily to two of their year to come and join them, to fill up the table and make sure there was no room for Mr Dedder when he returned. Soon Christopher and James, two of the more intelligent men in their year, were seated with Tabitha and Blanche. James, a bland and hearty pink-cheeked public-schoolboy, was into his fourth pint of lunchtime ale, his brightly coloured Skelmerdale scarf hanging loosely round his neck; Christopher, more studious and quiet, had contented himself with a single pint. Blanche filled her tumbler and that of Tabitha with Armagnac, and offered some to James. And he happily let Blanche tip a generous slug into his beer. Neither James nor Christopher could throw any light on why Blanche had not been able to find the works of Virginia Wulf in the library, and James suggested that she ought to ask at the enquiry desk. "Maybe the books are not in the library," he opined. "It's a pretty small library after all."

Blanche and Tabitha were now quite merry, and had decided that they would not bother to do any academic work that day. So they plied Christopher and James with drink and conversation, and Blanche boldly held out her empty pint glass for James to buy her a refill.

"Bloody good stuff, this beer," she said happily, lolling back against the cushioned seat, and letting her head fall on James's shoulders. "Did I tell you I had a bit of luck on the one-armed bandits today? Won me a packet - next round's on me."

2 p.m. came and went, and Christopher excused himself on the grounds, unusual for Skelmerdale, that he wanted to read a book. James, however, stayed happily gossiping to Blanche and Tabitha, until 4. 15 p.m., when he looked at his watch and said that he must see the repeats of the Magic Roundabout on ITV. And not all of Blanche's exhortations or pulling at the sleeves of his sweater, for she was by now pretty drunk, could deter him from leaving for the JCR TV room to watch this favourite children's series, which had a cult following at the University of Skelmerdale.

Thwarted, Blanche tottered to the bar, fished into her pouch for a dozen more coins, and returned with a second bottle of Armagnac. The bar was quieter now, though there were still a couple of dozen people drinking there. This was the quietest time of day in the Skelmerdale campus bars. Towards 5. 30 p.m., when the last afternoon lectures were over, the early evening and pre-dinner drinkers would come in, and then the after-dinner crowds, and then the evening recreationalists. From 9 p.m. to closing time at 11.45 p.m. the bar would be jammed to the doors. Blanche drained her tumbler of Armagnac, and chattered excitedly to Tabitha. Then she felt a little faint, and leaned her head back against the banquette seat of the bar. Soon she was nodding off. When she awoke, feeling somewhat refreshed, it was 5. 25 p.m., and the early evening drinkers were just starting to arrive. Blanche paid a quick visit to the ladies' to freshen up, and splashed some warm water from one of the washbasins over her face. Then she returned to the bar, ordered herself another pint of beer, three bags of crisps, and a sausage roll, and was soon making deep inroads into the bottle of Armagnac. A crowd of friends and freeloaders joined her table to assist Blanche in consuming her liquor and lightening her pouch of the gambling winnings. By 10 p.m. Blanche had had enough. She lurched unsteadily to her feet, swearing foully at those who tried to assist her. Reaching the door of the bar, she felt nauseous, and was violently sick into a convenient litter bin. Then, pale and queasy, she staggered up the stairs, pale about the gills, a haunted and nervous expression on her face. She vomited again in the corridor outside her room, and then, unlocking her room with difficulty, she lurched towards her bed, and passed out on top of it, still clad in her Merrywoman outfit of Lincoln green. Thus came to its close a typical day in the life of Blanche Quick, English and Communication Studies, 2nd year.

*****

Fawn and Florinda were feeling very pleased with the success of their classes. Things were going well for them. By photocopying words from a Chinese-English dictionary, and pasting them on to a piece of paper, they had now produced a Chinese version of their *Mill on the Floss* scenario. They now had six books to their name, had shot up to the very top of the department's publication list, and were in for promotion with a good chance of getting it. Freddie Frowstie had written another boastful piece for the *Skelmerdale Newsletter* puffing the Chinese connections of his department, and stating that when China joined the EEC an ERASMUS interchange between Skelmerdale and Bei-Jing would be a top priority, thanks to the excellent relations which had always existed between the Skelmerdale department and the People's Republic. And indeed, a Chinese mature student who had been an early member of the department had played a prominent role in purging Lin-Piao in the 1960s.

Fawn and Florinda's teaching too was going astonishingly well. Fired by the success of their experiment with the Early Learning Play Theatre, the two women were developing and deepening their teaching programme in juvenile communications. They had been much taken by the colourful bricks in different shapes and sizes that the Early Learning Centre had in stock, and so they had devised a project for the students to build the Mill on the Floss from these. And so, one Saturday, they had triumphantly spent

£200 on assorted boxes of bricks, chargeable to departmental funds, and from these the students would have a practical session in bodying forth their different ideas of what the Mill on the Floss looked like.

After her heavy day's drinking, Blanche Quick slept in later than usual, and so it was 12.30 p.m. before she had fully recovered consciousness, and smoked a couple of Gauloises to restore herself to something like normality. She felt dehydrated, so she swigged the last remnants of the bottle of Armagnac that she had bought in the bar the previous day. She had slept all night in her Merrywoman outfit, now crumpled and dishevelled, but she did not care about that. Blanche ran her fingers through her hair, and without bothering to wash hurried downstairs to get a quick fix of a cup of coffee and a couple of pints of real ale. Passing the one-armed bandits again, she lost five pounds before kicking the machine bad-temperedly and staggering into the bar. Tabitha was there already ensconced in the corner, and she looked at Blanche sympathetically as she ordered her a couple of pints of Owd Horizontal with a brandy chaser. Peyote had made Tabitha serene and unconcerned, as she stood in her pretty smock with the pipe in the corner of her mouth, inhaling deeply.

"Here you are kiddo, thith will put new life into you."

"Thanks, Tabby," said Blanche gratefully, tilting the pint glass down her throat and draining the whole in two large gulps, before swallowing a double brandy and starting more slowly on the second pint of ale. Ten minutes later, Blanche began to feel more human again.

Tabitha looked on sympathetically.

"Wow, I bet you needed that. You put away a packet latht night. Did you thleep OK?"

"Out like a light," replied Blanche proudly. "Slept the clock round till 11. 45 a.m., had myself a couple of ciggies, and here I am. How about you?"

"I wath OK," said Tabitha nonchalantly. "But then I didn't have ath much Armagnac ath you."

By 2 p.m., after a third pint and three more brandies, Blanche was fully recovered, and she and Tabitha walked happily to Fawn's room for their weekly class.

Fawn greeted them with her usual gushing laugh, and said: "We're going to have such fun today, we're going to build the Mill on the Floss. It's so important in a department of Communication Studies such as ours not to think that only words or books or films or TV can communicate. Everything is a text, as modern theory has shown - clothes are a text, tins of baked beans are a text, a sauce bottle is a text, a train is a text, an Inter-city train is a text connecting two cities, which are themselves texts, hence an inter-textual text, a car is a text equally, and so too are buildings texts. So today, in accordance with the Skelmerdale traditions of gaining practical hands-on experience of texts, we're going to carry further our deep studies of *The Mill on the Floss* by each of us building the mill. Look, here are some bricks for us to do it in, and so the first thing is for us to think about our concept of the Mill, and then to concretize, so to speak," - Fawn laughed - "or perhaps I should say to woodenize, our feelings in these bricks." Gaily she took the lids of the boxes, and tipped several hundred bricks on to the floor. "Look," she continued triumphantly, "some of them are blue and cylindrical, they can serve as chimney pots. And then after that, we come to the next stage - doing the same in Lego, because Lego is so much more expressive and life-like. It represents naturalism, as opposed to the more shadowy semiotics of the brick, which can only, as it were, rough-hue or block out the general idea."

Blanche squatted down eagerly on the floor. It was a long time since she had played with bricks, and certainly, after her drinking of the previous night, and her lunch-time hair of the dog, it was nice not to have to read a boring text in the book sense of that word. And how nice and shiny the bricks were!

Soon she and Tabitha were squatting happily on the floor, building the Mill on the Floss. Fawn and Florinda looked on benignly, sipping infusions of herb tea. After a while, Florinda started to crochet, while Fawn idly turned over the pages of some more books on costume. On either side of them, the other students in the class were busily engaged in constructing their own plans. Twenty minutes later, six very different higgledy-piggledy masses of bricks were ready for inspection. Fawn and Florinda were captivated by the enthusiasm and versatility of the students. They asked each member of the class to cast a vote by secret ballot on whose edifice was the nicest. And to her delight, Blanche Quick was the winner!

"Great, well done, Blanche, we must thelebrate that in the bar tonight!" exclaimed Tabitha.

Blanche Quick nodded happily, as Fawn entered a merit mark for creativity in her notebook. This would be transferred to the continuous assessment record which the Department held on all students, and would contribute at least 65% to the award of the final class of degree.

Then the class moved on to constructing the Lego models. This required a great deal of patience, for the Lego bricks were smaller, and needed a certain amount of physical force to make the bricks stick together. As the students built their Lego models, Fawn started to assess a pile of student projects, whilst Florinda happily knitted a pair of mittens.

Half-an-hour later the first of the Lego houses were built, though a couple of the boys were still scrabbling around.

This time, Tabitha's model was judged to be the best. Tabitha had ingeniously adapted some Lego roofing material to make the sail of a windmill, and this she had stuck with a pin into the side of her construction, so that the thing turned like a sail, and this was the crucial factor.

"Well done Tabitha," said Fawn enthusiastically. "That's terrific! And now we must make it more realistic by putting your model on the Floss itself. From underneath her desk she brought out a large, enammelled oblong casserole dish, with deep sides. As the students looked on somewhat mystified, Fawn placed the Lego model into this, whilst Florinda took a hosepipe from the desk drawer, and went out into the corridor, to connect it to the tap in the washroom two doors away. As Fawn held the hose over the casserole tray, Florinda turned on the tap, and a stream of water began to fill the dish. Then, quickly, Fawn took a length of plastic tubing from another drawer in her desk, puffed out her cheeks, and began to suck in the water from the casserole dish as if from a straw. Then, nipping the other end with her fingers, she flung open the window of her room, relaxed the grip of her fingers, and lo and behold a continuous stream of water flowed past Tabitha's Mill on the Floss, from the bathroom via the hose to the casserole, from the casserole dish via the tube to the window, and thence on to the ground below. Fawn's window overlooked one of the public footpaths that ran below Grace Darling College. Mr Dedder happened to be passing, on his way from one college bar to another, and he got a soaking. He spluttered angrily and shook his fist as the full force of the water splashed down his matelot's jersey, but he was too fuddled to see where the water had come from so nobody cared about that. The class watched in fascination as the water flowed by.

"It's symbolic, isn't it?" asked Fawn casually. "It's a symbol of change and transience in human life. As a Greek philosopher once said in a famous quote, we cannot put both feet in the river without getting them wet. The water, i.e. the river, is a text after all."

The class agreed wholeheartedly with these sentiments, even when Blanche, who had secreted a hip-flask of Armagnac in the quiver of her Merrywoman outfit, and had been slyly drinking it whilst she was squatting on the floor, decided to inject a little merriment into the proceedings by taking the hosepipe and spraying her old sparring partner Hugo with the cold water. Everyone shrieked and laughed at this sportive happening, even Fawn and Florinda. As the hosepipe soaked Fawn's carpet, Florinda ran to the bathroom to turn it off. And thus the teaching of the Victorian Novel was over for another week, and the class dispersed, heading in ones and two to the various college bars, there to meditate upon what they had learned, and to further their development by literary discussions of a more informal nature, washed down by copious quantities of liquor. For, as Roland Gasser the Shakespeare lecturer had often observed, it was the high quality of the talk at Skelmerdale that made the department of English and Communication Studies so renowned.

CHAPTER TEN

THE TEACHING QUALITY AUDIT (1)

'The Judge is at the Gate' (Bernard of Morlay, *De contemptu mundi*)

More and more Professor Freddie Frowstie had taken up residence in the well of his desk during office hours. There he could feel secure, protected womb-like by wood on three sides, invisible to anyone who casually opened his door to see if he was there, be they secretaries or students. There too he could sip whisky in secret, and smoke the occasional joint. He felt in need of these comforting stimulants more and more nowadays, and this was especially so when he opened the letter from the Higher Education Funding Council for England, giving details of the imminent arrival on campus of HEFCE's team of Teaching Quality Assessors for the subject of English and Communication Studies. The very lettering on the envelope, the blackness of the letter-head itself, were enough to alarm the fraught Frowstie as he swigged a quick sip of whisky from his hip-flask, and eased the letter out of the envelope, tugging fearfully at his wispy beard as he did so. He opened the letter with trembling hand, and propped a battered pair of spectacles precariously on the end of his mottled nose, leaned back against the side of the desk-well, and began to read what HEFCE had to say...

"The HEFCE audit team will arrive on Tuesday 25 October next at 5 p.m.," he read nervously. "They will need two secure and lockable rooms, one for themselves and one for their secretarial staff, together with 'phone, fax, telex and e-mail facilities, and message encryption capability for each of these media. The auditors wish initially to meet your staff informally - we suggest you arrange a sherry reception for 5.30 p.m. on the 25th, and then the visit proper will take place between the hours of 8.30 a.m. and 6.30 p.m. on Wednesday 26th - Friday 28th October inclusive. The auditors will prepare their report and deliver it to the Vice-Chancellor and such other members of the department as you wish to be present at 3 p.m. on Saturday 29th October... The team will be led by Professor Magnum, who will act as Reporting

Assessor." Professor Frowstie felt a fierce stab of pain to the heart. Professor Magnum! His contemporary at school and university, who had always been effortlessly superior to Frowstie! It simply was not fair, they had never been friends, and Magnum had rubbished all of Frowstie's early publications on D.H. Lawrence in the *Critical Review*! 'Mindless and rambling,' he had said of Frowstie's first essay, 'fails to rise even to the level of dullness'. By now, of course, Frowstie was used to such reviews, but when he was a young man of twenty-eight Magnum's remarks had struck home! Since then Magnum had moved on to higher things, had become an educational bureaucrat, and now he was to head the audit of the teaching quality of Frowstie's department... Frowstie lit a joint, and read on with hopeless despair.

"Other members of the team will consist of Professor Brootal from the University of the Wirral..." Professor Brootal! Another of Frowstie's enemies and *bête-noires*. Years ago, when Frowstie had just been appointed Head of the department, he had blocked an application by Brootal for a Readership at Skelmerdale. Brootal had promptly obtained a chair elsewhere, but he was not a forgiving man, he remembered slights, and he had pursued a vendetta against the Skelmerdale English department ever since. It would be hard to think of a more hostile and unwelcome auditor, for Brootal was a real thug with an aggressive manner. He did not frighten easily, and indeed relished his reputation for brusqueness and thuggery. Never fear, Brootal would find plenty to disapprove of at Skelmerdale! "Another member of the team will be Professor Maeve Dalrymple, from Palermo University in the United States, currently on three-year secondment as British Academy Research Professor in Cultural Studies and Literary Theory at King's College, Cambridge." Freddie Frowstie gasped again. Professor Dalrymple! English drama was not Frowstie's line, but even he had heard talk of the recent Nottingham Conference on eighteenth-century drama, when she had remorselessly torn to shreds the paper on Connbrugh's *Pish! If You Say So*, jointly presented by Skelmerdale's very own English drama specialists, Mr Cuthbert and Dr Codsworth, who had spent the last fifteen years of their lives writing occasional short notes about how that famous play worked on the stage. "It really wasn't fair," thought Frowstie to himself bitterly, "HEFCE had produced a team that knew Skelmerdale far too well to be objective." He toyed for a moment with the idea of exercising the theoretical right of appeal against any member of the Audit team, but knew in his heart of hearts that he lacked the guts to make such a gesture, for offence would certainly be caused if he did, and Frowstie never liked to offend anyone... The next name on the list made Frowstie cheer up a bit. "Ms Susan Simper, from the Selby University Polytechnic College of Further Higher and Advanced Educational Studies." That was a bit more like it, thought Frowstie - someone from one of the new universities, that had been a Teachers' Training College until last year. Now there was someone who would have an open mind, he thought, and would be impressed by the fame and standing of the Skelmerdale English department, there at last was someone he might be able to patronise a bit, and perhaps buy a drink in the bar with a view to influencing her views... The next name gave Frowstie another pang of anxiety. "Dr Ralph Grumbler, from the University of Rugby." And that for sure was the specialist in analytical and enumerative bibliography, who as Mr Ralph Grumbler had lectured in English at Skelmerdale twenty-five years ago, when he had arrived with his new bride to take up his first appointment. And whose attractive bride had been seduced by one of Frowstie's own post-graduate students within two months of the marriage, for Grumbler, in his passion for analytical and enumerative bibliography, had so neglected the young Mrs Grumbler that she had sought solace elsewhere. But there had been the hell of a scandal at the time, thought Frowstie, and not long afterwards Grumbler had departed in some bitterness, blaming Frowstie, as supervisor of the student who had cuckolded him, for the whole state of affairs. It simply wasn't fair, thought Frowstie, everything was going to go wrong, and he would get the blame. He started to whimper quietly, and drained the last dregs of his whisky flask. The last name on the list, Dr Gropper from English and Communication Studies at Skegness, meant nothing to him, so might just about be tolerable. Slowly Professor Freddie Frowstie lapsed into unconsciousness, and fell into a stupor still slumped away from sight in the well of his desk.

*****

"Well, this is a bit of all right," thought Professor Dalrymple to herself three weeks later, as she checked into one of the spacious and luxurious £500 a night suites at the Royal Skelmerdale Hotel that HEFCE had booked for its auditors. She had travelled up that morning by train from Cambridge to Skelmerdale, and now after a light lunch of smoked-salmon sandwiches from room service, she reclined in stockinged feet on the comfortable leather couch of her sitting room, her head propped comfortably against its deep cushions, a half-bottle of Puligny Montrachet in an ice-bucket on the table beside her, at peace with the world. This would be her third audit visit in the last sixth months - she had previously done the English departments at Sussex and QMC (both 'excellent'), and though the visits were time-consuming and took her away from her researches, at least HEFCE put one up in a rather decent hotel. In any case it was interesting and useful to see what was happening in today's British universities. And since the young professor had a wide acquaintance, there were usually people whom she knew in the departments that she visited, and the visits gave her the opportunity to do renew old friendships and maybe do her friends a good turn. "The Skelmerdale visit would be particularly interesting," Professor Dalyrmple thought, taking another sip of Puligny Montrachet. It would be interesting to see Cuthbert and Codsworth in action on their home ground, even though she had thought their Nottingham paper on *Pish! If You Say So* rather a feeble one. "I will really try hard to be fair to Cuthbert," she said to herself firmly, trying to repress the smile that came to her lips whenever she thought of him. "I know he's really very keen on practical theatre, and maybe it is true that if only Skelmerdale had a drama workshop like other universities, then Cuthbert would indeed be able to give some truly inspirational demonstrations to his classes of how plays worked on the stage..." And certainly, if one listened to the gossip of the profession, it did seem as if Skelmerdale was striking out in a very innovative way with its Glove Puppet Seminars, in which central literary texts such as *Daniel Deronda* were re-worked as ten-page Glove Puppet scenarios... It would be interesting to see if the reality lived up to the hype... It was a novel idea, certainly, though one did wonder if some of the complexities of the text might not be lost.

But Frowstie had made a big thing of this in his bid for 'excellent' to HEFCE. Apparently he was trying to sell the idea to the Bosnian Serbs, who were, so he claimed, "very interested in the whole project." Professor Dalrymple took another sip of cool wine, and soon drifted off into a light slumber, thoughts of Cuthbert as a glove puppet drifting irrepressibly before her eyes.

*****

At 6 p.m. Professor Dalrymple descended into the bar of the Royal Skelmerdale Hotel. She had slept a little, taken a short stroll round the old walls of Skelmerdale, and then showered and changed into a black cocktail dress, ready to meet her fellow auditors at the first 'get to know each other' dinner which had been arranged. She sat herself in a comfortable armchair near the open fire, enjoying the flickering and cheerful flames, munching peanuts, as the barman poured her a glass of Chardonnay. A tall, broad-shouldered, slightly stocky figure approached, and said, "It's Professor Dalrymple, isn't it? I heard your brilliant paper on disembowelment at the MLA in Chicago last year. My name's Brootal, Richard Brootal, from the University of the Wirral. I gather we are colleagues on this little audit job here."

Professor Dalrymple lifted her glass in a friendly gesture of welcome, and Brootal slipped easily into the chair opposite her, and signalled for the waiter to bring him a triple scotch on the rocks.

Brootal raised his glass to Professor Dalrymple, took a deep draught of the scotch, and swirled the liquor meditatively around the ice cubes, which chinked against the cut-glass crystal.

"Well," he laughed shortly, his voice deep and rather harsh, "we've got our work cut out here, no doubt about it. The Skelmerdale English department!" He snorted derisively and drained the rest of his scotch, at the same time calling for a refill. He placed his arms flat on the sides of the armchair, and looked directly at the young professor, his eyes direct, his shoulders well thrust back, his complexion healthy, looking keen and alert, and younger than his years. There was something of the air of a prize-fighter about the man, thought Professor Dalrymple, as she slowly sipped her Chardonnay and nibbled peanuts.

"Know any of the people from Skelmerdale?" Brootal asked her directly.

"Well, I can't say that I've heard of anyone here, except that I did once hear Cuthbert and Codsworth give a talk on *Pish! If You Say So* at a conference in Nottingham," she answered.

"And was it any good?"

"Well, since you ask, it was rubbish," she replied comfortably. "They didn't have a clue what they were talking about. I thought they were just a pair of dafties."

Brootal laughed heartily.

"Of course it was rubbish," he replied with great satisfaction. "After all, if ever a play has been worked over to excess, it's *Pish! If You Say So.* And those two haven't had an original thought in their lives. Let's face it, Skelmerdale is a pretty rotten department, everyone knows that, it's been going to the dogs for years. In the face of strong competition, one has to say, it must be the just about the worst and most complacent English department in the country."

Professor Dalrymple nodded thoughtfully. Indeed she had found Cuthbert and Codsworth complacent and self-satisfied and very pleased with themselves for their uninspiring paper.

"Still, one mustn't prejudge the issue," she remarked. "And I'm told they are doing great things with the glove puppets."

Professor Brootal leaned back and roared heartily with laughter.

"Glove puppets," he repeated. "glove puppets... yes indeed, yes indeed... but when did you last actually read a book by any member of the Skelmerdale English department? Ever read any of Frowstie's stuff?"

"No, I don't think I have," reflected Professor Dalrymple. "But then, I'm not really in his area."

"That's got nothing to do with it," said Professor Brootal firmly. "It doesn't make any difference if you're in his area or not. No one reads Frowstie's stuff at all. I looked him up yesterday in the on-line citation index, just to get the latest figures. He had four citations in the last twenty-five years, which is poor, very poor, and scarcely a member of the department can get into double figures. Whereas you, for example, have pulled in thirty-five citations in the last five years for your last book on the drama alone, let alone your papers on disembowelment and scopophilia, which have got twenty-five for the same period. Ah, I think that's Magnum over there."

Professor Magnum made his slow and stately progress across the room, a tall portly man, who declined Brootal's offer of a drink, and settled for a glass of iced water, which he sipped austerely. Brootal effected the introduction to Professor Dalrymple, for she had never met Magnum, and soon afterwards the three were joined by Ms Susan Simper, Dr Gropper, and Dr Grumbler, who was making notes about skeleton formes on little pieces of paper which he thrust into his jacket pocket.

Introductions all round were effected, and the newcomers ordered drinks, whilst Brootal and Professor Dalrymple had their drinks freshened. "They're an ill-assorted bunch," thought Professor Dalrymple to herself, after she had tried and failed to engage Grumbler and Ms Simper in conversation...."Oh well, it takes all sorts...."

"Well, I think we are all here," remarked Professor Magnum, "and as it's nearly 7 p.m. I think we can now go in to dinner." He gave a sign to a waiter, and shortly afterwards the party were escorted to the private dining room which HEFCE had booked for its auditors, a richly panelled room with deep carpets, a mahogany table laid with crystal and silver cutlery, and a pleasing array of glasses in front of each place. For this was to be a working dinner, and privacy was essential to the auditors.

Magnum sat himself at the head of the table, and placed Professor Dalrymple on his right, and Dr Gropper on his left. Brootal was placed to the right of Professor Dalrymple, and on his right sat Susan Simper, a slight and rather inconspicuous figure. Grumbler brought up the end of the table on the other side.

Magnum seemed to have very little social small talk, and such as he had was directed at Dr Gropper, so Professor Dalrymple was glad of the company of the loquacious Brootal to her right.

"Very drinkable Aligoté, this," he remarked, savouring the excellent wine that was served with the caviare. "One thing about HEFCE, they know how to treat their auditors well.... trying to put us in a good mood, I suppose," he laughed. "Not that I'd let myself be influenced by such a consideration, of course. No, from what I've heard, it's going to be very hard for any of us to find Skelmerdale English anything but 'unsatisfactory'... there are just so many hopeless incompetents in the department. One never sees them at any important conferences, they don't publish so that you would notice, their citation record is awful, none of them has moved about, most of them are over 55, they're incompetents who couldn't teach a dog to sit, and as for Frowstie, Frowstie couldn't punch his way out of a wet paper bag." Brootal drained his wine with great satisfaction, and, since few of the others apart from

Gropper and Professor Dalrymple were drinking at all, allowed the wine waiter to top up his glass again.

A fine second-growth claret, Ducru Beaucaillou, accompanied the delicious lamb that was served as a main course, with fresh home grown vegetables. Professor Dalrymple was resolved to be fair to Skelmerdale, in spite of her low opinion of Cuthbert and Codsworth, but she could not help laughing in spite of herself as Brootal regaled her with his endless fund of stories discreditable to the Skelmerdale English department. Brootal was well-known in his own field of 18th-century literature, he was visible on the conference scene, he gave and chaired papers and talks, wrote for the *Higher*, was in demand as a visiting lecturer, and was an indefatigable correspondent by e-mail with a wide range of contacts. And it was at conferences and via e-mail that the Skelmerdale stories circulated, with which Brootal proceeded to bring Professor Dalrymple up to date. How Frowstie was going to pieces and had taken to the bottle, how his latest book had been torn to shreds by the reviewers, how five members of the department had drunk themselves to death in the last six years, how Florinda Morrison had thought that Tom Brown wrote *Tom Brown's Schooldays*, how fighting had broken out at a staff meeting last year, how four members of the department were up on sexual harassment charges; how the drunks were always vandalising the memorial tree to Professor Bodgering, first department head at Skelmerdale before his transfer to Surleighwick; how 75% of the students had got firsts in 1995; how staff meetings were so incompetently chaired that they usually lasted ten hours; how the minutes were thirty-five pages long, because no one at Skelmerdale had ever learned to do précis, how a gaggle of campus geese had attacked Roland Gasser, the Shakespeare lecturer, and torn away a good deal of the remaining hair from his balding pate; how Mr Cuthbert had tumbled down a manhole whose cover had been carelessly left open, and was only saved from falling into the sewers below by the fact that he had put on weight and got wedged in the hole; how the Skelmerdale English lecturers invariably made mistakes in any language they happened to quote, and so on.

The lamb was succeeded by a compote of fruits served with a sweet syrup, and with this a rich and sweet desert wine was served. At last coffee arrived, and with it Professor Brootal took a glass of

Courvoisier, whilst Professor Dalrymple contented herself with a second glass of pudding wine.

Professor Magnum then addressed his audit team.

"Well, Skelmerdale," he observed, "the English department, that's our task, to audit it. You'll all have had the information which HEFCE requires as a matter of course - c.v.'s of the department, lists of their publications since they entered the profession, details of their degrees, copies of the department's correspondence since 1987, copies of minutes since 1986, copies of sub-committee meetings since 1985, and so on."

"Too right we have," answered Brootal. "Gosh, they are a lot of windbags. Talk about verbal diarrhoea...!"

"Now," continued Magnum, oblivious to the interruption, "the first thing to do is put the department absolutely at its ease. We have to come to the task with a completely open mind. We are here as friends, to help them."

"Absolutely agree, couldn't have put it better myself," replied Brootal, with a wink at Professor Dalrymple, who struggled to bite back a smile.

"Now, perhaps we can try to make a tentative schedule of classes for us to sit in on," mused Magnum. "The idea is that we will sit in on about twenty-five classes, either alone or in twos and threes. I have here the schedule of lectures for the day after tomorrow. Let's see, the first class is Mr Cuthbert on *Pish! If You Say So*. I wonder who would like to do that one?"

"Well, that's clearly one for Professor Dalrymple," put in Professor Brootal. "She has reviewed the nine most recent editions of the play, after all."

"And I'd like to sit in on that class too," interposed Grumbler, unexpectedly. "There are some interesting questions about setting by formes on sigs E and F that simply cry out for further investigation. I'd be interested to see how Cuthbert tackles those."

"Agreed then," said Magnum carefully. "Professor Dalrymple and Dr Grumbler to sit in on the Cuthbert class. And then we have Frowstie himself on 'How to read a poem'."

"I'll take that," said Brootal firmly. "There are some questions about that topic that I'd very much like to ask Frowstie...."

" - and then the big lecture on communication studies I think I'd like to take myself, "continued Magnum, "it's always been one of my interests."

The working dinner over, some of the party repaired to the comfortable lounge of the Royal Skelmerdale Hotel. Professor Dalrymple settled herself comfortably on a deep sofa, and leant her head momentarily against its back, replete and content after the evening's business. Professor Brootal gestured to a waiter and ordered drinks for the party. Professor Magnum had absented himself, party pooper that he was. Dr Gropper though had settled himself on the sofa next to Professor Dalrymple. Ms Simper too had joined the party, but had refused any further alcohol. Indeed, of the single glass of wine she had consumed at dinner, she had left at least half untouched. Ms Simper sat at some distance from the rest of the party, silent and withdrawn, and soon took out a Penguin paperback from her handbag, and started to read, lost within a private world of her own. Grumbler had not joined the party, opting instead for an early night and reading another article about skeleton formes in bed. Brootal excused himself for a moment to make a telephone call, and Professor Dalrymple found herself for a few moments alone on the sofa with Dr Gropper.

Gropper, thought Professor Dalrymple, was a not particularly imposing individual. His skin was sallow and oily, and there was a boil on the back of his neck. Gropper worked on Middle English religious homilies, and Professor Dalrymple was not familiar with his work, it being a long time since she had cultivated that particularly arid bye-way of English studies. Gropper however claimed to know Professor Dalrymple's work.

"It's so nice to meet you at last," he said with an ingratiating smile. "I've heard so much about you. Everyone speaks so well of your book." Dr Gropper was both a coward and a lecher. In days gone by, when it was safe to do so, he had pestered his female students for dates. When that became dangerous, he turned his attention first to the departmental secretaries, then to colleagues. Checked in that direction, it was his wont to annoy anyone in skirts under thirty-nine outside his own institution. Emboldened by the wine and whisky he had been drinking, he put his hand on Professor Dalrymple's knee and leered at her.

"We're going to be seeing quite a lot of each other in the next few days", he whispered. "I'm an old hand at this audit game. If you feel you need any advice, I'm always available. My room is 201, quite close to yours, I believe." How winked. "What about it?"

Professor Dalrymple removed his hand from her knee very firmly, and seizing the little finger of his right hand, bent it backwards with just sufficient force to dislocate rather than break it. "I think not, Gropper," she retorted coldly. Gropper let out a howl of pain, and left the room, clutching his finger in agony, at the very instant that Professor Brootal returned from making his phone call.

"What's up with Gropper?" asked Professor Brootal, puzzled, as Cropper left the room, his face contorted with pain.

"Gropper came a cropper," she replied laconically, and Professor Brootal divined from her reply the essence of the situation, and forbore to ask for further explanation. Ms Simper continued to read her book as if nothing had happened. Eventually tiredness overcame Professor Dalrymple, and as it was now nearly 11 p.m., she said a cheerful goodnight to Professor Brootal, and left him contentedly drinking scotch and puffing a cigar. She returned to her room to enjoy a deep sleep, interrupted only by fantastic images of Cuthbert, Gropper, Brootal, Magnum, and others, which flitted surreally through her dreams.

*****

The audit team was not due to meet the department till 5 p.m. the next day, so Professor Dalrymple spent the morning enjoying a lazy breakfast in bed from room service, reading the *Times* and *Guardian*, then glancing at some of the last-minute papers that had been circulated for the team's attention by Magnum's assistant the previous evening: percentage of firsts awarded in the department in the last six years (80%, 75%, 82%, 68%, 84%, 78%), the sign, as Roland Gasser, the Shakespeare lecturer and examinations officer had pointed out, of a truly outstanding teaching department. There was also a last-minute update on external lectures given by members of the department, from which Professor Dalrymple learned that the egregious Roland Gasser had recently given three lectures to the Skelmerdale Women's Institute on 'Shakespeare for the Glove Puppet Theatre of Today', and one lecture to the Skelmerdale Girl Guides on 'Introduction to Shakespeare for the Glove Puppet Theatre of Today'. Professor Dalrymple yawned, and pushed aside the papers non-committally, and at last got up.

*****

Professor Dalrymple had arranged to meet her old friends Professor Charles Hanwell and his wife for lunch, and perhaps to gain some inside information on life at Skelmerdale from his experiences as visiting professor there. The Hanwells had taken up residence in Skelmerdale a few weeks previously, and had found themselves an apartment in the centre of the city, having declined as pokey, dark, noisy and uncomfortable the accommodation which the university had offered to provide for them. At 12.30 p.m. the three of them were drinking an agreeable Australian Chardonnay on the balcony of the first floor of the Riverside Cafe, overlooking the tranquil waters of the river, toasting each other's health. Professor Hanwell and Dalrymple were old friends who were always bumping into each other wherever Renaissance scholars met, at the MLA, the RSA and the SAA, at the Huntington, the Folger, and the Newberry, and in Surleighwick, Arkansas. They had gossiped about science and gender in the Renaissance along the shores of the Pacific and the Gulf of Mexico, and on the banks of the Potomac, the St Lawrence and the Cam.

"OK Charles," said Professor Dalrymple when she had sipped a little of her Chardonnay, "so tell me frankly, what's Skelmerdale like from the inside. Is it a good university or not?"

"Not really," he replied cheerfully. "I should say its standards are in general rather low. For various reasons, not least that Ruth's great-aunt Flo flatlined a couple of months ago and she needed to be in the area to clear up the estate, it suited us to be here this session. It's basically a party school. From what I've seen so far, it's a pretty frivolous place, as you can tell by all the fruit-machines that litter the colleges. And everyone seems very fond of getting dressed up, or indeed, dressing down," he said with a smile as he recalled how he and his wife had met Tabitha in her role as Eve-before-the-Fall at the 'Writing Women' conference. "If you are auditing the place, I'd certainly ask them about their language teaching. Just look at the mistakes they have made in their 'Italian' translation of their glove-puppet scenario of *El Molino sopra lo Flosso,* as they so term it, which Ruth found lying around one day." Professor Dalrymple, who had both worked in Italy and spent a year as a Fellow at the Villa I Tatti, glanced at the first page of Fawn and Florinda's translation, and exclaimed with incredulity when she saw its errors.

"Yes, it's pretty horrendous stuff, isn't it?" remarked Professor Hanwell with a broad smile, as he refilled their glasses. "Even Ruth's ten-year old niece was able to correct most of the mistakes." Professor Dalrymple read out some of the extracts with increasing amusement and disbelief and in an affected accent, causing Ruth to dissolve in a fit of hysterical giggles, which only subsided when the waiter brought their smoked salmon entrée. Over lunch the three exchanged gossip of the profession, talked about books and movies and the progress of their researches. Professor Dalrymple had always been envious of the fact that her friend Charles had been present at the only English showing of Dick Domino's cult movie, *Bimbos Behind Bars*, one of the all-time-great chicks-in-chains movies, which was so politically incorrect nowadays that it could never be shown. Professor Dalrymple rationed herself to two glasses of Chardonnay, as she had to be on duty at 5 p.m., but Ruth and Professor Hanwell had no other plans for the afternoon other than to return home to make love, so they felt free to split an excellent bottle of Pouilly Fuisse between them, and follow it with a leisurely cognac or two as they sat there on the balcony in the mild sunshine, sheltered by the conservatory glass, watching the peaceful traffic on the river below them. At last it was time for Professor Dalrymple to take her leave. She went back to her hotel to shower and change before meeting her fellow auditors and awaiting the limousines that the take them to the Skelmerdale campus. Dr Gropper, she was pleased to note, now had his hand encompassed by a sling. He avoided catching her eye, and hastened to sit in the limousine in which she was not travelling. Professor Dalrymple found herself in the limo that contained Professor Magnum and Professor Brootal - the former stiff and taciturn, the latter with the eager light of battle gleaming in his eye.

Professor Dalrymple had dressed formally and conservatively for what was after all a formal inspection. She wore a dark suit and white blouse, with black tights and polished low-heeled shoes. She restricted her jewellery to a single silver brooch on the left lapel of her jacket. Her nails and lips were however scarlet, and she had dabbed a little Givenchy behind her ears and on her neck.

The limos deposited them at the entrance to Grace Darling college, the home of the English department. The porter led them past the crowds of students playing space-invaders and trying their luck on the fruit-machines. They passed the raucous jollity of the still-open bar. Soon they were approaching Freddie Frowstie's room. Frowstie had spent a long time preparing for the arrival of the auditors. He had swept the mass of papers that normally cluttered his desk away into a cupboard. He had tidied his book-shelves. He had had his room specially cleaned and redecorated. He had cleared out the well of his desk for the duration of the inspection. The carpet had been shampooed. Frowstie had been to the barber's and had his beard and eye-brows trimmed. Nervously he opened the door to the porter's knock.

"Ah, hum, hum, I'm Freddie Frowstie," he said nervously, as he saw the figure of Magnum and his colleagues.

"Yes, long time no see," stated the chairman flatly. "Let me introduce the rest of my team." Nervously Professor Frowstie shook hands with everyone, wincing as Brootal crunched his fingers in a vice-like grip. After a few pleasantries, Frowstie said, "Well, I gather that first of all I have to present you to the Registrar and VC. If you would kindly-er-follow me?" Frowstie led the way through the squalid surroundings of Grace Darling college, and out on to the grass, forgetting to warn his guests about the duck excrement that littered the campus. Professors Dalrymple and Brootal kept a sharp look out, and managed to tread carefully around it, but the unsuspecting Gropper, Grumbler, Ms Simper, and Professor Magnum, who followed immediately in Frowstie's wake, were less careful and soon found themselves fouled and smelly from the ankles downward, which did nothing to put them in a good mood.

"A curious place," reflected Professor Dalrymple, "which thus encourages these messy pests." For Skelmerdale was proud of its geese and ducks, and boasted about them in its prospectus. The party, led by the nervous Frowstie, passed by massive pieces of topiary, and approached the Palladian magnificence of the central Administration building, the old country house that had been the nucleus of the university, so unlike the rest of the campus buildings, with its thick deep carpets, its panelled walls, its Grinling Gibbons carvings.

The Vice-Chancellor and Registrar waited to greet the party, two wary professional administrators, with expressionless features devoid of all real emotion, coldly surveying the members of the audit team. It was their intention, if the audit produced a verdict of 'excellent' to claim all the credit for themselves. But if the result was only 'satisfactory' or worse, they would turn on Freddie Frowstie with concentrated fury, and witch-hunt his colleagues to distraction. Magnum was impassive as always, remote, like a stone, and no one, not even the shrewd Professor Dalrymple, could get a rise out of either the Registrar or VC.

The formal introductions over, the nervous Freddie Frowstie led the auditors back to Grace Darling College to meet the rest of the department. The SCR had been booked, and a few bottles of inferior sherry and some soggy cheese nibbles had been laid on, for Skelmerdale found difficulty in carrying off such occasions with any kind of style. It was simply too mean and poor an institution to do so, even if it had known how, which it didn't.

The forty-odd members of the Skelmerdale English department were mustered in the SCR of Grace Darling College, sipping sherry in a desultory fashion. Freddie Frowstie cleared his throat, and nervously said, "Um, ah, er, let me introduce Professor Magnum, the lead assessor." Professor Magnum moved to the centre of the room. "Now don't mind me, or my auditors, just think of us as friends, we are here to offer help and assistance, just academics like yourselves, here to help you do your job, that's what we are here for." His voice tailed off, and Magnum found himself the centre of hostile attention and disbelief from the assembled Skelmerdale academics.

Professor Dalrymple declined the glass of cheap warm sherry that was offered her, and, finding that mineral water was not available, settled for a glass of orange juice instead. The auditors dispersed to begin their uneasy informal introduction to the members of the English department, an introduction that was not helped by the small cramped room impeded by uncomfortable armchairs in which the reception was being held. At last Professor Dalrymple found herself backed into a corner, as a large corpulent figure in a clown suit bore down upon her.

"Hallo," said the clown excitedly. "We've met haven't we, you were at the paper on *Pish! If You Say So* that I read at the North East Drama conference at Nottingham last year. I've just been reading through *Pish!* with my class, and didn't have time to change. It's the very suit that was used in rehearsals for the Stratford production of *Pish!* at The Other Place," he boasted proudly.

Professor Dalrymple sipped her orange-juice coolly, and looked at the flushed face of the baggy-panted clown.

"Ah, yes," she replied at length, "It's Mr Cuthbert, isn't it - or perhaps I may be allowed to say Dickey? Well, Dickey, I see you are quite the Merry-Andrew tonight."

"I'm not Andrew," gasped the excitable Cuthbert, "I'm Beppo, Beppo from Acts 2 and 4 of *Pish!* Just think, this is the very outfit that would have appeared on the Stratford stage, but at rehearsals they decided that the buttons clashed with Millicent's shoes, so they let me buy it off them. I'm a friend of the Deputy Assistant Wardrobe mistress you know," he confided. Professor Dalrymple bit back a smile, for truth to tell Dickey Cuthbert looked an incongruous figure in his baggy pants and blue shoes, with big pom-pom style buttons in red and purple alternating down the front of his suit. A white ruff surrounded Cuthbert's bull-like neck, with pointed extensions that almost buried his jowly, fleshy cheeks. Cuthbert perspired in the heat of the cramped room as he sipped his glass of Dandelion and Burdoch. Professor Dalrymple was for the moment lost for words, but at that moment she observed another costumed figure squeezing towards her through the throng, a figure in full crinoline-like skirts, with white flannel pantaloons peeping out fully six inches beneath them. With a slight start, Professor Dalrymple recognised another member of the Skelmerdale English department.

"Hello," she said, putting out her hand "It's Dr - er - Codpeice isn't it? Didn't we meet last year when you gave a paper with Dickey Cuthbert? Your face seems familiar, it's just that I didn't recognise you in skirts."

"Codsworth," that worthy corrected her, taking the proffered hand. "Yes, I'm Millicent, in *Pish!*, which we're reading through with our students. It's a very demanding role you know. We're studying how it would work if we set it in the nineteenth century, hence the dress, just to help establish the mood - just got back from a class, didn't have time to change," he mumbled. Professor Dalrymple looked at Codsworth's greying hair, at the rouge upon his cheeks and the badly-applied lipstick smeared across his lips.

She looked at his thin waist, which must surely be nipped in by a corset, so slim was it. Again she had to repress a secret smile. Last year, during a brief discussion of transvestism and boy-actors at the Nottingham conference, Dr Codsworth had blushed so deeply, had seemed so embarrassed by the whole topic, that Professor Dalrymple had strongly suspected that Codsworth was a transvestite himself, and that suspicion had been strengthened when Codsworth had reached into his pocket for a handkerchief to mop his brow and pulled out a suspender-belt. Not that Professor Dalrymple thought the worse of him for that, she merely disapproved of his taste in underwear, the suspender-belt in question being a thick, stretchy elastic one with metal clips that positively screamed the 1960s. And indeed it was one which the adolescent Codsworth had filched from his elder sister's wardrobe twenty-five years ago. Why wasn't Codsworth more open about his predilections, she mused. Why didn't he go to somewhere like *Victoria's Secret* or *Knickerbox* and get himself some decent undies?

Professor Dalrymple detached herself from the ineffable Cuthbert and Codsworth, and helped herself to another glass of orange juice. She looked quizzically around the room. All around her the party was proceeding. At the other side of the room the odious Gropper was forcing his attentions on the newly appointed Dr Lucy Loveleigh, the prettiest (apart from Dr Codsworth) member of staff, who had been told by Frowstie to make herself amenable to the auditors. She stood there smiling nervously, as Dr Gropper's bandaged hand lightly rested on the shoulders of her blouse, searching for the strap of her bra. Magnum stood, a remote and lonely figure, in the centre of the room, insensitive and impassive as ever. Over the subdued babble of conversation, Professor Dalrymple could hear the brusque and confident tones of Brootal striking dismay into the hearts of his hearers. "Oh," he was saying, "so you gave up Pope and Dryden here five years ago because of the language difficulties, did you? I see." He laughed scornfully. "Of course at my university, we make all the first-years do a compulsory paper on the *Essay on Man* and *The Hind and the Panther*." To the right Ms Simper was asking questions about post-modernism and post-structuralism, a mousy figure over whom Freddie Frowstie hovered uneasily. As she looked around the room, Professor Dalrymple could not help but observe that she was both the most personable and quite the most smartly dressed woman in the room. Only Dr Loveleigh came remotely close. The young professor felt glad that she had chosen to make her career in the States, and that she was not part of the British academic scene, except for occasional periods as a visiting professor. For surely the Skelmerdale English department exemplified the current reality of that scene? Professor Dalrymple had been given the full c.v's and list of publications of the whole department as part of the audit briefing. And with the occasional exception, the record was not impressive. Fully three-fifths of the department had arrived at Skelmerdale in the boom years from 1963 to 1975, and there they had stayed ever since. They had arrived as bright young men and women of twenty-three to twenty-eight, with a great future before them, able to chatter brightly about a limited range of English texts. And since there were so few books in the Skelmerdale library, chattering had taken the place of reading. The best scholars had moved on to chairs and readerships elsewhere in more solid or more exciting universities. And now the remnants were still here, twenty to thirty and even thirty-five years further on, in this room with her, looking like extras from *The Night of the Living Dead* - a crowd of grey-haired greybeards, many of the men pot-bellied and fat and out of condition, mostly dressed in faded jeans and open sandals and some even with hippie beads; the women hideously dressed, in styles last seen most places in 1975, dowdy and dull, their faces all tired and lined, not one of them wearing any makeup, their personalities defensive, frightened, threatened. The early promise had gone, they had a great future behind them. New Criticism was dead, F. R. Leavis was dead, and yet the Skelmerdale department knew little else. Their individual sensitive responses to poems no longer mattered, and nobody cared what they thought any more. The department was now a city under seige, and already the enemy in the form of the auditors was within the walls. The staff rarely left Skelmerdale. The MLA knew them not. The Shakespeareans visited neither the RSA nor the SAA. The Medievalists were not seen in the halls of Kalamazoo. The Miltonists were unknown at Milton Society meetings. The staff were strangers to invited conferences in continental villas. The trans-continental jumbos passed them by. They were never asked to speak at other universities, or received personal invitations to read papers. So there they were at Skelmerdale, and there they festered, a great gene pool of the giftless and untalented, radiating a miasma of incompetence and tedium and despair, dragging down to their level such brighter spirits as had the misfortune to find themselves in that most unappealing of English departments....

Professor Dalrymple's reverie was interrupted by an excitable and hyper-active midget with elastoplast covering his greying and balding pate where he had been attacked by the Skelmerdale ducks.

"Professor Dalrymple? We work in the same area, I've read your book," he spluttered. "I'm Roland Gasser, the Shakespeare lecturer here. I expect you know my work, I once wrote an article on *Henry VI part ii* published in a collected volume at Aarhus in 1969, you must know it," he continued. "It's a pleasure to meet you at last, you will say we're 'excellent', won't you, it would mean so much to us. We should have a 'star' for research you know, we used to be Grade 5, but in 1989 we were put down to a 4, and in 1992 we were a 3, and in 1996 we only got a 2, but we're one of the very best grade 2 departments in the country, I was told in confidence on very good authority we very nearly got a 3b, it would mean so much to us to be 'excellent', you will help us won't you, we deserve it..."

Professor Dalrymple, unmoved, looked down with amazement at the diminutive Gasser, whose plastered pate was on a level with her shoulders. "I did read your essay as part of my homework for this visit," she replied, "but if I remember aright the whole volume was somewhat slated in *SQ*. Didn't the reviewers say that the book was worthy but dull, and the contributors might as well never have bothered? Personally I thought that a little harsh. Of course the arguments in your essay had all been advanced before, in the 1920s, and were abandoned by most scholars in the 1930s, but I thought it rather refreshing, indeed brave, on your part, to give them an airing again. Though I can't say that I've seen your paper much cited."

"No, it's not fair, nobody ever cites my work," said Roland Gasser, aggrieved.

"Ah well, you can't win 'em all," replied Professor Dalrymple, rather tiring of the tedious Gasser.

"You will give us an 'excellent', won't you, we deserve it," the importunate Gasser beseeched her retreating back. Professor Dalrymple endeavoured to find more agreeable company, but could not help overhearing the absurd Gasser approach Magnum, and say, "Hello, I'm Roland Gasser, the Shakespeare lecturer. I do admire your work tremendously. You know we're all hoping very much you'll give us an 'excellent', we deserve it really, our teaching is so good, can I get you another sherry, it's very nice you know, from Cyprus... it's very cheap and they make good sherries there."

At last the grisly meeting was over, and the audit team retreated to their limos to return to the hotel.

CHAPTER ELEVEN

THE GRAND AUDIT (2)

'And how his audit stands who knows save heaven'
(Shakespeare, *Hamlet*)

Next day the audit visit proper began. At 9.30 a.m. prompt, Professor Dalrymple and Dr Grumbler were waiting outside Mr Cuthbert's tiny room in the cramped corridors of Grace Darling college so that he could guide them to the seminar room. His face wreathed in nervous smiles, Cuthbert led the way along dark corridors, through the maze of student rooms, past kitchens and bedrooms and showers which abutted directly on to the corridors, for in the Skelmerdale colleges all these facilities were jumbled together as a result of its anti-hierarchical sixties architecture. Professor Dalrymple followed behind Dr Grumbler. At that moment a young man, dripping wet with nothing on, emerged from one of the showers and walked insouciantly down the corridor in front of her.

"Hallo," he said, turning to the young professor, apparently no whit disconcerted by her presence.

"Good morning," she replied, equally nonchalantly, though somewhat surprised.

"What are you doing here?" he asked. "We don't get many visitors in the corridor at this time of day."

"I'm one of the English auditors, just going to sit in on a class," she replied carefully, looking the dark-haired and lithe, but tired and blear-eyed, young man up and down.

"Hey, I do English, great party school," he replied, rubbing his unshaven stubbly chin. "What I like about it is that I don't have to do any work, it's just watching movies and glove puppets all day long. I'm just here to party, really... "

"So in that case I deduce that you must be going to bed rather than getting up?"

"Got it in one," he answered cheerfully. "I'm Chris. Here's my room, can I offer you some coffee or a joint?"

Professor Dalrymple recognised from his dilated pupils that the student was pretty much stoned. For a moment or two she was tempted to take advantage of his invitation, he seemed a rather charming and well-mannered young man and, after all, it would be useful to get the student view of the department directly. But the call of duty proved stronger, and she hurried along to catch up Grumbler and Cuthbert before they disappeared from view at the far end of the corridor, smiling to herself at the odd experience. Mr Cuthbert carefully guided his party past the prostrate bodies of students still zonked out in the corridors after the previous night's excesses. At last they arrived at a tiny, gloomy seminar room which faced out on to a brick wall. Three students were there, and two others wandered in zombie-like after a few moments. With an air of pride Mr Cuthbert, casually dressed in jeans and checkered shirt with open neck, pointed to his paper mock-up theatre, an elaboration of the common childhood toy. A box, with open top, perhaps three feet square, represented the theatre, and as the lecture progressed Mr Cuthbert introduced a number of cardboard cut-out characters on the end of pieces of wire. "I want to talk today about how *Pish!* works on the stage," he gasped. "You see here a cardboard miniature mock-up of the eighteenth-century stage. Of course we ought by rights to have a drama workshop on campus," he spluttered. "We've often applied for one to HEFCE but they've always turned us down. So we have to make do with this. It's not fair really." He glanced at the two auditors meaningfully. "Now I'll just draw the curtains, because what I want to talk about in today's lecture is costume." Cuthbert drew the curtains, and shone a torch down from the top of the cardboard theatre to represent a spotlight. It's all a question of colour contrast," he continued. "Look here is Beppo the clown, and see how if you put on blue shoes it doesn't work quite as well as if they're yellow, it just doesn't WORK with the lights the way they are. They had to change the colour of Beppo's shoes for that very reason at Stratford last year." Cuthbert fiddled around with the cardboard cut-out Beppo, and tinkered with magnetised cut-outs of Beppo's shoes, which he placed and removed in different colours to show the students how it worked. The students clustered around in a bored fashion.

"This is all very well," interrupted Dr Grumbler, "but what about the skeleton formes in Act II?"

"Oh no, there aren't any skeletons in *Pish!*" said Mr Cuthbert smugly. "You must be thinking of *The Chaste Maid's Tragedy*, there's a skeleton there all right, or at least a skull."

"No no, you misunderstand, I'm asking about the text," said Grumbler, in exasperation, "where do derive your text from, where did you get it?"

"Oh, we get them from the university bookshop," answered Cuthbert proudly. "The bookshop always stocks the course text books."

"But what edition do you use?"

"Oh, the paperback Mermaid."

"But that's an antiquated edition, do you think it's a satisfactory one?"

"Well, it's cheap and available, and anyway, our approach is very much centred on how it works on the stage, so the text doesn't matter," continued Cuthbert.

"But what about the textual cruces in Act III?" persisted Dr Grumbler. "I mean, the whole question of the compositorial practices in the different quartos has to be taken into account, surely?"

"Oh, we're not interested in that side of it," responded Cuthbert dismissively, "how it works on the stage, that's what we are talking about here. Now," he turned to his students again, "when I saw this play at The Other Place, Beppo was wearing red shoes, look." And Mr Cuthbert slipped two red shoes on to the cardboard cut-out of the Beppo figure, and waggled it up and down on the end of its wire.

"Why don't you have any green shoes for Beppo?" put in Professor Dalrymple suddenly.

"Because Beppo never wore green shoes in any production of *Pish!* that I have seen, and I have seen eight in the last fifteen years," answered Cuthbert proudly, glad to have scored a learned point over the young professor.

"But Beppo often wears green shoes in the productions I have seen in the States," said Professor Dalrymple.

"Oh, I have never been to the States," said Cuthbert, crestfallen.

Professor Dalrymple pursed her lips and looked disapproving.

"And he had green shoes too at the production done during the World Shakespeare Congress in Tokyo. Weren't you there?"

"No, I missed that one," confessed Cuthbert miserably.

"And Stratford, Ontario did it in green shoes, too, in their classic 1982 performance of *Pish!*. Olivier told me it was the best performance of *Pish!* he had ever seen," continued Professor Dalrymple remorselessly. "I agreed with him."

Cuthbert, who had never been to Canada, let alone spoken to Olivier, was crushed.

"What kind of petticoats did Millicent wear under her skirt?" interposed Sabrina, a blousy well-developed student who had apparently awoken from her slumbers.

"That's a very interesting question," said Cuthbert eagerly. "I know the Deputy Assistant wardrobe mistress at the RSC, and basically they use good quality underwear of the same period that the outer-garments belong to."

"So," remarked Professor Dalrymple, "If Millicent wears a crinoline and pantaloons, it would be reasonable to assume that she is wearing a tightly-laced corset underneath?"

"That's right," said Cuthbert, pleased that his point had been taken so quickly.

Professor Dalrymple suppressed the beginnings of a smile, and kept a straight face, trying not to laugh at the thought of Dr Codsworth in a corset.

At last the interminable seminar came to an end. When the students had left, Mr Cuthbert sat down, beaming, sure that his performance had made a good impression on the two auditors.

"What do you think?" he asked eagerly, "the kids liked it didn't they, they are fascinated by theatre and how it works on the stage you know."

"Well, we will be giving a detailed report in writing in due course," retorted Grumbler. "For myself, I'm not too happy about the way in which you seem to take texts for granted. And I think it became clear in the discussion that your knowledge of performance is rather limited, being confined apparently to the RSC and the Skelmerdale rep. - hardly very representative, some would say."

He looked at his watch.

"I think my colleague and I must be going," he said firmly. "We are due at our next assessment in a few minutes time, and this campus is so confusing we had better leave ourselves enough time to find the way. Shall we go?" he said to Professor Dalrymple.

"Yes, let's," she replied. "Goodbye, Dickey...it's been fascinating to see you at work." She wagged a scarlet finger-nail at him. "Now do remember what Dr Grumbler has said - a little more attention to skeleton formes in these classes would certainly not come amiss."

"But..."

"Skeleton formes, Dickey," Professor Dalrymple repeated firmly, as she pivoted smartly on her high-heels, and left the room in the wake of Grumbler, leaving the frustrated Cuthbert spluttering vainly to an empty room.

*****

That night, the auditors compared notes over dinner. Professor Dalrymple had changed into a long, cool evening dress of emerald green, and again found herself next to the amusing Brootal. Over the calamari the two polished off a bottle of Louis Roederer champagne, as they reminisced about the day's activities. Brootal had been visiting the library as part of his audit duties, to make sure that the holdings of books were adequate to support the range of courses that the English department put on.

"I thought they were adequate enough for Skelmerdale," he remarked easily. "You see I have always thought that Skelmerdale had a future if only it had a different view of its mission - I see their real future as lying in kindergarten and nursery education. Let's face it, that's the level at which the staff could best operate, and the library does have quite a good stock of children's books."

"It's true that they have a very nice large toy theatre," said Professor Dalrymple reflectively as she sipped her champagne. "And Cuthbert seemed happiest when putting shoes on his cardboard cutout clown - that's when he's not dressed up as a clown himself of course."

"Exactly! I see you take my point. And as for Roland Gasser - well, it's a clear case of a childish personality. And why do you think the *Peter Pan* and *Wind in the Willows* options are the most popular courses in the department? It's because the kids get money to go to Disney World in Paris to visit Peter Pan's Playground and Mr Toad's Mad Ride. It makes perfect sense to me. They'll never make the grade as an English department, but as a kindergarten institution they stand a real chance of finding a worthwhile niche." Brootal sipped his champagne with great satisfaction.

"Another thing," he continued, as they washed down a juicy corn-fed imported steak with a glass or two of excellent Pommard, "they wouldn't need as many staff to operate at kindergarten level. After all, they do very much go in for small group teaching you know. How many people at the class on *Pish!* ?"

"Five," answered Professor Dalrymple.

"There you are then. Now with a kindergarten you could have a class of twenty."

*****

'Some people haven't got brains, only straw. Some people without brains do an awful lot of talking.' (*The Wizard of Oz*)

The next day Professor Dalrymple had decided to sit in on one of Roland Gasser's Shakespeare lectures. It was a natural choice for her to make, for her own publications on Shakespeare, particularly her explorations of Shakespearean sexuality and gender, had been widely acclaimed. At 11.15 a.m. the next morning she found herself outside one of the few large lecture rooms on campus, capable of seating 220 persons. Neat as always in a dark grey suit and white blouse, she had first endeavoured to fortify herself with a cup of weak, cold, foul-tasting black coffee from the snack bar in Sir Roger de Coverley college. She entered the room, and took a place in the middle of the lecture theatre, a little over half-way down. Perhaps thirty-five students had turned out to hear Gasser speak, down from 200 at the beginning of term. Most of them were still yawning and only half-awake after the drinking parties of the night before. At 11.20 the white-haired balding figure of Gasser stumbled shambolically down the aisle, arms flailing. He dumped two or three books on the lectern, threw his scattered pile of notes on top of them, and began to gabble in an excited voice, as of one who had made a great discovery.

"I'm going to talk today about Shakespeare's concept of The Other in *A Midsummer Night's Dream* and *Hamlet* in particular," he gasped. "The concept of The Other, like that of what isn't there in an author's works, is an important one in modern criticism. We see it straight away in Shakespeare. Although he was English, Hamlet is set in Denmark, so Hamlet would of course have been speaking Danish, which requires a leap of imagination on our part. And the *Dream* is set in Greece, so the characters would be speaking Greek, those are two clear examples of The Other. Of course Shakespeare wrote a lot about foreigners. *Antony and Cleopatra* is set in Egypt, though Antony of course was a Roman, and again *The Merchant of Venice* is set in Venice, another town Shakespeare had not visited. Clearly he was fascinated by The Other. Some scenes in *Othello* also take place in Venice and Cyprus. Another play about an island is *The Tempest*. Of course Shakespeare lived on an island, but it was a big island compared to Cyprus and the one where *The Tempest* is set, wherever that is, we know it was small though. Shakespeare is also interested in the animal world, that is why his plays are full of references to them...especially the *Dream*, where Bottom is turned into a donkey," continued the ineffable Gasser. "I'm hoping to write a book on this theme. There are so many bits of OTHERNESS in Shakespeare. What we have to remember, though, is that Shakespeare was a very great poet, and however odd or strange or violent the plot, it is redeemed by the poetry, a point which I emphasise in my forthcoming school edition of *Henry VI part ii*..."

Professor Dalrymple listened to Gasser's ramblings at first with a kind of appalled fascination, and then with increasing disbelief. At some times she pursed her scarlet lips in disapproval, at others she fought valiantly to hold back the smile that threatened to turn into gusts of derision. All around her students had gradually stopped writing, baffled by the train of Gasser's thought, and from time to time some of them walked out. Professor Dalrymple too gradually gave up the vain attempt to follow the structure of Gasser's arguments, and tried to think of something else, though Gasser's voice intruded intermittently upon her musings.

"...it is of course very important how it works on the stage," she heard Gasser saying. "You would be able to see this if we had a drama workshop, which we unfortunately don't, but if we get an 'excellent' from HEFCE we might be able to afford one," he said looking hopefully at Professor Dalrymple, who returned his glance impassively, "but as Mr Cuthbert, one of the Skelmerdale English department's truly world-class scholars has shown in his brilliant analysis of *Pish!*, even though in a cut-out theatre simulation, what a character is wearing by way of shoes makes a very big difference to how we see that character. I once saw *Julius Caesar* done in jack-boots, and that really made it seem like a fascist state, which of course it was. That was a brilliant insight by the director I thought, only a real genius could have thought of it. Hamlet mentions too that his mother's shoes were fairly new when she married Claudius. Now in the last production I saw at the Skelmerdale rep. Gertrude was wearing a long dress which covered her shoes, so this point didn't come across very well, but when it does it is a wonderful stage effect."

At last the meandering ravings of Gasser came to an end. Those students who had been too timid to walk out of the lecture during its progress now fled from the room. Professor Dalrymple composed herself, rose to her feet, and smoothed down her skirt, as Gasser rushed up to her and said, "Was that all right? Will you give me an 'excellent' for that performance? I thought the students liked it you know, I think I have made the grade, I have, haven't I? It's very important to us that we are 'excellent' you know, we used to have a Grade 4 for research, but they took it off us most unfairly, we don't want the same thing to happen again in teaching, please give me an 'excellent', can I buy you a coffee?"

Professor Dalrymple closed her black notebook with a snap.

"Judgements on individual performances must remain confidential, as I'm sure you know," she said firmly. "But rest assured that what you have said today will be included in the overall assessment of the department. Now if you will excuse me I am due at my next assignment."

She turned on her heel, picked up her notebook and purse and walked briskly from the room, leaving the ineffable Gasser stuttering, "Oh, yes, of course, but there's no harm in hoping, is there, it would mean so much to me and all of us," he orated at her retreating back.

*****

The audit visit became a kind of blur to Professor Dalrymple. She was bombarded with statistics, snowed under with ever more pieces of paper in which the Skelmerdale department claimed to be excellent - its teaching was, so it said, outstanding. Its research was of outstanding international excellence, though it had been cheated of this by the last HEFCE research audit, which had maliciously given it a 2. Its staff-student relationships were outstanding. Its library, with its 325,000 books, was world class. Its research funding arrangements, £50 per head to all members of staff per annum regardless of whether they published or not, were outstandingly generous. Its committee structure and appeals system worked brilliantly. The classes Professor Dalrymple attended merged in her mind - she saw glove puppets dancing before her eyes, and was assailed by breathless voices saying, "We are wonderful aren't we, that class was SO successful, it really worked."

On the final Friday of the audit, the young professor returned to her room dazed, took a couple of Tylenol tablets with a large glass of Chardonnay, and fell into a refreshing slumber before the final working dinner of the auditors, in which they would discuss the draft of their report. The usual excellent meal was cleared away by the waiters, and the audit team was sitting round the polished table of the private dining room, with cups of coffee in front of them, and, according to taste, glasses of port, cognac, white wine or mineral water.

"Well," said Professor Magnum, "perhaps I could go round the table first and ask each of you for an overall brief impression of the Skelmerdale English department. Professor Brootal?"

"Essentially an inferior school," he replied without hesitation. "Poorly qualified staff, insubstantial, badly prepared lectures, hopelessly out of touch with the latest developments in the subject, just not with it, library very poor, none of them knows how to do a précis - I'd say it's an 'unsatisfactory'."

"Dr Grumbler?"

"Rather low-powered, I thought in the sessions I attended. Too much time spent on dressing up in costumes, and certainly not enough attention to the text. The drama lecturers did not seem to know about skeleton formes, and the nineteenth-century folks had paid no attention at all to the impact of stereotyping.... Agreed, it's 'unsatisfactory'."

"Hopelessly out of touch with modern theoretical developments in the subject: 'unsatisfactory'," was Ms Simper's verdict.

Professor Dalrymple tried hard to be fair. Her scarlet lips scythed vividly through the air as she briskly and incisively analysed the deficiences of the Skelmerdale department, notably the hopeless stupidities of Roland Gasser, Dickey Cuthbert and Johnny Codsworth. "I'm not saying that it is all bad," she concluded. "It's not a university calibre department, but it could be a very respectable Liberal Arts place with several staff changes, if they worked at it a bit. I agree: 'unsatisfactory'."

"Agreed, 'unsatisfactory'," put in Dr Gropper, who had at last been slapped in the face by Dr Lucy Loveleigh when he had slipped his good hand under her skirt and twanged her suspenders.

Professor Magnum had spent most of his time examining the department's administrative structures, which he also found 'unsatisfactory'. A rare smile flashed from his thin and bloodless lips.

"So we are unanimous then? That is rather rare. If you will allow me to consolidate your notes and written reports, I will produce a draft which we can examine in the morning for presentation to the VC tomorrow afternoon."

*****

The morning was spent hard at work preparing and consolidating and proof-reading the final draft of the preliminary report. And then at 2.45 p.m. the audit team made its way out of the hotel for the last time, to enter the limos that would take them to the campus. And this time a group of four, dark-suited, thick-set unsmiling men joined the party and led the way in a limo of their own.

"Who are those guys?" asked Professor Dalrymple, curious, as the convoy set off.

"They're from Pinkerton's," explained Professor Brootal cheerily. "Sadly, not all institutions can accept a verdict of 'unsatisfactory' with equanimity. There have been some nasty incidents in the past when auditors have been physically attacked when their classification is not to the university's liking. Hence the need for the heavies, which HEFCE automatically lays on nowadays when the verdict is 'unsatisfactory'."

"Ah, I see," responded Professor Dalrymple thoughtfully. It was a curious system, she thought to herself, that made the English universities police themselves. After all, since the total UK budget for English was a fixed one, the less money for Skelmerdale English, the more money there would be for English at Skegness and Rugby and The University of the Wirral, and all the universities from which the assessors came, so there was not much incentive for guys like Brootal and Magnum to give Skelmerdale the benefit of the doubt... not that there was much doubt in this case.

The limos arrived at the Palladian administration building, and the party advanced up the stairs to the VC's office. One look at the four heavies told the VC all he wanted to know, and he scowled at the Registrar. The Registrar in turn scowled at the hapless Professor Freddie Frowstie, the head of department. And he in turn scowled at his staff. Although an invitation had been extended to all staff to hear the verdict, the wiser ones had divined what it might be, and chosen to absent themselves from the scene of grief. But the more naive ones, who were hoping for an 'excellent' and had convinced themselves that they would get one, had turned out in force. Roland Gasser was there, dancing excitedly up and down just inside the door of the VC's office; Mr Cuthbert was there, wearing his customary clown suit, and so was the pantalooned and petticoated Codsworth, fresh from the most recent classroom recitation of *Pish!*. Roland Gasser could hardly contain himself, and whispered to Professor Dalrymple as she entered, "We have got an 'excellent', haven't we, we must have done, oh I do hope so."

Professor Dalrymple made no answer.

The party sat down, declining the VC's offer of tea.

Professor Magnum launched into his summing up.

"By way of introduction, let me say that my team found that most lectures were badly presented and ill-informed. Seminars and tutorials ranged in general from unsatisfactory to satisfactory. We found the administrative procedures of the department cumbersome and ill-suited to the turn of the millennium. Library facilities were poor. Student morale was acceptable, but chiefly, we judged, because they were out for a good time and found that the department made few demands on them. We found the staff qualifications poor in general, with not enough of them having a doctorate, an essential qualification nowadays even for a part-time temporary job. We found the department deficient in leadership. Our overall verdict can only be 'unsatisfactory'. Here is a summary of our conclusions. A more detailed report will follow in two months time."

The four heavies moved in to surround the auditors. Roland Gasser started to cry. Dr Codsworth pulled up his petticoat and wiped it sniffily across his face. Mr Cuthbert turned white and spluttered, "But that can't be so......I don't believe it." Professor Freddie Frowstie sat miserably in his chair as the audit team left the room, and the VC and Registrar closed in on him menacingly from either side.

The audit team returned to their hotel for a final farewell dinner and to collect their £5000 a head honorarium from Magnum's assistant. On the following day Professor Dalrymple returned by train to Cambridge to resume her researches.

CHAPTER TWELVE

THE CORRUPTION OF NARCISSUS

'Mirror, mirror on the wall,
Who is the fairest of them all?' (*Snow White and the Seven Dwarfs*)

'adstupet ipse sibi vultuque inmotus eodem
haeret' (Ovid, *Metamorphoses*, iii)

The University of Skelmerdale woke up, and admired itself in its reflection, as it did every day, in the vast and continuous lake that overspread the campus, the lake which passed from college to college, from Residence Hall to Residence Hall, and swirled placidly between the scattered buildings of the lonely and desolate campus, each building being linked by bridges and walkways, so that the members of the university had maximum opportunities to admire their reflections in the water as they wandered round.

'This is a wonderful, wonderful university,' thought Dr Winsome, the Vice-Chancellor, cutting himself in the face as he shaved, for obsessed by the image from the lake, easily visible from the window of his bathroom, he had failed to watch his face in the mirror. He laughed complacently at his mistake. What rich red blood he had!

'This is a wonderful, wonderful university,' thought Freddie Frowstie, as he strolled over a bridge into his office in Grace Darling college to deal with the morning's mail. And the Department of English and Communication Studies was the most wonderful department in it, quite the very best of the eighteen 'above average' English departments in the country, and certain to be getting a 'grade 5 star' when HEFCE carried out its next research selectivity exercise! It was a pity it had been dubbed 'unsatisfactory' for teaching, with very low scores out of 24, but everyone knew that the TQA exercise was arbitrary, and Skelmerdale was still the best of all the 'unsatisfactory' English departments in the country. How lucky he was to be its head of department!

'This is a wonderful, wonderful university,' thought Fawn and Florinda, as they made their way past the lake, across the muddy grass and goose-droppings, to give their next glove-puppet class! There couldn't be many English departments in the country which had better glove-puppet scenarios than Skelmerdale had!

'This is a wonderful, wonderful university,' dreamed Blanche Quick, still in her alcoholic stupor at 11 a.m. in the morning. She had been lucky again at the one-armed bandits, and had stood treat in the bar last night to the extent of £60 of liquor. Sprawled face-downwards across the unmade bed, wearing only her bra, Blanche snored happily, half-smoked cigarette-ends littering the carpet, which was scorched and burned from their effects. In her left hand Blanche still clutched the empty bottle of vodka which she had drained almost in its entirety the night before. Her dress and shoes and items of underwear were on the floor, lying where they fell, wedging open the door, for she had only just been able to stumble into her room and get undressed the previous night, before passing out on the bed. 'This is a wonderful, wonderful university,' dreamed Blanche, as images of slot machines and glove-puppets and convivial evenings in the bar danced through her stupefied brain.

'This is a wonderful, wonderful university,' thought Dr Charles Bright, the newly appointed young lecturer in medieval literature and communication studies, as he wandered up and down the corridor outside Blanche's bedroom the next morning. At Skelmerdale, to ensure a happy atmosphere and social and educational interaction, student rooms and teaching rooms and lecturers' accommodation were all jumbled up in a friendly mix. So Dr Bright strolled up and down all morning, book in hand, from his flat to his seminar room, from the departmental office to his teaching room, from his teaching room to the departmental library, enjoying the sight of Blanche's curvaceous bottom every time he passed her room. 'What a wonderful, wonderful. wonderful, university Skelmerdale was!' There couldn't be many universities which provided so many opportunities for such informal staff-student contact.

'Thkelmerdale ith a wonderful wonderful univerthity', thought Tabitha to herself, as she smoked her first Peyote of the morning, before wandering leisurely down to the showers to prepare herself for the new day. 'It'th thuch a relaxing plathe.'

*****

'The distinction between the Present of Vivid Narration and the Annalistic Present seems obvious now that it has been stated' (G. M. Lane, *A Latin Grammar* (New York, 1898)

'Nominis et formae pariter ludibrium gestans,
  Conventus nostros, Dumbule parvus, adis.' (*Anthologia latina*)

The petite three-feet high Dr Thumbelina Thrump was giving her class on medieval geese to the first-year historians at Skelmerdale.

"*Finitum ero*, I will be cooked, *finitum eras*, you will be cooked, *finitum erint*, they will be cooked," the historians were chanting. "*Finitae eramus, finitae ansera erint*, you will be cooked, they [neuter] the geese will be cooked. *Trois fois ils le faisaient*, three ducks they did this, *quatres fois elles assayaient*, the four female ducks sat down." Dr Thrump glowed with pride at their progress. Skelmerdale was a wonderful, wonderful university. And what wonderful progress her students were making in goose studies. For the Skelmerdale History department had a long-term collaborative and inter-disciplinary project on the go, studying the medieval goose in all its aspects, what it ate and who ate it, what it excreted, who kept it on which farms and where, the goose in the town and the countryside, geese, goose girls and gender, and so on.

"And now let's do some more words," Dr Thrump said brightly. "*Mogistra* that is medieval document-speak for cat. And *libros*, which means pounds weight. And *anser illuster* is a good example of an adjective agreeing with a noun. They both end in *r* you see. And *fois* is Norman-French and Provençal for 'duck'."

"Yes, Thumbelina," replied the students eagerly.

"And *barum* is the document word for sheep, you see it in this will here," continued Dr Thrump. "It's where the English word 'ba-lamb' comes from."

"It's so easy to remember," chorused the students, "*barum* equals 'ba-lamb' equals sheep."

"You see you are really getting the hang of this," said Dr Thrump eagerly. "These records are such fun, aren't they? And so easy, because there aren't any rules, you see, so you don't have to know any grammar and you don't have to know what it means.

You'll find that out quite soon as we get into my colleague Eduardo Bandilegs' big collection of medieval goose records on which he has been working for many years."

'This was a wonderful, wonderful university,' thought the colourfully dressed Thumbelina Thrump to herself. What wonderfully receptive and enthusiastic students it got!

'This is a wonderful, wonderful university,' thought the first-year historians to themselves.' Thumbelina Thrump made medieval goose records so easy to understand! It was wonderful to think that she had started out in life as a trick-cyclist in a circus.

'This is a wonderful, wonderful university,' thought the diminutive Professor Alan Dummkopf, the chairperson of the History department to himself, listening to the students as he passed Dr Thrump's classroom. What a wonderful department the history department was! Surely it would get a grade 5 star in the next HEFCE survey, along with a 24-point average for first-rate and excellent teaching of surpassing quality!

Professor and Mrs Hanwell were also passing Dr Thrump's classroom. They looked at each other and laughed out loud.

"Something wrong there," they said to each other with one voice, failing to notice the tiny and insignificant figure of Professor Dummkopf. (For Professor Dummkopf was also a dwarf, like many members of the Skelmerdale History department, recruited under the affirmative action programme for people of restricted growth.) "In fact lots of things, it's all wrong!"

"Let's face it, Charles, this is a pretty curious and screwed-up university, isn't it? Thank goodness you don't have to work here, and are only here for a term giving some visiting lectures for a high fee!"

They both laughed, and passed on their way.

Professor Alan Dummkopf overheard these words, and grew red with anger, and returned to his office to gnaw the leg of his table, and drum his yellow-booted heels in a frenzy on the lino of his office. How dare a mere visiting professor impugn the wonderful teaching for which his department was so well-known? No doubt about it, Skelmerdale was a wonderful wonderful university, and the History department was one of its star attractions... Professor Dummkopf's tantrums disturbed a pile of books poised precariously on the top of his bookshelf. All six volumes of Du Cange's *Glossarium ad scriptores mediae et infimae latinitatis* (Paris, 1733), which had reposed there unused and unread since a foolish benefactor had bequeathed them to the Skelmerdale history department twenty years ago, rained down on the luckless Dummkopf's head, knocking off his pixie-cap and rendering him unconscious, and leaving him with a large bruise on his diminutive forehead. Later that evening Professor and Mrs Hanwell were narrating what they had heard to Ruth's friend and bridesmaid Tamsin. Tamsin, who had done some languages in secondary school, laughed merrily when her friends told her what they had heard.

"Yes, Dr Thrump is well known for being a bit of an idiot," she exclaimed. "But that's nothing compared to some of the others, like Mr Bandilegs. History is one of the weak departments of this university, it only got a 1 in the last selectivity exercise, unlike English which got a 3. But all my friends think that History is a good subject to do because you don't have to work very hard, and that leaves lots of time for socialising." Yes, no doubt about it, Skelmerdale was a wonderful, wonderful university!

*****

Freddie Frowstie admired his reflection in the glass door of Grace Darling college, and fluffed his beard complacently. Yes, in spite of all his tribulations, Skelmerdale was a wonderful wonderful university! And English was sure to get a grade 5 at the next selectivity exercise, now that Fawn and Florinda had come on stream in a big way with all their publications..

*****

'Chop off his head, man. Somewhat will we do.' (Shakespeare, *Richard III*)

The mad axe-person, clad from head to foot in a black SAS-style outfit, emerged silently at 11 p.m. from the tangled thickets of undergrowth which separated Grace Darling and Sir Roger de Coverley colleges. The sparse and weak campus lighting threw only pale and widely scattered circles of light amidst the desolate wilderness of the Skelmerdale campus. The mad axe-person advanced, axe in hand. The head of the axe and its blade were painted black so as to reflect no glimmer of light. No doubt about it, Skelmerdale was a wonderful, wonderful university for mad-axepersons, muggers, robbers and other thugs! What a splendid setting in which to play out their rituals of violence! The axe-person slid silently across the grass, and walked slowly by the lake, unobserved by all save for the mournful geese. The axe-person arrived quite unnoticed at one of the forty-three unlocked external doors of Sir Roger de Coverley college. Skelmerdale was certainly a wonderful, wonderful university, a really thief-friendly and murderer-friendly place! And now the axe-person was in the ill-lit corridors of Sir Roger de Coverley college, and there was no need to worry any more about concealment, for any passing student would instantly take the axe-person for a member of the department of English and Communication studies, the most wonderful wonderful department in the whole university, executing a practical dramatic project. The axe-person climbed the ill-lit stairs, kicking aside the litter of discarded coffee-cups, torn crisp packets, ice-cream wrappings and empty bottles of beer and broken glasses from the previous evening's brawls. Soon the axe-person was on the top floor of the college. The axe-person placed an ear against the doors of the student bedrooms, listening for noise from within, until a silent room could be found. A stolen pass-key opened the door, and the axe-person settled down to wait for the occupant's return, which happened at 11.55 p.m..

Bill, from one of Fawn and Florinda's glove puppet classes, returned drunk from the bar and flopped down in a stupor, vomiting on to the bed-clothes. The axe-person lifted up the axe, and gleefully decapitated him with a single blow, severing Bill's head from his neck, before retreating unobserved and silent back to the undergrowth. This was a wonderful, wonderful university, thought the mad axe-person!

*****

'The crime-rate in Skelmerdale, as in all cathedral cities, is low, which makes for a safe and attractive environment.' (*University of Skelmerdale Prospectus*)

'Skelmerdale was a wonderful, wonderful university', thought the University's press officer, as she prepared the press release extolling Skelmerdale's excellent security after the unfortunate demise of Bill from English and Communication studies! There couldn't be many universities that had a twenty-four hour porter sitting in a watchperson's hut on the very edge of campus all the year round! And crime could happen anywhere. Skelmerdale was really a very safe university, once you ignored the axe-murders, vandalism, and thefts from bedrooms, as mere statistical aberrations! It just had to be the safest campus in the country, for after all, crime could happen anywhere, and there was absolutely no evidence that Skelmerdale was being deliberately targeted, it was clearly just a co-incidence that five people had been murdered there in the last few months.... No doubt about it, Skelmerdale was a wonderful wonderful university.

*****

Tamsin's friend Sophie Poppet had come round for lunch with Professor Hanwell and Ruth, and over the dessert wine, the talk turned to her course. Sophie was reading history, and was studying medieval geese as a special option with Mr Bandilegs and Dr Thrump. Sophie, a kindly young woman who had a sense of humour recognised her teachers' idiosyncrasies, but remained silent and concealed her smiles. No doubt about it, Skelmerdale was a wonderful wonderful university, always laying on something to make you laugh! In high good humour from the Muscadet and brandies dispensed after an excellent lunch by Professor Hanwell's generous hospitality, Sophie Poppet felt on top of the world, as she strolled across the Skelmerdale campus in the mild sunshine of an unseasonably warm January day. "*Finitae ansera erint*, their goose will be cooked," she called out impulsively at the top of her voice, as she passed the campus lake. The very Skelmerdale campus geese themselves heard Sophie Poppet's mocking laughter at the History Department's goose course, and cackled loudly as she passed, her long hair streaming behind her in the breeze. The geese cackled their laughter to the moor-hens, and the moor-hens squawked their message to the ducks, and the ducks flapped their wings and splashed in the water, before emerging to defecate with deep satisfaction by the rushes at the side of the lake. Sophie

Poppet jumped for joy, in high good humour after the excellent lunch, suffused still with laughter at the thought of the History department's goose course. Her short grey skirt flapped in the wind as she jumped up and down, before proceeding to cartwheel exuberantly along the gravel path by the side of the lake. On and on she cartwheeled, chanting her mantra to the birds in the sky as she went. It was good to be alive, and Skelmerdale was a wonderful wonderful university! Sophie Poppet cartwheeled into the bar of Grace Darling college, before collapsing on the floor with a fit of the giggles, spluttering out to her friends who came to her aid in helpless amusement, *"Perdibor, perdibiris, perdibetur*, I am undone, or rather they are undone." Her friends sensibly ordered her a very large brandy, and at length Sophie Poppet recovered her composure sufficiently to sit with the crowd of late afternoon drinkers in the bar of Grace Darling college, to tell her friends about the History department's fascinating goose course, to play a game or two of Space Invaders, and to hazard a coin or two on the one-armed bandits. Yes, no doubt about it, Skelmerdale was a wonderful, wonderful, university, always laying on something to make you laugh.

*****

Mrs Quick, arriving in Grace Darling college to pay an unexpected visit to her daughter, overheard Mr Bandilegs and Dr Thrump expounding goose records to their class *"Per aevis et aevis"*, Dr Thrump was saying, "it's masculine, it means 'for ever and ever'." The third-year historians, apart from the impassive Sophie Poppet, obediently took notes. What a clever teacher Dr Thrump was! *"In nomen sancti Trinitatis et filiu Dei,"* the students chanted and wrote in their books. *"Septe ansseras vendunt ob vig. oboleas.* The seven geese are selling halfpennies in lots of twenty. *Trois fois plus*, the three geese wore feathers." Skelmerdale was a wonderful wonderful university, they really made their students study primary sources, thought Mrs Quick, as she climbed the dark stairs at the end of the ground floor corridor leading to Blanche's room.

Outside Blanche's room, Dr Bright paused for the twentieth time that morning to untie and tie his shoelace outside the open door of Blanche Quick's room. He gazed yet again at the sight of Blanche sprawled across her bed naked save for her bra, until the sound of approaching footsteps on the stairs made him straighten up and pad silently along the corridors to his room. Yes, Skelmerdale was a wonderful wonderful university! Leaving the door ajar, Dr Bright heard Mrs Quick walk along the corridor, enter Blanche's room, and slam the door in an angry burst of temper. Once inside she draped a bath-robe across Blanche's prostrate form, and shook her angrily by the shoulders until Blanche awoke.

"What are you doing, Blanche," she said angrily. "Why are you still in bed at this time of day? Are you drunk? And why is your door open?"

Blanche awoke from her blissful slumbers, and smiled happily at her mother. "Hello, mummy, nice to see you," she murmured sleepily. "No, I'm not drunk, just had a late night last night, that's all. No need to worry. Didn't I lock my door? Oh well, not to worry, people are very honest here, look, my video and lap-top are quite OK, no one has stolen anything."

"But your door was open," chided Mrs Quick. "And you had almost nothing on. Anyone could have seen you."

Blanche tumbled out of bed and ran her hands through her hair. She felt a little frowsty, started to boil the kettle, and then collapsed into an armchair in her bath robe and lazily reached for the first cigarette of the day, inhaling the acrid fumes with satisfaction.

"Don't worry, mummy. You fuss far too much. It's all girlies on this corridor anyway, apart from one or two teaching rooms that are hardly ever used. Forget it - I'm quite all right now. It's lovely to see you." She gave her mother an affectionate hug. "What brings you up to Skelmerdale? I didn't know you were here. But since you are, you can take me out for a really nice leisurely lunch, and over a glass or two of wine I'll tell you all the news. Just sit there and relax whilst I have a shower and freshen up." Blanche slipped into her mules, and flip-flopped down the corridor on the way to the showers. Half-an-hour later, she felt more human again, and neat in blue sweater and smart flannel skirt led her mother out of the labyrinthine passages of Grace Darling college to the car park. She smiled politely at Dr Bright when she met him in the corridor, and he smiled happily back at her. No doubt about it, Skelmerdale was a great place to be.

*****

Outside, walking along the muddy campus pathways, Dr Winsome, the Vice-Chancellor of the University of Skelmerdale, slipped on a pile of goose-droppings which he had failed to spot in his general satisfaction at the state of the university. His feet shot from beneath him, and straightaway he was sprawled full length on the ground, his face coming to rest next to yet another pile of goose-droppings. His shiny grey suit was now soiled, muddied and torn, his knee was bleeding from a jagged cut where he had gashed it against a stone. The Vice-Chancellor breathed in deeply. savouring the rich mixture of goose-droppings, the keen wind, and the decaying stench of muddy leaves. As he rose to his feet he was knocked to the ground once more by one of the inconsiderate giraffes which were now running wild across the campus. Yes, no doubt about it, Skelmerdale was a wonderful, wonderful university, with quite the best and richest and most malodorous goose-droppings of any university in the country, and certainly the only university in the UK that was playing host to two giraffes! How lucky he was to be Vice-Chancellor there!

*****

'Latinas autem linguas quatuor esse quidam dixerunt, id est priscam, latinam, romanam, mixtam.'
(Hugh of St Victor, *De grammatica*)

From the History department common room overlooking the lake, those long-standing members of the History department, squat, fat, toad-like Mr Eduardo Bandilegs and the petite Dr Thumbelina Thrump eyed malevolently the English department corridors in Grace Darling college. The departments of History and English at Skelmerdale, the two largest and most important departments in the University, were jealous of each other, and often did regard each other suspiciously across the toadstools that flourished by the side of the lake, across the goose-droppings, across the dank and slimy scum that clung to the banks of the lake. Mr Bandilegs and Dr Thrump were reading the *Skelmerdale Newsletter*, with its by now familiar litany of English department successes - the planned Socrates exchange programme with Bosnia as soon as that country had been admitted to the European Union, the success of the glove-puppet dramatisations of major works of English Literature, the videos of project work, the success of the Italian and German translations of the glove puppet scenarios and so on. Both dwarfs, recruited, like many other Skelmerdale historians, under that department's access initiative for people of restricted growth with learning difficulties, were wearing yellow boots, both were bearded, both were wearing pixie hats.

Dr Thrump scowled through her pince-nez spectacles, and grouchily remarked, "The English department boasting again, I see. They're obviously busting a gut to get a grade 5 star in the next Research Assessment Exercise. But I see that a lot of their publications are in the *Analecta Skelmerdaliana* - not a series I'm familiar with."

"It's Swedish," answered Mr Bandilegs self-importantly, for he was an expert in many areas besides goose studies. "They've had to go abroad to get their work published, obviously."

"But it seems to be a publication of their course work," said Dr Thrump peevishly. "Eduardo, I've had an idea, why can't we get our lecture notes for our medieval geese course published? Why don't we? Our courses are such a wonderful success with our students, you know, we've always had such a good record in goose studies here!" And indeed the history department has just started a new MA course in Goose Studies, which drew heavily on the work of Bandilegs and Thrump, and had applications on the stocks for Leverhulme Foundation and Arts and Humanities Research Board funding for an interdisciplinary goose project on geese in country and city throughout the ages. "Maybe if the course were published, other universities would take it! And it would give us both a publication too!" And, to be sure, just like Fawn and Florinda not so long ago, Mr Bandilegs and Dr Thrump stood in sore need of publications.

Excitedly Dr Thrump waved a sheaf of her and Mr Bandilegs' course notes under his nose. "Look, publishing is so easy nowadays with camera-ready copy, all we would have to do is give the publisher the typed notes of your transcription of medieval goose records, add in my course-work exercises, and we would have a book!"

Mr Bandilegs looked doubtful.

"Oh come on Eduardo," pressed domineering Dr Thrump, waving her deformed hands in the air. "We are going to do this thing. Look, I saw an advert in the *TLS* last week, 'Writers, we will publish your work' - Print and Pay Books I think they were called. Now your aunty Polly died last year and left you £15,000, didn't she? Write me a cheque for say £14,500, I'll send off our notes, add in some nice pictures of birds and geese from an Art History book, and we too will have an illustrated inter-disciplinary book to our names quite soon. I'm sure we will get our money back, other universities are sure to want our course when they hear how successful it has been here."

Obediently Mr Bandilegs took out his cheque-book - he had cleverly left the money in his current account to take advantage of the attractive rates of interest the banks were now offering - and wrote out a cheque to Print and Pay Books. Soon Dr Thrump and Mr Bandilegs' course, with its striking illustrations of medieval documentary idioms, and its working appendix on geese records, '*Tris ansera furunt in agros*' was on its way to the printers. Seven weeks later, at a cost of £14,500, 3,500 copies of the *Skelmerdale History Department Illustrated Documentary Goose Course for Historians and Medievalists* by Eduardo Bandilegs, (MA Skelmerdale) and Dr Thumbelina Thrump (DPhil Skelmerdale) had been delivered. Proudly Mr Bandilegs and Dr Thrump posted copies to all ninety-five British universities, to the *Higher*, to the *Classical Review, Speculum, Classical World*, and the *Journal of the Association for the Reform of Language Teaching*, to the *Journal of Goose Studies*, to the *English Historical Review*, to *History Today*, and to the other leading historical journals in the UK, continental Europe and the United States, and sat back expectantly to wait for the rave reviews which would surely follow. Yes, no doubt about it, Skelmerdale was a wonderful wonderful university! That no one could deny.

Next morning Professor Alan Dummkopf sat in his office looking with pleasure at his presentation copy of the *Skelmerdale History Department Illustrated Documentary Goose Course for Historians and Medievalists*. It was dedicated to him and proudly inscribed 'To Professor Alan Dummkopf, scholar, teacher, and friend, from Eduardo Bandilegs and Thumbelina Thrump. Ad mogistrum nastrum hanc libelum donaberimus pro signa amictiae'. This was a wonderful, wonderful university, thought Professor

Dummkopf proudly. This would really be one in the eye for that impertinent wretch, Professor Hanwell, who had dared cast aspersions on the History department's course. There weren't many universities in the UK where the staff could produce stuff like that! It would also be a real blow to the English department! Nobody there could do a documentary course like that, that was for sure! Proudly Professor Dummkopf sat down to compose an 'Encomiam' of the Skelmerdale History department documentary goose course for the *Skelmerdale Newsletter*. What a wonderful, wonderful university he was in, to be sure!

With great satisfaction Professor Dummkopf turned again to his own very significant researches into the number of eggs laid by partridges in Suffolk in May 1472.

*****

Professor Freddie Frowstie had spent a few moments of a distracted morning composing the press release for the first of Professor Hanwell's lectures on 'The Languages of Scientific Poetry'. 'Distinguished scholar, privileged to have him here, author of a seminal work on Scientific Poetry,' the phrases tripped lightly from Freddie Frowstie's pen, practised as he now was at writing puffs for members of his department at promotion time and for the *Skelmerdale Newsletter*. That done, he wrote Professor Hanwell a cheque for £12,500, this being the fee for his first five lectures, popped it in the post with a note of apology for his own unavoidable absence from the first lecture, and went home happily to bed. Professor Hanwell received the cheque in the morning post three days before his first lecture, and thoughtfully paid it into the bank straightaway. Say what you like about Skelmerdale, there was no doubt about it, they paid visiting lecturers a handsome lecture rate! All around the university, large posters had been placed on boards and hoardings and trees, advertising Professor Hanwell's lecture.

Professor Hanwell had arranged to celebrate the delivery of his first lecture by taking Ruth and Sophie Poppet, Fiona and Tamsin out to dinner afterwards. At 5.15 p.m. promptly, at the advertised time of his talk, he marched in to the 250 seat lecture-theatre which Freddie Frowstie had booked for the occasion. There, seated five rows from the front, was Ruth, elegant as ever in high-heeled shoes and a smart black cocktail-dress which she had purchased in New York. To her left was Sophie Poppet, smartly dressed for dinner in a figure-hugging grey suit which her parents had bought her for her birthday, and to her right sat Fiona and Tamsin, the latter alert and quizzical, with a lively expression on her face, clad in a dress of deep rich purple which reached to just below her knees. Around her neck was a string of pearls. Professor Hanwell, in a dark suit and Sussex University graduates' tie, picked his way through the litter of empty coke tins and discarded polystyrene cups that impeded progress through the aisles of the lecture theatre, and made his way to the podium at the front. Save for Ruth, Fiona, Sophie Poppet, and Tamsin, the lecture theatre was empty. Professor Hanwell took off his watch, and laid it on the lectern, and checked the advertised time and date of his lecture against his watch. No, this was the Roger de Coverley theatre, it was now 5.17 p.m., this was Thursday 13 January! But there was no one in the room save his wife and her friends. For a moment or two Professor Hanwell was disconcerted. He arranged his papers on the podium, looked at his watch again, checked the time against the clock at the back of the room, and then, as a believer in punctuality and promptness, carefully delivered his brilliant lecture on the languages of scientific poetry, a version of the one he had delivered at the HSS in San Francisco, to his wife, to Sophie Poppet, Fiona and Tamsin, and to the empty walls of Skelmerdale's largest lecture theatre. Some of his quips and learned allusions were lost on Fiona, Sophie Poppet and Tamsin - but they clapped enthusiastically at the end of the lecture nonetheless. Professor Hanwell took Freddie Frowstie's letter from out of his wallet, and satisfied himself again from his hole-in-the-wall bank statement that the cheque had now been properly credited to his bank account. Then, re-assured, he summoned a taxi, and soon was sitting with his wife and her three glamorous friends on sofas and deep armchairs in the grand lounge of the seventeenth-century Amberley Manor, a country-house hotel and restaurant three miles away on the southern edge of Skelmerdale, sipping excellent champagne and nibbling at canapés as the party waited for their order to be taken. Say what you like, it was certainly very decent of the University of Skelmerdale to have spent some thousands of pounds in laying on a guest lecture for just three of its students. What a wonderful wonderful wonderful institution it was to be sure!

*****

A kind colleague had alerted Professor Freddie Frowstie at coffee time to the appearance of the first review of his book. Dismissing his last class of the morning early, Freddie Frowstie hurried over to the library. Eagerly he riffled through the pages of *The Review of English Studies* - ah yes, there it was! - Freddie Frowstie, *STUDYING TRAGEDY. THE DEVIL-OPEMENT OF A TRAD-ITION*. University of Skelmerdale Department of English and Communication Studies Occasional Papers, 26. Skelmerdale University Press, xi + 151 pp. £95.

"This latest volume of the Skelmerdale English and Communication Studies Occasional Papers is well down to the usual standards of this series," he read with growing irritation. "The subject of the book purports to be tragedy - perhaps the real tragedy is, they chopped down trees for this. This book may have needed to be written - it did not need to be published. Frowstie's argument seems to be that tragedy developed within a framework of tradition. Of course it did! Frowstie offers here nothing that is new. Instead we are given a tiresome farrago, a muddled and confused mish-mash, stringing together clichés from all the worst books ever written on this topic. It is hard to envisage the audience at which it is aimed - at first year undergraduates? Perhaps, but if so it is dismally off-target, and would in any event be ruled out by its price. Professor Frowstie painfully underestimates the intelligence of his audience. This book is not even worthy but dull, though dull it certainly is. There are too many factual errors for comfort. Erasmus's translation of Euripides's *Medea*, dismissed by Frowstie, was not into Dutch. Marlowe's *Dr Faustus* cannot have been written in 1598, since Marlowe was dead by then. *The Conquest of Granada* was not written in 1620. *Waiting for Godot* was not first written in English. Proof-reading too has been abysmal. As in all works emanating from Skelmerdale, all the foreign language quotations are incorrect. Other misprints are too many to list individually, though some 1,165 of the more serious ones are appended at the end of this review. The question inevitably arises, how did this volume get through the editorial department at the Skelmerdale University Press? In decency the

Skelmerdale Press should recall this shoddy book and offer those who have bought it their money back. Here at last is the definitive book which everyone, beginning students, scholars, libraries and the general reader can afford to be without. JAMES MASTIX, UNIVERSITY OF BLACKPOOL"

Freddie Frowstie grew scarlet with embarrassment. But after he had had a couple of drinks, he began to look on the bright side. Few of his colleagues read the journals, so maybe they would not see it. And say what you like, the fact was that he had now had a review in the *RES*! Not many people at Skelmerdale ever got their books reviewed in such a prestigious journal! Everyone in the profession knew that normally you had to be at Oxford for this to happen. And they had called it the definitive book! He could quote that remark out of context. Then too the *RES* had a large circulation throughout the profession. Certainly this would bring the book to the attention of librarians, scholars and maybe even some of the general public! It was almost as good as having a book reviewed in the *TLS*! How jealous his colleagues would be! And more than that, this would count as another citation, taking him into double figures at last! Yes, there was no doubt that this review could be presented as another feather in the cap, not only for him, but also for the wonderful University of Skelmerdale and its scholarly press. In a state of excitement he rushed back to his office to write a boastful note to the VC that his book had been mentioned as definitive in the *RES*, with particular reference to libraries, scholars, students and the general reader. No doubt about it, Skelmerdale was a wonderful university.

CHAPTER THIRTEEN

CRUMPET IN HAITI (1)

'Flectere si nequeo superos, Acheronta movebo' (Virgil, *Aeneid IV*)

'Jamais aucun Colon ni Européen ne mettra le pied sur cette terre en titre de maître ou de propriétaire.'
(*Constitution of the Republic of Haiti*)

A few months after the Skelmerdale conference on 'Writing Women Re-Vued', into the Magic Women bookshop had come a copy of *The Serpent and the Rainbow* (1983), by Wade Davis, the fascinating, learned and authoritative record of the researches of a Harvard anthropologist into the mysterious phenomenon of the Zombies, the Undead, the Walking Dead. Such zombies had been the inspiration for so many horror films, like *Plague of the Zombies*, one of the all-time great Hammer Horror movies, and especially that wonderfully atmospheric and evocative re-working of *Jane Eyre*, the classic *I Walked With a Zombie* (1943), which Mrs Quick had several times seen on TV. Mrs Quick had been captivated by Professor Davis's story, and in particular his gripping account of the Haitian zombie paste, the wonderful substance which turned people into zombies by sending them into a catatonic trance, in which state they became the undead, subservient absolutely to the will of their mistress.

"If only I could have some zombie paste, what could I not do with it," she exulted to herself. It would be fun to have some tame zombies around the house, to do the domestic chores, to dig the garden, to help with loading and unloading books, to serve drinks on the terrace to Tony and herself on the long summer evenings.

The scheming Mrs Quick was not one to let the grass go under her feet. Straightaway she phoned her travel agent in Hereford, and soon had purchased an economy class return ticket from London to Port au Prince via Miami in the name of Dr Antonia Crumpet.

That evening she outlined her plans to Dr Crumpet.

"I've a little treat for you, Tony dear, as a reward for all your hard work," she said ingenuously, flashing Dr Crumpet an insincere smile, as the two women sat munching nuts and sipping Sauternes in the dining room of their cottage late that April evening. "You need a holiday, and so I've booked you one in the West Indies, just as a little thank offering from me to you." Mrs Quick kissed her protégée fondly, and handed over the air ticket and hotel reservation, together with a second-hand copy of the Left Book Club's *Pride of the Black Republic*, published in 1932 by Victor Gollancz, a romanticised and idealised vision of life on the tropic isle, which Mrs Quick had found on the 5p stand of one of the general booksellers in Hay. "A holiday in the sunshine is just what you need, Tony dear, you've been looking a little peaky of late."

Dr Crumpet was as always overwhelmed by the kindliness of her mentor and lover, and snuggled up towards her to whisper her thanks.

"And whilst you're there, Tony dear, you could get me some zombie paste. Look, I have a little information about it here." And Mrs Quick handed over a little folder containing selected extracts of the relevant parts of the Davis book. "It would be a useful addition to our stock of charms and potions, Tony dear," she continued brightly. "I'd go myself, of course, but I don't know French - they speak French in Haiti of course - and anyway, I have to remain here and see that the bookshop is all in order."

Dr Crumpet was touched by Mrs Quick's selflessness and generosity. She read the extracts from the Davis book with fascination, and agreed with Mrs Quick that it should prove to be a comparatively simple matter to ask around and purchase a small stock of the potent powder.

"Just think who we could turn into zombies," exulted Mrs Quick. "That Dr Margaret Jacquasse for a start. And then there's that silly Frank in our second-year classes - he's practically a zombie already, anyway," she laughed. "Do try your hardest to bring some back, Tony dear."

Dr Crumpet promised to do her best.

*****

'Mes enfants, pillez en bon ordre' (The President of Haiti)

One week later Dr Crumpet was sitting happily in the First Class compartment of the British Airways flight from Gatwick to Miami. Mrs Quick had booked an Economy ticket for her, but when Dr Crumpet checked in at Gatwick, the counter clerk had taken a fancy to the glamorous young woman, and since Economy Class was nearly full, had upgraded her to First free of charge. So now Dr Crumpet, well prepared for the tropic climes in her elegant and flowery Laura Ashley English Country Garden summer-style dress, was revelling in the unaccustomed spaciousness of her surroundings, as she lay back almost horizontal in the reclining seat, and sipped the Louis Roederer champagne that was served in unlimited quantities. Haiti promised to be a delightful experience - elegant beaches free from the horrors of mass tourism, an atmosphere unpolluted by heavy industry, a happy, carefree, smiling populace uncorrupted by Western materialism, a real triumph for black democracy, as the Gollancz book had said. And the zombie paste would be a real attraction, if only she could find some of that and bear it back in triumph to Hay! It would be fun to turn some of her and Pauline's enemies into zombies! Two hours out from London, when Dr Crumpet had partaken of canapés, caviare, and smoked salmon, washed down with liberal quantities of excellent wine, and a few glasses of Cointreau, she settled down in her seat, and fell into a deep slumber. She did not awake till five hours later, when the plane was preparing to descend into the muggy heat of a Miami summer's day.

The plane landed, and Dr Crumpet retrieved her luggage, and had soon passed through customs and immigration. Within an hour of debarking from the plane, she had presented herself at the check-in desk of Air Haiti, ready for the final stage of her long journey. The check-in desk was pleasantly uncrowded, and the formalities were speedily and courteously dealt with by the young American woman in charge of the Miami airport desk of Air Haiti. When her flight was called, Dr Crumpet was somewhat surprised to find that the plane to Port au Prince was a tiny propeller-driven Cessna - and that she herself was the only passenger on the plane! Oh well, no doubt it was the low season for tourism in Haiti. She fastened her seat belt, and the plane took off. A little over an hour later, the plane landed on a bumpy runway, and Dr Crumpet was in Haiti.

The airport at Port au Prince was almost deserted that hot summer's day. Dr Crumpet was glad that she had brought a wide-brimmed straw hat with her against the heat, and she fanned herself with it whilst seated in the arrivals hall waiting for her luggage to be unloaded. She did not have to wait for long for her two large, light-weight Louis Vuitton suitcases to be unloaded. Two suitcases and hand-luggage was all the baggage that she had. It would not take her long to get through customs, and soon she would be relaxing with a gin-sling or a rum punch at her hotel, ready for a good night's sleep before rising to breakfast on paw-paws and pineapple juice and some fragrant Colombian coffee.

Dr Crumpet picked up her luggage, and moved into the customs hall. As she had anticipated, in this sleepy airport it was empty. Two guards with machine-guns patrolled the exit from the customs hall. It was good to know that security was so visible in Haiti. Dr Crumpet smiled as she heaved her case on to a table before two young and attractive black women of the Haitian Republic Customs and Excise Service, trim and elegant in high heels, blue shirts, and tightly-fitting pencil skirts, with snub-nosed automatics reposing neatly in holsters at the waist. They wore gold Rolex Oysters on their wrists, and their fingers were encrusted with sapphires and diamonds. "Vous avez quelque chose à declarer?" enquired one of the young ladies, looking at her companion with a mischievous smile.

"Non, seulement mes possessions personnelles," replied Dr Crumpet proudly, glad that she could speak the lingua franca of Haiti.

The other customs officer took Dr Crumpet's hand luggage, and tipped its contents onto the table. Out fell Dr Crumpet's powder compact, her sunglasses, her copy of *Pride of the Black Republic*, a copy of that morning's *Guardian*, a packet of tissues, and her wallet, stuffed with $2000 in small denomination US dollar bills - useful, as Mrs Quick had pointed out, in the event that the Haitian hotels and taxi-drivers did not take Amex or Visa.

The girls riffled through the dollar bills and confiscated them on the grounds that Dr Crumpet did not have a licence to import foreign currency. They then pretended that the face-powder in her compact could well be cocaine, and asked her to open her suitcases.

Dismayed, but still believing that she had nothing to fear, Dr Crumpet opened her Louis Vuitton suitcase. Scornfully, the two young ladies of the Haitian customs service extracted Dr Crumpet's dresses and nighties, her blouses, skirts, slips, and petticoats, her bras and other lingerie and stockings from the suitcases, holding each item up one by one and making scornful remarks, before flinging them contemptuously to the floor. When the suitcases were empty, they each took out a knife and slashed at the lining.

Dr Crumpet protested.

"Mais pourquoi faites-vous ça,"she enquired? "Je suis touriste, je ne suis pas smuggler."

The two young women laughed, pleased to be able to divert themselves with a young and attractive and unescorted European woman, a rare type of visitor to Haiti in these days of revolutions and popular unrest. Such of Dr Crumpet's clothes and possessions as they did not choose to keep for themselves would certainly sell for a good price in the bars of Port au Prince.

"Oui, c'est ça, vous êtes smuggler," said the first customs official. "Alors, deshabillez-vous."

"Mais non, pourquoi, je n'ai rien fait... "

But the cool steel of the snub-nosed automatic pressed against her temples meant that Dr Crumpet had little choice but to comply.

"Deshabillez-vous," hissed one of the customs officers. "Tout de suite. Maintenant. Otez vos vêtements." Dr Crumpet began to wonder if the trip to Haiti was such a good idea of Mrs Quick's after all.

"Mais, pas devant ces hommes-là," she said, pointing at the security guards (the Ton Ton Macoutes) who were laughing as they peered in at the door at the door.

The two young ladies shrugged their shoulders.

"Ça ne fait rien. Ce n'est pas de quoi. Alors, maintenant deshabillez-vous."

As Dr Crumpet removed each item of clothing, the two young ladies examined it throughly, running their fingers through the material and the linings to make sure, as they said, that no drugs were hidden there. Soon Dr Crumpet was standing naked, the scattered remnants of her clothes strewn all over the floor, cupping her hands over her breasts in an attempt to conceal them from the leering Ton Tons.

The two young customs officers pored for a long time over Dr Crumpet's passport, where her occupation was still shown as a university lecturer. Then they started to divide her Laura Ashley dresses and lingerie and other clothing and possessions among themselves.

At last they said to Dr Crumpet:

"Eh bien, mam'zelle, c'est fini. Vous pouvez passer."

They handed Dr Crumpet back her possessions.

"Mais comme vous êtes smuggler, toutes vos possessions sont confiscées." They gathered up all of Dr Crumpet's clothes, including the ones she had been wearing, bundled them into her suitcase, and made as if to depart.

"Mais, vous ne pouvez pas me laisser ici comme ça," complained Dr Crumpet.

The two young women looked at each other, and, rendered amiable by the $2000 in small notes that they had confiscated from Dr Crumpet, and pleased by the dresses and finery in her suitcase, relented a little. They rummaged through the case, and took out a white satin mini-slip which would at least cover Dr Crumpet from the waist to nine inches above her knees. This they tossed to her with a slight shrug of their shoulders, and then they departed, leaving Dr Crumpet bare-breasted in the customs hall with nothing but her scanty slip and passport. As the Ton Ton Macoutes peered round the corner into the hall and grinned, Dr Crumpet hastily donned her slip, and clutching her passport in her hand, she hastily scampered past the guards. She then proceeded into immigration, and there the two officers, happy at the opportunity to quiz an attractive and bare-breasted white woman wearing only a scanty slip, slowly examined her passport, and made her fill in many forms, and answer many questions, before reluctantly stamping her passport and letting her proceed on her way. Dr Crumpet scampered into the arrivals lounge. The arrivals lounge was not crowded, but, somewhat shaken by her experiences, Dr Crumpet judged it best not to linger there. She settled down to run at a steady pace, and was soon past the airport perimeter and running along the badly pot-holed road that led into Port au Prince. She began to curse Mrs Quick under her breath for misleading her about the tourist attractions of Haiti, and she blamed herself for having taken so much on trust. Soon she was running barefoot through the scrubland, and reached the sanctuary of a grove of rich tropical vegetation. And there she found a mango tree, and flopping down underneath it, sank her teeth into the rich fruit, and began to consider her position. She had, to be sure, had an unfortunate experience, but it was not the end of the world. Matters might have been much worse. At least she had her slip, and fortunately the weather was warm. Moreover, her SAS training had made her resourceful and resilient. Clearly, all she had to do was contact the British Embassy, explain what had happened to her, and all would be well. There, she could cancel her credit cards and arrange for money to be sent to her from Wales Poste Restante. Judging it better, though, not to wander through the streets of Port au Prince bare breasted and in her skimpy slip in daylight, she resolved to wait until the hours of darkness. And so, building for herself a little den of branches and leaves, so that she was securely concealed from view, Dr Crumpet munched another mango and stretched out on the ground. Soon the weariness of her long flight caught up with her, and she fell into a deep slumber.

*****

Five hours later, Dr Crumpet awoke. She came to with a start in the silence of that Haitian night, for a bewildering moment or two uncertain where she was or how she had got there. And then she remembered the long flight out, the humiliating search at the customs hall, her headlong flight from the airport into the protection of the undergrowth. She shivered in her thin slip, plucked another mango from the nearby tree, and began to consider her best course of action. At least she was in Haiti, that was the main thing, and she would trust to her native wit and resolution, and to her military training, to see her through the rest. The juicy fruit refreshed her, and she wiped her hands on her slip, being anxious to darken its bright whiteness. The first thing to do was hide her passport. Carefully she seized the hem of her slip, and ripped a segment from it, perhaps a foot by eighteen inches wide. Carefully she wrapped her passport inside that protective layer of material. Then, heaping together a small cairn of stones, and placing it carefully in the middle of them, she heaped a further pile of stones on top of it. That, she hoped, would be sufficient protection against wayward bands of insects, and the ravages of the weather. Then, crawling carefully to the edge of the road, she took good observation of her location. Yes, there to the left was a clump of three trees, over there a run-down gas station with rusty signs, there a leaning wooden sign. She would be able to locate the cairn again without too much trouble. Then, feeling that it would be a good idea to disguise the whiteness of her skin, Dr Crumpet went rubbed earth into her hair, face, arms legs and slip, so that she had a poor, decrepit, worn and haggard appearance. Then, carefully, she spied the lights of Port au Prince in the distance, and the hills beyond, and set out for the latter with the aim of making contact with native society and acquiring some of the wonderful zombie powder which Mrs Quick so dearly wanted.

The moon was bright behind the scurrying clouds, and Dr Crumpet made her way, slowly at first, through fields and sugar plantations and dense patches of scrub, tracking across dirt roads and bye-ways and the occasional stagnant pool and stream. Brambles caught at her legs and slip, completing her transformation into a wretched-looking creature. Dr Crumpet made good time. The first bright rays of dawn found her five miles on the other side of Port au Prince, on the edge of a sugar-cane plantation. Before it was fully light, once again Dr Crumpet made herself a little den on the banks of a shady stream. She gathered some berries from a nearby bush, and settled down to observe the activities of the plantation.

When the sun was fully risen, and Dr Crumpet estimated it was about 10 a.m. (for of course she now had no watch, this having been confiscated by the Haitian customs officers) three black women and half-a-dozen teenage boys arrived, and in a leisurely way started to hack at the sugar-cane. They worked in desultory fashion for ninety minutes or so, and then lay down in the shade of a tree, chattering and laughing. Their clothes were torn but brightly coloured. From the pockets of their dresses and trousers they pulled out little packages, and proceeded to eat a simply meal, the sight of which made Dr Crumpet feel very hungry indeed. On the other side of the field was a tumbledown house, from which a wisp of smoke was now arising. An elderly man with greying hair, and a pair of cheap spectacles perched on his nose, emerged, and sitting in a rocking chair smoked a pipe, surveying the scene and from time to time spitting tobacco.

After a two hour break, the party hacked down a few more sugar-canes, and then in leisurely fashion heaped the cut canes on to a waggon standing near the house. As the sun was setting, they pushed the waggon laden with sugar-cane down the lane, singing as they went. Soon the countryside was devoid of human habitation, except for the old man on the verandah, who had now apparently fallen into a deep sleep. As the sun was setting, the man awoke, went into the house, and eventually emerged with a pan. He placed the pan in an open fire in front of the verandah, and soon the smell of wood smoke and the savour of cooked chicken wafted itself across the fields to Dr Crumpet. Cautiously she surveyed the ground. She had seen no-one else in the house all day long. She crawled stealthily round the outside of the field, and approached the shanty from the back. She peered into the windows one by one. No, the old man was alone. This might be the opportunity for which she was looking. As the old man was hunched in front of his fire cooking his chicken, Dr Crumpet drew herself up, and, muddy and dishevelled as she was, approached him to introduce herself.

*****

Forgetting to speak her schoolgirl pidgin French, and distracted by the enticing smell coming from the frying pan, Dr Crumpet walked carefully up to the old man and said:

"Hullo, my name's Antonia Crumpet. I wonder if you can help me?"

The old man looked up without surprise. Dr Crumpet's eyes turned longingly to the frying pan.

"You look hungry," he said slowly. He took an earthenware plate, and with a battered spoon heaped some of the contents of his frying pan on to the plate. This he offered to Dr Crumpet with the generosity so characteristic of the Haitian people.

"You sit down here, missy blanc, and eat."

Dr Crumpet sank to the floor, and eagerly seized the chicken leg in her fingers, and tore at the flesh with her teeth. With her fingers she scooped up some of the sweet corn and other vegetables and wolfed that down too. The old man watched her for a moment, and then went into his hut, and returned with some bread, two small earthenware cups, and a jug of the potent locally distilled white rum.

"You am hungry, missy blanc," he laughed, "you sure am hungry."

"You speak English," said Dr Crumpet in surprise.

The old man made no reply, but watched impassively as she continued to eat her food. He lit up his pipe again, poured two generous portions of the rum into the earthenware cups, took a sip out of one himself, and handed the other to Dr Crumpet.

"Drink, missy blanc, drink," he laughed. "This will do you good."

Dr Crumpet paused uncertainly, but took a tiny sip, and then as the sweet and fiery spirit went down her that, took a deep gulp. The old man handed her the jug, and gestured for her to help herself. Dr Crumpet refilled her cup, and then more slowly took another deep draught, as she tore a fragment off the loaf and mopped up her plate. Hunger made the meal one of the most delicious she had ever had in her life.

"That was good, thank you, you're very kind," she said gratefully.

The old man looked on impassively.

"Tonight you eat, tomorrow you help cut the fields."

He gestured towards the lush acres of sugar cane, and pointed to a machete leaning gainst a wall.

Dr Crumpet nodded slowly. The old man seemed kindly, and she was willing to help him. Maybe she could stay with him for a few days, working in exchange for her keep.

"I'm from England, " she said, as the rum loosened her tongue, and felt that she would like to give some account of herself. "I came here on a holiday to see this wonderful country, but the customs officials thought I was a smuggler and confiscated just about everything that I had. They were outrageous. I shall complain to the consul when I can find out where he lives."

The old man puffed slowly and meditatively at his pipe, and offered Dr Crumpet a slice of mango.

It was the perfect accompaniment to the rich and powerful rum. Dr Crumpet sank her teeth into the juicy fruit, which oozed over her mouth and fingers, and on to her stained and muddy slip; but by now she was past caring about her appearance.

The old man tossed a couple of logs on to the fire, and they gazed into the flames in companiable silence. The sun sank below the horizon, and suddenly the darkness of the tropics was upon them. The moon was again visible behind the flitting clouds,. With darkness, the animals of the night emerged from their lairs. A wild cat crouched on a nearby wall, its eyes gleaming in the reflections of the fire. In the distance, the low and insistent throbbing of the drums could be heard.

Dr Crumpet started.

"What is that?" she enquired.

The old man made no reply. But Dr Crumpet thought she knew what it was - it was, for a certainty, the voodoo drums! She was on the right track after all, and would succeed in getting the zombie paste with a little bit of luck. There were many questions which she felt the old man could answer and which she wanted to ask, but she sensed that he would not do so just yet. So she sat staring into the flames, and shivering a little at the cold. At length the old man went into his hut, and returned with a cushion and a dirty blanket.

He placed them on the wooden and decrepit verandah.

"You sleep there, missy blanc," he said, and without a further word went into his hut, closing the door behind him. Dr Crumpet remained where she was, staring into the flames of the fire, and drinking another couple of cups of home-distilled rum, which she most certainly needed. and then, feeling strangely content, weary but with her spirits decidedly restored, she stretched down on the wooden verandah, lay her dishevelled tresses on the cushion and pulled the dirty blanket over herself, and was soon lost to the world in a deep and sound sleep.

*****

At 6 a.m., Dr Crumpet awoke, feeling much refreshed. She flung aside the blanket, breathed in the pure and unpolluted air of Haiti, where there was no heavy industry, and, observing a rain barrel half full of water, dipped her hair and face and arms in it. The cool water made her skin tingle, and she felt aglow with health again. Seizing the machete, she marched to the end of the field, where the Haitian women had left off their labours the day before. Dr Crumpet set to work with a will, and soon developed a regular and effective rhythm. Her gleaming machete slashed through the canes, scything them down in an efficient and regular pattern. She hardly paused for three hours, until, pausing to mop her brow, she became aware that the Haitian women labourers of the day before had arrived, and were gazing in amazement at the sight of her work - though whether because she was a 'blanc', or whether at the tremendous progress she had made, she was not clear. As she stood there uncertainly in her sweat-stained slip, she became aware of the old man coming towards her. Unobserved by Dr Crumpet, he had been siting on the verandah watching her progress for the last half-hour or so. He spoke sharply to the women, and they commenced their labours too.

The old man had brought Dr Crumpet a cup of mango juice and she drained it gratefully, before resuming her labours. When the Haitian women paused and took out their lunch, the old man beckoned her, and offered her some bread and fruit, which she gratefully munched. And then she set to work with a will again, and the sugar canes fell victim to her tireless energy. The Haitian women gazed resentfully, but made to effort to interfere, being evidently in awe of the old man. Dr Crumpet worked on indefatigably, until before she realised it, the Haitian women had gone. She felt a light touch on her shoulders, and the old man said:

"It is enough - come, we eat."

She followed him back to the hut, plunged her head once more into the barrel of rain water, and gratefully sank down beside the fire, on which a steaming pot of food was cooking. He brought out a full jug of rum once more, together with the two simple earthenware cups, and Dr Crumpet drank deeply, tired but happy after her day's labours. Perhaps now she would be able to win the old man's confidence again.

"What is your name? "she enquired. "I told you I am called Antonia."

"Me, Jean-Paul,"replied the old man slowly.

"Well, cheers, Jean-Paul," said Dr Crumpet, draining her cup of rum, and pouring out another. Goodness, she really needed a drink after her day's labours.

The old man sipped his rum meditatively, and puffed at his pipe. Normally, Dr Crumpet, as a non-smoker, would have found this objectionable, but here, in Haiti, where the smell of the tobacco mingled with the smell of the burning logs on the fire, everything seemed natural and acceptable.

The food once again tasted delicious, and a fresh and juicy pineapple made an excellent dessert. After five cups of rum, Dr Crumpet felt bold enough to turn the conversation to the subject of magic.

"Those drums we heard last night, they were voodoo drums, weren't they?" she asked.

The old man made no reply.

"Actually, I am quite interested in voodoo myself, and in the occult generally," she continued determinedly. "In fact, that's partly why I decided to take a holiday in Haiti, because I wanted to find out more about the traditions of the island. Lots of people in England are interested in them you know." Here in the tropics, Dr Crumpet felt that she could talk freely. "In fact, Pauline Quick - that's the lady I share a cottage within Hay-on-Wye - and I are in a way of being witches ourselves. There's quite a tradition of witchcraft in England, you know."

Jean-Paul looked at Dr Crumpet with astonishment, and then he began to laugh.

Dr Crumpet was puzzled.

"What's so funny, Jean-Paul, what have I said?"

Jean-Paul fell off his chair with amusement, and was now rolling on the ground doubled up with laughter.

"Oh, missy blanc, missy blanc," he roared. "English witches! Everyone knows they're no good!"

Jean-Paul went back into the house, still laughing uncontrollably, tossed Dr Crumpet her cushion and blanket, and returned to his hut, laughing uproariously still.

Dr Crumpet was left outside, a little resentful, to soothe her injured feelings with the remnants of the jar of rum.

*****

Three days later, when Dr Crumpet has finished her stint in the fields, Jean-Paul's eyes were still streaming with laughter.

"English witches," he remarked helplessly, pointing at Dr Crumpet with his left hand as he handed her her dinner.

"Missy blanc is an English witch! Ho, ho, ho ho!"

"But I am," responded Dr Crumpet, irritated. "Pauline and I have put curses on people, and soon after, Percy Bodgering, our head of department, died! We made a doll and stuck pins into him, you know. Anyway, we're not just English witches, we practice in Wales now, where we live."

"Dolls! Curses! Pins! Wales!" Jean-Paul was suffused with helpless laughter, as he tilted the jug of rum to his lips and drained a deep swig.

Dr Crumpet was hurt to be thus slighted by Jean-Paul.

"Of course," she sniffed, as she too drained a cup of rum, "I realise that by the standards of Haiti our prowess may not be all that marvellous. As I say, that's partly why I came here. But believe me, Pauline and I are quite advanced by English standards. There are not many more effective witches than us there."

Jean-Paul nodded his head in agreement.

Dr Crumpet was mollified somewhat.

"Actually, Jean-Paul, it was my friend Pauline Quick who suggested I come here. She had read this book about zombies, and how there is a poison which puts people into a catatonic trance, another which keeps them there, and a third which is an antidote. She thought that if I came here I might be able to get some. Can I? Can you help me in this? Do you know anyone who owns some zombies?"

Jean-Paul passed her the rum jug, took out his pipe again, and puffed contemplatively.

Dr Crumpet drank draught after draught of the rum, to which she had now become quite addicted, and felt its tingling warmth course through her veins. She stared into the fire, and clasped her arms round her shoulders, waiting for Jean-Paul to reply.

"Yes, I know of zombies, and of those who own them," he replied slowly. "But missy blanc, they are bad bad men, men such as you would not want to have to do with."

In the distance the sound of the drums started up again, and an insistent throbbing echoed in the otherwise silent night. Dr Crumpet lifted up her head.

"The sound of the zombie drums?" she enquired.

"The sound of the zombie drums," he agreed gravely.

"Jean-Paul, I want to meet them," she said insistently.

Jean-Paul inhaled his pipe of tobacco, and let the smoke drift out of his nostrils.

"Not tonight," he said at length. "In a few days time, perhaps. I need to make enquiries. But if I do, missy blanc, it will be at your own peril. And now I go to bed."

And once again Dr Crumpet was left by herself in the open air, with only the glowing embers of the fire and the jug of rum for company.

Two days later, whilst Dr Crumpet was loading the cut sugar cane on to the cart, and was struggling to push it down the rutted lane to the little mill where great stone grinders would extract the juice, she saw Jean-Paul slip away across the fields, with a bright red kerchief around his neck, and stained white straw hat on his head, carrying a staff in his hand. He was away for seven hours, and Dr Crumpet had finished her day's labours, and was sitting drinking rum by the side of the fire, stirring the simmering pot of food that she had ventured to prepare for their evening meal when Jean-Paul returned, mopping his brow with his kerchief.

He gratefully took the jug of rum that Dr Crumpet proffered him, and stretched out full length on the grass. They ate their meal in silence, both weary from their day's labours.

When he had eaten, Jean-Paul went into the house and returned with another full jug of rum, from which he helped himself liberally, before passing it to Dr Crumpet.   "Well, missy blanc," he said at last, as his strength returned to him. "I have been to see the zombie men. Tell me, my English witch," - again a bleak smile crossed his lips - "tell me, do you really want the zombie paste?"

"Yes," replied Dr Crumpet eagerly. "My associate Pauline Quick would love to have some."

Jean-Paul grunted.

"Well, the zombie men say you can have some - but at a price, a terrible price, my poor missy blanc. But you are young, and strong, and may survive the ordeal." He sighed. "In three days time they will initiate you into the order, as a favour to me. I have told them it will be good for people in England to learn from Haiti. So, for two more days you work, and then on the third you rest and prepare yourself for the ceremony of the night."

Jean-Paul went indoors with a sigh, as Dr Crumpet wiped her greasy hands in satisfaction on her by now stained and tattered slip, and drank herself into oblivion on great doses of rum. Rum, no doubt would anaesthetize her against the gruesome horrors of the zombie ceremony, and then she would get the powder and paste, and Pauline would be pleased and proud of her! Happy and stupefied, Dr Crumpet stretched out again on the verandah, and was soon fast asleep.

*****

With Jean-Paul in the lead, at last Dr Crumpet was on her way to meet the practitioners of voodoo. Before going to bed the previous night, she had rinsed her slip in the stream, and hung it out to dry over the railings of the verandah. The sunshine of the following day had done its work, and by mid-afternoon the slip, though still somewhat torn and damp, was cleaner than it had been for some days. Dr Crumpet had spent the morning huddled in a blanket, waiting for her garment to dry, whilst Jean-Paul busied himself in his hut. At four o'clock he brought her out a jug of rum and advised her to drink deep. So Dr Crumpet sank four cupfuls of rum to steady her nerves, and at length returned behind a wall to change back into her slip. It was a nuisance that Jean-Paul had no spare women's clothing in the hut. The sun set, and Jean-Paul drained his cup of rum, and picked up his staff.

He laughed a throaty laugh.

"All right missy blanc - we go if you are ready. Follow me, and say nothing, whatever happens."

Jean-Paul set off at a long loping stride, and headed across the cane fields towards the hills, whence the low rumble of muffled drums could now insistently be heard. They walked through cane fields and woodlands, and then after about an hour the track narrowed and led upwards into the hills through dense vegetation. The way narrowed to no more than a single track. Brambles and creepers caught at Dr Crumpet's slip, inflicting further tears. She was glad that her feet were hardened now by her days of barefoot labour in Jean-Paul's fields. They came to a gate, topped with a gleaming white skull. Dr Crumpet bit back a cry. They climbed over the gate, and followed a trail of bones to a clearing. The noise of the drums became louder and louder. And then they breasted a hill, and there, in a small clearing in a hollow on the other side, a hundred yards away, a crowd of Haitian men and women were whirling around a tree-trunk adorned with several human skulls and bleached bones. A great bare-chested giant of a man wandered around between the dancers, drinking a concoction of blood and animal entrails out of another skull. Three small fires were burning a short distance away. Dr Crumpet shuddered in spite of herself.

Jean-Paul pointed at the giant black man with the skull.

"That is Henri," he said. "He is expecting you. I have told him that you are an English witch, and that he should give you what you want. But you will have to pay the price, and be initiated into their circle. Do you want to go?"

Dr Crumpet gritted her teeth, and nodded slowly.

Jean-Paul looked sad.

"Then goodbye, missy blanc, and good luck."

He held out his hand sadly. Dr Crumpet took it.

"Thank you, Jean-Paul, I'm truly grateful for all your help."

Jean-Paul pointed to Henri.

"Go to him," he said. And then without a further word or backward glance, he turned around and left Dr Crumpet in the shadows of a tree on the brow of the hill. Dr Crumpet looked at his departing figure with some regret, feeling that she had lost a friend. She shivered, and put her arms around her shoulders. Then, softly and somewhat uncertainly, she began to approach the dancing throng below. The drums throbbed hypnotically in her ears. As she approached two grinning Ton Ton Macoutes stepped from behind a tree, with machine pistols at the ready, and asked who she was.

Dr Crumpet gestured towards Henri, and mimed that she was expected. In the distance Henri observed her, and signalled to the two guards to let her through. They thrust the barrels of their guns indecently into her body, laughed, and then she was through. She walked uncertainly to Henri, who laid the bloody skull from which he was drinking on the ground. Dr Crumpet put out her hand, but Henri ignored it. Then he laughed out aloud, his teeth gleaming white in the darkness.

"So, you want the zombie powder," he remarked. "I think I have what you want here. Perched on a rock behind him were three small dark green bottles. "Here it is - the powder to make people zombies, the paste to restore movement to their limbs when they are taken from the grave, and the antidote. That's what, you want, isn't it?"

"Yes, Jean-Paul said you would give it to me,"answered Dr Crumpet more confidently. "I can't pay you now, I'm afraid, as all my money was stolen when I arrived in Haiti, but I'll send you an American Express money order when I get back to England."

Henri laughed, and gave a sudden signal with his left hand.

Suddenly Dr Crumpet felt her arms being pinioned from behind, and from out of the shadows emerged a dozen Ton Ton Macoutes, half-a-dozen other villainous-looking thugs and two young women in leather boots, blue blouses and tight skirts with pistols slung around their waist. The very same women, as Dr Crumpet realised, who had searched and robbed her in the customs hall of the Haiti international airport! Suddenly Dr Crumpet wished that Jean-Paul were still here, and began to feel in very great danger. She had read that the Ton Ton Macoutes and officialdom in general in Haiti were deeply involved in the secret world of voodoo, and it looked as if this was true!

Henri stooped and brought his face to within two inches of hers.

"The zombie secrets are not for blancs," he hissed. "But we told Jean-Paul we would give you the powder. And so we will. We will sprinkle the powder on your skin, and you will be our white zombie, the first in these parts for fifty years."

He beckoned to the two young women of the Haitian customs service, who advanced with an amused and complacent expression, laughing at the helpless Dr Crumpet. They stood gloatingly before her, and at a further signal from Henri, as the first young lady laughingly pulled down her slip with two violent yanks, the second advanced with the intention of sprinkling the powder on the naked Dr Crumpet's breasts and stomach.

And now, in this moment of extreme peril, Dr Crumpet was glad that Mrs Quick had made her join the SAS a year before. Deftly kicking away the tattered remnants of her sip, she first kicked Henri in the groin with her work-hardened feet. A split second later she lashed out with her heels at the shins on the men who were pinioning her from behind, and with startled yelps they let her go. Freed, and angry but ice-cool, Dr Crumpet hurled herself forward and relieved the first of the customs officers of her two 9mm Browning automatics, a weapon she knew well from her small arms training at Bradbury Lines. Without a pause Dr Crumpet somersaulted forward towards the undergrowth, firing with deadly accuracy as she went, and leaving Henri, two Ton Ton Macoutes, and the second customs official dead in their tracks, with holes neatly drilled through the centre of their foreheads. A second later she was in the cover of the dense undergrowth, and two further shots dropped the two Ton Ton Macoutes with machine pistols to the ground. There was a sudden shocked silence, and the black men fled from the corpse bestrewn copse. The customs official whose guns Dr Crumpet had taken sank to her knees sobbing. Dr Crumpet remained in cover for a full five minutes. All around her she could her the distant sound of the remnants of the gang crashing through the undergrowth. The sounds faded into the distance, and now all that could be heard was the shocked sobbing of the weaponless young lady sobbing shattered on the grass. At last Dr Crumpet judged it safe to emerge from the undergrowth . With a gun in each hand, she stood naked over the sobbing figure of Nicolette, and gestured to her to rise to her feet. As she did so, Dr Crumpet backed away, the guns in her hand pointed straight towards Nicolette's heart.

"Ne me tuez pas," whispered Nicolette, in her attractive lilting patois. "C'était seulement une drôlerie."

Nicolette seemed unable to believe what had happened.

"Alright," agreed Dr Crumpet. "But I need your clothes. Votre jupe! Vos sabots, votre blouse. Donnez-les moi!"

The terrified Nicolette took of her skirt, blouse, lingerie and boots. Dr Crumpet made her stand with her hands behind her neck facing a tree trunk, and then thankfully she put on Nicolette's skirt, blouse and boots and gun-belt. Decently clothed for the first time for a fortnight, her morale rose considerably. She thrust one gun back into its holster, and kept the other trained on Nicolette. She picked up Antoinette's handbag, and tipped its contents out on to the grass. Then she carefully took the bottles containing the zombie paste and its antidote from the ledge, wrapped them in various items of clothing removed from the corpses scattered all around her, and placed then in the shoulder bag. Finally, she retrieved Nicolette's hat and put it on her head. Dr Crumpet then bound Nicolette's hands and feet tightly to a tree with belts taken from the dead Ton Ton Macoutes. Finally, the young Englishwoman ascertained the location of the British Embassy in Port au Prince from the terrified Nicolette. She debated for a moment whether to kill Nicolette in the approved SAS manner by putting a bullet through the nape of her neck, and decided that, since the survivors of the gang would already be trying to raise the alarm, to do so would be gratuitous and unnecessary. And so, when she was satisfied that the terrified Nicolette was clearly telling the truth, she gagged her with the dead Antoinette's blouse, then, feeling too exhausted to execute Nicolette in the approved manner, calmly pressed the gun against Nicolette's temples and blew her brains out. Finally Dr Crumpet departed from the scene with the zombie paste, leaving Nicolette's lifeless body with its bloody and unrecognisable features drooping like a rag doll from the trunk of the tree.

CHAPTER FOURTEEN

CRUMPET IN HAITI (2)

After she had escaped with the zombie paste from the Ton Ton Macoutes and the ladies of the Haitian Customs Service, Dr Crumpet travelled through the night, and then hid and slept throughout the day in the scrubland. Two nights later, after having made a detour to retrieve her passport, at 2 a.m., she was approaching the strife-torn city of Port au Prince, then in some disorder as a result of one of the abortive coup attempts that were so frequent on that unhappy isle. But in the small hours of the morning, few people were on the streets. Dr Crumpet had slung her boots around her neck so as to walk barefoot and in silence. With one of the automatics tucked into the waist of her skirt, she felt reasonably confident as she padded through the darkened streets. The city's power supply had failed, and there were no lights to be seen. Signs of disorder were everywhere - burned-out cars, rubble in the streets, houses scarred by bullet holes and shells, boarded-up shops. Once or twice Dr Crumpet heard the noise of drunken Ton Ton Macoutes as they roamed the streets at will, but she melted into the shadows and avoided them. At last she found the street on which the British Embassy was situated, and sidled from house to house until she came to it. Two Ton Ton Macoutes were slumped in slumber in front of the barred and bolted gates. Silently Dr Crumpet scaled the walls, and dropped down into the Embassy compound with a sigh of relief. She straightened up, and went directly towards the entrance porch. The whole building was silent and forbidding, its windows tightly shuttered. Dr Crumpet mounted the steps and prepared to bang on the door until she was admitted. And there she was transfixed by a fading typewritten notice:

'As a result of recent government cut-backs, the British Embassy is closed. All commercial enquiries and requests for visas should be directed to the Office of the British Consul in Miami, Florida, USA. Other British interests are now being handled by the Consulate of the Republic of San Marino, 625, Avenue de l'Indépendence, to which all other enquiries and requests for consular assistance should initially be made.'

Dr Crumpet's heart sank. Then suddenly she remembered that she had passed the Avenue de l'Indépendance a mile or so back. So she retraced her steps, and as the first streaks of dawn were rising in the east, she found herself outside a run-down white-stuccoed house, with a garden that had rather gone to seed, in what was clearly one of the more fashionable parts of Port au Prince. Once again the gate was locked, and once again Dr Crumpet made her way into the grounds without difficulty. There were no guards on duty this time. In the porch a small brass plate read: *Consulate of the Republic of San Marino: Acting Consul, Signor Jacopo del Amore.* Safe at last! Dr Crumpet felt tired but happy, and realising that it was still very early in the day, and thinking that she might get a more favourable reception if she presented herself at a more civilised hour, she reconnoitred the grounds, and then retreated to a slatted summer house in one corner of the rear lawn, there to doze fitfully in a canvass armchair until, waking with a start, she saw by the watch she had stolen from Antoinette that it was 10.30 a.m. She hid her automatic in her shoulder-bag, brushed the sleep out of her eyes, tossed back her mane of auburn hair, and returned, passport in hand, to the front door of the residence. She rang the bell, and it jangled within.

A moment or two later the door was opened by a lithe, dark-eyed, tousle-haired, handsome young man of some thirty-four years of age, dressed in a light-blue towelled bath robe, a cup of coffee in his left hand. His eyes brightened when they say the somewhat dishevelled, but still clearly attractive figure of Dr Crumpet.

"Hullo, I wonder if you can help me,?" she asked politely, holding our her passport. "It says at the embassy that you are now representing British interests here, and I'm afraid that I have got myself into a bit of bother."

The young man opened the door politely, and invited her in.

"But of course, please come in and tell me all about it. You must excuse me for not being dressed this late in the morning. The fact is," he laughed, "that business in the consulate is rather quiet now with all the trouble in Haiti. In fact, I rarely have any visitors at all."

He ushered Dr Crumpet into a light, bright room, clean and sparse, but furnished with cane and wicker furniture. One of the tables was set for breakfast, and Signor del Amore was clearly in the middle of this. The fragrant aroma of coffee and fresh croissants wafted across the room.

Signor del Amore looked sharply at Dr Crumpet.

"You look all in, my dear," he remarked. "Sit down and help yourself to some coffee and croissants. I was just in the middle of my breakfast. You'll join me I hope? You need have no further fear. This is San Marinan territory, and the Haitians respect it. And then you can tell me all about your troubles, and I shall endeavour to be of what assistance I can to a citizen of a country whose interests I have the honour to represent here."

He ushered Dr Crumpet into a chair, and taking a large continental-style cup from a glass-fronted wall-cabinet, he poured Dr Crumpet a delicious cup of strong black coffee. She drained it eagerly to the dregs, and closed her eyes in sheer sensual pleasure as the revivifying liquid trickled down her throat. Signor del Amore refilled her cup, and proffered her the basket of croissants. Dr Crumpet ate quickly at first, assuaging her keen hunger. The warm bread and comfits tasted delicious. She began to feel at peace with the world, as the strain and tiredness of the last days flowed out of her body.

Signor del Amore studied his guest attentively as she ate. She was dirty and a little travel-stained, but she seemed to have the most magnificent figure. Yet her knees were torn and scratched, her boots scuffed, and she was all too clearly wearing the uniform of a female official of the Haitian customs service! Ah well, he thought philosophically, the mystery would explain itself soon enough. "You look quite exhausted, *ma pauvre fille,*" he sighed. "Let me give you a little medicinal brandy." He went to the cabinet again, and brought back a tumbler filled with an exceedingly generous portion of Courvoisier.

"Drink this," he commanded. "Go on, it will do you good!"

Dr Crumpet drained it at a gulp, and held out the tumbler for some more.

Signor del Amore refilled her glass, and leaving the bottle on the table, told her to help herself. To keep her company, he poured a little in a glass himself.

"And now," he enquired, "Do you want to tell me all about it?"

"If I do, you will let me stay here, won't you?" asked Dr Crumpet a trifle uncertainly. "And you will help me get out of this infernal country? I heartily wish I had never come here, I've had some terrible experiences."

Suddenly, in a cathartic re-action from the traumatic events of the last few days, Dr Crumpet burst in to tears, and buried her face in her hands. She had after all only just escaped being assaulted, she had killed for the first time in her life, and she had nearly been turned in to a zombie.

Jacopo put his arms around her protectively, and raised her to her feet.

"*Ma pauvre*, you are quite safe here," he said re-assuringly. "Whatever you have done, I will not let the Haitians get you, you may count on me for that." He raised her hands to his lips, and kissed them reverently. "Certainly you must tell me all about it - but not now. First, you must bathe, sleep and rest. Come with me."

He led the trembling Dr Crumpet back into the hall, and up a flight of wooden steps to the first floor. Then he ushered her into a clean and spacious guest-room at the back of his residence. The shutters were drawn, but he turned on the bedside light, and revealed a clean and pleasantly furnished room, with stained and polished parquet floor, a massive old mahogany four-poster bed, a capacious wardrobe, a bedside table, a shelf of books, some cane chairs and a writing-desk, a wardrobe and two chests of drawers. In a spacious alcove, screened from the bedroom by a curtain and folding screen, was a bathroom, and Signor del Amore went into it and turned on the taps. From the wardrobe he took a pale blue full-length dressing gown of light linen material, and gave it to Dr Crumpet.

"Put this on," he commanded, "and let us get rid of that uniform of the Haitian customs service." He smiled. "Yes, it's very recognisable, I'm afraid. Come, go the bathroom, and give your clothes to me."

Dr Crumpet stepped behind the curtain into the bathroom, and slipped out of the blouse and skirt. She donned the dressing-gown, and handed him her clothes.

"That's all there is," she explained through the curtain. "As I said, I've had a terrible time. But you're right, I'm tired, and it will be better to tell you later. Perhaps you could get my clothes washed, they're filthy but that's all I've got."

"No, we burn them," he replied calmly as she emerged in the pale blue dressing gown, her golden hair tumbling down her shoulders. "You can wear whatever you like of these." He pulled back the doors of the wardrobe, and revealed large numbers of lacy slips and petticoats hanging there on one side, together with skirts and suits and summery frocks neatly arrayed on their hangers on the other. He pulled open the side drawers to reveal a quantity of lingerie. At the bottom was a rack of boots and shoes.

Dr Crumpet gasped.

"And in here also there are things for you - ." Jacopo pulled out the top drawer of the tallboy, and trickled a pair of filmy stockings through his hands. "I think you will find that all your needs can be met from here," he continued. "And now you bathe and sleep. Take your time. I shall be downstairs, and I am not going out today. And then you can tell me all about it."

Dr Crumpet felt that she could trust Jacopo. She smiled wanly, and went into the bathroom. She luxuriated for a few moments in the lovely warm water, letting the stains and filth of the last few days soak away. On the shelf by the bath stood a rich array of bath salts, unguents and perfumes, which she poured into the water in generous quantities. Then, returning to the bedroom, she saw that Jacopo had laid a white diaphanous nightgown on the bed. Gratefully she put it on, and slipped between the cool linen sheets of the four-poster bed. She was asleep as soon as her head hit the pillow.

*****

'Off with that girdle, like heavens Zone glistering,
But a far fairer world encompassing

....
Unpin that spangled breastplate which you wear
That th'eyes of busie folles may be stopt there.
Unlace yourself, for that harmonious chyme
Tells me from you, that now it is bed time.

....
Licence my roaving hands and let them go,
Before, behind, between, above, below'
(John Donne, *To His Mistris Going to Bed*)

Eight hours later Dr Crumpet awoke, feeling utterly refreshed. She bathed again in the blissfully hot water of the en suite bathroom, and luxuriated once more in the delightful unguents that adorned the bathroom shelves - rose water, perfume, green bath crystals, scented soap. Dr Crumpet dried herself carefully with a massive yellow bath-towel, and then carefully poured a liberal portion of talcum powder over her soft white skin. Then she went back into the bedroom, and examined the contents of the wardrobe, tallboy, and chest of drawers. She was a little surprised, but nevertheless entranced to find whole drawers full of lingerie, slips, stockings, girdles, and a wide range of frocks, skirts, blouses, suits and dresses. She dressed with some care, luxuriating in the feel of clean white satin and lace close against her skin. She donned a lacy blue bra, a matching girdle, filmy stockings, a satin slip, and pale blue summery dress, and polished black leather shoes. She felt like a million dollars, after the previous days of sweat and labour in the fields. She was a Western woman once again.

Merrily she tripped downstairs, her high heels clip-clopping on the wooden floor. Jacopo rose from his armchair to meet her, a glass of champagne in his hand. With his free hand he gently took Dr Crumpet's left hand, and raised it to his lips. He ushered her into the living room, a pleasantly uncluttered room with polished parquet floor, cane furniture, and a deeply cushioned sofa in one of its alcoves, and poured her a foaming glass of champagne.

"To us," he raised a glass in a toast.

"To us," responded Dr Crumpet softly.

When the first bottle of champagne has been despatched, and the second one opened, Dr Crumpet felt that she should give Signor del Amore a suitably modified and sanitised version of her tale.

"It's like this," she explained. "My friend and associate Pauline Quick and I run a bookshop in Hay-on-Wye in Wales. It's called the Magic Women bookshop, we specialise in works on women and witches. And Pauline thought that it would be worth while for me to pay a trip to Haiti, to check out the book-stalls and see whether there were any books on magic that it would be worth while buying. We had heard of the reputation of Haiti for voodoo, of course."

"Did you not know that your own Foreign Office advises all British citizens not to visit Haiti - because of the unrest?" asked Signor del Amore.

"No," replied Dr Crumpet simply. "Pauline never told me about that. I knew almost nothing about Haiti. When I landed at the airport, two dreadful young women from the customs service confiscated all my possessions, including all my clothes except a slip - they said I was a smuggler, which was absurd!"

"Quite," replied Signor del Amore indignantly.

"Anyway," continued Dr Crumpet. "I lived rough for a while, and then one day I met the very customs officers who had robbed me of all my stuff, walking in a country lane. So I knocked one out, and made the other give me her blouse and skirt, which is why I was wearing them when I arrived here. And that's about it, really. Of course, I didn't really get to see any of the bookshops."

"Fabulous," said Jacopo, raising Dr Crumpet's hands to his lips and kissing them again. "I think you were wonderful and very brave."

"Well, I like to give as good as I get," said Dr Crumpet with a smile, feeling a rapport with the sympathetic Jacopo.

Jacopo ushered Dr Crumpet into the dining room and sat her down at the polished mahogany table, and served her a delicious melon.

"How come you have such admirable arrangements here?" asked Dr Crumpet. "I thought the electricity in Port au Prince had been cut off?"

"We San Marinans know how to make ourselves comfortable," answered Jacopo with a smile. "The consulate here has its own power generator, there is plenty of wood in our extensive grounds to keep it going, and that takes care of the hot water, air conditioning, and the freezer. Once a year the San Marino government sends out a large container of supplies - tinned pineapple juice, cans of meat, wine and liquor and fruit and so on, and that keeps me going for quite a long while. And then one of the consulate servants shops for me in the local markets. Don't you worry, I know how to adapt to life here OK."

He smiled, his teeth gleaming white amidst his saturnine complexion.

For dinner Jacopo had prepared a simple chicken casserole, accompanied by local freshly prepared vegetables, and washed down by a really excellent Chablis. The casserole was succeeded by an ice-cream gateaux, and a bottle of sweet Alsatian pudding wine. They chattered happily throughout the meal, and enjoyed each other's company a lot. Dr Crumpet had not had such an enjoyable meal in such company for years, whilst Jacopo was entranced with his pretty and captivating guest.

Dr Crumpet felt languorous and very amenable to Jacopo's suggestion that they should take their coffee in the drawing room.

Dusk had now fallen, and Jacopo closed the shutters, and turned on the soft subdued lighting that illuminated a snug and cosily furnished room. A large and comfortable sofa stood before the hearth. The coffee was simmering in a percolator by the side of the hearth. Jacopo poured the delicate and aged brandy into two large balloon-shaped glasses, and then made Dr Crumpet a large and creamy cup of fragrant coffee, served with a delicate after-dinner mint. Jacopo placed a CD of Chopin's piano music on his CD player, and turned the volume control to low. As Dr Crumpet sipped her brandy, she was emboldened to enquire why he had so many items of women's clothing in his house.

"They belong to my sister," he replied easily, as the gentle music of Chopin resonated from the walls. "She's very much your height and build. She was going to spend the summer with me, and ordered a lot of new clothes for the occasion from the Italian fashion houses, and had them sent here in advance. But then because of all the troubles she decided not to come after all. As the postal service is now somewhat unreliable, she told me to keep them here. She always does keep a good deal of clothing here for her occasional visits - lingerie is hard to find in Haiti, you know, and it saves her a lot of trouble."

Dr Crumpet's curiosity was satisfied. Her well-being was complete, as she laid her flowing tresses back against the cushions, and Jacopo joined her on the sofa, both of them replete with food and good wine. And it seemed the most natural thing in the world that Jacopo was turning his sensitive features towards her, and gazing deep into her eyes as he smoothed her auburn tresses away from her forehead.

"*Ma chère Antoine, ma pauvre petite*, you have had a hard time. Has anyone told you that you are a very beautiful woman?" Gently and tenderly he laid a kiss upon Dr Crumpet's smooth forehead. He kissed the tip of her left ear, and then the tip of her right. He kissed Dr Crumpet's closed eyes, he placed a tender kiss upon her nose, and reverently and gently placed his lips against the softness of her own. And suddenly Dr Crumpet was kissing him, tongue to tongue with a warmth and ardour that she had never experienced from Mrs Quick's kisses. It seemed that every bone in her body trembled and turned to water.

"Be gentle with me, Jacopo, please' she said. "I am so nervous. I have never made love with a man before, only with a woman, Mrs Quick."

"Oh, *ma pauvre* Antonia," whispered Jacopo. "But why? You are so pretty. You are the sweetest and most wonderful and most beautiful woman. Have no fear, I will be very gently with you, and educate you in the ways of loving men. We will take it very slowly, step by step. We have time, do we not, *ma chère* Antonia? In any case there is no way of leaving Haiti for the next two weeks."

"We have time," whispered Dr Crumpet, feeling safe and secure with the tender and loving Jacopo.

"My dear Antonia Crumpet, my darling," Jacopo gazed deeply into her eyes. "You know I love you, my darling and charming Antonia," he said.

Dr Crumpet did not demur as Jacopo gently unzipped her dress, eased it from her and let it slide gently to the floor. Deftly and lovingly he raised her lacy satin slip up to her hips, and nuzzled her stocking-tops with his lips, placing tender and reverential little kisses on her stocking-tops and on the soft white flesh of her thighs, and then gently stoking them with his finger-tips. Dr Crumpet did not resist as Jacopo suggested that beauty so great as hers in very truth did not need the adornment of clothing. She lay there tranquilly as he removed her slip, then kissed her naked shoulders, her bra, her stockings, and her knees and feet. Soon they were fondling and caressing each other passionately amidst the deep and yielding cushions of the sofa, slowly shedding their apparel. Dr Crumpet felt at peace with the world, radiant and tranquil in her loveliness, fulfilled in a way which she never had been before through the tribadism of Mrs Quick. Jacopo fondled and caressed Dr Crumpet and kissed her tenderly many times as she lay there in her bra, her stockings, and her white girdle. Then he gathered Dr Crumpet into his arms, and carried her gently to the large bed in her room. There, with many endearments, he unclipped her stockings and removed her bra, before turning her on to her stomach, slowly pulling off her girdle, and patting her gently on the bottom several times in a friendly fashion. He slipped into bed beside her, and there they kissed and caressed with many tender embraces until slumber overtook Dr Crumpet's lovely eyes.

*****

Dr Crumpet slept a deep and dreamless sleep. It was half past ten in the morning when she awoke, the sun streaming through the gently opened shutters of her room, a light breeze wafting the scent of flowers over her balcony. She half rose, and shook her tousled hair, and stretched out her arms luxuriously. Jacopo entered the room wearing only a light blue robe belted loosely at the waist. He carried a tray on which reposed a plate of croissants, a steaming pot of fragrant coffee, and a jug of freshly squeezed orange juice. He threw off his robe, and clambered into bed beside Dr Crumpet, they kissed and cuddled again for a moment, and then sat happily snuggled up together munching croissants and drinking coffee. Then Jacopo carried Dr Crumpet in his arms to the bathroom, and placed her tenderly in the circular whirlpool bath, before joining her himself. They laughed and giggled as the water swirled around their soapy bodies. Tenderly Jacopo dried Dr Crumpet down with a massive and soft bath towel that covered her completely. He led her back into the bathroom thus wrapped up, and crossed the room to the chest of drawers and wardrobe.

"I will help you to dress," he laughed. "A summery outfit is appropriate for this morning, I think, for the day is fine." He chose for Dr Crumpet some filmy lingerie, and selected a pair of dark nylon stockings. He gently assisted Dr Crumpet into these garments, kneeling before her as he helped her put on her stockings, and pressed his lips against them in a loving kiss of respect. He then selected a peach coloured satin slip, and helped her step into a flowery Laura Ashley frock that clung sveltely to her waist, and fitted her to perfection. Finally Jacopo knelt before her and eased her feet into black and polished high-heeled shoes. Then he took a hair brush from the dressing table, and brushed Dr Crumpet's auburn hair one hundred times with gentle and caressing strokes. Standing before her, he embraced her gently, and placed a sensuous kiss on Dr Crumpet's lovely lips.

"There, that is perfect," he said. "Come now, I will give you a tour of the house and garden."

He held the door open for her to pass through.

"On this level are the five principal bedrooms," he remarked, preceding her into each of them and throwing open the shutters. "Upstairs there are some smaller rooms. Downstairs are the dining room which you saw last night, and some other reception rooms. Here is the entrance hall - and here is the library." He threw open a double door, and preceded Dr Crumpet into a carpeted room lined with books on shelves from floor to ceiling.

"You have catholic tastes," she remarked, as she ran her eyes along the shelves. Editions of the major European novelists, Tolstoy, Broch, Dostoevsky, Maupassant, Stendhal, Flaubert, Dickens, Thackeray, Henry James were clustered with biographies, works on military history, richly tooled first editions of modern poetry, and a large section of books devoted to travel. Jacopo pulled some of his treasures from the shelves, and stood next to Dr Crumpet as she bent over the table to see them, her auburn curls tumbling down her shoulders, her dress and slip rustling pleasantly over her stockinged legs as he brushed against her. The time passed pleasantly enough for her.

"And now I think an aperitif is called for," remarked Jacopo, leading the way into a smaller cosily furnished morning room, with a sofa, two easy chairs, a mirrored cocktail cabinet, and two chromium and leather stools at the bar.

He took a bottle of Krug champagne from the bar refrigerator, and poured the sparkling liquid into flutes.

Dr Crumpet settled herself into one of the bar stools, one high-heeled stockinged leg resting on the stool, the other pointing provocatively forward. She drained her glass of champagne quickly, and happily accepted another. This was a re-assuring way for her to get to know Jacopo, she thought. Dr Crumpet started to enjoy herself; it was agreeable to flirt with Jacopo in such a safe and civilised environment. She felt a pleasurable sense of sexual desire. Jacopo refilled their glasses, and padded around the room adjusting the cushions on the sofa. From the kitchen the delicious savour of roasting poultry began to emerge. Jacopo refilled Dr Crumpet's glass, and from time to time left the room to attend to some of the dishes he was cooking, before serving her a meal as the prelude to more passionate kissing and love-making on the sofa.

For two whole weeks Dr Crumpet remained as Jacopo's guest. She spent a large part of that time in bed, receiving a protracted tutorial in the arts of courtship and of love from the experienced Jacopo. She left the bed only rarely, late in the afternoon, to be bathed by Jacopo in the huge and gleaming bath, or to wander down to the kitchen, wearing only her slippers and one of Jacopo's unbuttoned shirts, to search for fruit and wine and bread to sustain them in the intervals of kissing, petting and fondling each other and lovemaking.

*****

'I have a journey shortly for to go' (*King Lear*)

But, eventually, Dr Crumpet felt that she had lingered long enough in the enchanted island of Haiti, and so she began to plan her departure back to England. Jacopo received philosophically and with understanding her announcement that she must soon return, and, lying in each other's arms, kissing and fondling each other passionately, they discussed the best way to get her off the island, and when they should meet again, something they were both determined to do before very long..

"Air services have been suspended because of the recent troubles," he reminded her. And all around them, revolution and disorder had been raging, as they had whiled away the days and nights under the protection of the San Marinan flag.

"You'd better get out on one of the refugee boats," said Jacopo. "I have one or two contacts, I'll see what I can do."

Jacopo left the consulate, and was gone for several hours. It was 7 p.m. when he returned,

"You leave at midnight tomorrow," he told her. "I've bought you a place on one of the refugee boats making the crossing to Florida. From there you can make contact with the British Consul in Miami, and he will get you home."

"Dr Crumpet hugged him.

"I shall miss you, Jacopo," she aid. "This past two weeks has been blissful for me. You've taught me so much. I didn't know love-making could be so wonderful."

On their last night they dined formally together. Dr Crumpet had dressed to please in one of the long-sleeved full-length evening dresses which she had found in her room. And, when she had consumed the best part of a magnum of champagne, she stood before Jacopo and slowly undressed to please, kicking off her shoes first. When she had taken off her clothes, she sat next to Jacopo on the sofa, and kissed him with a long and passionate kiss, putting her arms round his neck, and drawing him down full length on the sofa beside her. Jacopo and Dr Crumpet made love throughout the night, and slept till well into the following day. And then, at 8 p.m. in the evening, Jacopo stood sadly by as Dr Crumpet donned a khaki shirt, a light canvas skirt, a pair of sensible shoes, a cardigan, and a straw hat to protect her head against the sun. Inside the all important shoulder-bag was the zombie powder, paste and antidote, still quite safe, as well as the two Browning automatics. Jacopo had prepared for her a bag containing thermos flasks of water, a half-bottle of medicinal brandy, and several packets of biscuits.

"The journey should not take more than two days," he said.

At 11 p.m. they left the house, and drove through the deserted streets of Port au Prince. Soon they were on the beach, where Jacopo's contact was waiting to meet them. They kissed each other goodbye sadly and passionately, and agreed that Jacopo would come to visit Dr Crumpet very soon when he was next in Europe, or else that she would return to the West Indies, to a safer island like Bermuda, and that they would resume their relationship there...   The boat arrived, a small power-cruiser. Jacopo paid over the $1,000 dollars fare-money, and stood waving as the boat disappeared from view. There were eight other passengers in the boat - a middle-class Haitian family of four, and four gangsters. When the boat was out of sight of land, the gangsters pulled a gun and made the cruiser's owner and pilot jump overboard, where he soon fell prey to the circling sharks. Then the gangsters started to rob the family of four, gesticulating and joking and licking their lips as they leered at Dr Crumpet and joked about what they were going to do to her when her turn came. Dr Crumpet sighed. It was clear to her that her military skills would once again be needed. Calmly and unobtrusively she took out her Brownings, shot the gangster with the gun through the head, and made the other three kneel on the side of the boat with their hands on their heads. Then she executed them one by one, in the approved SAS manner, with a single bullet through the nape of the neck. The corpses toppled neatly into the water, and Dr Crumpet took the wheel of the power-boat and headed north for Florida. Thirty miles south of Florida, they were intercepted by a US Coast Guard cutter, and taken in tow. As it approached, Dr Crumpet casually tossed the two useful Brownings overboard with a sigh of regret. Fortunately, the family with whom she had completed the journey knew no English, but they were in any case unlikely to report Dr Crumpet's actions, for they were grateful to her for saving their lives.

When they reached Florida, the Haitians were taken to a detention camp to await repatriation to Haiti. Dr Crumpet waved her passport at the lieutenant in charge of the ship, and by him she was handed over to the State Police. The State Police drove her to the British Consul in Miami, and he arranged her return to England, endorsing her passport *Distressed British Citizen*, not to be let out of the country again until she had repaid her air fare to HM Government.

A little under eight weeks after having left for Haiti, Dr Crumpet was again flying the Atlantic in the British Airways economy class, feeling a much more mature and self-confident young woman than she had been at her departure.

"At least shooting a few Haitian bandits and brigands makes one see life with a proper sense of perspective," she thought to herself, as she eyed the confusion at Gatwick Airport in the cold grey light of a wet English dawn.

CHAPTER FIFTEEN

THE QUICK AND THE DEAD

'And the dead shall be raised incorruptible'
(The Bible)

Dr Crumpet had arrived at Gatwick from Miami. As she sipped her Chardonnay on the long and weary flight over the Atlantic in economy class, she reviewed in her mind the events of the last few weeks. She felt, in some respects, a changed woman. She had laboured in the fields cutting sugar cane, she had got the better of the female officers of the Haitian customs service, and of the practitioners of voodoo. She was returning to Wales with the zombie paste and its antidote. She had met Jacopo, and made love with him. For the first time in her life she had let a man undress her. Her experiences too had inevitably changed her relationship with Mrs Quick. Dr Crumpet felt a certain amount of distrust towards her mentor. Mrs Quick had failed to warn her about conditions in Haiti. She had given her the Gollancz book, *Pride of the Black Republic*, but that had presented a totally false picture of Haiti! Life in Haiti was not remotely as Mr Gollancz had pictured it, if indeed it ever had been.... and her experiences with Jacopo had altered Dr Crumpet's attitude towards life and love. She must try to sort out what she really felt about him.

Wearily and bleary-eyed Dr Crumpet disembarked from the plane, and made her way through immigration control and customs. Fortunately she only had hand-luggage - a grip containing some of the clothes belonging to Jacopo's sister, some toilet articles, and the zombie paste and its antidotes, so she did not have to wait for a suitcase to appear on the carousel. Soon she was on the Gatwick Express to London, and there she checked into the Dorchester hotel in Park Lane. Dr Crumpet felt that she needed to refresh herself after her long journey before meeting up again with her mentor in Hay-on-Wye. Dr Crumpet found herself in a luxuriously furnished room overlooking Hyde Park. Thankfully she flung her grip onto the bed, and stripped off her clothes to luxuriate in the foaming jets of a powerful shower, rejoicing as the travel stains were washed away by the liquid unguents of the bathroom. Then she washed her long golden tresses, dried her hair, and slipped into the clean white towelling robe that hung behind the bathroom door. Feeling refreshed, she opened the bottle of duty free Jack Daniel's that she had purchased on the plane, poured herself a generous slug, added ice cubes from the fridge, and with a sigh of relaxation sprawled herself across an armchair near the window of the balcony, as she consulted the room service menu. She rang down for a turkey club sandwich and a half-bottle of claret, and idly sipped her Jack Daniel's and channel-hopped on the TV until a knock on the door indicated the arrival of her meal. The lithe and attentive waiter placed the tray on a table overlooking the balcony, uncorked the bottle of wine, and poured a little into a glass for Dr Crumpet to taste, flashing his white teeth in a smile at the proffered £5 tip. Relaxed by the wine and Jack Daniel's, Dr Crumpet slowly ate her club sandwiches, gazing contemplatively into the distance at the green beauty and tranquillity of the park, and at the familiar London skyline. When she had sipped the last of her claret, and taken another draught of Jack Daniel's, tiredness finally overcame her, she drew the heavy curtains to block out the light of day, turned on the bedside lamp, removed her bath robe, donned the filmy nightrobe in which she had disported herself with Jacopo, and then at last laid down her head on the soft pillow, and fell into a deep slumber, overcome by languor and weariness.

It was 7 p.m. when she awoke. Dr Crumpet showered again, donned a girdle, stockings, a slip and a black cocktail dress, and rang down to the restaurant to book herself a place for dinner. She dined alone, sipping champagne with her roast duck and petits pois, pondering slowly and meditatively her future life. What was her future with Mrs Quick? Should she marry Jacopo, as he seemed to want...such matters were difficult to decide. Perhaps, for the moment, it would be best to return to the cottage she shared with Mrs Quick. Half of it was hers, after all, and she had a life to lead with her as a partner in the bookshop. Perhaps, though, she would not resume love-making with Pauline, pleading exhaustion after her ordeal...thus musing, she fell asleep again, and did not wake till 9 a.m. the following morning.

*****

After breakfast, Dr Crumpet sought out the San Marinan legation in Grosvenor Square, and, as had been arranged with Jacopo, asked them to send him a cable notifying him of her safe arrival in London. Then she did a little shopping, collected her replacement credit cards from the head office of her bank, and returned to the Dorchester to pay her bill and check out. Soon she was in a cab on the way to Paddington Station, from where she caught an Inter-City train to Hereford. At Hereford she boarded another cab to cover the final ten mile journey to Hay-on-Wye. Finally, at 5 p.m. that afternoon, Dr Crumpet arrived at the cottage. Mrs Quick greeted her cheerfully enough.

"Hello my dear, it's wonderful to see you back, did you have a good time? Come in and tell me all about it."

Dr Crumpet submitted to being embraced by Mrs Quick, and then went to unpack. Over dinner, she gave Mrs Quick a sanitised account of her experiences. She could not bring herself to state that she had killed people, or to tell her of her love affair with Jacopo, or of her ordeal at the hands of the voodoo gangs. Instead she gave a lacklustre and non-committal account of her doings in Haiti. But, of course, she had been successful in Mrs Quick's mission - she had obtained the zombie paste.

"That's great, Tony, I think you're terrific, I really do," enthused Mrs Quick when Dr Crumpet produced the potions - the paste that would send people into a catatonic trance and make it seem as if they were dead, and the antidote that would revive them, though without a will and consciousness of their own, and make them totally responsive to the demands of their master or mistress. "Now, Tony," said Mrs Quick with a frown as they sat down after dinner, sipping Cointreau and munching apples as usual, "the first thing we have to decide is who to give the paste to first. We want a student, I think, someone with no close relatives, someone with a weak will, someone who would adapt easily to being our voodoo slave..." Slowly they reviewed Mrs Quick's students one by one.

"Tamarantha would do," said Mrs Quick thoughtfully, "except that she's a woman, and we really want a male zombie. Anyway, Tamarantha does what I tell her to already anyway." The same objection applied to most of Mrs Quick's students.

"What about Frank?" said Dr Crumpet at last. "His only relative is a maiden aunt, I feel sure - he told me about her last term - and he's not over-intelligent. He would suit fine, I should say."

"Yes," agreed Mrs Quick slowly. "Frank would do fine. As you say, he has no close relatives. And not many friends either, no one would miss him, that's for sure. And he has quite a strong physique, he could do lots of the menial tasks, help us with our cottage garden, that kind of thing. Yes, Frank is certainly a possibility..."

"And how would we administer the paste?"

"Oh, mix it in with his drinks, I should think," responded Mrs Quick. "He's a rugby player isn't he? You could go to one of the Saturday night club parties and slip it to him then. Wait a minute, of course, Janet could arrange for you to be invited, she often goes, I believe, that's the way to do it."

At length Dr Crumpet excused herself, pleading tiredness and exhaustion, and retired to her small room under the eaves on the top floor of the cottage.

*****

'Now let the cannikin clink' (*Othello*)

'Gaudeamus igitur,
Iuvenes dum sumus' (Anon)

So it was that two weeks later Dr Crumpet found herself sitting next to Dr Janet French on the coach bringing the Hereford Polytechnic Rugby Club First Fifteen back to Hereford after a match with Malvern Academicals. The Hereford team had won by 75-15, and they were now celebrating their victory in the traditional way, by getting drunk. When Dr Crumpet, a few days previously, had expressed a desire to go to the club's Saturday night party, Janet had at first been surprised, and said, 'I shouldn't have thought that those raucous occasions were quite in your line, but if you want to come, sure, why not - but you'd better come to the match as well, that's the normal convention. Wrap up warmly for the match.' So Dr Crumpet, like Janet, had donned a thick woollen sweater and a grey flannel skirt, and black leather boots, and Dr Crumpet was wearing a duffle coat as well. She had watched the muddy match, in the shadow of the Malvern hills, without much enthusiasm, for organised sport bored her. But now, in the coach returning through the lengthening shadows of the coming twilight of that drowsy afternoon, as Janet passed her a silver hip-flask full of Irish whiskey, she started to feel better. It had been good at least to get out into the fresh air, and now she started to enjoy the change of company. On the back seat of the coach was a keg of beer, and already the team members were imbibing freely. Janet and Dr Crumpet too sipped some of the rich and potent liquid as the coach sped through the twilight on the way back to Hereford, and the customary and indelicate Rugby songs were roared out by the team. Dr Crumpet started to feel rather decadent, and to look forward to the coming party. She observed Frank roaring out the songs with the best of them, and started to feel a little superior at the power she held over him - once give him the zombie paste, and poor Frank's life would be changed for quite a while! Not that she had anything against him personally, of course.

The coach arrived at the large club house which was the headquarters of the Hereford Polytechnic team. The club house was situated not far from the playing-fields, on the very edge of the campus. There the team kept their kit and trophies, they kept fit in the gym, some of them even lived there. There were half-a-dozen bedrooms situated under the eaves on the third floor. In the basement were a locker-room, showers, a communal bath, and an adjacent bar. It was to the bar and the bath that the team made their way, with a good deal of pushing and shoving and ribald comment. Dr Crumpet sat with Dr Janet French on a stool at the bar, next to the locker room. Dr French pulled them both a pint of beer, and they sat there on stools at the counter, drinking from pewter tankards, as the sound of laughter and horseplay proceeded from the locker room next door. Eventually Alan, the captain of the team, and Frank and half-a-dozen other members of the team emerged laughing, with towels round their waists, and made for the bar, there to make a beeline for the pewter tankards that were hanging from hooks, and to pull pint after pint of foaming liquid. In the horse-play that followed, the members of the team tried to pull off each others' towels. Dr French smiled broadly, for she had seen such scenes before, whilst Dr Crumpet gasped and exclaimed, and then put her hand to her mouth, as two young men scampered past her back into the locker room without their towels.

"That was Sandy and Jason, our new members of the team," said Alan, the captain of the team, to Janet and Dr Crumpet. "As new members of the team they'll have to stand on a table upstairs and drink a yard of ale within a minute and a half without a pause." Alan pointed to the two long bulbous tubes hanging on the wall, which tapered outwards like a trumpet, and which held three and a half pints of ale. A few minutes later Alan shepherded the party, many of them now dressed, but Sandy and Jason still just wearing the towels they had recovered, out of the basement up the stairs, and back to the ground floor of the house. There several girl-friends of the team had been busy cooking a stew in the kitchen, and arranging the large front room for the festivities that were to follow. Half-a-dozen nurses from the nearby hospital had also arrived to participate in the night's entertainment, as was normal. Cheers and laughter erupted as the rugby players emerged from the depths of the bar. To cheers and squeals Alan escorted the two new members of the team into the lounge, and told them to climb on to one of the tables. Then he carefully filled the two yards of ale from one of the kegs of beer and handed one to each of them as they stood on the table in their towels. As Alan explained to Dr Crumpet, the yards of ale were apt to spill and the drinkers get drenched, hence the minimal attire. To cheers Jason and Sandy placed the lengthy tubes to their lips, tilted the bulb upwards and started to drink at a terrific pace, slopping beer over their neck and shoulders. The nurses, girl friends and other camp-followers clustered round the table, squealing and cheering and pointing excitedly. Dr Crumpet recognised several Polytechnic students of Mrs Quick amongst the noisy throng. There was Juliette in her red sweater and dark grey skirt, hopping around excitedly, trying to get a better view. There was Margaret and Anne, the former in a red dress, the latter in a blue one, as they stood at the very edge of the table, applauding the contestants. To cheers and squeals, Jason and Sandy drained the two tubes of ale. When the tubes were empty, Alan straightaway re-filled them, and made them drink again. The other members of the team clustered around, laughing and carousing, draining pint after pint of keg beer. It did not take long before a couple of mischievous team members had tugged off their towels again.

Dr Crumpet looked at Janet, standing there in her skirt and blouse, sipping wine languidly.

"Really, aren't they awful," she said. "Those poor young men. Are these parties always like this?"

"Usually," grinned Janet. "It's a fairly traditional rite - and I guess they are getting too drunk to care very much who sees them." Alan filled his tankard, drained a copious draught, topped it up again, and came over to speak to Janet and Dr Crumpet. Dr Crumpet looked on with wry amusement at the continuing contest as Alan approached. She felt rather decadent to be standing there in the midst of such drunken and informal scenes.

"Well, Alan," said Janet, "I see that as usual every one is letting their hair down...how much beer are those two on the table going to get through? That's surely the third tube they are on - that must be nine pints each surely?"

"That's right," agreed Alan. "We teach people to drink in this team."

"You rugby-players," laughed Janet.

More cheers erupted as Margaret eagerly climbed on to the table, and began to jive with the two drinkers on the table. She grinned and swung her hips, swirling her dress around and clicking her fingers in time to the music that came from the stereo. The two young men on the table also started to dance with her, holding the tubes by their sides and lurching around drunkenly. Dr Crumpet watched with enjoyment for a few moments, and then remembered Frank. She looked around the room for him - ah yes, there he was, bare-chested and bare-foot, also wearing only a towel loosely knotted round his waist. He was one of the crowd that had come up with her from the cellars an hour ago... Frank seemed to be having a merry old time, chatting to two or three of the nurses from the hospital, quaffing beer from his tankard in liberal quantities. Dr Crumpet thought that she saw an opportunity to slip the zombie paste in Frank's beer, and she moved over to join the group. Frank's face was flushed, his eyes were bright and merry. The party was now warming up. Dr Crumpet had switched from beer to wine, and after three glasses of that began to feel quite intoxicated herself. The nurses were now livening up too. Frank placed his half-empty tankard on the table next to Dr Crumpet, and as a raucous shout burst forth from Margaret and the table-dancers, the little group looked away. Unobserved, Dr Crumpet sprinkled a generous portion of zombie-paste over Frank's beer. By now he would be so drunk that he would not notice anything, or taste the tiny grains of powder that were lurking now in the froth. Frank turned back to his beer, tilted his head, and drained a good half-pint in a single draught. Dr Crumpet caught Dr Janet French's eye, and the two young ladies exchanged humorous glances. The wine coursed down Dr Crumpet's throat. She helped herself to another glass of wine, and to some nibbles and sandwiches from a buffet at the side of the room. She was glad that she had gone to the rugby match, and that she had come to the party. She hadn't really expected to enjoy it, but now she was. It was fun to see the young people letting their hair down, it took her back to her own student days.

Frank had gradually edged himself towards the bar, where he was out of the way of the crush in the middle of the room. He was standing there next to Dr Janet French drinking beer, and then a moment or two later they were joined by Julia, a merry-eyed young nurse. It would be fun to have Frank as a zombie, Dr Crumpet felt, looking at his bare chest with a sudden sense of triumphant power. He was a bit of a dolt after all, but a handsome and good-looking one, one had to admit, and with a fine physique, as she could clearly see, which would make him a most suitable voiceless servant for physical labour around the house.

"Of course you know my friend Antonia Crumpet," remarked Dr French to Frank. "I'm sure you must have seen her many times at Pauline Quick's."

"That's right," said Dr Crumpet, starting to tease Frank. "We have met before, though not perhaps in quite such informal surroundings as these!"

"Oh yes, we're always quite informal here," said Dr French, "especially on a Saturday night after an away match!"

As the party goers relaxed and started to enjoy themselves, Dr Crumpet looked with interest at Frank's flushed and semi-naked figure. How long would it be, she wondered, before the paste started to work? The manuals had been not very clear on that point. In the event it was quite a long time.

"So how is your course going?" Dr Crumpet asked Frank. "Are you doing single subject English or taking it with something else?
"

"I do English and business French," responded Frank. "Pauline is my tutor in English, and takes me for one class a week."

The party continued on its usual fashion. At length Dr Crumpet succumbed to tiredness. It had been a long day. She yawned, and took a final sip of wine as she cast an amused glance at the by now quite drunken scene. Frank was still chatting to Dr Janet French and to Julia and to two or three nurses.. And half-a-dozen other rugby players in various stages of undress were propping up the bar or dancing and lurching around the room. Dr Crumpet smiled at the sight, and then left the room.

Back at the cottage Mrs Quick enquired how the party had gone. "Did you give Frank the paste?" she enquired eagerly.

"Oh yes, I gave it to him," replied Dr Crumpet, yawning. "But it didn't seem to have any effect. Maybe I didn't give him enough. I'm tired now Pauline. I'm going to bed. Goodnight, see you in the morning."

She left Mrs Quick in the drawing room of the cottage, sipping her favourite Maid of the Mountains whisky, and gazing thoughtfully into the dying embers of the fire.

*****

' ....through all thy veins shall run
A cold and drowsy humour; for no pulse
Shall keep his native progress, but surcease.
No warmth, no breath shall testify thou livest.'
(Shakespeare, *Romeo and Juliet*)

Two days later Mrs Quick was sitting in her room with a box of glove puppets, preparing for her next literature class, when the phone rang. The college principal was on the end of the line.

"Pauline? Tragic news I'm afraid. Your student Frank Price has been found dead... I'm not sure why, the medics are investigating... I'll let you have details of the funeral in due course."

Mrs Quick's heart leaped. So the paste had worked after all! And soon Frank would be her zombie. All day long she taught with a will, her heart full of secret joy, longing for the moment when she could return home to Dr Crumpet to tell her the news. That night the two ladies celebrated with champagne and a delicious vegetarian moussaka, washed down with copious quantities of potent Lebanese wine. Over the second glass of nicely chilled pre-dinner champagne, Mrs Quick chatted to Dr French on her cordless phone.

"So it was a heart attack was it?" she said with apparent concern, winking the while at Dr Crumpet over the rim of her champagne flute. "I never knew that... yes, of course." She put down the phone. "That was Janet," she said to Dr Crumpet. "Apparently Frank had a weak heart. I never knew that. She has just signed his death certificate. The funeral is on Thursday at St Mary's church in Eastern Promenade... that will suit fine, that's great, we can dig him up again at the weekend, I bought two large spades the other day, and we will have him for our zombie next week. He can sleep in the barn - and his first task will be to chop up some wood for the fires this coming winter."

Dr Crumpet laughed, and draining her champagne held out her glass for a refill. It was a satisfying feeling to have carried out this little mission so successfully, she really felt quite proud of herself. She, Dr Crumpet, had been to Haiti and outwitted the local witch-doctors, and returned to England in triumph, and now she had successfully administered the paste! The two ladies enjoyed their triumph, and hugged and kissed each other excitedly, and then repaired to the dining room to eat the moussaka, excitedly discussing the details of Frank's forthcoming role as their future general factotum.

"He can wear overalls," said Mrs Quick. "And we can pass him off as a deaf mute whom we are employing out of the kindness of our hearts. And when anyone from the Poly comes to see us we'll hide him in the barn." They both sniggered. "And when he has chopped the wood, we can get him to paint the house - and he can mop the floors, and look after the garden, and wash the cars - oh yes, there are tasks a-plenty for Master Frank the Zombie." Both women broke out laughing.

When the moussaka was eaten, and the second bottle of Lebanese wine half-empty, the two ladies adjourned to the drawing room for fruit and dessert wine.

"You know I haven't felt so good for a long time," laughed Pauline Quick. "Not since poor old Jim Houghton died back at Surleighwick, followed by Percy Bodgering... of course, we had something to do with that as well, I believe. What a pity we didn't have the zombie paste then - I'd like to have seen Houghton chopping wood, though Bodgering would have been too wheezy to have been much good about the house and garden." They both laughed unfeelingly, and settled down to consume a heady bottle of rich and potent Sauternes, before gradually slumping into insensibility under the influence of the warmth, the alcohol, the food and the delicious feeling that everything was going their way.

*****

Thursday came, the day of Frank's funeral, and Dr Crumpet prepared carefully for the occasion. After breakfasting still in her nightgown and dressing gown, she had a long and leisurely soak in the bath, immersing herself in the foaming and soapy water, sprinkling bath salts in with lavish hand. Then she dried herself with a huge and fluffy bath towel, and then carefully donned a black bra and girdle and sheer black nylons. A dark but filmy slip went over these, and then she tied a black ribbon in her hair. She pulled on polished black boots, with high instep, gleaming to the knee. And then she stepped into a full skirted black velvet dress, belted at the waist with a black leather belt with a gold clasp at the front. She gazed at herself in the mirror, and rubbed a little powder into her cheeks. Finally she picked up a pair of black leather gloves and a wide brimmed flat topped black hat, and a gleaming leather handbag. She was ready for the event, and admired herself in the mirror, the very pattern of a pale and beautiful young woman in mourning attire, her well-brushed blonde hair offsetting the darkness of her clothes to perfection. Then she went downstairs, the soles of her boots clip-clopping on the bare boards of the stairs. Mrs Quick too was ready, also dressed in a dark blouse and a snugly fitting dark business suit. She ushered Dr Crumpet into the car, and the two ladies set off for St Mary's Church, Eastern Promenade.

They parked the car in the road outside. Two grave-diggers were steadily digging a fresh grave at the south end of the cemetery. "See," said Mrs Quick, pointing it out to Dr Crumpet. "That will be for Frank. Just by the wall, we'll have no trouble at all getting him out from there."

They took their place in church, and bowed their heads in prayer. A few of Frank's friends were there, and some members of the rugby team. The polytechnic registrar was there. Dr Janet French was there, trim and neat in a costume suit and black overcoat. Frank's distant cousins, two slim young women, Sandra and Joy, sat at the front, pale and composed. The organ sounded, the parson in his white surplice intoned the familiar words, 'Man that is born of woman hath but a short time to live...' Mrs Quick and Dr Crumpet sang the hymns, 'He who would valiant be' and 'Eternal Father strong to save' as lustily as anyone. The coffin was borne out of the church on the shoulders of six of Frank's fellow rugby players. They laid it reverently on the back of a hearse, and on the instant the hearse drove off to the crematorium followed by the principal mourners, Frank's two female cousins. There Frank was burned to ashes. Mrs Quick and Dr Crumpet remained disconcerted at the church porch, watching the two gravediggers finish their work in time for the arrival of the next party bearing the corpse that was to repose in it.

*****

Mrs Quick was unusually silent as she drove Dr Crumpet back to the cottage. She parked the car, and made her way into the drawing room. "I think I need a drink," she said. "I think perhaps we both do." She took two tumblers, and half-filled each of them with an exceedingly generous portion of Courvoisier. Mrs Quick proffered one to Dr Crumpet, and drained the other in two deep swigs, before refilling her glass. Dr Crumpet took off her coat and sat in black on the sofa with her legs elegantly crossed, sipping her brandy with a thoughtful expression.

"I think I made a boo-boo," said Mrs Quick disconsolately. "It just never occurred to me that Frank would be cremated... I mean how was I to know?" She took another deep swig of brandy. Dr Crumpet took another sip from her glass, more poised and thoughtful still. As a women who had killed Haitian bandits and customs officers, she was perhaps better able to cope with the situation than Mrs Quick.

"Well," she said lightly as she sipped her brandy. "It certainly was a most unfortunate mistake. I guess it was quite a boo-boo, as you put it. The revival paste won't work on an urn full of ashes, that's for sure."

"Yes, next time we must make sure that we choose someone that we know will be buried rather than cremated," said Mrs Quick.

Dr Crumpet started to laugh. "Pauline, you are incorrigible." You had to hand it to Pauline Quick, she was a pretty irrepressible personality. Her plan had gone badly wrong, she had unwittingly caused the death of an entirely innocent student, but already she had picked herself up and was thinking of her next victim.

Mrs Quick looked up, still doleful, and caught Dr Crumpet's amused eye. And then she too started to smile, her shoulders heaved, and in a moment she started to laugh too.

"Well, anyone can make a mistake," she said defensively.

"You should have seen your face," laughed Dr Crumpet. "It was one of the funniest things I have seen in my life. It was a scream, you did look a sight."

"Well, it was such a shock... but at least we know the paste works now, so that's something to the good."

"Poor Frank," said Dr Crumpet, helping herself to a refill of brandy, "but at least it was a quick death and he can't have felt anything."

"A *quick* death indeed," spluttered Mrs Quick, falling into an uncontrollable fit of the giggles.

"Mind, it's a pity really," said Dr Crumpet. "After all the trouble I went to to slip the paste in Frank's drink... I wonder how the rugby team will get on without him?"

"Speaking of rugby," put in Mrs Quick. "I suppose that in sporting terms our little mishap might best be described as an 'own goal'!"

"Oh Pauline," you are wicked, giggled Dr Crumpet. "An 'own goal' indeed!"

Gradually, as the brandy worked its soothing charms, both ladies started to relax. Mrs Quick left her armchair, carrying with her the brandy bottle and glass. She joined Dr Crumpet on the sofa, and casually put an arm around her and snuggled up to her. The two ladies embraced each other and kissed, then sat together for a while in companionable silence, sipping their brandies from time to time.

"I must say, Tony, that I do like your outfit. Black suits you, I think."

Mrs Quick went into the kitchen to prepare a light luncheon of omelette, green salad, fruit, cheese and wine.

They consumed this repast sitting at the kitchen table, holding hands and gazing fondly into each other's eyes. At the end of the meal, Dr Crumpet led the way upstairs to Mrs Quick's bedroom, and there she allowed Mrs Quick to undress her and take her to bed. Thoughts of poor Frank were soon forgotten.

*****

At length, having carefully considered the matter for several days, Mrs Quick decided that her student Tamarantha would make an ideal zombie. She was a Nigerian who had no relatives in this country, and moreover, an important point, Mrs Quick had ascertained that Nigerians did not go in much for cremation. It proved surprisingly easy to give the zombie paste to Tamarantha - Mrs Quick had mixed it with the coffee, and had watched with approval as Tamarantha had sipped three cups. Next day Tamarantha was 'dead', and Dr Janet French, suspecting a mysterious virus of African origin had signed the death certificate to that effect. In the absence of next of kin, Hereford Polytechnic had taken care of the funeral arrangements, and Mrs Quick, as Tamarantha's tutor, had played a principal part in these arrangements. Just a week later Tamarantha was laid to rest in the graveyard of St Mary's church, and that same night Mrs Quick had sat on the wall of that lonely churchyard, sipping whisky from a flask and keeping watch as Dr Crumpet got to work with pick-axe and shovel to recover the body. Dr Crumpet put the shrouded remains of Tamarantha in Mrs Quick's long-wheel base Land Rover, and refilled the now empty grave. Forty minutes later they were back in Mrs Quick's cosy cottage, and the shrouded figure was laid out before the flickering flames of the drawing room fire and unwrapped. Anxiously Dr Crumpet placed the bottle containing the antidote under Tamarantha's nose, and in a few moments the still figure was stirring.

"It works, Tony, it works," exclaimed Mrs Quick delightedly. "That's very well done, you are really the non-pareil, you have done splendidly."

Soon Tamarantha was sitting bolt upright in front of the fire, staring on front of her with fixed gaze. And a half-hour after that, she was walking stiffly up and down the room in response to Mrs Quick's commands. Just two hours after being recovered from her grave, Tamarantha in her catatonic trance was resting between clean sheets in one of the upstairs guest bedrooms of Mrs Quick's cottage. She now had her first zombie, and already her inventive brain was plotting how to entrap her next victims, Dr Margaret Jacquasse from Whitepool University, and Professor and Mrs Charles Hanwell.

CHAPTER SIXTEEN

RETURN TO HAY-ON-WYE

'Diffugere nives, redeunt iam gramina campis'
(Horace, *Odes*, iv)

It was April, and as the first flowers of spring were thrusting through the cold damp earth, the Hanwells were driving contentedly down from Skelmerdale to Hay-on-Wye. Charles's time as a Visiting Professor at Skelmerdale was almost over, and in a few weeks he and Ruth would be returning to Surleighwick, Arkansas. Professor Hanwell was reasonably content with his visit. His lectures had never attracted a larger audience than that which had attended his first one, namely his wife, Tamsin, Fiona and Sophie Poppet. But those four had been faithful attenders. Every fortnight on Thursdays at 5.15 p.m. he had turned up in the 250 seat lecture theatre and spoken of some different aspect of the languages of scientific poetry. His second lecture on 'Scientific Poetry: the Latin tradition' had been followed by 'The Versified Encyclopaedias of the Renaissance' and then by 'Noceti and the Italian tradition of Poesie Scientifiche in the Enlightenment'. The fifth lecture had discussed 'Humanism and the French scientific poets'; the sixth, 'The scientific poets of the Iberian peninsula', had discussed Diego Allati of Seville and the strangely neglected Portugese poems on natural philosophy of Pedro Nuñez of Valdosa. After each lecture, to celebrate and spend some of the handsome fee which Skelmerdale was paying him, he had taken Ruth and her three friends to dinner at a nice restaurant, unwinding in a leisurely fashion over an evening's good food and wine. He had the satisfaction of a job well done, and the knowledge that the lectures would soon be written up as chapters of his next book. As always, it was pleasant to listen to the light-hearted and inconsequential chatter of Tamsin, Fiona and Sophie Poppet, as the three young women, their tongues loosened by an excellent burgundy or sauvignon, gossiped about the latest happenings and events in the world of English and communication studies, the glove puppet theatre shows and the interactive tutorials they had been enjoying. And now the lecture series was drawing to its conclusion, and there were only two more talks to give. The talks were written, and needed only delivering, and so he and Ruth were at liberty to take five days off and revisit their old haunt of Hay-on-Wye, which they used to visit when they had both been at the University of Surleighwick.

They headed south down the traffic-clogged M6. It was a relief to leave that motorway just west of Birmingham, and to cut across country on the A456 to Bewdley, thence to Tenbury Wells, where they used to stop for coffee on their way to Hay from Surleighwick. Soon they were retracing their old route through Leominster and Dilwyn, and were back in Wales. The Hanwells were booked in to The Fisherman's Arms, a superior hostelry and country house hotel just four miles west of Hay, listed in *The Good Food Guide*, and popular with anglers since its verdant lawns abutted directly on to the river Wye. The Hanwells arrived at their hotel, checked into their suite, showered, and were soon sitting in the lounge over a welcome gin-and-tonic, studying the menu and recovering after their long journey down from Skelmerdale.

*****

The next day they arose late, read the newspapers over a leisurely breakfast, then strolled along the banks of the river Wye for an hour or so before driving five miles east to the town of Hay-on-Wye. The town had changed a little since they were last there. More bookshops had opened, and more fast-food eating establishments had appeared on the once tranquil streets. But it was still good to see the grey stone streets again, and the gaunt and ruined castle serenely dominating the town from its lofty battlements. They wandered round the bookshops in a desultory fashion, making the occasional purchase, but not finding any real bargains. The days of purchasing valuable books at low prices were evidently no more. At half-past twelve, for old times' sake, they drove across the border into England to the Wayside Inn, five miles east of Hay, and their favourite lunchtime hostelry in the days when they had made expeditions to Hay from Surleighwick. They both had scampi and chips, and downed a pint or two of bitter as they sat in the tranquil lounge of the Wayside Inn, with its picture windows overlooking the calmly flowing river Wye. After an hour and a half, they drove back to Hay, and there they separated, Ruth to look for novels, Professor Hanwell to look for books on military history. A little after three, bearing the meagre haul of the day's book-hunting, the Hanwells returned to their hotel, and were soon sipping Earl Grey in the lounge, whiling away the time till 7 p.m., when it was time to get a taxi to the cottage of Mrs Quick and Dr Crumpet, where they had been invited for dinner. They had not visited the Magic Women bookshop that day, reserving that treat until a later time during their visit.

*****

Mrs Quick was looking forward profoundly to the visit of Professor and Mrs Hanwell, when she fully intended to administer the zombie paste to them, and add the two to her collection. Her zombie Tamarantha, neatly attired in a black maid's outfit and white apron, had been employed dusting and cleaning the dining-room all day long. Mrs Quick herself had overseen the cooking of the dinner - wine in abundance, Chablis to accompany the fish-pâté that comprised the first course, a decent claret to go with the spicy cajun chicken and stir-fried vegetables, a Trockenbeerenauslese to accompany the strawberry gateaux, and brandy, strega, and whisky in abundance for post-prandial drinks. Sometime during the meal she would give the Hanwells the zombie paste, unknowingly they would drink it, and then they too would be her slaves. Mrs Quick luxuriated in the thought of having Ruth at her beck and call... as for Professor Hanwell, she would use him as a jobbing gardener and general handyman.

She greeted the Hanwells fulsomely as they were deposited by taxi at her cottage at 7.30 p.m. that evening. The Hanwells, anticipating that liquor would be served in generous quantities, had wisely decided to leave their car at the hotel. Ruth wore a snugly fitting dark cocktail dress with white lace cuffs, and her husband his customary dark suit. Mrs Quick was wearing her usual evening attire, a loosely-fitting flowery ankle-length frock, and Dr Crumpet her black velvet dress, belted at the waist, and polished boots of soft black leather. Dusk had fallen, and the curtains of Mrs Quick's cottage were drawn against the cold and darkness without. She greeted the Hanwells effusively, shaking Ruth's hand firmly and flashing them both a friendly smile with her gleaming white teeth.

"Hullo, my dear, it's good to see you here at last, now what can

I get you to drink? G and T, white wine, martini, whisky, I have most things I think."

"Gin-and-tonic please," said Ruth firmly. "Charles and I are both confirmed gin-and-tonic persons before dinner."

Mrs Quick went to the sideboard, and returned bearing two generous-sized tumblers heaped with ice and slices of lemon.

"And how are you enjoying Hay-on-Wye? You must look in on my shop you know, I have some items that might appeal to you."

"We were a little disappointed, to tell the truth," answered Ruth. "Hay is not the place it once was. But still I bought a few novels, and Charles got one or two military history books."

"You'll be interested in my stock, I know," said Mrs Quick. "Tny and I have been building up quite a collection of books on medieval and renaissance magic. And some of the books are in Latin, which I know you are fond of." She smiled knowingly at Charles.

"Well, we will certainly look in tomorrow and see what we can find," answered Ruth, draining her gin-and-tonic and holding out the glass for a refill.

It was a small party. Only Mrs Quick and Dr Crumpet and the Hanwells were present. Soon the four were sitting down to eat the fish pâté, washed down by the agreeable Chablis which Mrs Quick had chosen for the meal. When the first course was eaten, Mrs Quick and Dr Crumpet cleared away the empty plates and retired to the kitchen to make the final preparations for the main course. Out of sight in the kitchen Tamarantha the zombie drained the potatoes and placed them in a tureen, and placed the peas and other stir-fried vegetables in another couple of dishes. That done, Mrs Quick placed the cajun chicken on Professor and Mrs Hanwell's plates, and sprinkled the spicy mixture with a generous helping of zombie paste. "There," she said to Dr Crumpet with great satisfaction, "that will take care of those two I should think, they'll be a nice addition to our labour force, they can live in the barn."

All charm and effusiveness she carried the tray containing the plates back into the living room, placed it on the sideboard, and then proceeded to place the dishes of vegetables on the table, and to give the Hanwells their plates.

"Don't wait for Tony and me, help yourselves to veg, and do start. Charles, would you like to pour the wine?"

Professor Hanwell poured out four glasses of wine from the nearest of the two glass decanters, and took a first sip as Ruth helped herself to vegetables. Mrs Quick returned to the table, and looked on with pleasure as the Hanwells ate their chicken. Soon they would be zombies!

"So how have you been enjoying your time at Skelmerdale?" enquired Mrs Quick. "It's a lovely campus, isn't it, but I don't know very much about the university."

"It's a strange place, that's for sure," laughed Professor Hanwell, as he narrated the bizarre story of being paid £2,500 a time for lectures that no one save his wife and her friends ever attended.

"It's been an amusing interlude," he admitted, "and it's given Ruth an opportunity to clear up her great-aunt Flo's affairs. But I can't say I shall be sorry to return to Arkansas." He accepted a little more cajun chicken from Mrs Quick, and she watched him eat it with great satisfaction. Normally he would have declined a rich dessert, but to be polite he accepted a small sliver, and ate it slowly, sipping also the heady Trockenbeerenauslese. Mrs Quick and Dr Crumpet exchanged many covert glances, looking pleased at the success of the meal. Their zombie-experiments were turning out well, and soon their zombie Tamarantha would have company. The entrepreneurial Mrs Quick was already thinking ahead to the days when she would have whole colonies of them, and would lease them out to others as hired workers.

When the cheese and biscuits had been cleared away, the party moved into the lounge for fruit and petit-fours, for coffee and liqueurs, a Courvoisier for Dr Hanwell, a crème-de-menthe for Ruth, cointreau for Mrs Quick and Dr Crumpet.

Mrs Quick raised her glass to the Hanwells yet again as she served the liqueurs. "Cheers, Charles and Ruth, it's really great to have you here. Such a pity that we did not ever meet when we were at Surleighwick...ah well, it must have been fate."

At 11.30 p.m. the Hanwells' taxi arrived to take them back to the Fisherman's Arms. Mrs Quick bad her guests a fond and hypocritical farewell. "Next time we see those two they will be zombies, in our power," she said triumphantly as she poured herself the remainder of the Trockenbeerenauslese, and settled down to make love to Dr Crumpet.

The taxi deposited the Hanwells at their hotel a few minutes before midnight. They were by now both rather tired, hastily undressed, and clambered into their king-sized bed, and there, after a few kisses and murmured endearments, it was not long before they fell into a deep slumber, enriched by vivid dreams.

*****

Next morning, Ruth was thoughtful as she sat in her nightgown brushing her hair, after she and her husband had had a lazy breakfast of coffee and croissants in their room.

"Charles, can you amuse yourself this morning?" she enquired. "Why don't you go for a walk along the river bank, have a pint or so in the bar, and I'll join you at about three?"

"OK, if you want," replied her husband. "Or I could go and have a look at the Magic Women bookshop."

"No, don't do that," said Ruth firmly. "Don't ask me why, but don't do it." She looked her husband straight in the eye. "Trust me - just don't do it. I'll tell you why not in due course."

"OK, darling, since you feel so strongly about it," said Professor Hanwell, giving his wife a kiss. "I'll go for a tramp along the river bank. But what about you - what are you going to do?"

"Girl-talk," answered Ruth firmly. "I want to look up an old friend in Hereford. We'll save the Magic Women until we both can go."

Professor Hanwell donned an old anorak, with a cap in the pocket against the rain, kissed his wife goodbye, and set out to walk west from the Fisherman's Arms, further into Wales, towards the Brecon Beacons, breathing deeply the pure and unpolluted air.

Ruth slipped on the jacket of her suit, picked up her handbag, slipped her Psion communicator into it, and then called a taxi and settled down for the fifteen miles' drive to Hereford, where she had arranged to have lunch with her friend Dr Janet French, who had been her doctor when she was a student at Surleighwick, and had been five years ahead of her at the Bath School for Girls. They had continued to meet there at Old Girls' Reunions, and had resumed their friendship when Dr French came to the University Health Centre at Surleighwick, and Ruth had been assigned to her as one of her patients.

Ruth arrived in Hereford, paid off the taxi, and then proceeded to do a little shopping, followed by a quick look around the cathedral. She then strolled the three hundred yards to Janet's practice, and arrived as Janet was just showing out her last patient, a tall fair-haired member of the Polytechnic Rugby team who had sprained his ankle in the high-jinks after the previous Saturday's game. Janet greeted Ruth with a friendly kiss as her patient hobbled off, slipped off her white coat and stethoscope, donned a blue blazer, and locked the door behind her.

"I've booked us a table at the San Remano," said Ruth, naming Hereford's most fashionable restaurant, overlooking the cathedral.

"Great," said Janet, "my favourite place. So how are things?"

Ten minutes later, the two young women were seated in a comfortable and secluded booth on the first floor at the front of the restaurant, admiring the grey stone facade of the cathedral, and looking at the tranquil scene before them.

Janet's labours were finished for the day, and so she was able to sip without a qualm the excellent bottle of Frascati which Ruth had ordered to accompany the primi patti. With her excellent and idiomatic Italian she soon established a rapport with the waiters. They both ordered fillet steaks with vegetables, cooked in the Italian style, and Ruth ordered an expensive bottle of full-bodied and potent Barolo to go with it. As they nibbled and imbibed the Frascati, and waited for their steaks to be grilled, for the first half-hour or so they exchanged pleasantries, catching up on each other's recent news and gossip. Though they had corresponded and sometimes called each other on the international lines, it was almost a year since they had seen each other, at the last Old Girls' dinner in Bath.

The steak arrived, and for the next twenty minutes the conversation slowed, as they endeavoured to do justice to the thick and juicy corn-fed cuts. Both young women had excellent appetites, and so they followed their steaks with a light dessert of flaky Italian pastry. When the empty plates had been cleared away, Ruth ordered espressos accompanied by some of the really excellent grappa for which the San Remano was renowned. She downed a generous sip, and then started to broach with Janet the matter on which she wished to consult her.

"How well do you know Pauline Quick?" she asked. "I want to ask you some things about her."

Janet sipped her coffee and shrugged her shoulders.

"Not very well, I have known her off and on since we were at Surleighwick. She is more the friend of my colleague Veronica."

"I don't trust her," said Ruth quietly. "You do know that she is a witch?"

"Yes, of a sort," laughed Janet. "A lot of nonsense in my opinion. She worships Diana at a lonely spot on the Brecon Beacons. She has a coven, of course. It's a way of getting her acolytes to take off their clothes. I have driven them there sometimes, though it's not my scene at all. They prance around in the nude, sing and dance, invoke Diana in the cold moonlight, and return to her cottage to warm up in front of the fire and drink hot punch in the nude. Pretty juvenile and pointless in my view - but then I'm just the driver."

"She tried to turn Charles and me into zombies last night," stated Ruth quietly, signalling for more espresso and grappa. "You're a doctor, what do you know about catatonic trances?"

"Not very much," admitted Janet. "I know they can be very deep and long-lasting, and can go on for years even. You seem dead, but you aren't."

"That's about it," said Ruth. "The real expertise in this area is in Haiti - there's a book about it by Wade Davis, a Harvard anthropologist, *The Serpent and the Rainbow*. It got quite a lot of attention in the States when it came out in the 'eighties, less so here. Davis discovered that Haitian zombies were in fact unfortunates who had been cast into a catatonic trance - there is a paste or potion which they make in Haiti. Give it to your enemy, and they seem dead, and are buried. Then there is a counter potion - give it to the seemingly dead person, and they come to life again after a fashion, but have no will and will do whatever they are told. Such are the zombies, the undead, the walking dead. It sounds far-fetched, but Professor Davis proved his case beyond the shadow of a doubt. Now Mrs Quick has some of this paste. As you know, her partner Tony Crumpet was in Haiti this summer. She brought some back of it back, I feel sure, along with the counter-potion. She tried to give Charles and me some at dinner last night - in fact she did give us some. I shall know this for certain very soon, as I have sent some of last night's meal for analysis. It came with the cajun chicken, I feel sure. But fortunately for us, I was on to her little tricks. I know all about the Davis book

- my great-aunt Flo who flatlined last summer left me her books, and that was one of them. And when I was in San Francisco, I discussed the matter with Christophe, of Dr Zombie's Voodoo shop in the Haight-Ashbury - a charming fellow, we are big buddies, Christophe and I. And he gave me some powder that nullifies the zombie paste, and I was able to sprinkle it unobserved on Charles' and my meal last night - so her tricks had no effect on us. But I caught a glimpse of someone through the kitchen door - and I feel sure that that was a zombie - a dark girl. Tell me Janet, have there been any unexpected deaths in these parts of late - at the Poly, perhaps...?"

"Yes," answered Janet slowly, "what you say sounds rather fantastic - but yes, there have been. First Frank - and then Tamarantha - and they were both her students... But Frank can't be a zombie, he was cremated. Tamarantha was buried though... I wonder." She paused, lost in thought.

"It will be Pauline Quick's doing, no doubt about it," Ruth put in firmly. "Now, what are we going to do about it, that's the question. The woman is a menace..."

"Well, I am certainly tired of getting caught up in her affairs, driving the coven to midnight worship and that kind of thing," said Janet, sipping her grappa. "Maybe I ought to sound out Tony discreetly. I have had the feeling recently that she may be getting somewhat tired of being under Pauline's thumb the whole time. Pauline does exploit her rather, you know. Makes her do all the errands, that kind of thing... she doesn't really have a life of her own."

"Well, we ought to turn the tables on her somehow," continued Ruth. "She is a pest. I'm frankly very annoyed that she tried to turn Charles and me into zombies. I'm not going to have it, and I'm going to do something about it. Anyway, I'm glad I raised the matter with you. Let's keep in touch on this one. And now let's have another grappa."

Janet and Ruth continued talking and gossipping in a leisurely fashion, until 4 p.m., when, made mellow by the wine and spirits, they said an affectionate goodbye to each other, and went their separate ways, Janet back to her flat in Hereford, Ruth in a taxi to the Fisherman's Arms, where her husband was waiting to greet her. They embraced affectionately, and since Ruth did not feel up to eating a full dinner in the dining room, they remained in their suite and contented themselves with turkey sandwiches and a bottle of Chablis from room service. At 10. 30 p.m. Ruth was replete and drowsy, and she went to bed and fell asleep on the instant.

*****

The next morning, refreshed and clear headed, and firmly resolute, Ruth sent her husband out for a walk again whilst she made some telephone calls, sent some faxes, and checked her e-mail on her Psion Communicator. Her husband returned at 12 noon, they had a pint of beer and a ploughman's lunch in the bar of the Fisherman's Arms, and then called a cab to take them into Hay-on-Wye again, to visit the Magic Women bookshop. Ruth was interested to see what Mrs Quick's reaction would be when they walked in.

They approached the shop, its black sign with witch's hat in gold swinging in the wind. Boldly Ruth pushed open the door, a bell jingled, and Dr Crumpet gazed at them open-mouthed as they entered.

"Hello, Tony, here we are again," said Ruth, beginning to enjoy herself as she saw Dr Crumpet's white face and startled expression. "We've come to visit your shop as we promised. Is Pauline in? That was a lovely meal you gave us, wasn't it Charles?"

"Yes, it certainly was, a great meal, good to have seen you both again. I'm looking forward to seeing your stock. Of course magic is not particularly my line, but so many of the early magic books impinge on the history of science that I'll be interested to see what you have."

Dr Crumpet gazed at them open-mouthed. She had thought that the potion would have worked by now, and that Professor and Mrs Hanwell would have been in a catatonic trance in their hotel room or in the mortuary, pronounced dead.

"Is Pauline around?" continued Ruth cheerfully? "I know she's not here all the time, but I hoped she might be in today."

"Er, I think so," answered Dr Crumpet. "I think she's in the back room. I'll go and tell her you are here." She slipped way hastily, and went to tell Mrs Quick the news. And she too was flabbergasted to hear that the Hanwells had arrived, and disappointed to boot. Why were they not now in a trance? What could have gone wrong?

"Maybe we didn't use enough powder," she said at last to Dr Crumpet. "And yet I thought we had. I used more than for Frank and Tamarantha, that's for sure. I don't understand it, I just don't understand it."

Mrs Quick composed herself, took a nip of whisky from a bottle she kept in a cupboard, applied a little rouge to her cheeks, and then feigning a cheeriness she certainly did not feel she left her back room to greet her visitors.

"Hello, my dears, so very nice to see you," she said, assuming a smile which was however wan.

"Hello, Pauline, such a lovely meal you gave us the other day, wasn't it Charles?" Ruth turned to her husband, but did not pause for him to comment. "What a lovely shop you have here... I'm sure Charles will find some books that are right up his street here - look, Charles," she said, pulling a book more or less at random from the adjacent shelves, *"Warlocks, Wizards, Witches, Wantons, Werewolves and Weirdos*, that book might have been written just for you. He's interested in all these topics, you know," she smiled at Mrs Quick. "I remember the first time he took me out he lectured me on the differences between witches and warlocks, he knows all about it, never you fear. And what have we here? *From Abracadabra to Hey Presto! The Origins of the Magic Words of Power*, you'd better put that on one side for him too, and then I see you have some books on medieval and renaissance magic as well! Look, you had better let us both browse around for a while, and then we'll have another chat before we go. I wonder if you have anything that impinges on my own interests, such as cooking, say?" Ruth gazed quizzically at Mrs Quick, who gestured uncertainly towards a shelf at the far corner of the room.

Professor Hanwell was soon engrossed in the medieval and renaissance section of the Magic Women bookshop. He quickly found a rare treatise on the evil-eye, Leonard Vairus's *De fascino libri tres* (Venice, 1589), a book printed by the later Aldine press, priced at a very reasonable £250. And then he found an unusual book about Arab magic in the middle ages, and two odd volumes of the Greek Magical Papyri which were of interest to him. One had to hand it to Mrs Quick and Dr Crumpet, they had certainly assembled a very respectable collection of texts in their chosen speciality. Ruth meanwhile was buying some books about fairies - Hodgson's *Fairies at Work and Play*, Andrew Lang's *Yellow Fairy Book*, a delightful work of children's literature, and some of the seminal works on fairy-tales by Jack Zipes. She also was delighted to find a rare copy of F. Liebrecht's Hanover 1856 edition of some of Gervase of Tilbury's folk-tales. And at last she found a little book on *The Magic of Herbs*, a kind of white magic cookery book on a minor scale.

Mrs Quick retreated in somewhat disgruntled fashion to her small office at the back of the shop. Clearly Professor and Mrs Hanwell were in vibrant health, something had gone wrong, but what? She felt very put out, and cheated by it all. But, irrepressible as always, she began to make plans to have another go, to invite the Hanwells around for dinner again, and this time to double the dose...

Meanwhile the Hanwells had finalised their purchases and were ready to depart.

CHAPTER SEVENTEEN

RUTH IN A RUTHLESS MODE

'Hell hath no fury like a woman scorned'

Ruth had indeed learned all about zombie paste and its antidote when she had shopped at Dr Zombie's Voodoo Shop on Main Street of the Haight-Ashbury in San Francisco. Over coffee Christophe had told her all about it, for he admired her frank and friendly manner. And he had given her a little box of potions containing the zombie paste antidote, and other wondrous drugs, possets, and elixirs. And now she needed to contact Christophe again, in accordance with his offer to help her with matters occult should she so need. So that evening, at 6 p.m., after returning from the Magic Women bookshop, whilst her husband was chatting in the bar downstairs to the regulars over a pint of local ale, Ruth sat at the writing table of her suite sipping a gin-and-tonic. She looked at the slender diamond-encrusted Cartier watch which her husband had bought her for her last birthday. 6.15 p.m. in Wales, that would be 10.15 a.m. in San Francisco, and Christophe, no doubt, would be in his shop... She set up the Psion Communicator, and sent him a priority e-mail. 'Hi there Christophe from BG, it's Ruth from Out East again....what's the weather like in SF? Trust that all is well and that you are up and about. Christophe, I need some advice, reply when you get this if you have time.' Ruth sipped her gin-and-tonic, smart in the white blouse and dark-grey skirt of a formal suit. Within a few moments came the reply. 'Hello Ruth from Out East. It's Christophe here...always ready to give a young lady like you advice, how can I help?' Ruth picked up the phone, and in a moment was speaking to Christophe almost six thousand miles away.

"Christophe, I'm so grateful to you for your zombie antidote, it came in useful the other night when an acquaintance tried to turned my husband and me into zombies... Now I don't want to turn the perpetrator into a zombie, but I do need to paralyse her for a while. Are any of the potions in the box you gave me when I was in SF of any use?" Ruth poured out her troubles to the sympathetic Christophe, and he offered numerous suggestions and ideas. In the end he laughed. "OK, my little lady from Out East, I get the picture. Let me think about it for a little while, then just you go into fax mode, give me half-an hour, and I will have instructions in your hands very soon. When are you coming to SF again? Be great to see you again."

"Thanks Christophe, you're a pal. We'll be back in SF in a couple of months. I'll let you know when and will certainly call in again at the shop...be seein' ya."

Contentedly, Ruth slipped the jacket of her suit over her shoulders, and moved out on to the veranda, overlooking the river where a few hopeful fishermen were still lazily casting their flies over the water, as the midges hovered above the slowly running waters. Forty minutes later, the Psion communicator buzzed into life, and the first of three pages of Christophe's fax emerged from the machine. Ruth cast her eyes over them, smiled slowly, and then folded them carefully in her handbag for more detailed perusal later. She then went back into e-mail mode on the Psion and sent a message to Christophe to say that the fax had been safely received. She sipped the last of her gin and tonic, and then it was time for dinner; she buttoned up her jacket, and went downstairs to join her husband in the lounge.

Dusk was falling slowly as the Hanwells entered the elegant dining room of the Fishermen's Arms, and took their place at a table overlooking the soft green lawns and the slowly flowing river.   "Well, our time in the UK is coming to an end fairly quickly, isn't it?" remarked Professor Hanwell to his wife as they sipped some of the excellent Chablis which he had chosen to accompany the smoked salmon appetiser. "Only two more talks to give, and then I guess we could go back to Arkansas more or less any time. What about it, how much longer do you want to stay here? I suppose we could stay in Skelmerdale until the end of June if you really want to...."

Ruth frowned as she ate her salmon.

"I'm not really sure just at the moment," she answered. "Let's see, we're in April now - I've got one or two odds and ends to tie up before I leave - I think I'd like to stay till the end of May at least, maybe into early June. Would that be OK?"

"Sure," replied her husband easily, with the insouciance of one who rarely had to do any teaching.

*****

Two days later Ruth and Dr French were once again lunching in Hereford, laying their plans to turn the tables on Mrs Quick. The two young women put their heads together over lunch, trying out ideas on each other as they sipped gin-and-tonics, then glasses of potent Barolo with the main courses, and dessert wine with the fruit and cheese.

"One idea that did occur to me," suggested Janet. "A way to knock the enthusiasm for witchcraft and covens on the head - you know I told you she gets her acolytes to dance naked in the countryside and worship Diana.... I have driven them there myself on several occasions in the long-wheel-base Land Rover. A thought that just occurred to me - another group that I know that gets naked from time to time are the Hereford Polytechnic Rugby club - I have sometimes thought how the two would interact, I mean if I could drive the team after one of their jaunts to where the coven is dancing in the countryside - that would be a bit of a riot, and might lessen the enthusiasm of her devotees for such occasions."

"You know that's not a bad idea," answered Ruth slowly, sipping her wine in a meditative manner. "Or even better, get the two sides to meet at the post-match party. I know what Rugby clubs are like of course, I used to see their misbehaviour when I lived in Second Hall at Surleighwick... But would it be possible to arrange the meeting?"

"I rather think it would," said Janet. "You see the club here has an away match at Skelmerdale in three weeks' time, and it so happens that Pauline and her coven will be in Skelmerdale the very same weekend - there is a conference on feminism and gender that they are all going too, and last time Pauline and Tony were in Skelmerdale, they had an outing with the coven to an old stone circle on the moors..." She frowned. "It might be possible to arrange something, if I can swing it by myself."

"I'm willing to help, if I can," said Ruth. "Perhaps I could offer to help with the coven, attend as an observer, something like that?"

"Pauline would jump at the chance I think," said Janet. "She fancies you I think... I'll see what I can do. Maybe I could risk sounding out Tony, I have an idea she has been put upon, and might be willing to assist... I have the feeling that she is a bit fed up with Mrs Quick, you know. If we could fix this thing, maybe you could drive the Land Rover for the coven whilst I see to the Rugby club and get them in a party mood... or perhaps better to do it the other way round. Let's see, here's what we will do." The two young women put their heads together, and over a couple of glasses of excellent grappa started to flesh out the bare bones of their plan, before kissing each other an affectionate goodbye and arranging to keep in touch.

*****

Mrs Quick was having another meeting of her coven on the Brecon Beacons in two days time. Janet suggested to her that Ruth would like to attend as an observer, and Mrs Quick accepted the suggestion with alacrity. She was still greatly puzzled and disconcerted by the way in which the zombie-paste had failed to reduce Professor and Mrs Hanwell to zombies, but irrepressible as ever had soon put the matter behind her.

And on the Thursday evening Ruth bade her husband goodbye, leaving him to have an evening by himself at the Fishermen's Arms. "I need to have some girl-talk with Janet, and have a little other business to transact - don't worry, I'll tell you all about it in due course," she said, giving him a little kiss. "You get yourself a nice meal in the dining room, and then you can have a brandy or two in the bar, or watch movies on TV - I won't be back till the small hours, but don't worry, Janet will be with me all the time." And Professor Hanwell, who trusted his wife, was content not to ask further questions, but went to the dining room to dine on a grilled Dover sole washed down by some excellent Pouilly-Fumé, before retiring to the lounge for a large Courvoisier and a pot of coffee. Then he went back to their suite to watch TV, before turning in for an early night.

Ruth meanwhile had as a precaution fortified herself with all the antidotes recommended by Christophe of Dr Zombie's Voodoo Shop. She dressed carefully in a white sweater over a warm silk blouse, donned a warm and comfortable grey pleated woollen skirt, and sat on the bed to zip up her black-leather fleece-lined boots. Then she carefully checked the pockets of her anorak, which contained a powerful but slim flashlight, some more medicaments, a headscarf, a silver flask of brandy, and various other items suitable for a night on the moors. She arrived at Mrs Quick's cottage by taxi at 9 p.m., to find that most members of the coven had already arrived, and were imbibing freely from the copious bottles of liquor that Mrs Quick had provided. Ruth watched carefully, and then accepted a glass of Cabernet from the bottle from which she had seen Mrs Quick and Dr Crumpet drinking. She did not however on this occasion wish to drink too much alcohol, it was important for her to keep a clear head. Mrs Quick seemed friendly enough and unsuspicious, as did Dr Crumpet. They had decided that somehow they had failed to apply enough zombie paste to Ruth and Professor Hanwell's meal, or that the spicy cajun chicken had somehow nullified its effects.

"Lovely to see you again, Ruth," said Mrs Quick, kissing her lightly on the cheek. Mrs Quick was dressed, as was usual on these occasions, in a long white flowing robe, embroidered with occult insignia, with sandals over her bare feet, her ears adorned with long jade earings, and with a coral necklace around her neck. "You know Veronica, perhaps, from your days at Surleighwick, and these are Margaret and Catherine and Annabelle, my grad. students left over from that institution too. And here are some of my present students from the Poly - Cynthia, and another Margaret and Alice, and my assistant Samantha from the Magic Women, and Amanda and Henrietta, also from the book trade - well, we are going to have fun this evening, I was so glad to hear from Janet that you are interested in joining our movement. We regard ourselves as pioneers down here you know, reviving the old pagan and Celtic traditions which are so much more beneficial to humanity than conventional Christianity."

Ruth chatted agreeably to Dr Crumpet for a while, and then gossipped with Dr Chamberlain and some of the grad. students who had been at Surleighwick. She was glad nevertheless that Janet was there, Janet whom she felt she could trust in a crisis. Ruth nibbled carefully at the buffet which Mrs Quick had provided, and allowed herself another glass of wine, which she sipped slowly and carefully. Janet, as the driver for the night of the long-wheel base Land Rover, abstained from alcohol altogether, sipping instead peach-flavoured mineral water.

Half-past eleven arrived, and Janet looked at Ruth with wry amusement as Mrs Quick called on her coven to disrobe.

Mrs Quick's ex-Surleighwick grad. students led the way as usual, and stripped off in a giggly fashion, to be followed by Dr Crumpet, Dr Chamberlain, Annabelle, Samantha and the others. When her coven had undressed, Mrs Quick handed round a tray of crystal glasses each containing a double whisky against the cold. Ruth too felt that it was now safe to drink one, as she had imbibed comparatively little alcohol that evening, and with food at that. Janet however as the driver stuck to her peach-water. Ruth was glad that she had attended only as an observer - she would have felt very defenceless and vulnerable being naked in Mrs Quick's presence. Mrs Quick herself, still in her flowing robe as ususal, looked round with satisfaction at her undressed acolytes as she drained her whisky to the dregs. "OK, mes enfantes, allons-y. To the moors," she called gaily, clutching the long stick made of ash which she bore on these occasions.

The laughing acolytes scampered out of the front door, across the shingly gravel of the drive, to the Land Rover. Janet slipped on her driving coat, and opened the back doors of the vehicle.

Ruth too donned her navy-blue anorak, and slipped the silk head-scarf around her head.

"You come in the front with us," said Janet. "There's room for you in the front seat in the middle." Mrs Quick slipped into the left front seat when Ruth had got in, and Janet walked all round the vehicle and closed the doors, and then got into the driving seat, rolling her eyes slightly at Ruth in suppressed amusement as she caught her eye. Janet drove the customary route to the Brecon Beacons, then engaged the four-wheel drive and slowly and carefully directed the vehicle across the tufty grass and rock-strewn moorland to the lonely 'temple of Diana'. The front-seat party descended, Janet opened the rear doors, and Ruth watched in amazement as the nudes, by now surely rather cold she thought to herself, scampered across the moors to the ancient stones. Ruth and Janet remained watching at a distance whilst Mrs Quick led her party in the customary rites...

"Well," said the practical Ruth, watching the bizarre scene, "this really takes the biscuit... of all the daft things I have ever heard of this has to be the daftest... but I can certainly see what you mean when you say that a Rugby club could really set the cat among the pigeons in a situation like this... there were a lot of rugby players among the boys in Third Hall at Surleighwick. I went to some of their parties with the Second Hall girls, and they were fond of taking off their clothes too. I fancy they could teach Pauline's acolytes a thing or two about drunken misbehaviour. Your Hereford club is no doubt the same." "It is," said Janet simply. "Then indeed if you could unloose them on Mrs Quick's coven on an occasion like this, that might well put paid to it. It would teach them all a lesson, to be sure. And I should certainly like to do that," said Ruth firmly. "Her behaviour to Charles and me was unforgivable."

"Ruth, you are so determined!" said Janet. "Well, I'm game if you are. Let's do it in two weeks time. The coven will be in Skelmerdale for the gender conference, and the Hereford Polytechnic Rugby Club will be playing an away match there that same weekend. I think on the whole it's better for me to drive the coven to the Skelmerdale moors, and I'll fix for you to help with the Rugby club, and all we have to do is figure out where and how to bring the two together. Pauline and Tony usually hire a couple of self-catering cottages when they go up there, maybe you can find a room for hire on the Skelmerdale campus, and let the interaction begin!"

"We'll do it," said Ruth quietly.

The ceremonies were over, the coven scampered back across the grass and into the Land Rover. Soon the acolytes were back in Mrs Quick's living room, clustering round the fire and trying to get rid of their goose pimples. Mrs Quick happily served wine and whisky to her acolytes. Ruth, tired now after the long evening, refused Mrs Quick's offer of further refreshment. She called a taxi, said goodbye to Janet, and with a last look around the room at the still-unclothed would-be witches, she made her adieux to Mrs Quick and left for the Fishermen's Arms. It was five to three in the morning when she arrived back at their suite. Her husband was sound asleep. Hungry now, Ruth ordered herself a round of sandwiches and a large bourbon from room service, and consumed these in the drawing room of their suite. Then, tired at last, she slipped into bed besides her husband, who, himself sound asleep, did not stir. Ruth slept till 10 a.m. the next morning, and as she opened her drowsy eyes her husband tenderly brushed the hair back from her forehead and gave her a gentle kiss.

*****

The Hanwells had returned to Skelmerdale, and Ruth and Janet's scheme was falling nicely into place. Mrs Quick, Ruth learned from Janet, had hired a large self-catering house with a large mews stable in the village of Skittleton, where her coven would stay for the feminism and gender conference. And the Hereford Polytechnic Rugby team would be in Skelmerdale as well, for their away game with the Skelmerdale first fifteen, and their match on the Saturday would co-incide with the last day of the conference, and the night on which Mrs Quick and her coven would repair to the old stone circle on the Skelmerdale Moors to worship Diana.

*****

Three days before the fateful Saturday, when the Hanwells had just returned to their apartment from dinner at Giovanni's Italian restaurant in the centre of Skelmerdale, the telephone rang. Ruth answered it, and to her surprise found that it was one of her contemporaries from the Bath School for Girls, whom she had known at Surleighwick, but had rather lost touch with since she had moved to the States.

"Why Susannah," exclaimed Ruth delightedly, for they had been quite close at one time. "How nice to hear from you... so what gives?"

"You free for lunch tomorrow?" was the reply. "If so, let's meet and do ourselves proud at Mr Murdoch's expense..."

"Mr Murdoch's expense?" queried Ruth, then laughed. "Oh, I get it, you're a journalist now are you? So what's it like working for the *Times*?"

"Not the *Times*, silly," chided Susannah, "much more exciting than that, I work for the *News of the World*."

"OK, I'll look forward to hearing all about it," replied Ruth with genuine pleasure. "Where shall I meet you?"

"I'm at Bannerthorpe Hall," replied Susannah, naming Skelmerdale's most pricey and exclusive country house hotel on the very edge of town, with its five red rosettes and two Michelin stars for cooking.

"Well, I'm impressed," laughed Ruth, "Charles and I have eaten there once or twice, and it cost the proverbial arm and a leg."

"Great!" said Susannah, "I'll send a limo to pick you up and we'll have a really nice lunch. Tell Charles not to expect you back till 8 p.m. at least - they know how to look after a girl at the Bannerthorpe..."

Next day, Ruth rose late and dressed carefully in a light-blue tailored suit with yellow blouse and her most elegant pair of black high-heeled shoes, for she knew by experience how smart the Bannerthorpe was. The chauffeured limo arrived, and Ruth carefully checked her lipstick, picked up her white kid gloves and Gucci handbag, and was ushered into the rear seat of the capacious limo by the uniformed chauffeur.

As the chauffeur ushered her out of the limo after the short drive to the Bannerthorpe, Ruth was greeted by a liveried footman in knee-breeches, who escorted her up the flight of steps at the entrance. He led her into a spacious lounge, which was lined with seventeenth-century portraits. Susannah rose from one of the luxurious and chintzy sofas that were placed all around the room, and gave Ruth a friendly hug and kiss.

"It's wonderful to see you again, Ruth. You are looking well. Married life must suit you, I like your outfit."

"You're looking in fine form yourself, Sukie," answered Ruth, taking in her friend's elegantly-tailored and figure-hugging pink suit with high-padded shoulder puffs and matching pink shoes, her white satin blouse and the Ladies' Rolex watch on her left wrist. The attentive waiter instantly filled their order for gin-and-tonic, and brought a large plate of nibbles and celery, which he placed on the table in front of them.

"So tell me about life on the *News of the World*," said Ruth as she sipped her drink.

"I'm having a great time. I've been there for eighteen months now. I cover the social scene, pop stars' parties, political events, some of the sporting scene, strawberries at Wimbledon and Henley, that kind of thing. You don't perhaps read the *News of the World*?"

Ruth shook her head. "Sorry, no, I don't, but now that I know you write for it Sukie, of course I will."

"That's sweet of you Ruth. Of course I'm just a gossip columnist really. But it pays the bills, and they give me a great dress allowance."

"So I see - that's a terrific suit you are wearing."

"And of course the old expense account allows me to stay in places like this."

"It's a pricey place, no doubt about it. As I said, Charles and I have eaten here once or twice as a treat. The food is marvellous, and they have a great wine list."

"I know. And don't let's stint ourselves. Mr Murdoch is paying the bill." The two young women studied the menu, and then Susannah turned her attention to the wine list. Their tastes coincided, and they both ordered a first course of poached salmon, caught earlier that morning and specially flown down from a Scottish estate, and then the rack of lamb. Susannah ordered a bottle of really excellent Puligny Montrachet to accompany the first, and a spectacular claret, a Château Pétrus, to go with the second course. Some twenty minutes later they were ushered deferentially into lunch by the maître d' hôtel, and escorted to a light and airy corner table overlooking the beautifully landscaped grounds of Bannerthorpe Hall. The service was impeccable but unobtrusive, and the wine waiter replenished their glasses after every few sips. The two friends gossipped and talked in a leisurely fashion, and caught up on each other's lives since they had last met two years previously. For dessert they both partook of strawberries and cream, washed down with a bottle of Krug champagne. It was now 4 p.m., and the two young women, by now slightly bibulous and loquacious, returned arm-in-arm to the lounge for coffee and liqueurs. Ruth ordered her favourite crème-de-menthe, and Susannah a double measure of antique Hine cognac.

"I've been sounding out my contacts in universities," remarked Susannah. "News is a bit slack at this time of year as summer approaches, you know how it is, the government looks set to be in power for ever, it's getting difficult to find a good scandal with this lot around, but of course universities are always news. My paper as you know is always anxious to expose the corruption of public life - or to put it another way, anxious to increase its circulation by a nice sensational story or two. So I'm on the look out for a bit of appalling sleaze, and wondered whether you might have some from Skelmerdale?"

"I most certainly do," said Ruth, opening her handbag and fishing out a copy of Fawn and Florinda's translation, *El Molino sopra Lo Flosso*. "I mean to say, Sukie, look at all the mistakes in this, it makes a complete travesty of the Italian language, and to think that they foist this kind of stuff on to their students with public money, it really is appalling."

Susannah laughed, and laid the book aside.

"Ruth, you are so sweet. But no, that's not quite what I meant. That's one for our sister paper the *Higher*, I should think. If you like I'll pass it on to them."

"Please do," said Ruth vigorously, for her sense of propriety was offended by the numerous mistakes in language at Skelmerdale, and she was annoyed with the university because no one but her friends had been to her husband's excellent lectures.

"No, Ruthie, what I meant was scandal as in *scandal*... you remember, like at Second Hall in Surleighwick when the boys next door went wild and dunked people in the pond with nothing on, you know the kind of thing, 'Shock/horror/ students in nude/sex/drugs/orgy'. Our sister paper the *Sun* did an exposé of parties at the London medical schools in the autumn of 1993, and we did one on the freshers' parties at Dundee University too in 1988. There were boys with nothing on dancing on tables you know," explained Susannah, adopting the tone of moral disapproval that characterised her paper, as Ruth raised a quizzical eyebrow. "Look, I've a file of press cuttings in my room, all the way back to the 60s, I'll send one of the waiters to get it. Of course Surleighwick got worked over by the Murdoch press too," continued Susannah proudly. "Don't you remember, it was when we were third years, the English Department had an outing to Hay-on-Wye that ended with the riot squad being called out, and some of the boys from English being charged with indecent exposure. Ah, here's the file."

The waiter deferentially handed her a thick blue file of neatly photocopied press cuttings, and Ruth flicked through them with a slight smile. There was a certain sameness about the press cuttings, which started with the drunken strippings and anarchy of the Essex residential towers in the 1960s, continued via the famous nude protest at Keele University in the summer of 1970 and included such highlights as the riotous pyjama-jacket only and toga parties at Kent and St Andrews in that same decade, and ended with a streak through the library at Leicester a couple of months previously. Drunkenness, vandalism, indecent exposure, drug-taking and parties that had got out of hand were the familiar themes, which indeed, as Susannah had suggested, Ruth remembered from her own days in Second Hall at Surleighwick.

"Well, yes, I see the kind of thing you mean," said Ruth comfortably. "Of course Charles and I are not resident on campus, so we miss out on most of the action I expect. But yes, one sees a bit of it. I seem to remember there was a Dance of the Seven Veils by one of the delegates at the first conference that Charles and I attended here, and I suppose Adam and Eve acted their pre-lapsarian roles without clothing in the performance of the interminable Skelmerdale Mystery Plays, though I dare say they would justify that on grounds of realism. Maybe you ought to have word with Charles - I remember that he was very surprised at 'Eve-before-the-Fall'. And then of course at the conference there were the girls dressed in Rocky Horror outfits, he couldn't understand that either. One sees a good deal of drunkenness and fooling around late at night on campus if one happens to be there. As it happens I think I can supply you with what you want. I've been invited to a Rugby Club party here after Skelmerdale's home match with the Hereford Polytechnic team. So has Janet French, do you remember her? - she was ahead of us at Bath - well you know what Rugby Club parties are like, and Janet tells me that the Hereford Poly crowd are no exception. I'm pretty sure that next Saturday's event would provide you with plenty of copy, you see from what I've heard they are planning to burst in on a coven of feminist witches and upset things a bit. Why don't you come with me, and bring a photographer of course? I think there might be a story in it for you!"

"Ruthie, you're a genius!" said Susannah. "You have just no idea what I can do with this material. I got even Enid Blyton taken off children's TV you know," she said proudly, "there was a shocking scene in a *Famous Five* episode where Dick was in bed with his dog Timmy, and George, who is actually a girl, threw a plate of cornflakes all over his pyjamas. I mean to say, when you think about the Freudian undertones, it was absolutely shocking, it should only have been shown after 11. p.m. And yes, of course I know what Rugby Club parties are like. Don't you remember, I used to date Dave Chaloner, captain of the Third Hall team at Surleighwick, so yes, I've seen it all - the team streaking after training, the drinking contests in the bar with the losers losing their clothes, and do you remember the scandal when the whole team got drunk, wandered around Second Hall with nothing on, and then gate-crashed one of the God-squad revivalist meetings in the table-tennis room? Gosh, it was fun, wasn't it! I feel quite staid and respectable by comparison now. So yes, I'll crash the party, and I'll get my photographer up too, we could have a great story there. You devil, Ruth, still waters certainly run deep, don't they? And you were always so demure and respectable - Head Girl at Bath (natch!), 'A' grades all the way through at Surleighwick, never saw you drunk, your head always stuck in a book by that medieval character you were so fond of, what was her name, Matilda something, oh yes, it's coming back to me, Matilda the Hermit. Crazy lady, crazy name! And all the time you were romancing your tutor. You were a sly one and no mistake. Come on, let's have another liqueur."

Nothing loth, Ruth accepted a second and a third and a fourth and then a fifth crème-de-menthe, whilst Susannah knocked back doubles of antique Hine. At length the conversation petered out, and Ruth realised that she was very sleepy and that, if not drunk, she had dined well, as the Victorian novelists put it. Susannah meanwhile was clearly about to fall asleep.

"Come on Sukie, I'll put you to bed." Ruth took Susannah's bag and extracted her room key therefrom. With the help of one of the attendants, she walked the drunken Susannah to the lift, and thence to the door of her suite. Ruth placed the almost unconscious Susannah on top of the deep and comfortable king-sized four-poster bed, took off Susannah's red shoes, and eased her out of her skirt and jacket. She hung these in the wardrobe, and then placed a coverlet over Susannah's prostrate form. Ruth then silently let herself out, and from the lobby of the hotel asked for Susannah's chauffered limo to be called. Twenty minutes later she was back at home with her husband.

She gave her husband a woozy kiss, and put her arms around his neck. "Sorry, Charles, I am going to have an early night." (It was then just gone 8.30 p.m.) "I had a really serious lunch with Sukie - girl-talk, you know, and it's all catching up with me.... goodnight, sweet prince..." Ruth unzipped her skirt and stepped out of it, and carelessly tossed her suit jacket over the nearest chair. She just made it to the bed in her slip, and then crashed out at once. Her husband tenderly drew a coverlet over her, and kissed her goodnight. Then he placed her shoes and suit in the wardrobe.

"Sleep well, my dear Ruth," said her husband gently as he left the room. "And perhaps you'll tell me, some day soon, just what all this girl-talk has been about..."

*****

Mrs Quick and her coven had driven up, along with Janet, from Hereford to Skelmerdale. Mrs Quick, Dr Crumpet and Janet sat in the front, the eleven others in the capacious rear of the long-wheel base Land Rover. Mrs Quick had rented a large house in the village of Skittleton, just on the edge of Skelmerdale campus, large enough to sleep all the coven, some in double rooms and bunk beds. They came up on the Thursday evening, and arrived at 7 p.m., drove through crowds of students just finishing their lunch-time drinking at the Louis XVIII and Moonshine pubs, and spent a merry night drinking numerous flagons of Chianti to wash down the take-away pizzas they had ordered as the easiest solution to satisfy their hunger on the first evening. Friday was spent happily socialising at the conference on feminist and gender perspectives in hospital soap-operas on TV, a theme which allowed all the sisters to talk to themselves happily about the suppressed other, the Freudian shadow, the body, the feminised male, the hospital porter as icon of patriarchy, lipstick as a feminine signifier, the hospital canteen as metaphor for cross-cultural exchange, and such like topics. Many of those who attended the Writing Women Re-vue at Skelmerdale the previous summer were there, including Fawn and Florinda, Deirdre and Dr Margaret Jacquasse from Whitepool. Deirdre was now superficially friends again with Fawn and Florinda, mollified in part by pleasant anticipatory thoughts of the vengeance she was minded to exact against Fawn and Florinda on this occasion. Fiona, Tamsin, Sophie Poppet, and others of Fawn and Florinda's students had been again enrolled to act as thematic student helpers, dressed this time in blue white nurses' uniforms and starched white aprons and cuffs, with black shoes and stockings. Ruth looked in at one or two sessions during the day to satisfy herself that Mrs Quick and her coven had actually arrived, and to chat to Fiona, Tamsin and Sophie Poppet, who looked quite glamorous in their nurses' uniforms.

The conference continued into its second day, and ended with tea and biscuits at 4 p.m. in the Castle Island complex, after which most of the delegates returned home. Ruth slipped away from the conference in the late morning to join Janet and Alan, the captain of the Hereford Polytechnic Rugby team for a pint of beer in the Louis XVIII. Alan was quite amenable to the idea that Ruth would drive the team to the match and to the party afterwards, since Janet would, as she explained, be otherwise engaged for an hour or two that evening.

"But to make up for it," Janet smiled at Alan, "I've arranged a special treat for you. There are some innocent young women here who would just love to see a Rugby Club party in full swing. They are staying quite close to where you are, they want some excitement their lives, Ruth will drive you there in your mini-bus - and you won't mind if she brings a couple of her girl-friends I know... it should be fun, you can enjoy yourselves, and of course they will welcome your attentions, so you needn't mind your behaviour. We'll be with you about 11 p.m. It should be fun for you and the other members of the team."

"Sounds great to me," said Alan nonchalantly. "After eight or nine pints, my team are game for anything anyway... and now I suppose I must start to get ready for the match. I won't have another pint, thanks, one's enough before the game. I'll make up for it tonight afterwards though."

Ruth and Janet sat for an hour in the Louis XVIII finalising their arrangements. Janet was delighted to learn that Susannah and her photographer would be present at the party to take some photographs and report the happenings for the *News of the World*. No doubt about it, a free and independent press was a wonderful thing.

CHAPTER EIGHTEEN

BURN, WITCH, BURN!

'Venit ineluctabile tempus' (Virgil, *Aeneid*)

The final day of the Feminism and Gender Perspectives in Popular Television Hospital Narratology Conference was a fateful one for many of its participants. For Obadiah Ouimpe, Lecturer in Wimmins Studies in the Sociology department at Skelmerdale, it was the last day of his life. By special permission, since he cut such an unmasculine figure, he had been allowed to be the sole man present at the conference on condition that he wear a dress, all other applications from men to attend having been firmly rejected. He spent the whole of the conference vainly trying to flirt with Dr Jacquasse, but she ignored him. In the closing moments of the conference, over tea, the mutton-chopped pint-sized baldy was smothered to death, his head caught between the pneumatic bosoms of two amply-endowed delegates who failed to notice that he was there, such was his insignificance, and such the enthusiasm and warmth of the *conversazione* of the two ladies. As they turned tail and bad each other a cheery farewell, Obadiah Ouimpe's lifeless body slowly slid down the wall, and slumped on the floor, where it remained unnoticed until the early hours of the next morning.

*****

Mrs Quick and her coven returned to her house, where they showered, bathed, gossiped, and once again consumed large quantities of wine, whisky and brandy, before undressing as usual and scampering into the back of Mrs Quick's capacious Land Rover. Janet, in her customary boots, anorak, and sweater, drove the coven to the remote stones on the Skelmerdale Moors, where Mrs Quick and her acolytes indulged themselves in their routine pagan and uncomfortable rites. By 11 p.m., under the bright full moon, they were returning at a stately forty miles an hour over the lonely ribbon of road that led to the A641, and thence back towards Skelmerdale. Janet hoped anxiously that Ruth and her friends would have sufficiently warmed up the Rugby Club for things to develop in an interesting manner.

*****

Ruth and her husband, and Susannah and her photographer, and Fiona, Tamsin and Sophie Poppet had all dined earlier that evening at a cheerful but traditional Italian restaurant in the centre of Skelmerdale. 'No doubt about it, Ruth has some vivacious and pretty friends,' thought Professor Hanwell to himself as they ate pasta and drank a variety of bottles of fresh and fruity Sardinian wine, both red and white. Susannah was dressed casually in a grey skirt, blouse and sweater, her fleece-lined long leather coat draped over the back of her chair. Rita, her 'snapper', as Susannah casually called her photographer, wore a leather skirt and bright green blouse, dark stockings and flat casual shoes. Fiona, Tamsin and Sophie Poppet were so taken with their fetching nurses' uniforms that they were still wearing them, chattering away brightly and admiring the London sophistication of Susannah and Rita. A Barbour anorak, with capacious pockets in which to place her variety of cameras, lenses, light-metres, filters, lap-top, digital camera and all the transfer paraphernalia, completed the latter's outfit. The two young women from the *News of the World* had the light of battle in their eyes. They enjoyed stirring up scandal and luring unsuspecting unfortunates into indiscretion. The party consumed several rounds of excellent grappa, and Professor Hanwell and Rita indulged in Villiger No 3 cigars before Ruth looked at her watch at last and said: "Well, I think it's time for us to be off. It's good of you not to ask too many questions, Charles. Just some girl-type things we've got on the go tonight, you know. *Aliqua nescire*, as Bernard of Chartres put it. There are some things one ought not to know. I'll tell you all about it someday..." She ruffled his hair and gave him a kiss. "You go home and have some brandy and a cigar, and I have a present for you that you can watch on the video." From her anorak Ruth took out a tape of *Viking Women and the Sea Serpent*, a film she knew her husband had often wanted to see.

"OK, my dear Ruth," said her husband philosophically, reaching for his wallet to pay the bill.

"No no no, Charles," said Susannah reprovingly. "This is business, you are Mr Murdoch's guest tonight." She beckoned to a waiter, told him to leave the remainder of the bottle of grappa for Professor Hanwell, and paid the bill by her company charge card, leaving the waiters a £60 tip. "Don't worry, Charles, we'll bring back Ruthie safe enough tonight, but don't wait up for us." The six young women left to hail a pair of taxis, with Ruth rather enjoying the feeling that she was indulging in a raffish and uncharacteristic fashion for a change, and looking forward to the dissipation of the forthcoming night. Professor Hanwell remained contentedly in the restaurant, lighting a large Macanudo cigar, chatting to the waiters, and sipping a further two or three glasses of excellent grappa, before returning home to read in tranquillity a couple of hundred lines of an eighteenth-century Italian poem about centipedes which he had recently bought, and then to watch the classic Roger Corman movie which Ruth had bought him.

*****

By ten o'clock that evening, the Hereford Polytechnic Rugby Club party was in full swing. The team had beaten Skelmerdale, a university with a low profile in most sports, by 75-15, so they were in a mood to celebrate. They too were in a large self-catering house a few hundred yards further down the main street of Skittleton from where Mrs Quick and her coven were staying. Ruth and Janet had seen that the house was supplied with spectacular quantities of beer, wine, and whisky. The dining room of the house had been converted into a bar, and five large 70-gallon barrels of Roger's Owd Horizontal were more or less sufficient to slake the capacious thirsts of most members of the team. Several cases of red and white wine and one of Johnny Walker black label whisky supplemented the supplies of beer. The loud noise of amplified pop music and the hubbub of loud conversation and shouting could be heard as the two taxis deposited the young women in the drive of the house. The team's mini-bus was parked on one side of the drive. The door was wide open, and they all entered. The house was warm and noisy, and permeated by an overpowering smell of liquor and stale tobacco smoke.

The arrival of Ruth and her party was generally welcomed by Alan and the team. Owing to the distance, only a couple of their female camp-followers had made it to the match and party, so the additional female company was welcome news indeed. Alan was soon dispensing glasses of red wine to the new arrivals in a hospitable fashion. Tamsin, Fiona and Sophie Poppet were soon jiving with members of the team. Susannah and Rita declined to dance, but stood gossiping with Alan at the side of the room. Ruth meanwhile checked her handbag, and unobserved by the inebriated team sprinkled a few drops of the potent elixir that Christophe had Fed-Exed to her the previous week into Alan's beer and into the wine-glasses of other members of the team that had been abandoned whilst they jived around the room. 'No need for zombie-paste' Christophe had told her. 'This elixir from BG, taken with alcohol, destroys the will and makes whoever has imbibed it obedient to whatsoever commands. Two drops in a glass of wine or beer, and half-an-hour later the subject is in a trance-like state, responsive to commands, which they will not afterwards remember. So much simpler than Haitian zombie-paste!' he had said proudly in his fax, a Guyanan from a superior magical tradition looking down at the cruder Haitian endeavours.

Then Ruth looked at the time; it was now just gone ten o'clock, and if all had gone to plan Mrs Quick and her coven would now be nearly at the stone circle on the Skelmerdale Moors, in Mrs Quick's Land Rover with Janet at the wheel. She whispered to Susannah, and donning her anorak slipped out of the room. Mrs Quick's lodgings were surprisingly close, and Ruth decided that when the time came she could get the Rugby team there on foot rather than driving them there in the mini-bus. Ruth went up the drive, and entered the house using the spare key which Janet had had cut and given to her earlier that afternoon. The house was warm, and the lights were still on in most of the rooms, but the curtains were of course drawn.

The floor of the living room was covered with the scattered shoes and clothes of Mrs Quick's acolytes. Ruth seized a large wicker basket from the conservatory, piled the shoes and clothes into it, and dragged it out to the back-garden shed, which she had previously reconnoitred, locking its hasp firmly with a new steel padlock which she had brought with her in the inside pocket of her anorak. Then she placed some drops of her will-paralysing potions into the half-empty wine glasses and bottles that were lying around the room.   Yes, thought Ruth, all is developing quite nicely towards the dénouement of this story.

*****

Meanwhile Deirdre was in her hide, carefully smearing her face with mud, and preparing to exact the final revenge on the University of Skelmerdale and the wretches who had declined her paper on the *Lady of Shalott* at the Writing Women conference the previous summer. She had thought that the fact that she had already axed to death five students might have damaged the reputation of the university, but no, Skelmerdale's publicity machine had been good. Skelmerdale had managed to turn the murders into a plus point for its own campus security, which was, so it maintained, excellent. The murders could have happened anywhere, they were nothing to do with Skelmerdale as such, they had taken place on campus, to be sure, but that was just mere chance... 'Well', thought Deirdre grimly to herself, 'let's see what they have to say for themselves after tonight.' She zipped herself up into her tight black boiler-suit, and finally donned the long black leather coat whose right pocket contained a 9 mm Browning automatic; inside, on the left, a short-barrelled Chinese-made Kalashnikov assault rifle hung from a loop. Deirdre had obtained both these weapons for £2,500 from a soldier who had recently brought them back from Kosovo, and a further £500 had procured several clips of ammunition and two lessons in how to use the weapons at a remote and disused quarry five miles outside Whitepool. Deirdre breathed deeply, and took a sip of whisky from a pewter flask. She had been psyching herself up all week for this consummate act of vengeance, first by watching twenty-five times an uncut DVD of the banned feminist revenge movie, *I Spit on Your Grave*, in which a young woman had wrought a bloody revenge on those who had done her wrong, and secondly by reading a volume of Dr Goebbels's collected speeches, for she had read that serial killers were often interested in the Nazis, and she wished to conform to the stereotype. 'And so my party comrades and party comradesses' (*parteigenossinnen* - Deirdre approved of the flexible feminine endings of the German noun system) 'I feel that in these difficult times the Führer is absolutely right to feel that he can count on his people one hundred percent... Terror can only be broken by counter-terror. Do you want total war? Total War is the shortest war... *Glauben, Kämpfen, Siegen,* Believe, Fight, Conquer!' Deirdre buttoned her coat and emerged from the undergrowth on to a path, to mingle unnoticed with the varied congress of people that characterised the Skelmerdale campus on a Saturday night. She strode firmly towards Fawn and Florinda's cottage, unremarked by anyone.

*****

A few moments later Ruth had slipped unnoticed back into the Rugby Club party, which was now beginning to warm up. Two young men clad only in towels around their waist were standing on a table, racing each other in the usual drinking contest to see who could drain first the long thin bulbous yards of ale, each holding a little under four pints. Fiona, Tamsin and Sophie Poppet clustered eagerly around the table along with the other camp followers and members of the club. Alan noisily exhorted them from the sidelines, and Susannah and Rita looked on at a distance, the latter smoking another Villiger No 3 and checking her camera equipment. Ruth carefully broke the seal on a new bottle of whisky, and poured herself a generous slug. She looked at her watch and decided that it was time to see if the potions were working. She went up to Alan, who greeted her jovially.

"OK Alan," she said casually. "I think you as Captain of the team should take the lead here. On to the table and get your kit off, the young women you are going to meet will be disappointed otherwise."

Alan immediately filled up his tankard of beer, clambered on to the table, and started to strip off. Soon he was parading up and down the table with nothing on, cheered on by his audience. Not to be outdone, the two team members who were draining the yards of ale also removed their towels, and started to gyrate and jive. Rita puffed contentedly on her cigar, and started to take some shots with her digital camera, which did not need a flash, as it automatically compensated for the light levels.

Susannah came up to Ruth. "This is fun isn't it, Ruth, it takes me back to my student days...oh really, whatever next!" she exclaimed, as the laughing Fiona, Tamsin and Sophie Poppet in their nurses' uniforms joined the nude young men on the table and started to dance with them, clicking their fingers, their frocks swaying around their knees. Susannah shot an anxious glance at Rita, and was re-assured to find that Rita was busily snapping away. The pictures would look great in the *News of the World*. For a moment Susannah idly wondered if she could blackmail the Skelmerdale VC and ask for money not to print her story, but journalistic ethics got the better of her and she repressed such unworthy thoughts. Mind you, this would give the Skelmerdale VC apoplexy, she thought, he would really hate the bad publicity!

"There's more to come, I think," said Ruth calmly, pouring herself another whisky. She caught Alan's eye, and beckoned him down from the table. Alan immediately climbed down and wandered over to her, tankard in hand. "OK, Alan," said Ruth calmly. "Tell the rest of the team to get undressed, it's time to meet those girls Janet and I were telling you about."

Instantly Alan shouted in a loud voice to his team mates to get undressed, and without a quibble they did so. Ruth by now felt totally confident that the potions which Christophe had given her were effective. She stood there sipping whisky and observing the dissolute scene, as Fiona, Tamsin and Sophie Poppet scampered round the room laughing with excitement at the sight of the team. She checked her watch. Janet and Mrs Quick's coven were due back soon, and it was important to get the timing right. To Ruth's relief, however, the team members seemed to feel no inclination to get dressed again, but were happy to help themselves to more beer and wine. Susannah, smiling a little, started to ask Alan about his studies at Hereford. Three other members of the team moved over to Rita to try to chat her up, but she warded them off with the glowing tip of her Villiger cigar whenever they became too impertinent in their demeanour. At last Ruth's mobile phone rang. It was Janet, reporting that the Land Rover with the coven had now turned into the main street of Skittleton. Twenty minutes later Janet rang again to say that the coven was safely back home. It was time for the scenario which Ruth and Janet had devised to begin in earnest.

"OK," said Ruth to Alan, "line up the team in single file and follow me..."

*****

Deirdre meanwhile had reached Fawn and Florinda's cottage on the edge of campus. She crouched by the garden wall and peered over it. The curtains were not drawn, and Deirdre could see that Fawn Fern was in the living room, by herself. Fawn had a glove puppet on her left hand, and was dreaming idly about her next glove-puppet class. Deirdre saw no reason for further delay. She drew the Browning from her pocket of her leather coat, smashed the front window with its butt, and as Fawn advanced towards the window to see what was happening, shot her three times, killing her with the second shot. "That will teach her to turn down my paper on *The Lady of Shalott*. Total war is the shortest war, terror can only be broken by counter-terror," she thought grimly, as she disappeared to the rear of the cottage. The sound of her shots passed unnoticed, for it was party time at Skelmerdale, as the evenings of the summer term lengthened, and there was the sound of revelry by night throughout the campus. The doors and windows of bedrooms and the colleges were open, the bars were doing a roaring trade, there were discos blaring out loud music. Smoke rose from barbecues, potatoes were roasted on tiny bonfires, and Sir Roger de Coverley College was holding its May Ball by the lake, with a bonfire and firework display about to get under way.

*****

"OK" said Ruth to Alan, "the party is at no 22, on the right, about four hundred yards away. The big house with a gravel drive - there will be a long-wheel base Land Rover at the front, you can't miss it. Off you go!"

The Rugby club started their streak through the village of Skittleton, with Ruth, Susannah, Rita, Sophie Poppet and the other guests jogging along in their wake. As they passed the Moonshine pub, packed to the doors with student revellers, and with others sitting on the grass and wooden benches outside, a great cheer went up, and six more intoxicated students disrobed to cheers and joined the streak.

The coven had returned, Janet had parked the Land Rover on the gravel drive, and the undressed acolytes had scampered into the house to warm up with another glass or two of wine, though that evening the weather had not been so cold as usual. Led by Alan, the drunken team and their newly acquired hangers-on surged up the drive and burst in upon the coven through the front door. There was consternation among the coven at the arrival of the Rugby team - the acolytes looked around for their clothes, and noticed for the first time that these had gone. From inside the house Ruth could hear shrieks and screams and cheers and howls of delight and outrage. Rita was inside, snapping the decadent scene as members of the team embraced and kissed the acolytes, some of whom succumbed, others of whom fled in all directions. Margaret and Annabelle dashed upstairs, hoping for refuge there. But most of the coven sought refuge outside the house. Mrs Quick lead the way, her robe flowing out behind her, her staff in her hand, and with the advantage that she was wearing sandals. Behind her in a cluster came Dr Crumpet, Dr Chamberlain, Susannah, Henrietta, the other Margaret, and Alice, pursued by Alan and ten other members of the team grouped together. They raced up the gravel drive at a fast pace.

"This will burn the..." said Janet, but the final words of her sentence were drowned by a drunken cheer.

"Burn the which?" enquired Ruth in a loud voice above the din. (Janet had been trying to say, 'burn the calories off the team.')

Alan overheard her, still in his suggestible mood.

"Burn the witch," he called out in excitement.

"Burn the witch," was the cry taken up in a raucous voice by the drunken members of the team. "Burn the witch," called Dr Crumpet and Dr Chamberlain excitedly, for they too had drunk wine laced by Ruth with the potion provided by Christophe.

Mrs Quick turned right and headed down the main street of Skittleton, heading for the vastnesses of the Skelmerdale campus, hoping to find refuge there. Her pursuers straggled out behind her, Rugby clubbers and acolytes, united now by the cry, "Burn the witch!" And indeed Dr Crumpet and Dr Chamberlain at this moment felt consumed with animosity against Mrs Quick for landing them in this embarrassing situation, caught without their clothes by drunken Rugby players. Susannah and Ruth remained standing in the garden, unobserved as the remainder of the team and coven spilled out in a confused mass, some following Mrs Quick's lead, others trying to escape drunken groping and assaults.

"This is great, Ruth," said Susannah excitedly, "this will make a wonderful story." Rita came out of the house smiling broadly, followed by a giggling Sophie Poppet and the others. "I've got some great pix, none better. We have a sensational story here, Susannah."

"Come on," said Susannah. "We have got to see how this ends. I'm sure there is much more to come." Speedily the young women brought up the tail of the chase, as Mrs Quick approached the edge of the Skelmerdale campus. Again, more revellers joined in from the Louis XVIII as the curious cavalcade made its way throughout the village.

*****

Deirdre meanwhile was roaming the campus looking for more victims. Dusk was falling, and lights were showing from many of the uncurtained rooms on the ground floors of college buildings of Skelmerdale. Deirdre sidled round the English Department wing of Grace Darling college; through one window she saw Mr Cuthbert and Dr Codsworth chatting to each other, dressed as usual in a clown suit and a crinoline. Mr Cuthbert was admiring a new model of a cut-out theatre which was on the middle of his desk. Glass tinkled as she smashed in the window, merrily sprayed a long burst from the Kalashnikov into their chests, and the two fell twitching and bloody, dead by the time their bodies hit the floor. Quickly Deirdre merged into the tangled undergrowth that bordered Grace Darling college, and carefully got her bearings in the vast campus. 'This would really screw up the Skelmerdale English department teaching programme!' she thought to herself with gleeful satisfaction. It would take some time to advertise and fill all these posts. Windows were opening in Grace Darling College, and people were looking out, but as yet no general alarm had been given. For noises off were a typical part of the Skelmerdale scene, and still no one knew that an armed serial murderess was on the loose. In the distance fireworks went off, and the occasional rocket fizzed into the air from the Roger de Coverley College summer ball. Deirdre moved on to another part of campus.

*****

The music from several bands was playing loudly at the Sir Roger de Coverley College summer ball. There was dancing in the dining room of the college, and food in the JCR. On this most formal of occasions the students and their guests and other attendees were smartly dressed, the men in dinner jackets, the women in long dresses. A group of them were standing on the terrace, wine glasses in their hands, watching the firework display. In the distance Mrs Quick appeared, robe still flying in the air behind her. She was beginning to lose her lead over her pursuers, for she was middle-aged and unused to running long distances. Behind her, Dr Crumpet, with her SAS training, and Alan and the Rugby team, who were also physically fit, and practised, too, through long experience, in running even when under the influence of drink, were gaining upon her yard by yard. The audience on the terrace gasped and cheered at the bizarre sight, and at the nurses (Fiona, Tamsin and Sophie Poppet) and other young women (Ruth, Rita and Susannah) bringing up the rear. Among the guests on the terrace was Dr Margaret Jacquasse, who had been invited to stay on after the feminism and gender conference by her latest conquest, the newly arrived Professor Clarence Cranborough, the sharp-tongued and unpopular Canadian who had recently joined the English department as a specialist in the late Victorians.

The two left the terrace and strolled hand in hand towards the runners, curious to see what was happening. That was a mistake on their part. From the cover of the undergrowth Deirdre took off her coat, unhooked the Kalashnikov, took careful aim, and let fly half-a-clip in the general direction of the two lovers. Dr Jacquasse was shot through the heart, and then Deirdre's aim faltered. Professor Cranborough was merely wounded in the thigh; he fell to the ground with non-life threatening injuries. The crackle of the automatic weapon was unmistakable; the dancers fled from the terrace of Roger de Coverley College to call the police and tell them that a deranged sniper was at loose on the Skelmerdale campus. Fiona and Tamsin dashed towards the slumped figures of Dr Jacquasse and Professor Cranborough, who was conscious still but groaning and clutching his leg, through which blood was seeping. "Good heavens, look, it's 'el diablo'," said Fiona to Tamsin in surprise (for such was the unpopular Cranborough's nickname among the students). Taking the scissors from her uniform pocket, she slit the left leg of his trousers to expose the wound, and tried to staunch it with a handkerchief. The doctors and paramedics were on the scene before the police. The latter had sensibly declined to attend until their armed response unit could arrive, and that took a little time. The first doctor to arrive took a speedy look at Professor Cranborough. "Non-life threatening wound, nurse," she said, throwing a medical bag at Fiona and Tamsin. "Just apply a tourniquet will you, and he'll be OK."

"But - ."

But the doctor had gone in search of others who needed her attentions more urgently.

"What's a tourniquet?" said Fiona to Tamsin.

"It's French for elastoplast," said Tamsin confidently.

The two 'nurses' opened the medical bag, took out the tin of elastoplast, and applied the biggest one they could find to the wound. The blood continued to pour out.

"It's not working," said Fiona doubtfully.

"Don't worry, give it time... look, there's nothing much we can do here, I need a large drink. Come on, we've done our duty." The two young women beat a hasty retreat to the bar of Tristram de Burke college, leaving 'el diablo's' lifeblood to rapidly drain away, and twenty minutes later he was no more. Rita was just in time to photograph his last twitchings for the *News of the World*, whilst, as the crackle of the AK47 continued to be heard, Susannah used her mobile phone to call the editorial desk of her newspaper and told them to hold the front page for the sensational and exclusive story of the Skelmerdale campus massacre that was now beginning to break.

*****

'O let the glorious news be spread,
    The wicked old witch at last is dead!' (*The Wizard of Oz*)

Her frenzied pursuers caught up with Mrs Quick in a sheltered part of campus, just inside a sylvan walk where the flames of a student barbecue were flickering quietly away. 'Burn the witch,' was still the call of Alan and Dr Crumpet and Dr Chamberlain as their followers caught up with them. Alan quickly seized a handful of brushwood and fanned the flames, and the eager members of the team, taking up the chant of 'burn the witch', quickly heaped up the flames with leaves and twigs and dry branches of trees. Mrs Quick struggled, her hands pinioned firmly behind her back by Dr

Crumpet and Dr Chamberlain. The fire was blazing nicely now, and a moment or two later they hurled her into the flames, still to the noisy chants of 'Burn, witch, burn'. As Mrs Quick's clothes and hair caught fire, Dr Crumpet seized Mrs Quick's staff and using it like a pitchfork transfixed her body to the flames with it. Mrs Quick struggled and screamed but was soon horribly burned. Footsteps were heard, and Florinda, carrying two glove puppet dolls, suddenly burst upon the scene. "Witchcraft," cried the hysterical Dr Crumpet, with memories of the voodoo dolls she had made at Surleighwick . "Witchcraft," Alan took up the cry. "Burn, witch, burn!". Soon Florinda too was hurled into the flames and burned alive, and rapidly lost consciousness, her dolls falling to the dusty ground. Alan and his team members and the acolytes heard footsteps approaching, and satisfied with the vengeance they had exacted, decided to run off. A moment later Ruth and Susannah and Rita and Sophie Poppet arrived breathless on the scene. Florinda was dying, Mrs Quick was still twitching and screaming horribly, and clearly had not long to live. They stood there for a moment or two whilst Rita photographed the hideous spectacle. Then Ruth calmly hitched up her skirt, and from the lacy holster strapped to her left thigh near the top of her nylons she extracted the tiny but potent .38 ivory-handled ladies' gun made from hardened plastic which she had seen advertised in *Women and Guns* and had purchased whilst in the United States. "I think I'd better ice them," she remarked compassionately. Ruth fired just three shots. The first two, to the head, put a merciful end to the life of Mrs Quick and Florinda. Ruth re-loaded the gun, and with her third shot, a silver bullet to the heart, she destroyed all supernatural remnants of Mrs Quick's occult powers, and interdicted her spirit, be she werewolf or vampire, from ever returning to these mortal abodes.

"Gosh, I need a drink," remarked Susannah. In the distance the crackle of shots was heard as Deirdre fired off her remaining ammunition, fatally splattering Thumbelina Thrump and Eduardo Bandilegs of the History department, and wounding the dwarfish and illiterate Professor Alan Dummkopf. His legs were shattered below the knees, and later had to be amputated. Through the trees flashing blue lights were seen, as armed police, paramedics, and ambulance units started to arrive. The four young women walked slowly and thoughtfully to the bar of Tristram de Burke college, and ordered themselves a pint of beer a-piece to quench their thirst. The bar was deserted except for Fiona and Tamsin, the other drinkers having left to investigate the happenings outside. Susannah took a sip of two of foaming ale, and then called on her mobile to update her editorial desk on the latest happenings.

"Eight people were killed tonight in a sensational mass attack at Skelmerdale University," she dictated. "A crazed gunman, armed with an AK47 and 9 mm Browning automatic" (Ruth had correctly identified the weapons for her friend from their sound) "executed several members of the Skelmerdale English Department" (extrapolating from the incidents of Professor Cranborough, identified for her via Tamsin and Fiona through Rita, and of Florinda, identified by Sophie Poppet). "Police suspect the killings are drugs-related, centring on a drugs, witchcraft and white-slavery ring based in the department of English and Communication Studies at Skelmerdale. An in-depth undercover investigation by our Special Correspondent Susannah Travers has revealed that the department was a front for a criminal gang specialising in drugs, witchcraft and pornography. In a shocking development, it can now be exclusively revealed that Skelmerdale students are taught to make voodoo dolls in English classes" (for Fiona and Tamsin had been chatting to Susannah about their glove puppet classes), "are regularly shown pornographic films in class, and indulge in nude orgies. See our exclusive pictures on pages 2,3,4,5,6,7 and our exclusive background exposés on pp. 8, 9, 10 and 11etc. A key figure in the movement was Mrs Pauline Quick, senior lecturer in the department at Skelmerdale" - ('she was at Hereford,' whispered Ruth: 'I know that, but I've got to keep the story simple for our readers,' retorted Susannah) - "who was burned to death in the aftermath of the shoot-out."

"There, that will do for starters," said Susannah proudly. "I've scooped the Street. Now Rita and I will finish off here in an hour or so when I've done an interview with the top cop and updated the body count... look why don't you take these three back to my suite at the Bannerthorpe, Ruth, and we'll join you a.s.a.p. for a nightcap?"

"Suits me," said Ruth easily. "I could do with a stiff drink, that's for sure." Accompanied by her three friends she walked back into the village of Skittleton, hailed a passing cab, and was soon back at the Bannerthorpe once again. In the distance she could still hear excited screams and yells as the Rugby club players and the late Mrs Quick's acolytes ran amuck.

*****

Deirdre had fired off all her ammunition, and it was time for her to make her getaway. She returned to her hide, dismantled her tent, and rolled all her paraphernalia up into a back pack. She took off her boilersuit, and changed into a long and flowing dress, slung the back pack across her shoulders, and carried the leather coat containing her weapons over her arm. She looked innocent enough, and nobody challenged her. She trudged calmly to the distant car-park on the edge of campus where she had parked her car, and was soon leaving Skelmerdale and on the motorway to Whitepool. Unobserved at 2.a.m., she dropped her weapons and the spent magazines from a bridge into the Whitepool river, where they were soon buried in silt. Deirdre was never brought to justice for her murders, since the Skelmerdale Police, less politically correct than Skelmerdale University, were looking for a gunman. The thought that the mass-killer might be a woman did not enter their minds. Exhaustive enquiries at hospitals and nursing agencies also failed to trace those valuable witnesses, the nurses who had been first on the scene to administer to the injured Professor Cranborough.

*****

Dr Crumpet meanwhile was slinking from tree to tree, trying to get back unobserved to the house where she had been staying. Her head was aching, she had very little recollection of what had happened since she had returned home with the coven and been so rudely interrupted by the Hereford Polytechnic Rugby team and their hangers-on. She crouched behind a bush waiting for a moment of tranquillity when she could, she hoped, dash unobserved over the next open patch of ground to another clump of trees. Suddenly she saw a familiar figure. Surely that was her lover Jacopo over there, Jacopo, whom she had last seen in Haiti? She waited for a moment to be sure, and then dashed towards him, arms extended, collapsing into his embrace with a sob.

"My poor Tony, what have they done to you?" he exclaimed, quickly taking off his jacket and draping it over her shoulders.

"They told me in Hay that you had gone to Skelmerdale, I went to your house, and everything was in disorder - one of your friends, Margaret I think, told me you had all been assaulted by some rugby players, and had fled to campus. So I came to look for you. Come on, my car is here, let me get you out of this."

Thankfully, Dr Crumpet let herself be led away by Jacopo, who drove to the nearest motel and booked them both a double room. That night he asked her to marry him, and next morning he drove to the nearest Marks and Spencer's to buy clothes for his fiancée, before driving south, south, away from Skelmerdale.

*****

Dr Chamberlain had similarly found refuge in a clump of trees. Like Dr Crumpet she advanced towards safety from clump to clump, crossing open expanses of the campus when all seemed quiet. Only once was she caught in the open and pursued by a clutch of whistling, jeering, drunken revellers returning from Skittleton. These however she eluded without too much difficulty, entered Tristram de Burke College through a back door, streaked through the ground floor till she found a staircase, and was soon in the study-bedroom area. She soon found several bedroom doors unlocked, and stole some clothes, heaving a deep sigh of relief once she was respectably dressed. Janet was waiting for her by the Land Rover. Dr Chamberlain climbed into the front seat. "That's the last time I ever go to a coven," she said bitterly. "Anyway I think Pauline's dead now. They burned her, you know, burned her as a witch." Silently Janet let in the clutch, and the two doctors drove slowly and carefully back to Hereford, anxious both to put the events of the night behind them.

*****

The remaining acolytes and members of the Rugby team merged into the normal colour and background of the Skelmerdale campus towards midnight, when the drunks habitually spilled out of college bars and the Skittleton pubs, and parties formed to go clubbing in the night-clubs in the centre of town, or to continue drinking in the study-bedrooms. Alan and two of his friends crashed the May Ball in Roger de Coverley College, now in full

swing once again, and helped themselves to wine and whisky from
the bars. Most of the dancers gave them a passing glance or two
and a cheer, supposing them to be a strip-show forming part of the
night's entertainment. Gradually, as a sense of modesty crept upon
them one by one, Alan and his friends purloined table cloths from
the tables of the buffet, and made their slow and stately way back
to their quarters in Skittleton. The acolytes too scattered in all
directions, acquiring scraps of clothing here and there; they were in
any case mostly students at Hereford, and had little difficulty in
blending into the Skelmerdale student scene. The police and
paramedics fanning out across the campus glanced at them
curiously, but had other things to worry about than student antics,
so the acolytes escaped closer scrutiny.

*****

Ruth, Fiona, Tamsin, and Sophie Poppet arrived at the
Bannerthorpe, and went straight to Susannah's suite. Ruth took her
place behind the bar in the corner of the large drawing room of the
suite, as her three friends perched on high stools waiting for their
drinks. "Ice-cool Heinekens all round, I think," said Ruth. "Gosh,
I'm parched!" The party sank a round of Heinekens in frosty lager
glasses, and then Ruth opened four more bottles. "And I think we
all need whisky chasers. Wow, what a night!"

After a while the party moved over to the more comfortable
surroundings of the sofas and armchairs under the tall windows of
the drawing room. They had just started on their third round of
Heineken, for they were very thirsty, when the fax machine on the
writing desk began to clatter. Ruth strolled over to find that it was
the front page of the latest edition of the *News of the World*,
containing Susannah's scoop about the drug and witchcraft-related
massacre on the Skelmerdale campus. Blaring black headlines
announced the truly sensational news. **CAMPUS MASSACRE
AT SKELMERDALE!** Then much to Ruth's surprise, for it was
still only 2.30 a.m., page after page of that Sunday's edition of the
News of the World was faxed through, each devoted to the affairs
of Skelmerdale. ***Degrees in Pornography!*** screamed page two.
EXCLUSIVE EXPOSÉ. By our Special Correspondent Susannah
Travers. 'Students at Skelmerdale, it can now be authoritatively
revealed, are studying salacious pornographic films like *Nurses on*

the Job! for their degrees in English. Sleazy sex films that mark the nadir of British film making, many of them banned by the censor, form the staple of a course in censorship and modern morals at Skelmerdale....' Ruth tossed aside page two, and came to page three. Page three of the *News of the World* was traditionally devoted to an at-least-topless pin-up. And this week Ruth recognised some familiar features. There was a picture of Eve-before-the-Fall who had greeted her husband and herself on their very first visit to Skelmerdale! *EEEve! I could FALL for you!* read the caption, as the picture showed Tabitha posing nude in front of a full length mirror, one hand holding an apple, complacently smoothing her hair with the other.

'You devil Sukie,' thought Ruth admiringly, 'you certainly don't let the grass grow under your feet do you? Of course I had mentioned Eve to you at lunch the other day.' "Tabitha pulls it off!" she read, "She may be a toff, but stuck up she ain't! Yes, folks, she sure is a lady, but the Honourable Tabitha Dagger, daughter of Viscount Dagger, Vice-Chancellor of the University of Skegness, aims to please all in her role as Eve, pictured above. Tabby has no inhibitions about facing up to the bare facts. 'I'm just being true to the part,' she explained. Betcha she's a real big hit with the lechering staff!"

Another fax reproduced page 4. **WITCHCRAFT AT SKELMERDALE! WE DEMAND AN ENQUIRY. GOVERNMENT MUST ACT NOW!** *Students taught to make Voodoo dolls. Heavy emphasis on occult in Skelmerdale courses. Students study 'Dracula' and 'Lair of the White Worm'! Plays with ghosts predominate in drama courses. Seances held in tutorials. Nude midnight witchcraft orgies on campus! See pix on next five pages...* and sure enough there was a picture of Mrs Quick's coven viewed from the rear streaming past a college clearly marked Grace Darling college. Ruth was at first staggered by the speed of it all. And then she realised that these must be pictures from Rita's digital camera, downloaded to the latest laptop and electronically transmitted in colour to the picture editing department of the *News of the World*. And now printed, no doubt in colour, and faxed to Susannah's room. Then came the next page, **SEX PARTIES AT SKELMERDALE SOLD FOR PORNO MOVIES!** (Susannah had made up this story from her fertile brain.) **EXCLUSIVE PIX SHOW SHOCK HORROR NUDE**

STUDENT SEX ORGIES! PORNO RING RUN BY ENGLISH DEPARTMENT. And there were pictures from the rear of Fiona, Tamsin, and Sophie Poppet in their nurses' uniforms dancing on the tables with the undressed young men of the Hereford Rugby team! Scenes that Ruth had witnessed in person not three hours ago... She hoped that Susannah and Rita would have had the sense to keep her friends from being identified, which was certainly the case for the present picture. You had to admire Susannah's cheek, no doubt about it, according to her story, which Ruth knew to be quite untrue, these were scenes from a porno movie made under the sponsorship of the English department as a way of supplementing the salaries of the Professors...

Just then Susannah and Rita arrived, embraced and kissed Ruth, kissed Sophie Poppet, kissed Tamsin and Fiona and danced gaily hand-in-hand round and round the room in a Scottish reel, their skirts flying in the air. "We are famous, hurrah, hurrah, we've scooped the Street, this story is sensational, the whole of Fleet Street is on its way here, our editor is so pleased with us, the whole crime team is on its way, so too are the reporters from the *Higher* but we had the story first, Ruthie darling I can never thank you enough, and you too Fiona, Tamsin, Sophie, come on, this calls for champagne. And I'm ravenous, let's order some bacon and eggs." Susannah rang room service, and ordered a vast assortment of eggs and bacon and sausages and kedgeree and fried bread and devilled kidneys, and opened a magnum of champagne, and tipped it hastily into six flutes. Susannah downed a glass of champagne and then another and another, and then opened another magnum. "This is a really great day for me, the best of my life," she said, "I am so happy." Behind her the fax continued to spew out the story. **HUMAN SACRIFICES AT NUDE WITCHCRAFT ORGIES.** *It can be exclusively revealed in our pages that two Skelmerdale teachers, Senior Lecturer in English and Drug Czarina at Skelmerdale, Pauline Quick, and devotee Florinda Morrison were put to death as human sacrifices by a vengeful coven in a perverted rite designed to raise the dead....*

"Hang on a minute, Susannah, you may have something there, talk about raising the dead, it reminded me " put in Ruth. "Here's a story for you Sukie. Mrs Quick did indeed keep zombies - that is, she used zombie paste from Haiti to put people into catatonic trances. Tell the police to go to her cottage at Hay - you'll find there a young black woman zombie sleeping in the shed I expect."

"Ruthie, you are absolutely fab. Let me get the story to my editor first, we can just make the last edition at 4. 30 a.m."

Rapidly Susannah dictated another exclusive about zombies in the Welsh countryside. Meanwhile Rita was working frantically at her lap-top and uploading and downloading further material from her cameras.

"OK children, gather round," she said proudly. "This is the tops. I filmed tonight's party from a hidden DVD camera in my camera bag. This will be on the Internet in five minutes time, available for viewing by our readers for two pounds a time. I've tweaked it a bit to protect our identities." Rita had the very latest technology, a recordable DVD drive in her top-of-the-range portable laptop. She inserted a disc, connected up the laptop to the TV, turned on the TV, and pressed play. And there in full colour were the risqué and decadent scenes of the three nurses dancing with the undressed Hereford Rugby team! Rita had digitally added masks to the nurses' faces, so they were indeed unrecognisable, unless you happened to know who they were already. And there too in the background were Ruth and Susannah, also now digitally masked. "This will go like a bomb," she prophesied. "Soft porn, of course, but the way we'll tell it it'll sound worse than that." She lit another Villiger. "That little movie, my children, is already on its way to our Website. Downloadable at two pounds a time by those punters with Real Player Plus G2 software, my guess is it will net a few hundred thou' at least for the old rag."

The telephone rang, and Susannah had another scoop. The young policeman whom she had cajoled with a false promise of sex in return for providing her with the inside track rang with the exciting news that two tranvestite lecturers at Skelmerdale had been found dead. The bodies of Obadiah Ouimpe and Dr Codsworth had at last been discovered, the former still wearing his dress, the latter his crinoline. *Transvestite lecturers murdered in drugs scam, Cuthbert the Clown was drugs link to circus underground*, Susannah coolly dictated to her newsroom.

The bacon and eggs arrived, along with two large pots of freshly made coffee, and the young women, hungry now, tucked in with hearty appetites, washing the bacon and eggs down with coffee and champagne. Susannah tuned on the TV, and sure enough the Skelmerdale story was running continuously on BBC1's News 24, on Sky News, and on CNN. But all their information clearly derived from the *News of the World.* "We scooped the broadcast media as well," she called excitedly. "Gosh, what a day."

Ruth looked at her watch, and suddenly felt rather sleepy. It was now almost 5.30 a.m. She called a cab and left her friends, and had just sufficient energy to undress and clamber into bed beside her husband before falling into a long sleep. It was almost mid-day when she awoke, feeling much refreshed, the sun streaming into her room. Her husband brought her a cup of tea which she sipped gratefully as she lay there and relaxed.

"You were out late last night," he remarked. "Did you have a good time? Whatever kept you out so late?"

"Oh, just girl-talk, Charles," she smiled contentedly, stretching out her arms to embrace her husband, "girl-talk you know..."

CHAPTER NINETEEN

A BLACK WEEK FOR SKELMERDALE

'Dies irae, dies illa,
Solvet mundum in favilla' (Thomas of Celano)

The first calls from journalists started to come through to Freddie Frowstie at half-past three that morning, rousing him from his slumbers. He was ex-directory, but even so the ladies of the press had soon obtained his number. Jackie from the *Sun* wanted a quote about the nude witch orgies in his department, about which the bewildered Frowstie of course knew nothing. "Oh, come off it," was the exasperated retort. "Don't you never keep up with the news? Just turn on the TV." The bewildered Frowstie did so, to watch the stories about the decadence of his department. Within the next half-hour he had fielded calls from the *Mirror*, *Daily Mail*, *Daily Express*, *Daily Record*, *Western Daily Press*, *Skelmerdale County Post* and from the *National Enquirer* in the USA. To all of these he mumbled that he had no comment. Professor Freddie Frowstie knew exactly what to do in such a situation. Taking the phone off the hook, he quickly packed an overnight bag, and drove his car out onto the drive. He paused to gulp down a cup of tea and snatch a hasty slice of toast. He locked up his house and went outside to flee from Skelmerdale. Then with sinking heart he saw that a sinister black van had drawn up outside his house, blocking his way out. Four heavies descended from it, as another van with a further four security men sealed off the rear of the house.

"Professor Frowstie?" said the leading heavy, lifting his bowler hat with a sarcastic grin. "Not trying to do a flit, were we Sir? It will have to wait, I'm afraid. I have orders to carry you straight to the Vice-Chancellor."

For Dr Winsome, the Skelmerdale VC, had been awoken by the importunate press even earlier than Professor Frowstie, and he had correctly divined that the cowardly Frowstie would run at the first opportunity. So he had sent in the heavies from Pinkerton's to stop the man and bring him in for an urgent interview. The Skelmerdale VC was pole-axed and flabbergasted as he watched the all-night news on television, and read fax after appalling fax of the pages of that day's *News of the World* which that paper had kindly transmitted to him. Thunderstruck the VC telephoned the Registrar and the Public Relations department to try to decide what to do. The VC scowled. That awful Frowstie! A real no-good no-hoper; his head would roll, that was for sure.

*****

"Well, it looks as if it was a dramatic night on campus last night," remarked her husband to Ruth when she had got up, as they strolled down the street on their way to lunch. "I see your chum Susannah got the story - did you see much of the action yourself?"

Ruth shook her head. "Not really. We were drinking in the bar at Tristram de Burke. I heard a few shots, and Susannah and Rita got the story and pix - but no, I really can't throw much light on what happened. It wasn't me if that's what you are thinking! I left my assault rifle and automatic in the States." Professor Hanwell laughed. "I'm glad you were OK, and that I didn't know anything about the story till I saw it on teletext when I got up on Sunday morning. Otherwise I might have been worried about you."

Ruth squeezed his arm. "That's sweet of you Charles, but really you had no need to worry. I can take care of myself, and in any case Sukie and Rita said they would bring me back safely."

*****

The Skelmerdale VC gasped like a fish as the overwhelming tide of bad news engulfed him. The campus PR person had arrived, but for once her feeble publicity releases had had no effect, indeed had made the situation worse. 'Massacre could have happened anywhere' was speedily re-coded by Susannah and her ilk as 'Skelmerdale admits: Massacre could happen again anytime! Security powerless to prevent it!'. Meanwhile Susannah with great relish was working up her material. **'Axe murders were failed white-slave abduction bid. Special Correspondent Susannah Travers exclusive. The axe murders at Skelmerdale, which the university tried to hush up, were, it can be exclusively revealed, failed attempts to abduct female students which went wrong. Police are working on the theory that Cuthbert the**

Clown was link to circus underworld which spirited victims to Middle East. High demand still in Eastern harems for white students....' 'Transvestite Link to White-Slave Drug Ring!' 'Skelmerdale's Transvestite Lecturers were Key Links. Ouimpe, Codsworth, die in gang feud! Student Lovers of Ouimpe, Codsworth, were Axe Victims!'

"You know, Ruthie, I'm having a great time. What matters is not what is true or false, but exclusively what is believed," said Susannah, drunk still with happiness, over tea to Ruth the next day. "One thing I like about the English libel laws, the dead can't sue, I can say what the hell I like about the corpses. You know, Ruthie, I think I'm going to get a book out of this, I've got so much material."

*****

Blow after blow rained upon Skelmerdale. The Minister for Higher Education, in response to public demand, had prevailed upon the University and College Admission System to allow applicants to Skelmerdale to reconsider their positions and opt for another institution. A torrent of withdrawals ensued. Then all that week a horde of reporters from the press had been trapping students into indiscretions. **'Students dressed as women in tutorials!'** screamed the *Sun*, which had investigated some of the English department's theatre workshops. **'Drugs rife on campus!'** was the cry from the *Mail*. At Ruth's suggestion, Susannah had called Professor Dalrymple, who had now left Palermo University to take up the Cuchulain Distinguished Professorship of Renaissance Literature and Cultural Studies at Berkeley. Professor Dalrymple had heard of the recent events without surprise. "Well, yes, I thought it was a bad department," she told Susannah. "We gave it an 'unsatisfactory' for TQA. Nude orgies? Wouldn't surprise me, come to think of it, I did meet a naked student in the corridors when I was doing my audit. He invited me into his room," she continued, thinking of the time she had met Christopher in the corridors of Grace Darling college. "And I guess he had been taking drugs, he seemed pretty high to me." **'Nude male students used as honey trap for female auditors'**, screamed the next day's headlines. **'Nude male students set up by department to blackmail or bribe female auditors. Sex scandal continues at**

Skelmerdale! By Special Correspondent Susannah Travers.'
The VC sat at his desk, sobbing. He did not know what to do. He
had sacked Frowstie, he had given notice to his PR officer, and
still the tide of awful stories continued. Susannah telephoned all
the auditors, and all was grist to her mill. Grumbler was still
complaining about skeleton formes. It did not need much
imagination to see how Susannah would interpret this as further
evidence of black magic in class. A remark of Professor Hanwell's
about thinking he had seen Snow White on his first visit, when he
had seen a student helper helping the dwarfs of the History
department became **'Snow White was Skelmerdale crack
queen'**. Professor Brootal too cheerily put the boot in. 'Yes, my
love, the department was a complete shambles, and be sure you
quote me on that! It's double *o* mind in my surname, not a *u*,' he
laughed.

*****

'Where got'st thou that goose look?' (*Macbeth*)

The bad news continued to flood in thick and fast all week at
Skelmerdale. Hordes of journalists from the tabloids had
descended on the student pubs, and more and more stories of wild
parties emerged. Meanwhile the police were making no progress
whatsoever in solving the massacre. They were hampered by
having no motive to go on. They had no weapon. They had no
suspects. And perhaps, given that they were inclined to believe the
News of the World, they felt little sympathy for the witches,
transvestites and drug traffickers who had been killed. On Friday
of the same week, the *Higher* appeared, and the massacre was of
course the headline news. Inside were many background features
on the University of Skelmerdale. The essential points of
Susannah's story were re-written from a high-brow angle. The
professor of Film Studies at Warwick criticised the choice of
movies shown in the Skelmerdale course. *Nurses on the Job!* was,
so he maintained, a poor movie, unsuitable for work in class. Then
the Serena Professor of Italian Language and Literature at
Skegness tore to bits the 'translation' of *El Molino sopra lo
Flosso*. 'Illiterate and disgraceful balderdash, shows complete
ignorance of the language' were among his choice phrases, and he

was easily persuaded by the *Higher*'s attractive female reporter to suggest that the errors in the Italian were in part due to the corrupting influence of badly printed and illiterate Italian magical texts which the witches had been reading. *Der Müll auf dem Floss* received similar treatment from the Professor of German at Doncaster. One by one the linguistic experts tore to bits the translations emanating from the University of Skelmerdale. They then started a trawl through the other publications emerging from that University. A Bulletin Board was set up on the Net, and soon 8,500 errors in Italian, French, German, Latin, Spanish, Dutch and Portugese had been listed from Skelmerdale publications of the previous ten years. These were then grouped into sections and published by the *Higher* over the next few weeks, to the general amazement of scholars in normal, literate universities. All this was not to mention the shock and outrage with which the *Documentary Goose Course for Historians and Medievalists* was greeted. Up and down the country scholars happily joined in the criticism, and one by one the courses at Skelmerdale were taken out. The MA in Embroidery Studies was one of the casualties, leaving Fiona and Tamsin uncertain quite what to study for their MA year.

*****

The Honourable Tabitha Dagger had been withdrawn from the University of Skelmerdale. Viscount Dagger had telephoned Dr Winsome. 'I want my daughter out of there,' he had said curtly. 'See to it, will you?' Dr Winsome without more ado had sent for Pinkerton's, and two burly female heavies had forthwith entered the Hon. Tabby's room with a master-key, dragged her out of bed, bundled her kicking and screaming and still in her nightie into the back of a car, and taken her to Viscount Dagger's manorial home on the outskirts of Skegness. The noble lord was not best pleased with his daughter. In the first place, he had not liked receiving several hundred anonymised e-mails from students at Skegness to the effect 'Phew, what a scorcher! Will you get her to do her act here please?' Nor had he relished the knowing leers of his colleagues on Whitehall committees. A stern Victorian parent, the Viscount had raided his daughter's room and found her peyote pipes, which he had broken in a fit of furious anger. He had looked at the books on her shelves, and angrily confiscated several lurid titles such as *The Confession of the Black Penitents* and Carol Clover's *Men, Women and Chainsaws*. He had been through his daughter's collection of video-tapes, and had been even more shocked. The subsequent explanation that *Emmanuelle in Hong Kong*, *Sex for Sale* and *Women in Love*, with its nude wrestling scene, had been films prescribed for her course in communication studies, left him even more dissatisfied. He felt a great urge to thrash his daughter, an urge which only with difficulty, for he had just sufficient sense in his rage, was he able to contain. He did however forcibly commit his daughter to a rehabilitation clinic, so that Tabitha could dry out, and repent the error of her ways for a fortnight at leisure, over lemon tea and Ryvita.

"You know, Susannah," said Ruth to her friend over coffee a couple of days after the appearance of Tabitha's pose in the *News of the World*, "I think it was perhaps a tiny bit unkind of you to have put Tabitha into your exposé."

"Not a bit of it," answered Susannah, unabashed. "It was a great career move for her. In the first place we gave her £2,000 just for stripping off, and she was glad of the money. She went into this with her eyes open, and knew what she was doing OK? Second, she wants to be an actress, and already she has had film and stage offers as a result of this. The Royalty theatre are interested in a reprise of her role as Eve-before-the-Fall. And third, and best of all, Hugh Hefner - a charming man, by the way, do you know him? - thinks she would make a great centre-fold for *Playboy*. *Playboy* is offering her $200,000 if she will do a spread with them. I mean to say, she's on the way to fame and fortune! You needn't feel sorry for the Hon. Tabby at all."

*****

Ten days after the Skelmerdale scandal broke in the *News of the World*, Professor and Mrs Hanwell were on their way to lunch with Viscount Dagger in Skegness. They passed a crowd of carpenters busily adapting Professor Alan Dummkopf's Wendy House. The illiterate dwarf historian had had to have both his legs amputated just above the knee as a result of Deirdre's activity with the assault rifle. But fortunately, when the legs of the tables and chairs in his Wendy House had been similarly shortened, he could lead much the same life as before. The carpenters carried out the sawn-off legs of the tables and chairs, and their job was done. The Hanwells arrived at Viscount Dagger's Palladian mansion on the outskirts of Skegness, and rang the bell. The door was opened by a pale, subdued, young woman with curly hair, wearing an austere dark skirt that came well below her knees, a white blouse, low-heeled black leather shoes and dark stockings.

"If you'll follow me pleathe?"

She led the way up the stairs, ushered the Hanwells into the library, and poured them each a glass of sherry from a cut-glass decanter.

"Pleathe be theated. Lord Dagger will join you prethently."

Professor Hanwell sipped his sherry. "That girl's face seems familiar," he said to Ruth. "I'm trying to remember where I have seen her before."

"You're slipping, Charles," said Ruth with a smile. "But I daresay you didn't recognise her with her clothes on. That, my dear Charles, is the Honourable Tabitha Dagger, whom I'm sure you will remember better as Eve-before-the-Fall. You were quite taken with her, though you also thought she was Lady Godiva, which she couldn't have been as she didn't have a horse. I'm surprised you recollect her face at all; I seem to remember it was her other features that held your attention."

Professor Hanwell coloured, but was saved the need to reply by the entrance of Lord Dagger.

"Charles, delighted to see you again!" said that worthy, for the two had met from time to time at History of Science Conferences, and Lord Dagger had occasionally tried to tempt Professor Hanwell to come to a chair at Skegness. "It's been far too long since we last met."

"John, may I introduce my wife, Ruth?"

"Delighted to meet you, Mrs Hanwell."

"How do you do, Lord Dagger."

"Oh, John, please, and may I call you Ruth? No need for formality. Charles and I are old friends."

"Thank you, John."

Viscount Dagger helped himself to a glass of sherry, and topped up Professor and Mrs Hanwell's glasses. Soon afterwards the maid, trim in black frock and white apron, entered the room to summon them to lunch. Lunch was served at a bench-like table in a room lined with books overlooking the extensive grounds of Lord Dagger's house.

"Now Charles," said the latter, as they sipped their soup and the maid poured out tall glasses of Kendall Jackson Chardonnay, "I'll tell you what I want your advice on. It's that wretched University of Skelmerdale. Of course I know it's nothing to do with you really. Still, it struck me that since you have been there for a while as a visiting prof., you might have some observations that would be worthwhile. As you may know, I'm joint-chair of the humanities advisory panel both for the Arts and Humanities Research Board, and for the Higher Education Funding Council for England. I've been asked to sort the place out - the announcement will be made in a day or two. Question is, a) what the hell has been going on at Skelmerdale, and b) what are we going to do about it? The whole business is damned embarrassing, let's face it. Dammit, I feel personally involved. My daughter Tabitha is studying there - or was until I withdrew her. You may have heard that she ill-advisedly got herself into the tabloids. Damned unfortunate, but there it is. Confounded interfering journalists, she was set up, no doubt about it. Point is, this kind of thing would not have happened in a decent university. So my question is, what do you think of the place? Is it worth saving?"

"Well, John," replied Professor Hanwell, "fact is I've seen very little of the place. I've given my one lecture a fortnight and that's about it."

"I'll tell you one minus point about the place, John," interposed Ruth. "And that is that Charles's lectures were absolutely brilliant, but nobody went to hear them. At the HSS in SF his lecture on Crocodiles and Insects pulled in 600 people, at Skelmerdale the only people who turned out were myself and my bridesmaids, who are reading English and Communication studies there."

"Well, I'm not exactly complaining," said her husband. "The pay was good, I got £2,500 a lecture, and I was left with lots of time to research poems about centipedes and so on. The cathedral library has a fine collection of books, but of course since they aren't in English no one at Skelmerdale can read them."

"Still, even so, it's a damned scandal," said Viscount Dagger, filling up their glasses. "So far as I can gather the whole place is a complete mess. How will they ever live down this publicity about orgies and white slave rings and drugs and so on?"

"Well, John," said Ruth, "I daresay they could live that down eventually. You know what the popular press is like, they do tend to exaggerate a bit. Much more serious in my view is their horrible illiteracy in language. I mean to say, just look at this, it's a complete scandal. How can they possibly allow this rubbish to be given to their students at public expense?" Ruth gave Viscount Dagger a copy of *El Molino sopra lo Flosso*. Lord Dagger took the booklet, started to read, and exploded immediately with anger and disbelief.

"And their German is no better," continued Ruth, handing Lord Dagger a copy of *Der Müll auf dem Floss*. "It really is appalling, a complete linguistic travesty."

"And then there's that ghastly farrago, the *Documentary Goose Course for Historians and Medievalists*," put in Professor Hanwell. "Ruth is right. The whole place is a shambles really. And so far as I can see every volume in their vanity press, or *Analecta Skelmerdaliana* as they call it, is a complete mess so far as languages are concerned."

"But this really is appalling!" said Lord Dagger, flicking through the Bandilegs/Thrump booklet, and then throwing up his hands in despair. "Good heavens, I suppose that people in my position get cut off from what is actually happening on the ground. I had no idea that any British university could sink so low. *Goose Course for Historians* indeed! Well, really! What is the British university system coming too? How did Thrump and Bandilegs ever get jobs, one wonders?"

"I believe they came from the circus," replied Professor Hanwell. "They worked as trick cyclists, riding monocycles on tight-ropes and that kind of thing, till the History department took them in. Still, as for the English department's booklets, certainly Freddie Frowstie ought to have been aware of what was happening in his department, I think," said Professor Hanwell. "He was keen enough on publishing the booklets, I believe. And Dummkopf knew about the *Goose Course for Historians* - it was dedicated to him in fact."

"Frowstie has gone," replied Lord Dagger. "We can forget about him. Winsome demanded his resignation the morning this whole affair broke. Frowstie was trying to do a bunk anyway. He didn't have the guts to face the music. As for Dummkopf, we can always redeploy him to the maintenance department - there are some very tiny corners of the Skelmerdale buildings that only little people can get into to clean properly. Now tell me," he continued, pouring them both an excellent Macon as they started to eat their Beef Stroganoff, "what do you think of Winsome, the Skelmerdale VC?"

"Winsome?" said Professor Hanwell thoughtfully, "I can't say I've ever come across the guy."

"Yes, you have Charles," pointed out Ruth. "You know, he's the narcissist that I've pointed out to you a few times - the chap in the shiny grey suit who's always admiring himself in the little pocket mirror he carries around in his jacket."

"Oh, him! Will he survive this, I wonder, John?"

"I doubt it," Lord Dagger replied cheerfully. "He'll have to go, I think. Not one of our alpha VCs I'm afraid. I think the powers that be will make him go as the price of cleaning up Skelmerdale."

"Of course I'm not saying the place is all bad," continued Professor Hanwell. "Ruth's bridesmaids are at Skelmerdale, and intelligent and personable young women they are too, but I fear that at Skelmerdale they are not really stretched. They have been spending a lot of time making glove-puppets, fooling around with cut-out theatres and that kind of thing, instead of studying texts. Well really, that's not much of an education is it? And as for the historians, well, I have no objection to the affirmative action policy for people of restricted growth, but the point is they should be literate dwarfs, not illiterate ones like that awful Dummkopf." Professor Hanwell showed Lord Dagger a specimen or two of the latter's writings, full of mistakes in languages, and Lord Dagger groaned. "As I say, Charles, I'm afraid that folk like me just find it so hard to know exactly what is going on in the system nowadays. Of course what you are saying is more or less what the TQA assessors reported," continued Lord Dagger. "But from what I hear, the English department's two chief puppeteers were shot or burned in the massacre, whilst another of their crazes, cut-out theatre, suffered from the death of Cuthbert the Clown. And I gather that, co-incidentally, the killer managed to take out some of the illiterate dwarf historians too, which is certainly a bonus. Still, I think it's pretty clear that Skelmerdale needs sorting out in a major way. Come on, let's have our cognac in the library and see what can be done to put the place in order."

Lord Dagger led the way to his well-furnished library, and the three settled down in deep and comfortable armchairs. Lord Dagger and Professor Hanwell savoured an excellent Courvoisier, whilst Ruth contented herself with a Drambuie, since Lord Dagger, who did not often entertain young women to lunch, unaccountably had no crème-de-menthe in his stock of liquor. Lord Dagger offered Professor Hanwell a Bolivar cigar, and lit one for himself.

"As I see it, John, there are three essential weaknesses to Skelmerdale," said Professor Hanwell, taking the first satisfying puff of the Cuban tobacco. "First, the department of English and Communication Studies. Second, the department of History, and third, the fact that there is no History of Science department there. Now if you are in the business of remaking the university's reputation, why don't you close down the first two to finance the third? You and I both know that the first two subjects attract pseuds and dreary bores respectively in considerable numbers, whereas you have to be intelligent and know something to do the latter. You could swap the lecturers who wrote *El Molino sopra lo Flosso* and all that nonsense for a historian of science who actually knew Italian properly and could do some proper work on Galileo and Leonardo da Vinci - and as you and I both know, there are far too many people nowadays who think that Galileo wrote in English! After all, let's face it John, one more or less department of English or History in the world's universities makes not a ha'porth of difference. Whereas a really good History of Science department could really put Skelmerdale on the map. It could take over, in a proper professional fashion, the languages that History and English so mangle at the moment in Skelmerdale. There's no reason, in fact, why you shouldn't have a transitional period. Bacon, for example, is an Eng. Lit. author, isn't he? Well, you could get the students to do not only his *Essays* but also the *History of Winds* as well. You could start the students on Burton and Browne, and introduce them to seventeenth-century medicine and so on. How about some lectures on Shakespeare and Paracelsus? And similarly, you could alter the emphasis of history. Get rid of all this goose-girl nonsense, and shift them over to intellectual history in a big way."

"Well, OK, I like the idea a lot," said Lord Dagger. "Let's see, what are we talking about here? We would need say four people in ancient science, with competence in Latin and Greek of course.

Let's say another half-dozen Latinists for medieval science. And another six again for the Renaissance - Kepler, Copernicus, Harvey, Vesalius, Agricola and so on. Four Italianists, say, four Hispanists, and four Portingales."

"And let's not forget Middle High German," put in Ruth decisively. "I know Charles once wrote an article on alcohol which drew heavily on Middle High German sources."

"Oh, absolutely, I entirely agree," said Lord Dagger. "We'd better say two of those, and of course we need some Frenchies. Let's have four of those perhaps. Let's see, where does that leave us? I make that thirty-four posts for Historians of Science competent in those languages. Let's say we need another half-dozen research posts, that would make a department of forty. And let's see, after the massacre, I still make it that English and History have forty-eight posts between them. So if we clear them all out, that still leaves us eight posts to play with."

"Do you think you can swing that?"

"Oh absolutely, no doubt about it," opined Lord Dagger confidently, pouring Professor Hanwell and himself another brandy. "Winsome is running scared at Skelmerdale, he'll do what I tell him in his last weeks, before we get a new man in. And HEFCE and the AHRB will go along with my plans, I'm sure of that. Let's face it, the reputation of the University of Skelmerdale is absolutely in tatters, they will simply have to face up to what's coming to them, and there's an end to it. My guess is that people at Skelmerdale will be delighted to get off so lightly, if all they have to do is close down English and History and start up History of Science. Brootal from the Wirral will deal with the former - I've already had words with him, and he's willing to be seconded for a year to sort the department out."

*****

Roland Gasser the Shakespeare lecturer could not bear to think of what had happened. He had a painful interview with Professor Brootal, on the very day that the latter arrived in Skelmerdale as head of department on secondment. Professor Brootal told Gasser to get a PhD and write a book. The very next day Gasser slunk off campus and never re-appeared. No one noticed his absence, and he was soon forgotten. Professor Brootal set out to see what could be salvaged from the wreck of the English department. He happily decided that almost nothing could, and sent out UB45s to most of the department.

*****

Professor and Mrs Hanwell enjoyed their final weeks at Skelmerdale. Professor Hanwell gave his final lecture, 'Erasmus Darwin and the Italo-Latin centipede poem tradition' to his usual audience of Ruth, Fiona, Tamsin and Sophie Poppet. For his last lecture the audience was however increased by one. Lord Dagger had decided to support his friend, and found time from his busy schedule to attend the lecture. Professor Hanwell discoursed happily about centipede poems in late antiquity, and made some amusing jokes about the late grammarians' observations on centimetric metres. He discussed a little-studied manuscript of a ninth-century Latin poem by Joachim of Milan which had never been studied by scholars of insect poetry. Picking up some unusual features of Joachim's poem, he was able to show that this poem was clearly well-known to English writers from the twelfth to the seventeenth centuries. He showed that there were manuscripts of this poem in English libraries, manuscripts which wrongly attributed the poem to John of Calais, which explained why Joachim's influence had never been recognised. Finally he showed that Dr Moffett knew the poem well, and that several sections of Erasmus Darwin's poems were virtually a hitherto-unrecognised translation of Joachim. Afterwards the party went out to dinner as usual.

"Brilliant lecture, Charles," remarked Lord Dagger, as the party strolled across campus to pick up a taxi in Skittleton. He waved a cheery hello to Professor Brootal, who was tending a large bonfire at the side of one of the campus lakes. Professor Brootal was leaning on a stick, happily watching the remaining members of the English department toss glove-puppets on to the flames. One of his first actions had been to call in student project work and order it to be burned, and now a vast pile of junk was going in to the flames, glove-puppets, embroidered handkerchiefs, Mills-on-the-Floss by the score. A little further away, by another bonfire, the illiterate dwarfs of the Skelmerdale History department were also grumpily consigning great piles of their department's *Documentary Goose Course for Historians* to the bonfires.

Fiona and Tamsin were somewhat disgruntled about the withdrawal of the MA in Embroidery Studies. That had gone, along with all the glove puppet and drama options. The English department was in now the transitional phase of being phased out and replaced by a History of Science department. As a concession, MA courses in English and Communication studies were still available for a further year. In this transitional period, puppet and drama options had been replaced by a courses on Early Modern Natural Philosophy, devoted to a close reading of the works of Francis Bacon, William Gilbert, and Timothie Bright. Cuthbert the Clown's workshop course on the Fool in Eighteenth Century Drama was also no more. It had been replaced by a course on Renaissance Platonism: set texts, Marsilio Ficino's *De triplici vita* and Symphorien Champier's *Opera omnia* (Paris, 1520).

"Oh, well, I suppose I had better brush up on the *Descriptio globi intellectualis*," put in Tamsin resignedly. "It's been some time since I read the work."

They were booked in to the Bannerthorpe as a treat, to mark Professor Hanwell's final lecture for Skelmerdale. Fiona and Tamsin and Sophie Poppet exclaimed with delight at the luxurious and antique ambience as they sat on the chintzy sofas of the enormous lounge, drinking gin-and-tonics.

"I was interested in what you said about the influence of the natural philosophers on centipede poems," remarked Fiona to Professor Hanwell as she sipped her gin. "You said that heat, radiation and mobility were the essential environmental factors, but surely Telesio, for example, and other Renaissance natural philosophers said that tenuity was also essential - heat, radiation, tenuity and mobility is what he said."

"Yes," put in Tamsin, "and if animals and plants derive their organized structures and capacity for nutrition and growth from the vital spirit, and the spirit works nobler effects in animals than in plants, then by virtue of the spirit animals have a greater diversity of internal organs. The point is worth emphasising, I think."

Lord Dagger gaped at Tamsin and Fiona.

"Telesio? You've been reading Telesio?"

"Oh yes, we've been reading the books Charles has recommended in his lectures," answered Fiona casually.

"Aldobrandinus and Zanchius and Obbadinus's *De avibus et creaturis minoribus* - that kind of thing you know. We had plenty of time in the intervals of making glove-puppets, and it was really much more interesting you know."

"And I've been reading Vincent of Beauvais on geese," interposed Sophie Poppet. "So much more interesting than the goose course. As well as the various goose poems Charles alluded to in his lectures, like Cruceius's *De anseribus* (Padua, 1542), Tammarino's *Anseres curiosi* (Milan, 1578), and Facciolus's *Altilia* (Paris, 1594). Fiona is quite right. Tenuity is stressed is all these works."

Lord Dagger gaped at Tamsin, Fiona and Sophie Poppet, drained his gin and called for another one.

"Good heavens! I have never met a student who has read such works. Well, Charles," said Lord Dagger, "I certainly see what you mean about Skelmerdale not really stretching its students. But you have obviously had a good influence on them. Now," he said, turning to the three young women, "do I gather that you three are planning to do graduate work at Skelmerdale? I wonder if you have thought about coming to do your grad. studies at Skegness instead? We don't have such a large pond, but we do have a rather better library you know."

"Really, Lord Dagger, do you mean that?" said Tamsin fluttering her eyelashes.

"Yes certainly, there's a place for all three of you if you want, I can guarantee it. And I think I can say that young women like yourselves who have read Telesio, Cruceius and Tammarino would certainly be awarded graduate bursaries available at my discretion, which would cover your fees and provide a maintenance allowance of £12,000 a year each. You would carry the title Vice-Chancellor's Graduate Scholars."

"Thank you, Lord Dagger. You are so sweet," said Tamsin, puckering her scarlet lips and bestowing a light-hearted kiss on that startled, but not altogether displeased, functionary. "We accept."

They finished their aperitifs, and were summoned to dinner. Thus three more bright students were lost to Skelmerdale.

CHAPTER TWENTY

ALL'S WELL THAT ENDS WELL

Back at Whitepool Deirdre was happy at last. She felt fulfilled as never before, and revelled in the secret knowledge that she had been the catalyst which had brought down Skelmerdale. As the days went by, she felt more and more confident that she had got away with her crimes, and happily relived her highly enjoyable private memories of zapping Fawn Fern, Dr Codsworth, Cuthbert the Clown, and all the others she had killed. Gosh! It had been great fun, a deeply satisfying experience, to see Fawn Fern fall fatally, flatlining just like that, to blow away the corpulent Cuthbert, red nose, pom-poms and all, and to cut down the corseted, crinolined Codsworth! Deirdre had exorcised a demon, she had expelled the hate from her system, and she felt a whole lot better for it. Deirdre started a new chapter in her life. She abandoned her interest in feminism and *The Lady of Shalott*, and decided to sharpen up her interest in languages, in conformity with the reforms that were on the point of being introduced at Skelmerdale as a result of her actions. Soon Deirdre was drafting notes on the language of *Beowulf*, and brushing up her Old High German, Old Icelandic and Old Gothic. Thirty years later she was to publish a massive and authoritative tome on *The Heroic Ideal in the Early Germanic Literatures*, before dying, in 2045, as a Dame of the British Empire, a Fellow of the British Academy, and a still undetected mass murderess. The magisterial authority of her chapter on 'The Hero as Killer' was, as more than one critic remarked, absolutely unsurpassed.

*****

After the death of Obadiah Ouimpe, his room was cleared and his papers thrown away, and the scholarly world was thus spared his still unfinished opus, riddled with linguistic error, *Pins, Purses and Petticoats. The Leisure Expenditures of Skelmerdale Teenage Girls.*

*****

Lord Dagger, shaken to the core by what he had found out about the current state of English and Communication Studies and History at Skelmerdale, had made immediate enquiries of the History and English Departments at Skegness. He made the professors of English and History take lie-detector tests, but he found to his relief, and as he had indeed expected, that in the English department there were no glove puppets, no cut-out theatres, no models of *The Mill on the Floss*, no lecturers in clown suits and crinolines, no risqué movies; rather the students and teachers were quietly studying texts. Neither was there a *Documentary Goose Course* in the Skegness History department. Lord Dagger looked at some of the books and articles that had come out of that department in the last fifteen years. In none of them was there a single mistake in German, French, Latin, Italian, Spanish, Dutch or Middle English. Neither were there anacolutha, errors of punctuation, wrong references, gross inconsistencies of editorial practice, or rambling repetitions. The teaching material given to the students was, without exception, literate. Reassured, Lord Dagger allowed those two subjects to continue at Skegness.

*****

In November, the Honourable Tabby was *Playboy*'s Playmate of the Month, and, later, Playmate of the Year. She appeared in the centre-fold wearing only the mortar-board she had earned as a new BA (Skelmerdale) in English and Communication Studies. Her acting career did not however take off; her figure, appearance, and gestures were fine, but her lisp proved a great impediment. She used the nearly half-a-million dollars which her contract with *Playboy* had earned her to start the first nude table and lap-dancing club in the centre of Skelmerdale. Blanche Quick was one of her first artistes, for it was proving difficult for Skelmerdale graduates in English and Communication studies to get jobs in the immediate aftermath of the Skelmerdale scandal. Blanche soon formed a troupe of female graduates in English, the Elegant Ecdysiasts, and Tabby's, as it is now known, is a popular establishment with the students at Skelmerdale, both male and female, who are given a 20% discount on production of their union card. Tabby went on to enjoy a certain fame as an icon of the free and liberated young women of the turn of the millennium. Gradually, very gradually, her loving father came to accept his daughter's new role in life, and to accept also with a certain kind of pride the secret, often unspoken, raffish admiration that accrued to him from friends and colleagues. 'At least,' he thought silently to himself, 'I now know which of my friends and colleagues actually does read *Playboy*.'

*****

After their marriage in San Marino, Dr Crumpet and Jacopo returned to Haiti. Under the protection of a diplomatic passport, Dr Crumpet was not molested by the Haitian Customs and Immigration service. She still collects books, and on Tuesdays and Fridays browses the Haitian bookstalls in Port au Prince, occasionally finding an interesting volume. After the death of Mrs Quick, she inherited the entire stock of the Magic Women bookshop. Her experiences in Hay, Haiti and Skelmerdale had however considerably reduced her interest in the occult. She sold off the stock as a job lot, and invested the proceeds in works of romantic fiction and pornography. She now trades as Women in Love, over the Internet, as www.womeninlove.haiti.com and crumpet@womeninlove.freeserve.haiti.com,   and   makes   a sufficient income to indulge her taste in clothes.

*****

Susannah's investigative journalism at Skelmerdale won her a prestigious award as Journalist of the Year, and a massive increase in salary to £200,000 a year. She speedily wrote up her notes as *Massacre on Campus: the Skelmerdale Psycho-Slaughters!* The book sold 50,000 copies in hard-back, and was then published as a Penguin Special which sold another 200,000. It was paperbacked in the States in True Crime Library, and translated into French, German, Dutch, Spanish, Italian and Japanese. The book was fully illustrated with Rita's snaps of the Rugby club party and of the corpses, and developed in lurid detail Susannah's theories about the links of Cuthbert the Clown to the circus white-slave underground, the putative gangland connections   between the axe-murderer and the harems of the Middle East, and the campus porno-movie rackets.

*****

Dr French and Dr Chamberlain returned to Hereford, and resumed their medical practice. After her bad experiences, Dr Chamberlain abandoned her interest in witchcraft. She threw herself whole-heartedly into her medical practice, but still relaxes by accompanying Dr French to the rugby club parties at Hereford. She is wary now of taking off her own clothes on social occasions, but still encourages the rugby players to take off theirs.

*****

Vice-Chancellor Winsome received the usual rewards meted out to high-level failures in British public life. His University Council dismissed him, but authorised a 'Golden Goodbye' of £5,000,000 as a parting *douceur*. Dr Winsome bought a house in Skelmerdale, and is sometimes to be seen, a lonely and desolate figure to whom nobody wishes to speak, wandering through the melancholy wreck of the Skelmerdale campus, and lamenting what might have been. 'I should have sacked Frowstie years ago,' he thought to himself. 'I should have smelt a rat as soon as he started to talk about a Socrates scheme with Bosnia, but I was too eager for good publicity and cheerful, upbeat stories. I shouldn't have trusted my professors, they always told me lies. I should have had the glove-puppet scenarios checked out, and not allowed vanity publishing by the University of Skelmerdale. I should never have been conned into employing learning-impaired dwarfs. I should have black-listed former circus employees. I should have insisted that my historians were qualified and knew languages. And I should have had the campus wired off and proper security checkpoints installed.' The former vice-chancellor sighed as he looked at the twenty-feet-high barbed wire coils which now completely surrounded the campus, and pulled out his laissez-passer as he joined the queue for the security barriers and screens, staffed by Pinkerton's, which now controlled entry to and egress from the University of Skelmerdale and its constituent colleges.

*****

Professor and Mrs Hanwell were once again flying the Atlantic, returning to Surleighwick, Arkansas. His book on *Crocodiles and Insects* was now complete, and he had sent it off to press a week before leaving Skelmerdale.

"Well, it was quite an eventful term, wasn't it?" remarked Professor Hanwell to his wife, as they sipped Wild Turkey on the rocks in the spacious and comfortable first-class compartment of the British Airways flight to Washington D.C., where they would stay the night before proceeding to Arkansas. "Not perhaps the most stimulating of universities, but at least it enabled me to finish off my book. The Cathedral library had some surprising old editions of insect poems, and no one at Skelmerdale seems ever to have looked at them."

"Yes, and I was able to do a good deal of work on my thesis on Agnes of Anieto too," said Ruth. "And it was nice to meet up with my old friends like Susannah, and my bridesmaids Tamsin and Fiona. And to meet Sophie Poppet too of course."

"Of course the events of the last few weeks were pretty startling," said Professor Hanwell, as the stewardess brought him another extra-large glass of Wild Turkey along with the wine list and the lunch menu. "I wonder if the police will ever catch the gunman? It's beginning to look a little unlikely. I mean to say, what could have been the motive?"

"Probably just a mindless impulse," said Ruth. "Some poor frustrated soul wanting to shoot off their guns in a fit of anger or something like that. Personally, I would suspect a member of the Skelmerdale staff. After all, you know how irritating some academics can be, it must be a real temptation to blow them away if you have the guns."

"Of course it was terrible too about Mrs Quick," mused her husband. "To be burned as a witch at the close of the twentieth century... it's a pretty unusual way to go isn't it? *Was* she a witch, I wonder? I always thought of her as an amiable airhead myself, hardly a witch... of course I know she sold magic books, but still, that's hardly conclusive. I buy magic books myself."

"She did have a coven, I believe," said Ruth idly. "But it was pretty low level stuff I should think."

Professor Hanwell looked at his wife closely.

"You know, Ruth, I've always had the feeling that you know more about Mrs Quick than you have let on," he said, sipping his

Wild Turkey. "I get the feeling that you didn't like her, and are not sorry that she has gone."

Ruth sipped her Wild Turkey, demure in a newly-purchased figure-hugging pink suit with matching accessories, laid down her copy of the latest issue of *Women and Guns*, and turned to face her husband, arching her eyebrows with the mischievous smile her husband found so devastating.

"OK, Charles," she whispered conspiratorially, "I don't see why you shouldn't know the truth. Mrs Quick *was* a witch and was trying to turn us both into zombies. So I decided to burn her alive. But her coven got there first, so I blew her brains out and put a silver bullet through her heart so she couldn't do us any more harm either in this world or the next."

Professor Hanwell laughed, and took his wife's left hand in his right, and raised it to his lips, and kissed her wedding and engagement rings.

"You know, my darling Ruth, there are many reasons why I love you so very much - because of your *sprezzatura*, because nothing fazes you, because you have a great sense of humour - and perhaps because you are a good shot too!"

Ruth kissed her husband tenderly on the cheek, and then dissolved into a fit of the giggles. Professor Hanwell laughed again, and Ruth laughed with him too. They were still laughing and holding hands as the stewardess refilled their glasses, and the plane, heading north and west, passed over the former campus of the University of Surleighwick, now doing sterling service as an Open Prison and on-shore oilfield. The Hanwells were still laughing as the plane flew further north and west, over the derelict campus of the University of Skelmerdale, smouldering with the ashes of glove puppets and project work and theatrical costumes and the burning pyres of the illiterate publications of the Skelmerdale press and the dwarf historians. North and west onwards, laughing still, over the Irish sea and into the Atlantic, heading for Arkansas, to the pool and the Chardonnay and the corn-fed steaks, to the abundant leisure and the further works of scholarship, to lazy gossip in the afternoon sun, to the visiting lectures that were to come, to the myriad adventures that awaited them still in the unending human comedy of academic life.

THE END

ALSO AVAILABLE FROM ZOILUS PRESS

Silviano Santiago in Conversation
This is the first book to introduce the renowned Brazilian
novelist, theorist and critic, to an English-speaking
audience. It includes essays and an interview.
ISBN 1 902878140   £6   paperback

Macdonald Daly, *A Primer in Marxist Aesthetics*
Aimed at readers with little or no knowledge of the field or
its vocabulary, this book includes succinct extracts from key
texts with a commentary and aids to study.
ISBN 0 952202816   £10   paperback

Ellis Sharp, *Driving My Baby Back Home*
The latest collection of 35 surreal stories from a master of
postmodern wit and experimental narrative. It includes a
new version of Joyce's *Ulysses*, reduced to five pages, a
startling solution to the mystery of who shot JFK and the
astonishing theory of Tympoptanomania.
'He is stranger than Burroughs and often funnier' *Zene*
ISBN 1 902878 00 0   £6.99   paperback

John Herdman, *Four Tales*
The major early writings ('A Truth Lover', 'Memoirs of My
Aunt Minnie', 'Pagan's Pilgrimage' and 'Clapperton') of a
classic Scottish writer, together with an authoritative
introduction and bibliography.
ISBN 1 902878 45 0   £10   paperback

Ronald Binns, *J.G. Farrell*
The first, pioneering book-length critical study published on
the Booker Prize winning novelist, who died in 1979, and
who is best known for his 'Empire trilogy'.
ISBN 0 9522028 9 1   £9.99   paperback

George Gascoigne, *Selected Poems with 'Certayne notes of Instruction concerning the making of verse or ryme in English'*
The first new edition of Gascoigne's verse for twenty years, and the only cheap paperback edition now available in print. This new selection includes Gascoigne's major lyric verse together with his pioneering essay on prosody and an authoritative introduction and notes to the poems.
ISBN 1 902878 59 0   £12   paperback

Charles H. Cutting, *The Surleighwick Effect*
The classic novel which explores the vibrant new commercial values of modern academic life, as well as its more traditional features such as fraud, stupidity, drunkenness, witchcraft, ignorance and lechery.
'A campus novel of wild comic caricature which bounces along with unflagging zest' *Times Literary Supplement*
'Comic but chilling Jonsonian satire' *The Library*
ISBN 1 902878 76 0   £7.99   paperback

Macdonald Daly, *Crackpot Texts*
A dazzling and idiosyncratic collection of essays on contemporary and post-modern fiction and literary theory. It includes an anatomy of nonsense and the sensational exposé of the most scandalous literary plagiarism of recent times.
ISBN 0 952202859   £10   paperback

Ronald Binns, *Malcolm Lowry*
This critical introduction to Lowry's life and writing career offers numerous original insights into the twists and turns of Lowry's life as a writer, as well as a full account of the multi-levelled meanings of Lowry's masterpiece.
'Lively and enlightening... sophisticated and subtle'
Contemporary Review
ISBN 0 9522028 8 3   £9.99   paperback